Also by

Brittany Larsen

BRITTA & THE BEACH BOY

BRITTANY LARSEN

To Emma

My favorite barista, My firstborn, My heart

CHAPTER ONE

Britta

G oodbyes suck.

I hate them almost as much as I hate bad coffee (looking at you, Starbucks). At their best, they're watered down and marginally satisfying. At their worst, they're full of sugar, yet somehow still bitter.

What I'm saying is that filling a complicated coffee order is much easier than saying goodbye. That's what people in Paradise, Idaho, don't understand. For the past month, my regulars have been tiptoeing around me, ordering their coffee black, then taking their mugs to the condiment bar where they pour in way too much cream and even more sugar. And I have to watch it all. I don't know who winces more with the first sip, them or me. We all know that I can make them the perfect cup of coffee if they would just ask.

The locals giving me space would be bad enough, but the vacationers do the same thing. I've looked forward to the first day of the summer season being so busy that I wouldn't have to think about anything else besides coffee, but their orders are basic, not the usual bougie brew out-of-towners want.

Maybe someone posted a notification about Mom somewhere or they're picking up on a vibe. I don't know. It's not like I hung black crepe in the doorway—or whatever they used to do back in the day when a family member passed—so I can't figure out why they're being so careful with me too. It's irritating.

So, when a disheveled guy in board shorts steps up to the counter, I expect nothing other than a basic coffee. Then he opens his mouth, and in a—sweet mercy—*Australian* accent says, "I'm guessing you use ristretto in your flat white. Being that you're American."

For the first time all morning, I actually *look* at the person across the counter from me. I don't see disheveled anymore. Nope. This guy is all shiny and gold, like the first day of the summer season usually is. Eyes the color of a dark Ethiopian blend flecked with amber; honey brown curls swirled with shocks of blond; bronze skin dipped in sunshine.

He literally glows.

And I *feel* a spark of something for the first time since Mom died. Not just because of how he looks, but because I've heard Aussies are snobs when it comes to coffee—deservedly so, according to everything I've read.

I smell a challenge, and I'm here for it.

"If you've got time..." I drop my gaze, taking in his beach attire, and leave unsaid my *which, obviously, you do.* "I'm happy to make it the way you like. Espresso instead of ristretto?"

He answers with a nod, then points to the sign on the wall above my head. "That's quite a claim to live up to."

I crane my neck to read the words I've known by heart since I was five years old, when my mom took over this shop from her grandma, Britta Neilsen. They were the first words I learned to read. *Breakfast at Britta's: Coffee so good, it's only found in Paradise.*

I shrug. "I've had no problem living up to it so far."

The corner of his mouth pulls up. "You're Britta then?"

I nod and bite back my own grin. It's too soon. Not because of him, but because of Mom. It's barely been a month since she lost her fight against early-onset Alzheimer's. Everyone—including her—knew she'd lose, but we still weren't ready to say goodbye.

"I'm Dex." The Australian juts out his chin. "I'm here visiting Cassie and Georgia. They were my neighbors in LA, before your brothers got hold of them. They're your sister-in-laws, yeah?"

"Yeah." I think I've heard them mention a guy named Dex, but I stop myself from correcting him.

Not just his grammar—it's *sisters*-in-law—but also his understanding of our relationships. Technically, Cassie is only engaged to my brother, Bear. But Georgia is very much married to my brother Zach, so I'll give him that.

"What's e-bell-skiveh?" Dex points to the menu posted on the back wall; the *r* at the end of ebelskiver gets lost in his smile.

This time I do correct him. "Ay-bluh-skee-ver." Some things have to be said right. "Danish pancakes. First order is on the house." For him, at least. Not for other short-timers. "So is the flat white, if it doesn't live up to the claim." I tip back my head toward my *Britta's* sign.

Dex's smile dimples. "Sounds like a fair deal."

"I think you mean a fair *dinkum* deal, mate." I cringe as soon as the words escape.

"Were you trying to speak Australian there?" Dex sends me a much-deserved smirk—my Australian is terrible. "Only pensioners say fair dinkum anymore."

"And a pensioner is—"

"—an older person, yeah." Dex's eyes dance with the smirk still plastered on his face.

Almost everything I know about Australia, I learned when I was ten from an old movie about an Australian going to New York. I only remember two things: he had a big knife, and he said *fair dinkum* a lot. Then, for about two weeks, *I* said fair dinkum a lot.

And while I'm enjoying 'fair dinkuming' with Dex, there's a line forming behind him, and I've got to get to work on the best flat white of my life. I'm not about to give away my coffee.

"You want your order to stay or go?" I know which one I want, and I hope he hears my invitation.

"Reckon I'll stay for a bit."

Invitation heard, accepted, and, if I'm not mistaken, he's given an invitation of his own. I'm not sure to what yet, but I'd like to find out.

"Find a seat. I'll bring out your order when it's ready." I let my smile grow wider after he has turned away.

The next hour is crazy busy with people in and out, the bell above my door continually ringing in the official start of the summer season. The weekends before Memorial Day bring in a few visitors, but May thirty-first marks the beginning of the busiest three months of the year. And while I don't get any orders as challenging as Dex's, the day seems brighter with him sitting in a corner, trying to hide the fact his gaze keeps drifting back to me. But I don't miss that his eyes are on me as often as they're on his phone.

Maybe I should be creeped out by that, but his smile is too boyish to give off stalker vibes. Plus, he's in Paradise to see Georgia and Cassie, which gives him instant credibility. Georgia might be taken in by a charmer (she got taken by Zach, after all), but Cassie is ex-LAPD. She'd handcuff a player for hitting on me.

Just as things slow down, Dex stands. He ambles to the counter and lays down a ten-dollar bill.

"The e-bell-skiveh was excellent. The flat white coulda been a bit stronger but was almost as good as in Aus."

I assume when he says *oz*, he means Australia. I push his money back to him. "A deal's a deal. You can pay me when my flat white is better than what you've had in Aus."

Golden rays of laughter flicker in his eyes. "Cracker idea, Britta. I'll see you here tomorrow."

Dex ambles out the door in the same easy gait he used to approach the counter. Like he's got all the time in the world, and no cares weighing him down. No business to run. No family to help whenever they need an extra hand—which is always. No mom he's watched slowly slip away too soon.

Having things you care about is a good thing—I'm aware of that. But Dex's worry-free air is infectious. I want some of that.

Dex keeps his word and comes back the next day, and the next.

Whatever makes everything shiny when Dex is around, I'm into it. Over the next five days, he spends every morning at *Britta's*, his gentle teasing pushing me to make coffee as good as what he's had at home. And when he lets slip he's a professional surfer, I tease him about getting an actual job. If pro-surfing is anything like the pro-rodeoing some cowboys around here do, Dex makes a little money but mostly spends his time chasing both cash prizes and girls.

His laugh lightens the atmosphere like a blue sky after a hailstorm, so I don't mind him flirting with me. He can chase all he wants. He's not going to catch me. We both understand he's here for a week, maybe two, and then he'll go back to his life a long way away from here. Even further in lifestyle than miles. There are no professional surfer positions in Paradise, and I'm not going anywhere.

He tries to pay for his coffee each day, but I'm determined to get him to say my coffee is as good as—if not better—than an Aussie brew. I barely know Dex, but this is important, and I'm up for the challenge.

Except, he's only in Paradise for a week, and by the end of his stay, I still haven't beaten all of Australia at coffee. The morning he's headed to the airport to fly back to LA, I don't expect to see him. But when he saunters in during a lull between customers, I'm thrilled to have one more chance to prove my mettle as a barista, and to look into his copper-toned eyes one last time.

By some miracle, Dex is the only customer in the café, and my employees are in back doing dishes and prepping ebelskiver batter. For the first time, we're alone.

I don't bother asking him what he'd like before I make it. He leans against the condiment counter instead of taking a seat, so I pour his flat white in a to-go cup before carrying it to him. Dex takes the cup from me, his fingers brushing mine.

"You should try it before you go." I want to see his reaction when he tastes the last cup of coffee I'll ever make for him.

I know what I've accomplished with this flat white. I've spent the little free-time I've had researching how the best baristas make them in Australia and then done my best to copy the method: finely ground beans and perfect water to bean ratio. If this cup doesn't convince him that at least one American can brew coffee as good as any Australian, he's lying to himself. Which is fine, but he won't get away with lying to me.

Dex takes a slow sip, and his eyebrows go up. His lip follows, curving with satisfaction behind his to-go cup.

"You can say it. You won't lose your Australian citizenship." I step closer, just in case he tries to escape before admitting the truth. Also, he smells really great. Like coconut sunscreen and a fresh, salty, summer breeze.

"I might." He lowers his cup and my stomach dips at the sight of his dimples. "But I'll take my chances."

He sets the coffee on the counter, then hooks two fingers around the apron strings I've wrapped around my back and tied in front, just below my belly button. Despite the layer of apron and shirt, his fingertips scrape the top of my jeans as he pulls me closer.

I'm surprised by this, but I don't resist when Dex draws his hand across my stomach to my lower back then slides his other hand to my jaw. I need no more prompting than this to tip my chin to him. I expected enthusiasm for my flat white, but until right now, I never expected he'd show his enthusiasm by pressing his lips to mine, kissing me with an eagerness that turns my legs to jelly.

Apparently, Dex *really* likes my coffee.

His lips are Chapstick smooth, and he tastes rich and spicy with the exact right amount of sweet. Like a good brew should.

"Best flat white I've had...in the States," is the last thing he says to me before leaving.

And it's the perfect goodbye.

Chapter Two

Dex

The sun's first rays break through the cloud cover as I bob in the lineup, watching the horizon for a good set. The wave is even more packed than usual for a dawny, but it's September, which not only means perfect wave conditions at Lower Trestles, but also heaps of Southern California high school surf teams taking advantage. A few surfers recognize me, but most of them are focused on the waves. I'm okay keeping a low profile.

A cleanup set of big waves rolls in, and the less experienced surfers wipeout, making space for me to drop in to a perfect groundswell wave that curves high enough for me to carve its face twice. I build enough speed to launch off the lip into an aerial. It's only a simple one-eighty, but

I catch enough air to leave me satisfied that the whole morning wasn't a waste. I land it perfectly, kick out, then dive into the water.

When I surface, I'm keen to paddle back out now that the waves have finally picked up, but Archie motions me in from shore. I pretend I don't see him and take another wave. It's nothing special, but it gets me closer to the beach, so I don't have to paddle the entire way in.

By this time, Archie's waving his arms. I can't hear him, but I can guess what he's shouting. "Time for the shoot, mate!"

"I know, Archie," I grumble to myself. Time to do the part of my job I don't love.

I pause long enough to glance between him and the next set rolling in. The wind has changed, and the wave is good. But over the crashing surf, I hear Archie calling my name again. Against my will, I paddle all the way in.

I'm grateful every day that I get to surf for a living. That doesn't mean I don't miss just being able to surf for the love of it. My passion is my career, and I reckon that's a rare privilege, but I've traded away some of my freedom for it. Days like today are a reminder of that.

I drop my board on the sand next to Archie and look back at the swell. "If sponsors want me to win, they shouldn't schedule publicity nonsense days before the biggest event on the tour."

"It's not picking up. You caught the biggest wave of the day." He's trying to make me feel better, but we both recognize I'll miss some good sets.

"Come on." Archie slaps me on the back. "Let's get you some brekkie before you put that ugly mug in front of a camera."

As much as I hate to walk away from the ocean, I *am* hungry. And with the World Surf League Championship coming up in a few days, it'll only mess with my head to stay too long on the wave I'll be competing on. I've made the drive south from LA to Lower Trestles every day this week to practice, and I've reached the point where I might be too comfortable.

Lower is a consistent, predictable wave, but that doesn't mean it's easy. I can't go into competition thinking I've got it figured out.

With surfing, confidence can be as dangerous as fear because, ultimately, Mother Nature is the one who has all the control. And she can be nasty. Too much confidence can lead to serious injury. The right mindset means respecting who's in charge, and it's never the surfer. The understanding of what I can control and what I can't is just as important as technical skill. I've learned this the hard way. Twice.

Archie picks up his board and we head for the wide dirt trail that leads to the car park. "I got everything on video. We can watch over brek. You looked good, mate."

On our way up the trail, I recognize Griffin Colapinto on his way down and regret even more that I came off the water. He's got the same intense look on his face I'm sure I had on the way down to the beach this morning, gazing straight ahead, seeing nothing but how he's going to surf. It's the same look we'll both have next week when the waves are competition-level and the waiting period is over.

"It's mushy out there today," I say, and my American rival for the world title—who grew up surfing here in San Clemente—looks up to give me a wide smile of recognition.

"This wave knows me. It's just waiting for me to pick up." Colapinto meets my eye with a confidence that's meant to be both friendly and intimidating.

"Nah. I already tamed it for ya, mate." I smile back as we clasp hands and bump shoulders in a side hug. "You should be able to handle it now."

Colapinto laughs, but his home court advantage is no joke. He surfs every day at Lowers, where the world title competition is about to be held. He knows this wave better than anyone else on the Championship Tour, but, as I told myself a few minutes ago, familiarity isn't always the right edge.

We give each other a shaka—the "hang loose" Hawaiian hand signal every surfer is pretty much born knowing. Come competition day, things won't be so cozy between us, but today we can appreciate that we've both fought hard to be on the Championship Tour this year. Difference is, he hasn't fallen off the Tour the way I did when I was his age.

As a rookie, I let the fame and success go to my head, my first time on the Championship Tour, and ended up falling out of the ranks before the championship event. My second time on Tour, I pushed myself too hard and ended up with a serious back injury that took me out halfway through the year.

This time, I'm taking care of myself—physically and mentally—and I'm in it to win it, even though I'm nearer the age most surfers hang up the leash than I am of those who usually win the WSL Championship. With every year that passes and every minor wound that inevitably comes with surfing—and the genuine fear of another serious injury—my chances of taking the title decrease.

"Don't let him get in your head, mate," Archie says once we're out of earshot—and just in the nick of time, as my doubts threaten to set in. "Eye on the prize, and all that."

I nod, pushing away all the other comparisons trying to crowd my brain.

"Got it." Eye on the prize; it's the only thing I've got space for.

Archie leaves it at that. He's not just my best mate. He's the guy who pulled me up from rock bottom, then pushed me harder than anyone ever has to get me where I am now. He gave up his own race for a title to become my coach and it's made all the difference—I wouldn't be here without him, and we both know it.

By the time we get to the Sprinter van, the last of the clouds have disappeared, and the day is poised to be hot and sunny. The wind has shifted from cross-shore to offshore, and Colapinto will probably get the wave he wants. I try not to obsess about that and focus instead on the fact that with a good swell coming in, I'll have my chance soon to beat him, *and* the three other surfers in the top five with me. This is my year. I can feel it.

I climb into the passenger seat and grab my phone from the glove box. When I pull up my messages, there's one from Georgia Beck that wipes away some of the disappointment of missing the rest of the morning waves.

> Britta's coming to take over the last six weeks of my apartment lease while her coffee shop is under construction. Stella's coming for part of it. Keep an eye on them, will you?

> Happy to.

I've only met Stella once, but Britta, I haven't stopped thinking about since the day I walked into her coffee shop.

"What's put a smile on your dial?" Archie asks.

"Nothin', mate." I try to pull back my grin, but can't. Not while I'm picturing Britta's full, pouty lips, her blonde hair pulled back with a few locks falling in gentle waves to her jaw, and her eyes the turquoise color of the water around Whitsunday Islands. She's going to be across the hall for the next six weeks. How about that?

It's been three months since I spent a week in Paradise, Idaho, flirting with the local barista. It was fun, and I was careful not to let it get out of hand. Georgia had told me back then that she thought it was a good idea for Britta to take a long vacation here in LA, once the summer season ended in Paradise—if she could talk Britta into it.

I didn't let myself think too much about the possibility because I sort of loved the brief flirtation we'd had being exactly that. I should have remembered that Georgia generally makes happen whatever she wants.

As to what "keeping an eye on Britta" will actually look like, I'm going to have to sort that out later.

"Brekkie here?" I ask, waving toward our favorite spot for breakfast that's coming up on the left.

"You'll order the egg whites and veggie option?" Archie's already turning into the car park, though, so he knows the answer. I'm rigid about nutrition during competition season, but he likes to boss me, anyway. "And we have to get it take away or we'll be late."

No sooner do we get in line than someone recognizes me, and Britta is pushed out of my mind completely. People are already arriving in San Clemente for the world title event next week, and I'm asked for more autographs than usual. I'm alright signing them, but Archie knows the attention is a distraction for me. People's expectations get in my head, and I can't afford to let that happen so close to competition.

Plus, I've got the photoshoot to do for a new wetsuit ad—hence why I'm headed back north toward LA to hit a different wave in Huntington Beach. I hate that modeling gear is part of my contract with my sponsor, but at least I'm actually getting paid. That wasn't the case even ten years ago for young surfers coming up, including me. We got cut out of a lot of earnings.

The real money in surfing is in sponsorships. I've been surfing professionally since my teens, and in the early days I couldn't cover entry fees or equipment and travel costs without a sponsor. Now that I get paid for wearing their brands, I can actually make a living, even without the prize money that comes from winning events.

But staying on the Championship Tour is key to keeping the big sponsors. On Tour, there are ten events per year—including the World Title event—but only thirty-six spots for men and eighteen for women. Halfway through the season, that number gets cut to twenty-four men and twelve women, based on the number of points each surfer has earned at the first five events. Doesn't matter if you won the World Title Cup the year before. High points are the only thing that keeps you from being cut. And the five men and five women with the highest points at the end of the season compete in the final event for the World Title.

If you're not winning, you're not earning from events or sponsors. I've learned this from experience. I've made it to, then fallen off, the Championship Tour twice and been dropped by sponsors because of it. That, and my attitude. The only reason I'm on the Tour now is because I earned enough points last year from winning events in the Challenger Series to qualify to get bumped up to the 2024 Championship Tour.

People think surfing is all about being chill and riding waves, but at this level, there's intense pressure to perform. I feel that pressure every day. So even though I'm smiling on the wave during my photoshoot, and even enjoying myself, there's always a voice in my head making an old steam engine sound, chugging *keep your focus* over and over and over again.

It's close to dinner by the time the photoshoot ends, and Archie and I get back to the van. I'm knackered and hungry, and neither of us is up for preparing a meal at home. We stop long enough to eat high protein salads at Organic Greens.

Between surfing for practice and getting back in the ocean as part of the photoshoot, I've spent most of the day in the water. My lips are chapped, my skin is pickled from the salt water and it's the best feeling in the world. The only thing that could make it better is a stubby, but I've committed to stay away from alcohol before events. And there's always an event in surfing. I'll have a celebratory beer after I win, but that's it.

Archie, though, hasn't given up beer. Since he's had a few to wash down the salad I guilted him into eating, I drive back to our unit. As I pull into my parking spot, I notice a car with Idaho plates parked in Georgia's old spot, and I can't stop the grin that creeps across my face.

Britta's here.

In my town this time. I wonder if she'd like to get a coffee.

"Is Georgia back?" Archie asks as he takes notice of the unfamiliar car in the spot that's been empty for most of the year.

"It's a relly of hers—her sister-in-law, Britta," I say as casually as I can manage. "I met her when I visited Paradise. She's the girl who made the ripper flat white." I leave out the part that I left her with a Hollywood-worthy kiss any director would've been proud of.

"Ah, right. I've heard you mention her. What's she doing here?"

"Finishing out Georgia's lease." Again, I'm super casual about this. But Archie sees right through it.

He peers at me once I'm parked in my spot. "You can't afford to get distracted right now." His voice is stern and paternal, and my glare tells him exactly what I think about his tone. He puts his hands up as though in surrender, but he's not backing down. "Sorry, you're paying me to coach you. I'm just doing my job. No grog. No girls. Those are your rules, mate.

I stare at Britta's car as I consider his advice. "It's not like that," I finally say, because it isn't. "We're not even friends, really, just acquaintances." Although, that doesn't sound quite right. "She's probably as exhausted as I am if she's been driving all day," I add, more for myself than for Archie.

I don't miss Archie's sigh of relief. "Let's get the boards put away and I'll get your yoga video set up. Then meditation and bed. *Alone.*"

"Got it, boss!" I salute Archie, who salutes me back with his middle finger. "Won't hurt to take her some coffee in the morning, do ya think? Just to be neighborly," I say as he shuts his door. I'm goading him, but also, I did promise I'd keep an eye on her.

Archie shakes his head while walking to our apartment. But he doesn't say no. Wouldn't matter if he did. He knows he can't keep me away from Britta Thomsen if I decide I want to pursue something with her—whatever that might be. He's my mate and my coach, but he's not my keeper.

He also knows I'm not letting anything get in the way of winning the world title in a few days. Not even the woman I haven't stopped thinking about since the day I met her.

CHAPTER THREE

Britta

The first morning of my extended vacation in LA, I wake to a hazy dawn instead of the buzzing of an alarm. It's not a terrible start to the day, even if I have to force myself to stay in bed and enjoy the quiet. I think that's what you're supposed to do on a vacation—enjoy relaxing. This is all new to me.

I make it five minutes before I'm so bored watching the ceiling fan turn in slow circles that I have to get up. Old habits die hard. I've spent too many years getting up before dawn, to make coffee and ebelskiver, to sleep in.

The first thing I do is text Dad to check on him, then my brother, Adam, to check on *Britta's*. I get a long response from Dad about how he's doing great—I don't believe it—and that he misses me. Adam's reply is short.

> demo starts today.

Taking a deep breath, I repeat the mantra I've said no less than a thousand times since driving out of Paradise. *Everything will be fine without you.*

I wait a few seconds to see if I believe myself this time.

I don't, but I'm getting closer...maybe.

Then I pad into the hallway, stopping long enough outside a second bedroom door to confirm Stella—my cousin, bestie, and assigned vacation-enforcer—is still asleep. When Georgia talked me into taking over the last six weeks of her and Cassie's lease while *Britta's* undergoes some much-need renovations, she insisted Stella come with me for part of the time.

She'll need her back in Paradise once *At Home with Georgia Rose* starts filming again; Stella keeps all of Georgia's social media accounts updated with fresh content during the show's season. Until the season starts in a couple weeks, though, Stella's unofficial assignment is to make sure I'm okay.

My dad and brothers weren't crazy about the idea of me coming here at all, let alone by myself. I wasn't privy to the backdoor bargaining, but my guess is that Georgia offered to let Stella come with me to ease their worries before proposing her LA idea to me.

At first, coming to LA appealed to me, but the idea of Stella coming too didn't—as much as I love her. I thought I wanted time to myself. But if I'm already going stir-crazy in the first five minutes of my suddenly too-quiet vacation, my family probably wasn't wrong about sending her to keep things lively. I've got maybe an hour before she wakes up and puts my scheduled, unscheduled time into motion. Until then, I'm going to enjoy sitting on the small patio watching the morning move from gray to gold with the sound of lapping waves in the distance.

I just wish I had a good cup of coffee to go with it, and if Stella would wake up, I could make one. I didn't pack a lot, but I made sure to bring my espresso machine and some of my favorite gourmet roasts. Taking a break from work doesn't mean I'm taking a break from coffee. But setting up my essential coffee maker will take a minute and, more than likely, wake Stella. No one needs to poke that Bear. I'll let her come out of hibernation on her own.

An hour later, when someone knocks at the front door, I haven't changed out of my pajama pants and T-shirt—no bra—and it's not even eight am. Stella is still in bed. I still need coffee, and I really don't want to open the door to a stranger when I'm not dressed. Or even when I am. I've met one person in LA—barely—and I'd be lying if I didn't admit that all Dad's warnings about "big cities," aren't running through my head as I open the Ring app he insisted I set up.

I look at the live feed of the doorbell camera. Two men are at the door, both in board shorts, one in a tank, the other shirtless. The taller one swipes at the air around him, looking annoyed while the one with shaggy hair—Mom would have called him unkempt—is barefoot. I don't recognize the tall guy, but the unkempt one is the single person I know here. And his hair actually looks shorter than it did the last time I saw him, which would make Dad happy. He's suspicious of any man with hair past his ears—my brother, Adam, being the one exception to that rule.

Aside from the shorter hair, Dex looks the way I remember from the beginning of June, when he showed up in Paradise, perpetually shirtless and smiling. Which makes me happy.

I've missed admiring his well-formed pecs, the curve of his biceps, and the way his waist tapers into his low-cut board shorts. He's not big and muscular like my hockey-playing brothers, and I like that. There's a lean, natural athleticism to his shape that I could admire all day. In fact, I took the *no shoes, no shirt, no service* sign out of the window at *Britta's* after the first time Dex came in, just so I could admire his bare chest for at least part of the day.

The thing I'm most interested in at the moment, though, is the takeout coffee cups he's holding.

I do a nip check, then grab a hoodie to throw on, even though it's already over seventy degrees in this apartment. I'm surprised how many women in LA don't wear bras. Or much of anything, really. No judgement on them, because bras are the worst, but I'm not there yet seeing as how I've been a California girl for exactly fourteen hours.

And Dad might die of a heart attack if I ever do get to the point where I stop wearing a bra and let my bum hang out of my shorty short shorts. My brothers would have opinions about that too.

I don't care what they think about LA or the people in it. I feel lighter being somewhere besides Paradise than I have in months—years, really.

Some of that may have to do with the man on the other side of my door who rings the bell a second time. Georgia gave me Dex's number, but I haven't reached out. Haven't known exactly what to say, but I guess that's irrelevant now.

I throw open the door. "Hi, Dex. You're up early."

I say this as though we're old friends, and I was expecting him. Is that the wrong approach? I'm not sure what the right approach is.

Dex steps inside, warming me with his amber-flecked eyes ringed with gold. "Ah, I'm always up early." The letters in *early* blend, the hard r disappearing almost entirely, so the word roll over me as gentle as a breeze before he hands me a coffee. "Thought you might need this. Welcome to South Bay."

My smile disappears when I see the brand on the coffee cup. Honestly, I'm as surprised to see Dex as I am to see the logo of the company known for speed, not quality.

I take the coffee from him, and he leans close. Before I know it, he's kissed my cheek, sending a rush of heat across my entire face and reminding me of our last kiss.

Dex's friend follows him inside and tsks. "You've embarrassed her."

He has the same accent as Dex and waves his hand toward my red face, which only makes me blush more.

"Britta and I are old friends," Dex says, then hands me the other coffee. "This one's for Stella. She came too, yeah? Georgia messaged me, saying I should keep an eye on the two of you."

"Did she? She told me you'd probably be surfing somewhere." I sip my coffee to be polite, feeling more comfortable now that he's referred to me as a *friend*.

As I sip, his eyes sparkle with laughter, and I think he may be teasing me with this coffee.

"Treating me to something exotic today." I tip the cup to him and take another sip.

He cracks a smile, and he turns to his friend. "Told you she'd hate it."

"You're the whinger who told me to grab something else if *Annie's* was too busy," the friend says. "What else is there besides Starbucks? You set me up."

"Let me guess." I look in Dex's direction and raise an eyebrow. "You figured bad coffee was better than no coffee? At least for an American?"

The friend barks a laugh and steps around Dex. "You're right, mate, she's funny. I'm Archie." He lifts his chin in greeting. "Nice to meet you."

Something flickers in Dex's eyes that takes me back to summer and the heat that simmered between us. "I'll bring the good stuff later. We're in a bit of a rush this morning if I'm going to catch any waves today."

"That's right. You've got a *job*." If my hands weren't full, I'd make air quotes around *job*, but Dex knows what I mean.

"Best job in the world." His smile fills the room, briefly pushing away the sadness I still wake up to every morning since Mom died.

The sadness that brought me here because, after four months, I still can't seem to move on. It doesn't escape me I've felt better in these last few minutes than I have in all these months—which means Georgia might have been right about California sunshine being what I needed. Dex is his own sort of California sunshine.

I take another sip of my coffee, and for a few seconds, Dex and I grin at each other. Then I turn to Archie. "Are you a surfer, too? Or do you have to wear a shirt to work?"

Archie shoots Dex a look, and I worry I've offended him, but Dex jumps in. "He used to surf, but now he's my manager and my coach. I even pay him to do it."

Archie's face holds a question that I can't figure out before it passes, and his grin comes back quickly. "Doesn't pay me enough, but I let it slide, because I'm a good guy, and he wouldn't survive without me."

"That's mostly true," Dex suddenly grows serious. "I wouldn't be the surfer I am without Archie."

"Well, I'd love to watch you both sometime if you ever surf in California. Georgia says you're always traveling somewhere else to surf, so maybe you're bored with California waves?" I let my gaze linger on Dex, wondering for the first time why he spends most of his time in California instead of Australia if he's always leaving, while also hoping he's going to be around for a while. Six weeks, ideally.

Dex tips his head and gives me a curious look. "California has some good waves," he says in a voice dry enough to make me think he's understating the fact.

"Some of the best in the world." Archie adds with a gentle scoff. "This dingbat," he wags his head toward Dex. "Is about to surf one of them."

"This morning? Just one wave? Seems like you go to a lot of work to only surf one wave." My eyes dart to Archie back to Dex.

Archie's green eyes cloud with confusion. "He'll surf more than one wave. Probably a few sets."

Dex barks a laugh. "We mean the *type*, not the number, when we say wave. Every surf spot has a unique type of wave based on the wind and seafloor, but I surf as many good waves as I can catch no matter the location or what type of wave I'm on." Dex answers, his lips pulling into a smile. "I forget you don't speak surf."

I raise my eyebrows. The air snaps between us, throwing off more heat than the griddle back at *Britta's*. "I guess you'll have to show me what you mean."

"You can come watch right now. We're headed to a beach a few minutes south." Dex's eyes don't leave mine, and I almost say yes.

But I shake my head instead. "Stella's got plans for us today...if she ever gets up." As much as I'd like to have a beach day with Dex, Stella already told me she's found somewhere we *have* to go today. "Tomorrow, maybe?"

Dex shakes his head slowly. "I've got a competition that starts tomorrow."

"A competition? I thought surfers were too laid back to compete."

Dex laughs. "Professional surfers are a competitive bunch."

His voice has the dry-as-burned-toast tone I've learned he uses when he's understating something. But when his eyes travel over me, sizing me up, I get the sense I've underestimated what being a professional surfer means.

"It's no biggie," Dex says in that same tone. "But if you wanna watch, you can."

"That's *not* a good idea," Archie says, stepping closer to Dex, telegraphing a warning to me that's loud and clear. He doesn't want me there.

To be honest, I was more interested in flirting with Dex than actually watching him surf. I'm not really the *rah-rah-sit-on-the-beach-and-cheer-for-a-guy* kind of girl. Plus, hockey is my sport, not surfing. Not much surfing in Idaho, unless wakeboarding counts.

But Archie not wanting me at the competition, has me curious. Is it a private VIP event that will be hard to get me into? Maybe Dex really does make money surfing, and it's not just a hobby. Maybe I've just been invited to an event that only Hollywood stars who care about surfing can get into. Like...Keanu Reeves—I think he was in a surfing movie back in the day. He's old, but still hot.

I let my eyes roll over Dex. "I think I'd enjoy watching you at work. Seems only fair after you spent so much time heckling me about my coffee."

Dex's whole face cracks into a wide grin, but at a look from Archie, he smooths it away. "Get Stella and come with us to the beach today. That'd be less trouble than going to the competition, and you'll be more entertained watching me surf for fun. We can hang out." Dex says casually, but there's a dare in the way he traces his tongue along his bottom lip. Like he's throwing me a crumb to see if I'll go for the whole sandwich.

I do love a good sandwich.

"Watching you surf for fun sounds a little like you watching me make instant coffee at home." I match Dex's casual tone, but the return of his grin sets off a chain reaction that starts with blips in my pulse and ends with a tingle skipping along each vertebra of my spine. "I think I'd rather watch you at your competition."

Dex meets my gaze. "It's a fair drive to the competition. All the way in San Clemente, and it starts early. The traffic and parking will be chock-a-block and it's a ridiculous hike to the beach."

If he's trying to talk me out of going, his rich, coffee-brown eyes aren't doing him any favors by inviting me in for a sip.

"I'm on vacation." I shrug. "I've got all time in the world. I want to see as much of LA as possible, including San Clemente."

Archie laughs, and Dex's smile grows. "San Clemente is halfway to San Diego, in Orange County. Hours away, but not that different from South Bay. All multi-million-dollar beach shacks and girls in bikinis." His gaze drifts all the way to my toes and back. "I wouldn't mind seeing you in..."

I raise an eyebrow, waiting for Dex to finish his sentence.

"...The audience." He pulls in his lips, and I narrow my eyes, sure that's not what he was going to say.

"Sounds lovely." I sip my coffee, keeping my gaze on Dex. "What day and time?"

Archie crosses his arms like he's Dex's bodyguard. "You'll be a distraction."

"A distraction from what?" I look around like the answer might appear. "Hanging out at the beach, catching a few waves?"

Dex steps in front of Archie, who is visibly annoyed now. "Waiting period starts tomorrow. We're headed down later this arvo, so we're ready when the wave is."

I blink. "Sooo, you'll surf tomorrow?"

Archie's shoulders sag, and Dex laughs. "If the wave is good. But the swell reports say it'll likely be another day or two. Maybe even a week. The event is set for any day between September tenth and eighteenth."

"You just wait around to surf? There's no schedule?" Which, I guess, tracks for a surf competition if every stereotype of surfers being flakey and laid back is true. But I keep that opinion to myself.

Dex runs his tongue over the grin playing at his bottom lip, firing up memories of him kissing me in my shop that day. Man, that had been a nice kiss.

"The only place to schedule good waves is Kelly Slater's Surf Ranch," Dex says. "Mother Nature doesn't care about surfers or a schedule, so we have to wait on her. First thing surfers learn is to let go of any ideas about humans having control over anything."

I shift my gaze to Archie, who lifts a shoulder. "You want to go; you wait for the wave, same as the rest of us."

I think I understand the waiting thing, but now I'm caught on this surf ranch thing. I suspect it's some kind of Australian humor. "So, someone has a ranch, like, in the ocean? Where the waves are always good?"

Archie rubs his brow. "Not that kind of ranch."

At the same time, Dex says. "You've never heard of Kelly Slater?"

I shake my head, forcing myself to keep my gaze on his eyes—not his lips—but those are equally distracting.

Archie and Dex look at each other, then back to me, both their faces indignant. Archie is the first to speak. "He's literally the best surfer who's ever lived. He's in his fifties, still competing and still *winning*."

They stare at me as if I should be impressed, and I look back and forth between them, wondering why.

"And that's unusual?" I ask.

An awkward silence follows, so I lean against the sofa behind me and sip my coffee. It's lukewarm and not good, but I need to do something. Judging by their disappointed looks and sagging shoulders, I've offended them. The least I can do is pretend to enjoy my watered-down coffee.

"It is *exceptional*." Archie rakes his hand through his red, wavy hair. "You seem like a nice girl, Britta, but you've got no business at the biggest surfing event of the year if you don't even know who *Kelly Slater* is."

I laugh, assuming he's teasing, but his face only grows more serious.

"Really? I can't go? What do you think is going to happen? My lack of knowledge about surfing will spread like a nasty virus on a cruise ship?" I try to keep my voice light, but the more Archie doesn't want me to go, the more I want to.

Dex's mouth twitches while Archie's face flushes with anger.

"This competition is a big deal, no matter what Dex says. He needs to stay focused if he's going to win." Archie's words are measured and even, despite the irritation that underscores each one.

Dex turns to Archie. "The crowd will be too big for me to even see her."

They stare at each other, Dex lifting his chin to meet Archie's downward gaze. Finally, Archie lets out a loud, annoyed sigh. "Fine."

Just as I'm about to make a snarky comment about two men deciding what I can and cannot do, I hear Stella's bedroom door open. I take a few steps backwards to peer down the hall. She takes one step out of her room, wearing a T-shirt that barely covers her thighs, her black hair tumbling from a loose bun on top of her head.

"Do you have the TV on? Or are our neighbors just really loud?" she asks in a tired voice, rubbing her eyes.

I scramble around the couch and spread my arms and legs wide in the hallway entrance to block Dex and Archie's view to the opposite end. Stella will never forgive me if they see her with bedhead.

"We have company, Stella!" I call to her before glancing back at our guests.

Simultaneously, our "company" both crane their necks to see down the hallway.

She stops in her tracks, and her mouth drops open. "It's barely nine o'clock. On a Saturday."

"Eight o'clock California time," Dex yells to Stella as though they've met more than once. "But we brought coffee."

At the sound of his voice, Stella jumps back into her room.

"It's Starbucks," I warn as I jog down the hallway to hand her the cup.

"Thank you?" Stella, still in an early-morning haze, calls around my shoulder to Dex even though he's out of sight in the kitchen. Then she gives me a look and mutters, "Guess I'll get dressed."

When I come back to the open kitchen and sitting room area, Dex and Archie are already at the door.

"We'll head out," Dex says. "But bring Stella, too, if you can make it. I'm not allowed on my phone this close to an event." He sends Archie an accusing look, making it clear who's made the no-phone rule. "So, I'll give Archie your number, and he'll give you all the info about times and how to get there."

"You have my number?"

Dex stops his exit long enough for a confident grin to tug at his lip. "Course I do."

"Good." I smile back, ignoring Archie shaking his head—again—and my own doubts about what I've gotten myself into. "So, do I wear a swimsuit? Or what? Are you the only one getting in the water? Or can we swim?"

Dex's expression is both puzzled and amused. "Whatever you wear to the beach. There's no formal dress code."

"Sunscreen and a bikini." Archie gives Dex a pointed look when he says *bikini*. Like he's reminding him that's the only reason Dex wants me there. Dex only smiles.

Archie turns back to me, and in a resigned voice, adds, "And a jumper. I'll bring towels and chairs for you. And an Esky with drinks and snacks."

"Excellent. Thanks." I pass on asking what a jumper and an *esky* are. I've already made it painfully obvious how little I know about surfing, the beach, and California in general. An esky holds drinks and snacks. That's all I need to know.

"And thanks for stopping by and bringing the coffee," I add, as I follow them to the front door.

"Yeah. See ya soon," Dex says with a slow smile that sends a charge of electricity through me.

"Yeah." I return his relaxed goodbye with an even more casual one before shutting the door and letting out my own smile.

I've been in LA less than twenty-four hours, and already Dex and I are back to the easy banter that came so quickly the first time we met. I have a feeling my time here will be fun whenever he's around. Just like when he was in Paradise, there's no risk of attachment. I'm only here six weeks, at the most.

In the meantime, Dex will take my mind off worrying about what's happening at home. No expectations. No commitments. Just easy.

And easy is exactly what I need right now.

CHAPTER FOUR

Dex

"Wasn't a wipeout, but you scored pretty low there, mate," Archie says as soon as Britta closes her front door. "I take it you didn't tell her you're one of the top surfers in the world?"

"Didn't come up."

We walk into our apartment across from Britta's. Our units are steps away from each other, but oceans apart in décor. While hers was decorated by Georgia—the big-time designer who used to live there—and has a comfy California vibe, ours is more surf-bum thrift-store.

A line of surfboards, in an open rack, we've installed along one wall; weights; a giant TV; a second-hand sofa; and an old table with a couple of chairs. Neither of us is around enough to really care how it looks, but

I'm always surprised Archie doesn't want something nicer. I didn't grow up anywhere fancy like he did, so it doesn't bother me.

"Don't get discouraged, Dex. Eye on the prize." He pulls a surfboard from the rack. "This okay?"

"You need a new catchphrase, mate. 'Eye on the prize' is a bit tired." I take the board from him, tucking it under my arm. "Besides, she's a girl, not a prize. And I'm not chasing her."

Archie assesses me, his brows drawn together. "I wasn't talking about her. I was talking about the title. The *world* title. *Britta* is the distraction, definitely not the prize."

My face heats, and I turn from him to head out the door. Archie follows behind with his own board, his loud steps made louder as they echo off the metal stairs outside our unit. The waves are small this morning, so he'll be okay, even though he misses surfing the big ones. A colossal wipeout five years ago left him with a serious concussion and inner ear problems that knocked him clean out of competition. Now my career is as important to him as his used to be.

That's part of the reason I often value his insight more than my own. My career isn't mine alone, it's Archie's too. When I win, he wins.

Which is why, if he thinks Britta will be a distraction, I have to prove to both of us she won't be. The six weeks she'll be here are off season. I'll still train, but with the next event in January, I've got some time to relax.

And the brief time I spent with Britta this past summer was relaxing. I came back stronger, more focused, and confident. I can't point to the exact reason beyond Britta not knowing anything about me or having any expectations of me. That takes a lot of pressure off a fella.

That will all change if she comes to the World Title event, and I can't predict how she'll react any more than I can predict a rogue wave. Sure, I can read the signs that she's not intimidated or impressed by fame. Georgia Beck is a bigger name than I am, and Britta acts like Georgia's a regular person.

So, it's possible, she could show up for the event and not think twice about the crowds of people wearing T-shirts with my name on them and waving cut-outs of my face. She may not even notice.

Or, like other girls I've dated, she could get caught up in it and think what I do is more important than who I am. Yeah, I'm a surfer, but that's what makes me a one-trick pony. If surfing goes away—whether because of poor performance or injury—then so does everything else, and I'm left just being...me.

And I'm still trying to figure out who that person is. If I had time to get serious with anyone, she'd have to go on a journey of self-discovery with me. Because I'm at the very beginning of that trip and I don't know what to pack or unpack or even where to start.

Britta's not that girl. She's only here for six weeks. Maybe not even that long. So, I definitely won't get distracted by her long term. In fact, having her around may help me relax not just in the coming weeks, but right when I need to most. At the biggest competition of my life.

With Britta at the event, I'd have one person in the audience who sees me not as a pro-surfer, but as I am at my core. A guy who loves coffee and waves. That's the simplest, easiest version of me. And that's the version I need to be to win the title.

I've put all I can into training for the championship event. Now it's time to sit back and let muscle memory and Zen take over. Britta might be the good luck charm I need to do just that.

But I'll have to convince Archie first.

When we reach the sidewalk leading to the beach, I slow to walk beside Archie. "There's really not a way to uninvite her," I say.

"I don't send her the info. Problem solved." There's relief in his voice, but his solution isn't right, and we both know it.

"She's going to be next door for weeks, and Georgia asked me to keep an eye on her." I match his longer steps when he speeds up. "She's had a rough go the past few months, losing her mum and all."

"She knows *nothing* about surfing. What are you supposed to talk about? You need someone who understands the sport and the pressure you're under." Archie sighs, but his words lack conviction.

"I'm talking about her coming to the event tomorrow, maybe spending some time with her while she's here. I'm not marrying her." I clap my hand on Archie's shoulder. He tends to make things bigger than they are.

"Maybe not yet, but you've mentioned her more than a time or two since you came back from Paradise, and you couldn't take your eyes off her just now." Archie stops and faces me. "Every time you fall for someone—which is a lot—you lose focus. The no-dating rule this season paid off big. Maybe it's not realistic forever, but when you date girls who've been around the Tour, they cause less of a disruption to your training schedule. They understand they have to come second to that, even in the off-season."

"That was before. I'm more mature now. I'm focused." I scoff. Obviously, the no-dating rule worked this season, but Archie's got it all wrong about who I should fall for when I'm ready to date again. "I've dated plenty of girls on the Tour. Never been so under the pump as I am with surf bunnies and women pros. There's too much pressure. We're powder kegs."

Archie's thongs thwack with every step he takes, taunting me to deny that the only time I stop thinking about Britta is when I'm in the water.

Lucky for me, I spend a lot of the time in the water. "Not interested in dating anyone right now, anyway. My eyes *are* on the prize, and I'm not letting anything get in the way of the title or staying on the Tour next year."

The only answer I get is the sound of Archie's thongs. When we hit the sand, they go quiet, and he finally speaks. "She shouldn't come Monday. She'll be a distraction. Worse, she doesn't respect the sport. Only fans should be on that beach."

"Yeah. You've got a point."

I say nothing else until we get close to the water. We drop our bags on the beach and take out rashies. I get mine on faster than Archie. I'm pulling the spandex over my chest and stomach, while he's barely got one arm in his.

I grab my board. A wave crashes, and I offer Archie a broad grin. "On the other hand, I'm keen to show her what I can really do—you heard the dig about me not having an actual job, right?"

Then I jog to the water, duck dive under a wave, and paddle out to the lineup. The waves come to me like Britta's smile when I tease her—easy and heart-pumping—and I surf better than I have in weeks.

CHAPTER FIVE

Britta

Stella keeps me busy all day Saturday. After exploring the Farmer's Market at the Grove, the surprise she has planned is a live music screening of *La La Land* in the LA Historic Park. I'm not sure what any of that means until we get to an enormous park in the middle of LA. A giant movie screen is set up in a grassy area and an orchestra is warming up next to it.

"How did you find out about this?" I ask as Stella spreads a blanket for us to sit on, along with at least a thousand other people laying down their own blankets.

"I've done my research." She lifts a shoulder and closes her eyes like she's waiting for me to throw flowers at her feet.

For the record, I don't, even though we've watched *La La Land* together roughly one million times and can sing every song. So, the fact we're here, about to sing along with the composer who wrote all the music leading a live orchestra, is pretty epic. Definitely not something we could do in Paradise.

Stella is four years younger than I am, but we grew up surrounded by her brother and all three of mine. We banded together out of necessity, but as we grew older, we became genuine friends. Especially over the past year, after she came back to Paradise to work as Georgia's social media manager. Stella is the one person I've talked to about Mom.

Which, I guess, is why the following day, she thinks she needs to fill our entire Sunday, too. She, more than anyone, knows how broken I am.

So, we check out the stars on the Walk of Fame, eat delicious Mexican food in Koreatown, and go to a Dodgers game. It's not hockey, but it's fun, and while I'll never stop thinking of Mom, I almost don't have time to think about the fact Archie hasn't texted me any details about Dex's tournament.

Tournament?

No, he called it a competition.

When Monday morning comes, I wake after the sun, which is something I haven't done in years. I sit with my back against the headboard and scan the still-unfamiliar room. Thin lines of daylight poke through the vinyl blinds opposite my bed. Everything is quiet except for a low hum coming from the ceiling fan. I close my eyes and breathe in the silence, bracing for the morning's first sense of urgency to pummel me.

Then I remember: I have nothing to do today. *Nothing*. Nada.

The stillness that should be peaceful is disconcerting. The usual urgency I feel every morning is replaced with anxiety. A few days without obligations or responsibilities is a vacation. But a few weeks? How am I supposed to fill entire *weeks* with no coffee or ebelskiver to make? No dad or brothers to help. No mom to take care of.

I haven't unpacked my bags yet, despite Georgia's empty dresser and closet. I haven't had time, but suddenly, I'm not sure how long I can stay.

I wanted to be here. Living in LA was a dream of mine in college—a dream I gave up when Mom got sick. But when Georgia offered me the opportunity to visit LA for six weeks, it sounded like a chance to at least get a taste of something I'll never fully experience. Like a magic pill offered to someone who's lactose intolerant that allows her to have one scoop of the best ice cream in the world before going back to her boring, dairy-free life.

Now that I'm here, though?

Six weeks feels like a lifetime. My skin itches when I think about whether Dad is lonely and wonder if the construction at *Britta's* is going okay. I can't get over the nagging feeling that I should be back home with Dad and *Britta's*.

Then I remember, *Britta's* isn't mine.

We chose not to read Mom's will until after the summer season. The grief was too much, and we all needed to focus on our businesses. When we finally read it last week, I learned she'd left *Britta's* to my whole family, not just me.

I was so angry at Mom; I couldn't stand to look at all the places that held memories of her. She might call my expectation that *Britta's* would be mine a sense of entitlement. I call it what I'd earned by working there, with her, for most of my life.

That's what finally pushed me to accept Georgia's offer to take advantage of her empty apartment. I thought LA would be an escape from my anger and hurt—a way to work through it. But two days in, I can't stand *not* to see Mom everywhere I look.

Maybe that's the reason I haven't unpacked. Stella and I have no plans today, so it'd be easy enough to get out of bed and empty my suitcases. Tuck them away with my hurt until it's time to go home. Hopefully, by then, I can leave the hurt smoldering here in the closet and go back to Paradise healed and happy.

But I don't get out of bed. I can't. The more I think about the empty day ahead, the more my heart picks up speed. So does my breath. I see my chest move up and down, but I don't feel air reaching my lungs.

I hear a knocking sound, and Stella pokes her head in the door. "Hey! What should we do today?"

Her voice sounds far away as I turn to her bright, smiling face with every intention of returning her cheerful greeting. But I can't. Nothing comes out but a cry.

"Are you okay?" Stella rushes to me, climbing onto the bed to wrap me in her arms.

I can't hug her back. My arms are numb. My whole body is. I think I might be crying. Someone is making a whimpering sound, and I don't think it's Stella.

Stella shushes me, rubbing my back while also rocking me back and forth. "You can let it out. You've held it in too long," she whispers gently.

I hate those words and that she's saying them to me. She's not the first person to tell me it's okay to cry and that I need to grieve, but she is the first to see me break down. I guess I'd rather it be her than my dad or brothers, but I'd prefer not to lose control at all. That's not who I am.

I inhale and force the breath to reach my lungs. Then I do it again and again until my eyes are dry and I can pull away from Stella.

"I'm fine." I mutter before sliding out of bed to dig through my suitcase for something to wear. "We can do whatever you want. We've got the whole day and lots to explore!"

I'm relieved when my words come out sounding normal and not like I've taken her hostage on my crying jag. But I don't trust myself to look at her yet. I stare at the empty closet, wishing my clothes would magically hang themselves up or, at least, tell me what I should put on. Every decision feels heavy.

Stella stays quiet for too long, forcing me to look over my shoulder at her. She's studying me like a math problem. As though there's a formula to solve what's wrong with me. I tense, waiting for her to tell me what I should do to stop being sad. To feel like myself again.

Her dad died when she was a baby. She never knew him. I had a lifetime with my mom compared to what Stella had with her dad. I shouldn't be sad. I should be grateful for the amazing years I had.

"Let's find some good coffee," Stella says with a soft smile instead of the advice I expected. "That's the only assignment for the day. We wander and try whatever coffee house or café we find. After that, maybe we go to the beach or unpack a little more..."

I send her a worried look, and she quickly adds, "Clothes. Not emotions." She glances at my mess, then back at me. "Or we keep living out of a suitcase. We can do whatever you feel like."

The knot behind my ribs slowly unravels. "Coffee sounds great. Let's start there."

"Good plan. Let me throw on some clothes." Stella scrambles off my bed and hop-skips to the door, making me smile.

"Thanks, Stel," I say quietly before she goes through the door.

Without turning around, she waves off my gratitude. "Love you, cuz. We'll get through this!"

Stella is an eternal optimist, which makes me want to believe her. I'm not there yet, but right now, I'm more grateful than she knows to have her here with me. And grateful to Georgia, not just for this apartment but also for letting Stella work remote while we're here. I didn't think I'd need my younger, bouncier cousin, but she's already proven I do.

I sort through my suitcase until I find a pair of linen shorts and a t-shirt. While the weather is getting cooler in Paradise, it's still hot here. I guess I'm grateful for that, too. I'm dreading the cold months ahead when business will slow to a crawl, and I won't have Mom to fill my empty hours.

Fifteen minutes pass and Stella still hasn't told me she's ready to go when I decide to search for her. I find her in her bedroom, still in pajamas, staring at her already-organized closet.

"What are you doing?" I stand next to her and stare at the same spot, but I don't see what she's trying to see.

"Finding something to wear. Sundress? Or workout clothes?" Her closet is full of the first, and I'm sure her dresser drawers are full of the second.

I look down at my cut-offs and the signed, but old and coffee-stained, Post Malone tee I've had for at least five years. "We're just going for coffee."

"We're in *LA*. There's no such thing as just 'going for coffee.' Famous people live here. I need something casual but chic." Stella pulls a short, white, spaghetti strap dress from her closet and examines it.

"And I need coffee." I open one of her drawers and find a pair of Lulu shorts and a tank top, and hand them both to her. "Let's go please."

She rolls her eyes, but with a grin, she takes the clothes from me. "Fine."

I walk away to let her get dressed, but before I get to the door, Stella says, "My goal is to get you to relax before we leave here. We're not on any kind of schedule." Her voice raises as I shut the door. "You're allowed to slow down and enjoy yourself!"

She's loud enough I can hear her through the door, but I don't need to. I've heard it a million times from my dad, too. If I wanted to slow down, I would. Slow isn't enjoyable. It's only long moments filled with too many thoughts. That's why I never thought about taking a vacation until Georgia talked me into it.

"Two minutes. Then I'm leaving without you."

I go back to the sofa in the front room and scroll through TikTok. We both know she'll be longer than two minutes, and I'm not going anywhere without her, so I might as well enjoy some Coffee Tok. I'm laughing at a barista I follow, sharing her Most Ridiculous Drink of the Day when a message appears on my screen.

> **This is Archie. Event is on. Be there by 7 am tomorrow if you're coming. No obligation. Just let me know.**

I read the text a second time, scoffing at his *no obligation*. Will getting up early to drive a couple hours to watch people surf all day be the most fun I've ever had? Doubtful. But there's no way I'm not going. If Archie's *no obligation* is his passive-aggressive way to tell me not to come, I am officially obligated to show him his passive-aggressiveness won't work on me. I've played more than one hockey game where I was the only girl on the ice and up against guys twice my size. I don't back down.

Stella comes down the hallway wearing the outfit I picked out, her hair in a made-to-look-messy ponytail, and her face done up to look like she doesn't need to wear make-up, when clearly, she is. Basically, she looks California native, while I look...basic.

I grab my wallet from the kitchen table and stuff it in my back pocket while she slings a designer purse Georgia gave her across her shoulder. I could take a lesson from her, but I've never worried too much about fitting in here or anywhere else. I won't be here long enough for it to matter.

"Okay, listen to this," I say to Stella as we walk outside, then read her Archie's text. "Is there subtext there? Or am I reading too much into it? I get the sense he still doesn't want us to go, even though Dex does."

We stop at the bottom of the stairs, deciding which direction to go before Stella slides her arm through mine and turns me right. "I think the only question you should be asking is how early we'd have to leave to get there by seven am."

"True." I speech-text the question to Archie as we wait at the crosswalk for the light to change.

It's nine in the morning, but cars are already backed up as far as I can see. Our apartment is a block from the beach in one direction and a block from Pacific Coast Highway in the other. Even with summer coming to a close, Georgia and Cassie warned us traffic would be bad on sunny days, especially when waves are good. I haven't looked at the ocean yet, but the sun is out and the traffic is bad, so the waves must be good.

Shops, restaurants, nail salons, and bars are packed tight on both sides of Pacific Coast Highway, and a million distinct smells waft from open doorways as we stroll past. Stella and I haven't done a lot of exploring around the neighborhood yet, but my pulse is pounding in a much different way than it did an hour ago.

I'm energized by everything there is to look at. Within walking distance of our apartment, there are restaurants that serve a dozen different foods: Japanese, Mexican, Vegan, Columbian. Every one is different, and I want to try them all, especially the New Zealand ice cream. What even is that?

Then there are the people.

Paradise was settled by Danish immigrants back in the day, and it's still full of a lot of blond-haired, blue-eyed people whose names end in -sen—including mine and my family's. There's some diversity—Latino families, the Native Americans who were the original settlers, and one Asian family. But not compared to this. In the twenty feet we walk, I hear at least three different languages, and I can't identify any of them.

The people who pass me on the sidewalk and the street have every shade of hair and skin color. I've never seen so many different people in one place. Some walk toward the beach, surfboards tucked under their arms. Others are on big-handled bikes blasting music from handheld speakers. A BMW with its top down pulls up to the light and the dad driving blasts some old eighties song while the teenagers in the backseat look close to dying of embarrassment.

The whole scene excites me in the same way Memorial Day weekend does in Paradise when the summer tourists show up. Some of them have been coming long enough that I know them now. Others are new, and I get to intersect with their lives for a brief moment. I may never see them again; we likely won't remember each other, but because our paths crossed, we're part of each other's lives forever. I love that thought. When Paradise feels too small, I remember that I'm connected to something much bigger, even if it's only by a gossamer thread.

"I think that's the main square. There will be coffee there." Stella points right toward the beach and the wide street perpendicular to it. It's closed to cars and parking, paved with bricks, and lined on both sides by restaurants with outdoor seating and stores providing every beach accessory possible. People mill around, lingering to pet dogs or window shop.

The atmosphere reminds me of Paradise's town square during the summer, especially the week of Huckleberry Days when there's a farmer's market and craft fair. I'm about to follow Stella to the square when I look the opposite direction and see people walking down the hill, carrying to-go coffee cups.

I wave Stella back. A man with shaggy hair and no shirt who looks like he just rolled out of bed walks past me and pulls the lid off his coffee cup. As he does, I get a whiff of something nutty, almost spicy, and slightly chocolatey that can only come from a good medium roast coffee bean.

"Excuse me." I tap his shoulder and he turns, holding the same to-go cup I've seen other people carrying. "Where did you get that?"

He glues his gaze to my chest, then nods and smiles. But just before I'm sure I've made a huge mistake and will never speak to a stranger in LA again, he says, "Post Malone. Cool, man."

I look down and remember what I'm wearing, then return his smile. "Yeah, I ran into him once in Utah while I was wearing this shirt, so he signed it for me."

"Very cool." He's still nodding, but he drags his eyes and points up the street. "*Annie's*. Best coffee in LA, and I've tried them all."

"Thanks!"

He wanders away, and I grin at Stella. "Bingo!"

"That could have gone very bad, you know."

"What?" I'm already following my nose in the direction my fellow Post Malone fan pointed.

Stella scurries to keep up with me as the light changes and I cross the street. "Talking to a complete stranger in the middle of LA. He could have been a creeper or a kidnapper or...worse."

"Would have been worth it. You heard him. Best coffee in LA." My phone pings, and I pull it from my pocket to see a message from Archie answering my question about what time to leave in the morning.

> **Pretty early. No later than 5 am. It's okay if you can't make it.**

I show Stella my screen. "There's nothing passive about that. He's being aggressively aggressive."

Her eyes go big. "Five am? That is aggressive. I don't want us to go either," she says firmly.

"It's not that early." I head up the steeply rising street, looking over my shoulder to make sure Stella is following. "And like you said, we can do whatever *I* feel like, right? And tomorrow I feel like slowing down and relaxing on the beach while watching a surf contest."

Stella drops her head more dramatically than her four-year-old niece when she has to go to bed early. "Fine."

I grin and pick up my pace. The air hangs heavy with a briny, ocean smell, but under it I can smell an amazing brew. I can tell we're getting closer to our destination by the people streaming by, coffee cups in hand, smiles spread across their faces.

One block later and a left turn on a side street, we find the pot of gold at the end of the rainbow.

Annie's is the cutest coffee shop I've ever seen—aside from mine, obviously. Painted blue on the outside, it's an old beach cottage that's been transformed into a bakery and coffee shop. A line of people winds out of a weather-worn wooden door that looks original to the house. Flowers peep out of window boxes, also adorned with pinwheels that spin slowly in the gentle breeze.

I take it all in, but the thing that holds my attention the longest is a chalkboard sign under a white-shuttered window that says *Help wanted to train staff. Experience necessary.* Taped to the board is a flyer, and I step closer to read it. *Annie hires people who are experiencing homelessness. She trains them here, then helps them get jobs at other coffee shops and works with housing agencies to find them shelter.*

"Don't even think about applying for a job here," Stella warns as we get in line.

"What? I'm not thinking about anything." The fact I'm still staring at the sign gives me away before I finish my sentence, but I can't stop myself. The word *help* calls to me as much as the story of what Annie is doing.

Stella snaps her fingers in front of my face, breaking the sign's hold on me. "Hello? Come back to me, Britta."

"Sorry." I shake my head to clear it, but that doesn't keep my eyes from sneaking back to the sign.

"Britta..." Stella warns.

"Stella..." I mimic her tone exactly. She rolls her eyes, which I answer with an eye roll of mine before letting out a sigh. "Look, I've spent nearly five years not only helping Mom with her illness, but also all the people I love most with their businesses. I can't take a vacation from being a helper. It's part of who I am, and this sign feels like a sign. I could train people to make coffee while I'm here. That's something I could *do* instead of spending the next six weeks stewing over *Britta's*."

"Let me explain how vacations work." Stella takes me by the elbow and moves us both forward with the line.

I pull my arm back and shoot her a bored look, which she ignores.

"People—*normal* people—go on vacation to *not* work. That is the foundation of every vacation—the very core, even—*not* working." Stella wags her finger every time she emphasizes *not*. "Now, granted, sometimes people have to do work on vacation—like I'm doing for Georgia with her social media accounts."

"Have you got a point, Stella?" I tap my foot and stare her down.

"Yes. I'm so glad you asked, because this next point is the most important element of a vacation." She hinges forward, rising to her toes to meet my eye. "Getting a *new* job, while on vacation, doing the same thing you do at your regular job, not only defeats the whole purpose of a vacation, but actually—in a cosmic, butterfly-effect kind of way—undoes vacations happening across the world."

"I'm not thinking about getting a job." With my arms still crossed, I face the shop, away from her.

Stella scoffs. "You're not *not* thinking about getting a job either."

"Only because I could learn some things about how another shop is run while teaching them some things, too. It seems like they could really use the help, too. This line is barely moving," I say loud enough for the woman in front of us to glance over her shoulder.

"We passed other coffee places. Let's just go to one of those." Stella turns, but I don't move.

"It's worth the wait. I promise," the woman says. As if in response, the line inches forward. "It's not usually this slow, but Annie's daughter, who works here, was in a serious accident recently." She slides her sunglasses to the top of her head and hooks her thumb around her bag's straps.

"Oh, no." I glance at Stella, who gives me a stern headshake that I pretend not to see. "How hurt is her daughter?"

"Pretty bad. She was hit by a car, and the last I heard, she may be paralyzed," the woman sighs. "Annie should really be with her, but if she closes it for more than a few days, her employees who need the paycheck she provides are at risk of being unhoused again."

"Why are there so many homele—" at her raised eyebrow, I correct myself. "Unhoused people in LA? That sounds naïve to ask. I hope it's not offensive. Is it because it's warm here?

I asked the same question yesterday when Stella and I drove around downtown LA, through entire blocks with tents and pieced-together shelters set up on both sides of the street. Neither of us had an answer other than California doesn't get very cold, so it's easier to be outside most of the time, but that seems too simplistic.

"I'm Britta, by the way." I hold out my hand, which she shakes. "This is Stella."

"Karen." She returns Stella's wave, then faces me. "Warm weather makes it less dangerous for people to sleep outside, but very few people choose to be unhoused here because the weather is nice. There are dozens of reasons LA has a problem keeping people housed that have nothing to do with the weather. High-priced rent and low wages, addiction, lack of mental health care, other states offloading their own unhoused people on California, just to name a few. There's no one solution that will solve the problem."

We move forward with the line, and I ask a few more questions. It turns out Karen does free legal work for unhoused mothers in her spare time. As we enter the air-conditioned shop, she adds, "Annie is doing good work. It's a drop in the bucket, but every drop makes a difference."

Karen nods to a black woman behind the counter who has spiral braids peppered with gray. She's wearing a brightly patterned caftan that reminds me of a sunset.

"Hi, Karen! You got company with you?" The woman—who I have to assume is Annie—asks with a wide smile that doesn't hide the worry in her eyes.

Karen introduces Stella and me as out-of-towners. At the same time, people walk out the exit calling out, "Thanks, Annie!"

She says goodbye to them by name, which really makes me miss *Britta's*. I miss knowing people's names, making small talk as I get their orders ready. I miss meeting new people who may just be passing through. I miss comping someone a good cup of coffee and some ebelskiver because I can tell they need it. Mom taught me that was the most important thing about running Britta's. It's not just about the coffee.

We don't have a homeless population in Paradise, but we have people with mental illness and other problems that, anywhere else, might leave them unhoused.

Like Lynette, who wears a tinfoil hat to protect herself from aliens and has squirrels for friends. I give her free ebelskiver and coffee almost every day even though she has money, but she doesn't always have the wherewithal to take care of herself. I take care of her in my small way, as do other people in town. But she's one person.

I'm a little embarrassed at how distant this problem is from me in my safe little town. And how very present it is here.

My family doesn't do vacations very often, but after my conversation with Karen, the fact they've arranged for me to not work for six weeks hits different. I'll still have food and shelter when I go back to Paradise. A couple of missed paychecks won't put me out on the streets, living in a tent, washing in public restrooms.

I wonder how many people Annie is training. Behind the counter with her are two employees who look a little lost, and not just because they're staring at the order screen with wide eyes. Both are missing a few teeth, and uncertainty drips off them like water from a leaky faucet.

"I'm ordering for the office today," Karen says and hands a sheet of lined paper to the pierced and tattooed barista, whose eyes go even wider.

But then Annie says in a soothing voice, "that's a big order. I'll get it while, Diva, you take this order out to those gentlemen, Joe and Paul." She points to two men sitting at a table in the corner. "Don't let them give you a hard time," she jokes. "Mitzi, you come take the next order."

"Really nice meeting both of you," Annie says to Stella and me. "Sorry about the wait. I hope you'll stop by again while you're here."

"I can help you!" I blurt as Annie is about to turn toward the espresso machines.

She blinks a few times. "With what?"

"Britta!" Stella hisses, but I step in front of her and lean over the glass covered display of pastries.

"I saw your sign." I point toward the chalkboard, even though it's out of sight. "I own a coffee shop in Idaho. I can make that cappuccino for you. Or take the drinks to the customers. Whatever you need."

With a serious expression, Annie studies me before finally saying, "Why? I thought you were on vacation."

"Because you have a help wanted sign up, and I'm good at helping. But mostly because you're doing a good thing.

Annie turns to Karen. "What does my lawyer say?"

"Your lawyer wants her coffee, so she says yes. As long as it's 'volunteer' and not paid work. That saves you both a lot of forms to fill out." Karen glances at me, then back at Annie.

"Totally volunteer." I can't stop the excited grin spreading across my face.

Annie reaches under the counter, then hands me an apron. "You can start by taking orders out." There's hesitation in her voice, but she adds, "And thank you."

I slip the apron over my head, then meet Stella's annoyed gaze.

"Really?" she says.

I slowly lift my shoulders in a shrug. I'm not sure what I've gotten myself into either, but in the middle of my sternum, there's an inkling of the purpose I used to feel before Mom died.

"Only for a few hours." It's not a question, but the words come out sounding like I'm asking for permission, and Stella's face softens.

"Get me an iced mocha. I saw a bookstore next door. I'll find something to read and hang out while you *work* on vacation."

"Thank you!" I squeeze her close, but she keeps her arms by her side.

I let go and hurry to pick up an order before Stella can change her mind.

From that point on, I'm so busy, I barely notice when she leaves or when she comes back into *Annie's*. For two hours, the line of customers never shrinks. As soon as one person leaves, another two or three fresh faces show up to replace them, and Annie seems to know them all. The energy is familiar and invigorating but lacks the bittersweet aftertaste I get being at *Britta's* without Mom. I'm doing what I love without missing someone I love, and it's exactly what I need.

Sometimes work is rest.

Things slow down around one, and Annie hands me an iced chai tea latte. "Time for a break. Your friend needs some attention." She points to Stella sitting at a table in the back, looking bored with whatever book she's trying to read.

I take the seat next to her. I'm about to apologize when I notice a wall of photos behind her. There are a dozen of them, all different-sized, framed and signed by the people in them. But my eye is drawn to the one in the middle of four people on the beach holding surfboards with the title *Surf City High* scrawled across the top.

I vaguely remember an old TV show with that name. A teen-drama kind of thing that I never watched. That's not what's got my attention, though. It's the guy standing on the left side of the group.

"Is that..." I squint and step closer. "Dex?"

Chapter Six

Britta

Stella and I both study the picture like it's a famous piece of art in a museum. The guy in the picture is definitely a younger, much, much blonder version of Dex, even though the printed name at the bottom of the picture identifies him as Liam Dexter.

"Dex is Slater?" Stella says excitedly.

I whiplash between her and the picture. "I have no idea who Dex is anymore."

"Wait! Did you say his friend who came over was Archie?" Her voice grows more excited as she points to the tall auburn-haired surfer next to Dex in the picture. "Like, Archibald Forsythe?"

I look closer. "Yeah, that could be him."

"Britta!" She grabs my shoulders, her face inches from mine. "If Dex knows Archie, then he knows Frankie Forsythe, too. They're twins on the show and in real life." She suddenly goes still, her hands dropping from my shoulders as she pivots back to the picture. "And if he knows them, he knows Rhys James," she says reverently.

"You mind taking this order out, Britta, while I help Diva make an Americano?" Annie says from behind me over the clatter of coffee cups clinking, espresso machines hissing, and customers chatting.

"Of course," I answer before taking a second look at the picture.

"If Dex is in the picture with Rhys and Frankie," I say to Stella. "He's met them at least once. I think he said Archie's his manager, so he obviously knows him well." I grab the cups from the counter and carry them to the table outside that Annie points to.

Stella follows me, talking the whole time. "How are you not freaking out right now? We are *definitely* going to that surf competition. Rhys James could be there. Archibald Forsythe will be for sure. No one's seen Frankie in ages... but, oh my gosh, what if *Rhys James* is there?"

I walk back to the counter with Stella still trailing behind.

"Why would Rhys James be there?" That's the one name I recognize. I don't listen to his music, but everyone knows who Rhys James is, and I'll admit to feeling a whisper of excitement at the possibility I might meet him. I'm not getting my hopes up or anything, but I've never met anyone famous in Paradise. Rubbing elbows with celebrities is kind of the dream for anyone who comes to LA, and I might actually get to do it.

Wait...

Technically, I already have. Because, apparently, Archie, at least, is famous, and Dex may be semi-famous himself.

"This order goes to the Gupta family over there." Annie says when I return to the counter. She points to a mom, dad, two young girls, and a poodle-looking dog. "The cookie is for the dog."

"They were on *Surf City High* together," Stella says behind me, and I realize she's still talking about Dex's connection to Rhys James. "But they were friends before that. All four of them, if I remember right." Stella helps me carry the order to the Guptas, setting the dog treat in front of Yogi.

When our backs are to the family, we exchange a look, and I'm sure we're thinking the same thing; a dog is being served food in a restaurant that's for people? We are *not* in Paradise anymore.

We both pull back a laugh before Stella picks up the thread she'd set down long enough to play waitress to a dog.

"I can't believe I never made the *Surf City* connection before. I thought Dex looked kind of familiar when he came to Paradise, but he was only in the show for one or two episodes. I'd kind of forgotten about him." She wags her finger toward the photo, then goes back to stare at it up close again.

I leave Stella to study the *Surf City High* crew and return to the counter where Annie is taking orders again. When Stella notices I'm gone, she finds a table close to the counter and pulls out her phone.

Annie moves away from the register and motions me to her. "You seem to know what you're doing. Can you take orders while I do a little training? Neither of these gals has done the espresso machine before, so I'm having to do all those orders. The point of sale is pretty intuitive. If you have time to make the orders yourself, great. If not, send them back here and we'll get them."

"No problem." I take her spot, and she gives me a thirty-second tutorial on her system. When she turns back to the staff, I smile at the waiting customer. "What can I get for you?"

"A flat white," he says, and I breathe a sigh of relief that it's a simple order and, thanks to Dex, I've had plenty of experience making it. But then he adds, "Quad shot, extra hot, extra foam, lactose-free milk."

There it is. But I've got this, and it feels good.

My experience and ability to pick things up quickly doesn't mean things go smoothly. There's some confusion as I learn how to call back the orders and communicate with the staff. But we fall into a pattern within the first twenty minutes I'm at the register that, while not completely smooth, speeds things up.

While I work, Stella sits at her table, eyes glued to her phone screen. She only lifts them long enough to call out something new Google has revealed about Dex and his *Surf City High* friends.

"Britta! Dex is really good at surfing! Like, one of the best in the whole world!"

I roll this over in my head. I don't think there are many surfers in the world, so does being one of the best come easy? Or is it so rare that it takes loads of hard work and talent?

A few minutes later, Stella adds, "Britta! This competition is huge! He'll officially be *the* best surfer in the entire world if he wins!"

Followed by, "Archie *is* his manager."

"That's what I thought."

The fact Archie is his manager seems like the least important thing I knew about Dex, considering everything else I've learned this morning. I had no idea he was so good, and I'm slightly humiliated that I teased him about being a slacker with no ambition. To be fair, I didn't realize surfing was as big a deal professionally as it is.

The line of customers finally slows to a trickle, and in between customers, Stella moves closer so that she's leaning her elbows on the counter, still holding her phone in front of her face. "Archie, Rhys, and Frankie were all competitive surfers, too, until the show started. They came here together from Australia to model for Rip Tide, then got recruited for the show. Rip Tide came up with the idea for the series and financed it; that's how they all got involved. But Dex is the only one who stuck with surfing instead of the TV show. They had no idea it would take off the way it did after the pilot, and he backed out of his contract only a few episodes in. They all stayed in America, but he was primarily in Australia until 2021."

Annie comes up next to me. "Learning about our local celebrities, are you?"

Stella lowers her phone and lifts her wide-eyed gaze to Annie. "You know them?"

"They've been coming in here since they were kids. Their show was filmed at our beach and the local high school." Annie wipes her hands on her apron, reaches into her pastry case to pull out what looks like a piece of custard pie, and hands it to Stella. "They were all so homesick. I wanted to do something, so I told them I'd add an Australian dessert to my menu. Rhys gave me his grandma's recipe for it. Lemon and honey Anzac biscuit tart. This one's on the house."

Anzac? I've never heard this word in my life.

Speechless, Stella takes the plate to her table. While I'm waiting on another customer, Stella lets out a borderline inappropriate moan and says, "this is amazing! It's as delicious as Rhys's voice."

Annie laughs. "Enjoy it. That's probably as close as you'll get to him. Fame makes it hard for him to come in anymore or even go to Dex's competitions. He hates the attention off stage."

"We're still going," Stella says around her bite of tart. "At least I can meet Archie."

"I never said we weren't going," I say. "You're the one who was complaining about the early morning."

I glance over my shoulder at Annie, almost regretting my new "job" now that I know Dex is *famous*-famous, not just semi. I want to see him do the thing he's famous for.

"Dex is a... friend." I don't know how else to explain our relationship to Annie. "He invited us to his competition tomorrow. We thought we'd go, unless you need me here."

Annie shakes her head. "You're volunteering. I'll take you whenever I can get you, but if you've never seen Dex compete, you need to watch him. That boy is magic on the water."

A large group walks through the door and Annie calls for Mitzi and Diva to come off break. Stella scrapes the last bit of tart from her plate, then reaches for her phone again.

"I bet we can find footage of Dex from other competitions," she says, typing.

Something flutters behind my ribs, and I have to fight the overwhelming urge to pull up a chair next to Stella and watch every video I can of Dex—including his two episodes of *Surf City High*.

I pick up the tart plate and wipe down her table to keep from looking over her shoulder at the video that's made her drop her jaw. I'm working—or volunteering, anyway. I have to stay focused.

I hand Stella her half-full iced mocha—her second of the day—that she's been nursing for an hour. "Maybe the bookstore has some books or magazines about him, since he's a local celebrity. I'll find you there when things slow down here. Or I can meet you back at Georgia's."

Stella gives me a questioning look before noticing the growing line at the counter. "I'll meet you at the bookstore." She drops her phone in her bag, then waves to Annie. "Thank you, Annie!"

Without Stella interrupting me every few minutes with more info about Dex and his friends, I'm able to keep my head where it should be—on my non-money-earning job. By the end of the day, Annie lets me take over the espresso machines, and I feel the sweet satisfaction of her trust. The worry in her eyes has almost disappeared and her voice is lighter.

After locking the door at three o'clock and turning the closed sign—an old school one that reminds me of *Britta's*—Annie lets out a long sigh.

"Britta, thank you," she says, tearing up. "Karen probably told you about my daughter. Things have been pretty rough without her. You were an answer to prayer today."

Annie wraps me in a tight embrace, and I fight back tears as I'm engulfed with the scent of coffee and browned butter. She smells like Mom. This takes me off guard, but is such a sweet realization that I give her an extra squeeze. I've missed Mom so much, but realize that more than that, I've missed the sweet memories of her. The last few years were so difficult that maybe they crowded out my memories of the mom I had before she got sick. That's made it easier to be mad about *Britta's*.

"Thank you, Annie." I pull away and smile. "You've helped me as much as I've helped you."

She smiles softly. "Get out of here before Stella comes back asking more questions about my Aussies."

I take a second to realize she's talking about Dex and his friends, but when I do, excitement bubbles up the center of my chest. I tap it down, afraid that acknowledging my feelings would be like popping the tab on a can of Coke that's been rolling around the backseat of a truck after that truck's been four-wheeling.

"Let me help you clean up first." If I leave now, I'll give into the temptation to google Dex and re-read everything Stella's already told me about him.

"Absolutely not. Mitzi and Diva will clean up." There's no room in Annie's stern voice for argument. "You've got an early morning tomorrow if you're going to make it to that competition. I'm packing up some of Dex's favorites that I made for after the competition. Since you're going, will you get them to him? He's going to be nervous; some lamingtons will remind him of home."

"Okay." I reluctantly slip off my apron and hand it to Annie.

In the time she takes to grab the box of goodies in the back for Dex, I've already texted Archie back, finally answering his message from this morning.

> **Send directions, please. We will be there with delicious baked goods from Annie.**

With the box in hand and plans to help Annie again the day after Dex's competition, I send Stella a text to meet me outside the cafe.

She's there when Annie lets me out the front door. There's a huge smile on her face and her hands are behind her back.

"Did you find a good book?" I ask, holding back a yawn. It's only three o'clock, but I'm wonderfully exhausted, and I've barely thought about Dad or *Britta's* all day.

Stella nods enthusiastically, then whips her hands from behind her back to show me a softcover photo book emblazoned with the stars of *Surf City High*. A whisper of disappointment runs through me when I don't see Dex's face on it, but I quickly brush the feeling aside.

I still take the book and flip through it, stopping only long enough to look at the one page devoted to Dex's character Slater—named in honor of famous surfer Kelly Slater, who I'd known nothing about until Dex's tutorial this morning. Then I hand it back to Stella.

"That's a good find."

She lets out a dismissive laugh. "I found better than that. Check out this video of Dex."

She holds up her phone, and for the next thirty seconds, I watch a very young Dex in a Rip Tide commercial. It has over two hundred thousand views on YouTube. That number doesn't take into account how many people saw the commercial when it first aired.

And my earlier feeling of humiliation from not understanding who Dex was, grows from slight to utter and complete. Dex is a VBD—very big deal, and I had no clue. Because I've spent my life—the past five years in particular—in a little town serving up coffee instead of experiencing the world. I'd planned on seeing the world, but then Mom got sick, and I got... stuck.

I chose to go back to Paradise after college instead of taking an internship opportunity right here in LA, a city I'd always wanted to come to. It was the right decision, but I guess, somewhere in those years of taking care of Mom, I decided I'd never be able to leave Paradise again. I can't even pinpoint when it happened. Especially since I just noticed it right now.

Watching Dex ride the inside of a wave opens something inside of my chest, releasing the tightness that's been there so long I've forgotten it. His hand outstretched, gliding through the wall of water at his side and the smile on his face softening his look of intense concentration feels like freedom.

Stella tries to show me more videos, but I wave her off. Instead, we window shop, sit on the beach, get some dinner, and basically do nothing until all I want to do is curl up into bed. Which is exactly what I do once we return to the apartment.

But I don't close my eyes. Once I'm snuggled into Georgia's downy comforter, I pull up the videos of Dex and watch him surf wave after wave until I fall asleep.

CHAPTER SEVEN

Dex

I'm in a quiet spot overlooking Lowers sitting cross-legged on a towel when Archie taps my shoulder and holds up both hands while he mouths *ten minutes*. I give him a shaka then close my eyes again to focus on the meditation music flowing through my headphones and the breath flowing in and out of my lungs.

When I first made not only the Championship Tour but also the final five, I was a nineteen-year-old rookie. That was nearly ten years ago. Back then, my music of choice before my heats was rap. Kendrick Lamar, Eminem, Kanye. They all got me amped up before hitting my wave. I'd go out fast, angry, and aggressive.

Too aggro.

That was my downfall. Over the following four years, I sank in the rankings, losing more and more sponsors every year.

I replaced my dad with Archie as my manager in 2021, the same year I moved full time from Queensland to California. Things have been better since then, even with my back injury in 2022. I worried I wouldn't surf again, but Archie stuck by me, making sure I got all the medical care I needed through six months of recovery. It's because of him I'm at the World Championships today.

Once I finish the meditation practice I go through before every competition, Archie and I navigate around arriving spectators to walk from a corded off spot on the beach to a cluster of temporary and permanent structures set up for this event. A few of the other surfers in the finals linger outside them, and I nod to Caitlin Simmers and fellow Aussie, Molly Picklum. They're not my competition, and I'll be cheering for Molly in her heats.

We climb the stairs to the changing room where I've stored my boards, giving a nod to Jack "Robbo" Robinson. He's another Aussie who's in the first heat against me. He's a good fella, a little younger than me, but he came up the ranks around the same time I did. He's got focus, determination, and a fresh silver medal from his Olympic surf. A medal I might have had if I'd not been such a screw-up when I was younger.

We'll talk after the heat, no matter who wins. He's got his AirPods in, doing the same thing as me—focusing on nothing but the wave, even though we're only seeing it in our heads right now. He's already pulled his green jersey on over his wetsuit that signals to everyone that he's number four in the World Surf League rankings. I've got orange for number five.

There are nine pre-World Title events on the Championship Tour, each comprised of rounds and those rounds are made up of heats. Two-to-four surfers can be in a heat, and the two who earn the most points move on to the next round. The others are eliminated, but compete in an elimination round to earn more points and a higher ranking.

The events can take days, and at the end, the surfer with the highest points and rank wins the whole thing. But every surfer leaves with points based on where they ranked. Those points add up, and the ten surfers—five men and five women—with the highest point totals at the end of the season move to the finals for the World Title.

In the World Title event, only two surfers compete at a time, and if you lose a heat, you're out. If you win, you move to the next heat. The heat you start in is determined by the number of points you've earned in the nine previous events of the season.

Because my overall points for the entire tour are lower than everyone else here today, I start in the first heat. I'll have to win three heats to stay in competition for the title, then two out of three more heats to actually win the title. That means a lot of surfing for one day, and I'll be up against guys who are fresh and rested. Very few surfers have ever surfed all five heats and won the Title.

I plan to take my place among those few today.

After stretching for a few minutes, I turn off my music so Archie can give me some final pointers and encouragement. I listen carefully to all the words I've heard before. I'll put them on repeat when I'm paddling out, along with the order of maneuvers I'm planning to do. If the waves cooperate, that is.

When the first horn blows, signaling I have two minutes until I have to be in the water, Archie and I head toward the beach, scanning the crowd on my way down the stairs. I've resisted the urge to look for Britta since I got here. The sand was already full then, but now it's packed shoulder to shoulder, standing room only.

We stop at the bottom of the stairs, and I peer down the roped off path from the WSL building to the entry point, hoping to see her among the fans cheering on both sides of the sandy path.

"Forget about her, mate. Focus," Archie says, sterner than usual.

He's right. He kneads my shoulders and points me to the water where the wave is coming in as reliable as ever. A perfect A-frame, high in the shoulder, spilling on the outside, and plunging on the inside. A wave that can be ridden right or left, which makes it perfect for a goofy-footer like me who prefers a left break.

"You *know* how to surf this wave." Archie's tone is still stern but also confident. "You *know* how to win this wave."

He knows what I need to hear, and my confidence surges. I've fought hard to get where I am, and I will not lose now. Not to this wave and not to my competition.

Regardless whether Britta's here to see it.

I leave Archie and walk the path to the end of the sand, then hop gingerly across the smooth, wet rocks the tide has carried in. The last thing I need is to hurt myself before I even get into the water, especially in front of a wall of spectators. My head is high, and I'm feeling good. I've still got around thirty seconds to make it to the water when I hear a familiar voice call, "You're up against Robbo, Dex. Good luck."

I know exactly who it is, and I stop in my tracks. Without thinking, I turn away from the water to get in the face of Brandon McVey, the surf journalist who's followed my career since I was in the juniors and who's been a ratbag from the get-go.

Brandon puts up his hands, feigning innocence. "I mean it."

He's trying to rattle me. I've never won against Jack, but after a deep breath, I pivot back to the water. I'm not letting Brandon get to me.

But then he asks, "How's Frankie?"

That does the trick he was aiming for.

People can say what they want about me, but they cross the line when they bring up my friends. McVey isn't asking about Frankie's health. He's goading me for information, and he knows he's got under my skin the second I trip. I catch myself, but I don't have to see him or hear him laugh to recognize that he's loving it.

When I made the finals my first year out of the juniors, I thought I was invincible. All the attention I got from the media and sponsors played that up and I spent way too much time giving interviews and flirting with girls and generally acting like an idiot, up to the point of punching McVey when he called me out for my behavior.

He ended up with a busted lip, but also the last laugh. I went into the Championship event sure I'd take the World Title. I ended up losing in the first heat with an embarrassing score.

The next year, I fell off the Championship Tour all together. Didn't even make it through the first cut because I couldn't place higher than fifteenth in any heat in the first five events of the season. Part of the problem was *Surf City High* taking too much time away from surfing, but Dad thought I could do both. It cost us a pretty penny to get out of that contract when we figured out I couldn't, but I was able to get back on the waves.

The following three years, I fought hard, determined to beat the most powerful waves in the world.

I should have been respecting them instead.

Off the waves, I was worse. I partied too much and trained too little.

A serious wipeout at Pipe two years ago—the second time I'd made it to the Championship Tour—and the six months it took to recover, finally knocked some sense into me. Now, I'm all about focus. I've shifted my mindset a hundred-eighty degrees. No more fighting the waves. No more distractions or glamming for the media. I work with the wave, not against it. We're partners. An old married couple who can finish each other's sentences.

I'm in a better place.

But Frankie's not, and that's McVey's fault.

I try to put McVey's taunt out of my head as I jump on my board and try to catch up to Jack, who's already paddling out. A good set is coming in, and I know he's seen it. That's one of his talents—reading the ocean and picking the best waves. I need to get to it before he does.

But I lose the paddle battle to him, and he gets that first wave. Usually, I'd be on the other side of it and not able to watch him, but he was so far ahead of me I have a front-row seat to his carves and the aerial that follows. I'll have to score a seven or higher, which is not the pressure I want to feel dropping into my first wave.

Every heat is the same in that we get thirty-five minutes to surf as many waves as we can. Five judges score each ride, with ten points being the highest. The highest and lowest scores are dropped and the other three are averaged for total points for that ride. At the end of the heat, the best two scores are added together for a final score out of twenty points.

A perfect ten for a single wave has never happened in the finals. And a perfect twenty rarely happens in any event, let alone in the Worlds.

Scoring a seven or above on a first wave, like Jack just did, is an excellent position to be in. Being the guy following the one who scored that high—*me*—is not.

That's what's in my head when I drop too early into my first wave. I do exactly what Brandon dared me with his taunting to do and lose my focus. The wave collapses under me before I can do anything more than carve the face once.

That'll be a zero score.

As soon as I'm out of the wave, I see Jack patiently studying another set of waves coming in, but he doesn't go for any. He'll wait for just the right wave, possibly only taking two waves total, maybe three. That's the other thing he's known for—patience.

That's something I'm still working on, and I'm already under the pump because he won the first wave, so I focus on settling my nerves. I wait until I spot a good set coming in. Jack starts to go for the first wave, then turns back. He'll wait for something better. I don't have that luxury, so I paddle.

I'm ready to pop up on the second wave of the set when I spot something ahead of me.

A fin.

I change direction, paddle out of the wave, and sit up. I can't put my legs on my board, but if the fin belongs to a shark—not a dolphin—I don't want him mistaking my dangling legs for seal fins, so I hold as still as possible. I glance over my shoulder and catch Jack getting ready to paddle toward another wave. At the same time, the sound of a jet ski in the distance confirms the Safety Crew is on their way.

I wave my arms over my head to get Jack's attention. When he sees me, I shake my head and point to the jet ski. Jack sits up quickly. If Safety is coming for us, they've spotted at least one shark from the shore or from the copter above us.

Jack cups his hands around his mouth and yells, "You see it?"

"Yeah!" I yell back and point to the spot where I saw the fin.

Both it and the wave are gone now, but no one takes risks when it comes to the "men in grey suits." Tamayo Perry's death from a shark attack in Hawaii earlier this year is still fresh in everyone's minds. The professional surfing community is still small enough that when we lose someone, we all feel it.

Jack swears loud enough I hear it and shakes his head, visibly annoyed but fighting to stay calm. He's no more worried about the shark than I am. Every surfer deals with them, and the chance of attack is slim. We worry more about a serious injury taking us out than we do being eaten by sharks, but the World Surf League guys won't take any chances.

Jack had a good chance of winning this heat, but it's over now. We'll have to wait for the all clear to get back in the water. We're not going back out until Safety is certain the shark, or any others with it, is gone. That may mean calling off the comp for a day or two.

The interruption could be devastating for him, but could be good for me. I've got time to clear my head and get back in the mindset I need to win the title.

The jet ski pulls up next to me, and I scramble with my surfboard up the rescue sled to sit behind the driver. I hold the strap and scan the water for more fins while a second jet ski picks up Jack.

Water sprays my legs and face as my driver speeds back to shore. When we get close to the beach, I jump off and carry my board through the shallows to the shore. Archie is there to meet me. I sense more than see Jack behind me. I wait to talk until we get past the disappointed fans.

"Sorry, mate," I say to Jack once we're in the locker room and our boards are put up.

Jack drops his chin to me but stays silent.

We've already been on standby for four days, waiting for good waves. Now we may lose them. Staying in the mental zone it takes to win, while twiddling your thumbs on the sidelines, is excruciating.

I'm too nervous to stay put, so I peel down the top half of my wetsuit and head toward the outdoor shower. Archie follows me there, staying silent while we wait for the judges to make their official announcement about when we'll get back in the water. I wouldn't be getting in the shower if I thought it was going to be soon.

What I'm most nervous about, though, is whether I'll get a second shot or if Jack will get to take his score and advance to the next heat.

"You may have caught a lucky break," Archie says after I turn off the shower. "I didn't see you coming back from that first round. Your head wasn't in it."

I nod and tell him about McVey. Archie's face goes dark as soon as I mention the journalist's name and what he said about Frankie. Archie doesn't like him anymore than I do, and for better reasons than mine. He opens his mouth, but then holds back the million insulting names probably running through his head. Instead, his eyes go to a spot over my shoulder.

"We've got some company." Archie lifts his chin, and I turn to see what he's scowling about.

I smile, though, when I see who it is.

"You should have told her to bring something warm to wear. Bit chilly out here this morning," I say in a low voice before waving back to my "company."

Without being asked, Archie makes his way to the security guard, who's blocking Stella and Britta from approaching. At the same moment, I'm hit with a sense of relief. This is the first thing that's gone right for me today.

Britta is here.

CHAPTER EIGHT

Britta

Dex and I lock eyes as Stella and I step past the security guard with Archie. I hear a distant introduction between Archie and Stella, although Stella makes it clear she knows who he is as soon as she calls him Dylan, his character's name on *Surf City High*.

I stay focused on Dex. His lip pulls into a slight grin, as though he's happy to see me, but he's holding back just how happy. So, I temper my own excitement.

The closer we get, the harder I have to work to keep my smile in check and my eyes on his face rather than his bare chest. I succeed at only one of those things, and it's not keeping my eyes up.

Dex has peeled off his wetsuit to his waist, and I have a front-row seat to a water show that could rival the spouting-fountain shows set to music at any fancy Vegas hotel. Tiny droplets fall from the tips of his brown curls to his tan shoulders. There, the hardiest of the drops continue their journey down his pecs, then his abs, all the way to... whatever he has on under his form-fitting, neoprene work of wonder.

Do surfers wear anything under their wetsuits?

I immediately banish the question. Totally inappropriate. None of my business. I will never say that out loud. Ever.

"Did you already surf, Dex?" Stella asks when we're within a few feet.

Dex drags his eyes from me to her. "Yeah."

"Really?" Stella's face drops. "We left at five—maybe a little after—but it was crazy getting down here. Then it took forever to find a place to park. We had no idea there would be this many people here!"

I let her do the talking while I go back to Dex's water show. I can't say whether it's true that watching paint dry is boring, but I can confirm that watching water dry on Dex's chest and shoulders isn't boring at all.

National Geographic could do a whole, award-winning documentary on the phenomenon.

While Stella goes into too much detail about traffic and parking, people pass Dex with a wave and a "tough break, man." Or "hope you can get back out there soon."

Then Stella asks, "Do you wear anything under that wetsuit?"

"Stella!" I hope the shock in my voice covers any anticipation in my face, because a beat of silence follows where we both wait for Dex to answer.

"Wouldn't you like to know?" Dex is full-on grinning now, but before he can answer, Archie steps protectively in front of him.

"Sorry, you girls came all the way down here for nothing. We just got word competition's been called off for the day." He crosses his arms, going into bodyguard mode again. A tall, lanky, not-very-scary bodyguard.

"We did?" Dex asks.

"I got a message from the Judges' box." Archie points toward a two-story structure that's as much windows as wood and full of people wearing headphones, looking at computer screens. "You'll be able to repeat the heat. They're deciding whether Jack gets to keep his first score. They'll announce everything soon."

Dex gives Archie a high five.

"Called off?" I direct my question to Dex, since seeing Archie in person has only confirmed that he didn't want us to come.

"Shark sighting." Dex shrugs like he's talking about a puppy and not the many-toothed, man-eating monster of the sea.

"Shark sighting? Like, someone saw a shark in the ocean?" I point to the large body of water that's hidden by the event tents and stands in front of us. "That ocean right there?"

Dex laughs. "That's the one."

"But nobody was out there, right?"

"Just yours truly there," Archie points to Dex. "And his competitor. Their heat was called off and now officials have called the day."

My eyes bounce from Archie back to Dex. I hadn't added sharks to the whole surfing equation until just now, and I'm seeing Dex in a whole new light. That's no small thing, swimming with sharks. "Did you see it? Was it close to you?"

"Did you have to punch it?" Stella asks excitedly. "I just watched a video of a surfer punching a shark in the middle of a competition."

"That'd be Mick Fanning. That story is legendary." Archie's lip twitches like he might smile.

Stella's excitement ratchets up from a five to a seven—which is around eleven out of ten on a normal-person range—when she faces Archie. "Do you know him? You've got to know him, right? I mean, you're both famous."

Archie's face cracks wide open. And Stella's done what Stella does best. She's won him over.

"I'm not that famous," Archie says, his cheeks going pink.

"Whatever. I'm totally star struck, and I work for Georgia Beck—it's not like I'm unfamiliar with stars," Stella gushes. "I can't believe Georgia and Cassie never mentioned Liam Dexter *and* Archie Forsythe were their neighbors. I mean, come on! Who doesn't brag about that?"

"I'm guessing someone who's already famous, like Georgia," I answer, because I texted them both the same question yesterday after we discovered who Dex is. "Or someone like Cassie, who grew up in LA and has arrested a few celebrities."

"That's no excuse. Georgia knows I want to grow my business, and I need more than one celebrity who I'm related to if I'm going to prove myself." Stella turns to Archie. "If you or Dex need any help with your social media accounts while I'm here, I'm offering my services for free—mostly. You could pass my name onto Frankie and Rhys, if you're happy with my work. And you will be."

Archie allows a laugh to escape. "I don't have social media, but I'll keep you in mind for Dex's accounts. And I can introduce you to White Lightning. He's probably the biggest star here today."

At Stella's confused expression, Archie points to an open tent behind us where a man is sitting at a high table talking to a woman holding a microphone. "Mick Fanning—the guy who punched the shark. White Lightning is his nickname. That's him right there, being interviewed."

Stella rises on her tiptoes for a better look, then takes Archie by the arm and drags him to the tent where other people milling around immediately say hi to him.

I turn my attention to Dex. "You didn't tell me your name is Liam."

"Ah, no one calls me that but my mum." He looks a little sheepish, which is completely adorable.

"Your mum and me, from now on." That's my sorry attempt to keep our attraction in check. I have to maintain some control here, what with his bare chest and butt-hugging wetsuit working to lure me closer.

Dex chuckles, then rakes a hand through his wet hair. When he pulls it out, a section of curls folds in on itself, like even his hair is one with the waves.

Which is what I've learned about Dex over the past twenty-four hours. Since being back on tour, commentator after commentator has mentioned how Dex is "one with the wave" in a way he never used to be.

I'm not entirely sure what that means, but I've watched enough footage to recognize that what Dex does on the waves is riveting. I can't get enough of the videos I've scoured the internet for, and I couldn't wait to see him surf in real life.

"I'm sorry we missed you surf," I tell him.

"I'm not sorry you missed it. I crumbled."

"Crumbled?"

"Lost my focus."

"So, is that it? Is the competition over? Will you get another chance, or is this shark territory now?" I stop myself from making a *West Side Story* joke about the Sharks and Jets. Mom loved musicals, so I've seen them all, but I've had more than one joke fall flat when no one under sixty understands my reference.

"The ocean is always shark territory, but the judges and safety team obviously have to be careful. They'll keep us out a day or two until they're sure there aren't any aggressive sharks close by, then the competition will start back up." Dex says this with a nonchalance that could only come from spending more time in the ocean than outside of it.

"What qualifies as a less 'aggressive' shark? The ones that only nibble on you? They take a limb or two instead of eating all of you?" I shiver as a breeze wisps across my shoulders.

Dex laughs. "The ones that aren't looking for their dinner." He nods his head toward a portable building. "Come on. I've got a jumper you can put on."

I follow him to a room full of surfboards and lockers, where he pulls a sweatshirt from a locker and hands it to me.

"Oh, *this* is a jumper. I didn't think it would be this chilly on the beach." I slip the hoodie over my head, then glance down at the Rip Tide logo across my chest. "Are you supposed to wear this? You know, because they're your sponsor?"

Dex's eyebrows go up. Maybe impressed I know this.

Or, possibly, concerned that I'm stalking him.

"No worries. I've got a million of them. You can keep that one."

"Well, thank you... Liam." I take a step back to put an appropriate amount of non-stalkerish space between us and step on bare toes.

I jump and glance over my shoulder to see another surfer. "Sorry 'bout that," he says in an accent close to Dex's, but slightly different. Definitely Australian, but maybe from a different part of the country.

"My fault. Sorry." I back up away from him and Dex until I hit something that digs into the space between my shoulder blades. I turn to see what it is, but somehow knock loose a surfboard from the open-frame storage thing I've backed into.

The board slips out of its spot, diving for the ground. I grab for it, but it slides out of my fingers and falls to the wood flooring with a hard smack.

I raise my eyes to meet a look of horror in Dex's. "Oops," I mumble. "Sorry."

The other surfer looks even more horrified than Dex, which tells me exactly how big my oops is.

Big.

But Dex recovers quickly and turns to the other surfer. "I'll take care of it, mate. I'll get the shaper to check it."

With one irritated glance at me, the other guy grabs a duffle bag and walks out.

"Is a shaper bad? Did I break it? Was it that guy's board?" I resist the urge to help Dex set the board upright. Clearly, I'm not to be trusted around surfboards.

"Nah. Shapers sand down the boards... shape 'em into what the surfer wants. Jack and I use the same guy. If there're any nicks, he'll sand them out. No worries. Everything will be fine." Dex gently puts the board back into place. "These boards are used to getting knocked about more than you just did. Jack's just cranky because he was on track to beat me before that shark showed up."

I nod and let out my breath. "So, the shark did you a favor?"

Dex lets out a laugh that already is becoming familiar to me. It's a low, gruff sound that comes from the back of his throat but loses steam before it makes any actual noise. Like he wants to keep what he's laughing at between the two of us.

"I'll give that one a thank you if I see him again. Because of him, I get a chance to do better than I did this morning. Jack, though, had a great start that might not count anymore. Judges are still deciding." He faces me with a smile, like everything is fine. "But I'm sorry you drove all this way for nothing."

"Me too. I'm bummed I won't get to watch you."

He gives me a playful look. "Sure. You're just trying to make me feel better because I don't have an actual job."

"I'm serious." I've teased him a lot about surfing, but that's because I didn't understand it.

So, I take a breath and come clean. "I watched a lot of videos yesterday of you surfing and they're..." I don't think there's a word big enough to describe it, but I land on "incredible. You've spent your whole life learning to do what you do, haven't you? I'm sorry I put it down." I put my hands up to stop his pleased grin. "Don't let that go to your head."

I gather my thoughts, then go on, even though I suspect his grin will only grow bigger. But something's shifted in my thinking about Dex. We're not as different as I thought.

"This isn't a perfect comparison, but the look on your face when you ride a wave reminds me how I felt when I played ice hockey." I don't talk about playing hockey very often. It's a dream that didn't materialize, and it's painful to rehash. But it's also why I understand Dex.

Except the question on his face makes it clear he doesn't understand where I'm going, so I scramble to explain.

"The two things I did growing up were dance classes and hockey. Hockey I've just always loved. Dance I did because that's what was available for girls, and I figured out pretty quick that the coordination it took translated to the ice."

Another surfer comes into the locker room, and Dex guides me outside—away from the surfboards—where we have a little more privacy.

"So, you're saying you love hockey the way I love surfing? I didn't know that about you." He's pleased with that bit of information, but I shake my head.

"There's more to it than that. Paradise didn't have a girls' team, but I loved playing. And I was good enough that sometimes I'd play with my brothers and their teams." I swallow back years of disappointment in order to get to the hard part. "I'm not trying to brag, but I had more than one coach say I could play college-level if I had more time on the ice. I don't know... maybe now that there are women's pro teams, I could have even made it to the big leagues."

"I'm really sorry, Britta." Dex's apology is sincere, even though he's not the one to blame.

I shrug, because there's nothing to be done now. "The point is, in those videos, it's obvious how much you love not just surfing, but competing. That resonates with me. The work and sacrifice you've put in to get where you are...it's impressive, that's all."

"Thanks." Dex smiles in his self-deprecating way, brushing off the compliment. "Usually only other surfers understand the passion. I never thought a hockey player would get it."

"Hockey and surfing aren't *that* different," I say.

Dex raises his eyebrows, unconvinced, so I continue. "One thing I loved about hockey was anticipating other players' moves and finding a way around them while also staying in control of my balance and navigating the rough ice."

His forehead crinkles as his eyebrows go higher, and I search for the right words. "The close-up shots of your face and your body in those videos? I saw the same thing. You're watching the other surfers while also reading your environment. That takes a skill that's more than learned."

I know I've connected the dots when Dex's face lights with understanding. "Yeah, when things go right, I feel a synergy out there, biding my time, waiting for my wave, but also trying to determine what my opponent is planning."

His excitement draws me closer.

"It's a dance, right? So many things are in motion that your steps have to come naturally. You have to let go of what you know and trust your intuition." Our eyes lock, and I feel a connection I haven't felt with anyone in a long time. "I would get in a zone where I could *feel* what to do. No matter how loud everything was around me, I heard nothing but the sound of my blades slicing through ice. If I followed that music, I could score."

"Yeah." Dex moves closer too. "I like that. I think of it as following the right energy. Being in tune with yourself and the world around you."

We nod together, totally in sync.

And then I hear Archie's voice behind me.

"Did you hear that announcement, Dex?" he asks.

Dex and I both look at Archie. I'm not sure if Dex heard something, but all I heard was some mumbling coming from the speaker pointed toward the beach.

"Britta..." Stella says, breathless. "Matthew McConaughey is here. At this beach. To watch Dex. Apparently, he's a huge fan of surfing."

"Yeah, too bad we'll all have to wait until tomorrow. Jack's keeping his score, and he has priority in the first heat. Judges just made it official with the announcement you missed." Archie gives Dex a searing look that I'm sure has something to do with Dex being "distracted" by me. "Let's clear out so you can relax before then."

I turn to Stella. "I guess that means us, too." Then I face Dex again. "We'll try to make it back tomorrow, but is there TV footage we can watch if we don't?"

Dex glances at Archie, who gives a stern, micro-shake of his head, that Dex promptly ignores, and blurts, "Or you could skip the drive tomorrow and just stay with me tonight."

CHAPTER NINE

Dex

W*hat. Did. I do?*

Britta is staring at me, her shoulders pulled back, both surprised and guarded. Archie looks ready to knock some sense into me, and an awkwardness hangs over us, thicker than a soft squelching noise that could be nothing or could be someone breaking wind. I want to take back all the words that just spilled out of my mouth, because I think I just asked Britta to stay the night with me.

"Us! I mean us!" My voice squeaks in my rush to walk back what I've said. "Archie and I are both staying down here."

Britta's blush covers both cheeks. I feel mine all the way down my spine and Archie's mad as a cut snake. Stella is the only one whose face isn't some shade of red.

"You have a house here?" she squeals.

"Not my house. The house we're staying at." I point between Archie and me, just to clarify, again, that I'm not inviting Britta to spend the night with *me*.

"It's the Rip Tide house," Archie says, like I've just offered to throw a party at his parents' house while they're away on vacation.

Which, to be fair, I did do once. Maybe twice. His parents are gone a lot.

"We're the only ones there. They won't care." I say to him and only him, because they're *my* sponsor, not his and even though I'm a little nervous about the invitation I just issued, I'm not going to show it.

Britta stays quiet, and I barely breathe. She'll either say yes or she'll say no. But I don't want her to think I was hitting on her.

Was I hitting on her?

"You just got back in their good graces." Archie crosses his arms and stares me down. This isn't his usual stern look. He's genuinely mad. "If you don't win and they find out you had girls over, they'll think you got..." His eyes dart to Britta then back to me. "distracted."

He's used that word more than once about Britta, and I'm getting bothered by it. Judging by the annoyed look on Britta's face, she is too.

"Women," Britta says, and Archie turns his head only enough to peer at her. "We're women, not girls."

Archie rolls his eyes, which ratchets the awkwardness up to an uncomfortable tension.

"He doesn't mean anything by it." I jump in to diffuse the situation, mostly to protect my mate, but also because I want Britta to stay.

Few people have the guts to stand up to Archie. Not because he's intimidating, but because of his last name. It packs a lot of power in

Australia, and that—plus our long history—packs a lot of influence on me. I know Archie has my best interest at heart, and he's a ripper coach, but sometimes he's too protective of me, and I feel isolated from the real world.

Britta is a nice counterbalance to his certainty that he knows what's best for me.

Her eyes narrow in his direction, but she directs her words at me. "We didn't plan on staying. We don't have any extra clothes or toiletries, but thank you for the invitation."

Archie holds back a smile. He thinks he's won this little battle.

But Britta's answer isn't a no. It's a problem I can solve.

"The pharmacy will have toiletries," I shrug. "Rip Tide headquarters isn't far. They'll give me samples." *Easy.*

"Samples of what?" Britta asks.

"Clothes!" Stella grasps Britta's arm. "Yes, please! We're in!"

Archie lets out a loud sigh at the same time Britta says, "No, we're not!"

As much as I'd like Britta to stay, I won't push Britta to stay if she's not comfortable.

But then Archie says, "Good. Dex needs to focus," and Britta's eyes shift from the turquoise of Pipeline to the mottled blue of Lowers.

She doesn't like to be told what to do.

"We really couldn't let you give us clothes," she says to me with no conviction.

"Yes! We can!" Stella looks ready to burst out of her skin.

"But we don't want to *distract* you." Britta sends an angry glance Archie's way before looking at me again. "I know what a big deal this is. If we interfered with your win, I'd feel terrible."

Her eyes are back to the startling turquoise color of Pipe. They're as beautiful and as dangerous as that wave.

I've wiped out more on Pipe than any other wave I've surfed. I've broken my back there and nearly lost my career to it.

But I've also had the best rides of my life on Pipe. I'm mesmerized by its beauty. Tempted by its perfection. Scared by its power. And I'm never more alive than when I catch a perfect barrel there.

Britta's eyes tug at me in the same way.

So, trusting my instincts, instead of agreeing and sending her on her way—knowing I'll get my hopes up she'll come back tomorrow—I say, "You won't be a distraction. We'll hang out a bit, grab some dinner, then Archie will put me to bed early."

That gets a quick smile from her.

Archie throws up his arms and shakes his head. "Fine! But I get to choose what's for dinner—no burgers or tacos or anything heavy. Nutritionist approved only!"

He wags his finger at me like an old nun we had as a teacher in primary school.

"Yes, Sister Patricia." I fold my hands together, same as we had to for prayer, and bow my head.

Archie mutters, "Dimwit," then goes into the tent to pack up my stuff.

But Britta smiles. "I need to text Annie to tell her I won't be there tomorrow. Hopefully, she's more understanding than Archie. I think we're both in trouble with him."

"His bark is worse than his bite. Let me get some trakkies on and we'll get out of here." I wave my thumb toward Archie and the tent, then close the flaps behind me.

By the time we walk to the Sprinter van, Archie has already calmed down a bit. Stella talks his ear off as we load our stuff, then she sits up front by him. She's not his type—too peppy—but I think he gets a kick out of her.

We take Britta and Stella to their car, which is parked at least a mile away, then drop it at the house so we can all go to lunch together. When Britta comes back to the van, she's carrying a paper bag with thin handles, and I know exactly what it is.

"Don't let Archie see that," I whisper to her as soon as she climbs in.

Archie breaks in before she can respond. "Too late. Already saw it. No lamingtons until after you win." Archie motions for Britta to pass it to him, and, for whatever reason, she follows this order.

"Sorry!" she says and hands the bag to him. "I agreed to not be a distraction."

"Annie's cake doesn't count as a distraction. She makes it for me special." Does a whine creep into my voice? Yes. But that's because I'm hungry and nervous and Annie's cake always soothes what's bugging me.

"It's not on your nutritionist's list, so it's a distraction." Archie meets my eye in the rearview mirror while backing out of the tight driveway. "No sugar."

I growl, and my stomach joins me. "Then we need to get lunch now."

After some back and forth about whether ten o'clock is too early for lunch, Archie drives us to a farm-to-table restaurant that makes healthy food so delicious you forget it's healthy.

Another bonus is that it's twenty minutes from the beach, so there are fewer people to recognize me or ask about the finals, the shark, or anything else having to do with surfing. I don't want to talk to strangers about surfing. The only people I want to talk to about the Finals are the people on my team, including Britta.

Thirty minutes with Britta has convinced me I didn't make a mistake inviting her to stay. Even though, technically, she's a traitor for taking Archie's side about the lamingtons, joking around with her gives me something else to think about other than how I *will not* make the same mistakes tomorrow that I made today in the water.

She is a distraction, but exactly the distraction I need to keep from losing my chill.

While we wait to get into the restaurant, my phone buzzes. I take it from my pocket, then smile when I see whose face is on the screen.

"Rhys wants to FaceTime." I hold my phone for Archie to see. "Should I answer, or does he count as a distraction?"

Archie glares at me, then swipes the phone from my hand.

"Rhys James?" Stella's eyes fill her entire face, and she looks like she's not sure if she should faint, scream, or yak.

She goes on her toes to peek over Archie's shoulder as he accepts the call.

"You want to talk to Rhys?" I ask Stella while Archie lectures Rhys about what he is and isn't allowed to say to me.

"Do I want to talk to Rhys James? *People* magazine's official 2024 Sexiest Man Alive? Over Face Time?" she says dryly.

"So that's a no?" I take my phone from Archie, hold it close so she can't see, then dodge the bullets she shoots from her eyeballs. "Hey, mate! How's London? Did you hear about the shark?"

"Rainy, and I'm not allowed to ask you about the shark. How close was it?" My best mate's face fills the screen, his black hair sweaty and sticking to his forehead.

"Three, maybe four meters." I don't miss the surprise on Britta's face. "That's not so close," Rhys says.

"Closer than you've ever been, outside an aquarium."

Britta is playing cool. Her tapping foot is the only tell that she's interested in my conversation with one of the biggest musical artists in the world. Stella, on the other hand, may spontaneously combust if I don't give her at least a peek at Rhys.

Despite his fame, though, Rhys is shy. He gets nervous meeting new people, almost to the point of panic attacks. There's a physical and emotional distance between him and a crowd of people that makes him feel safe. One-on-one, though, isn't his thing.

"Hey, we've got a couple friends here who'd like to meet you," I say to him. "You up for it?"

His shoulders drop, and I already know the answer.

"No worries if it's not a good time," I say.

"I just got back from the gym," he says, like an apology.

It's an excuse—a flimsy one, at that—but it's fine. He has to protect his privacy in a way I only get a tiny taste of.

"Another time. They're rellies of Georgia and Cassie. You'll like them."

For a second Rhys looks like he might change his mind, but he changes the subject instead. "Did you get the tunes I sent you? For meditation?"

"Yeah. I used them this morning. They worked until I let McVey throw me off."

"What was McVey doing there?" Even separated by a screen and thousands of miles, I see Rhys's eyes go dark.

"Same as always. Stirring up trouble."

While I tell Rhys what happened, Britta gets her own call. She turns her back to me, and I can't hear her over Rhys, but I keep an eye on her.

Georgia didn't say specifically why she wanted me to keep an eye on Britta, but Georgia mentioned to me once in Paradise that I'd made Britta smile for the first time since losing her mum. I suspect that's what she wants me to do while Britta's here—get her smiling again.

So, when Britta's shoulders drop, I have a hard time focusing on what Rhys is saying. I want to make sure she's okay.

After a few *uh huhs* to what I'm only half-listening to, Archie motions our table is ready.

I interrupt Rhys. "We're grabbing some lunch. Thanks for calling, mate."

"Kill it tomorrow, dude. You can do it."

We end the call, and I hold open the door for Stella and Britta. As Britta passes, I ask, "Everything okay at home? Your dad all right?"

"Yeah, he's good. There're some problems with the construction on *Britta's*, but I'm sure that will be taken care of." Her expression doesn't hide the worry that her voice tries to cover.

But then she brightens. "Nothing I can't handle, though."

I squint, trying to determine if she really believes that, but she schools her face into a big, but empty, smile before I can.

"Did it help to talk to Rhys? That was nice of him to call. Does he always do that before your competitions?" She peppers me with questions that don't leave any room for my own questions about whether she really is okay.

I get the feeling this isn't the first time she's evaded concerns about herself by plowing the questioner in the opposite direction. In fact, as I think about it, she did it at *Britta's* once when a customer asked if Britta missed her mom.

Britta answered with a smile and a, *we all do, but we're doing great. How's your family?*

At the time, I thought she was being strong, but now I wonder if evading and redirecting is a defense mechanism.

I'd know. I do the same thing when anyone asks what my plans are once my surfing career is over.

I want to ask Britta more about her coffee shop and whether she really is okay, but I don't want to fill her with the kind of blinding dread and anxiety about the future that I get thinking about life after pro-surfing.

Beyond the coffee shop, I hope Britta has some sense that eventually she'll be able to answer questions about her mum and what life looks like without her.

I don't know if I'll ever be able to do that with pro-surfing. Partly because I love it as much as I do, but mostly because it's all I know how to do.

The thing with chasing a dream as big as being the best surfer in the world is that surfing is the thing I've spent my life focusing on. Not school, not vocational training, not a future that doesn't involve surfing. I've spent the last twelve years chasing nothing but waves.

Dad always said that kind of single-mindedness was exactly why I would be the best. I believed him for a long time. But the older I get, the more I can't keep from worrying about what happens if I'm not the best.

Not if. *When.* It's inevitable. I've been up and down the rankings so many times. Even if I beat all the odds and win the WSL Championship this year, it could be my first and only win.

Being around Britta makes that even clearer. She has *Britta's,* Paradise, and her family. She knows where she fits. She knows what her future looks like.

And maybe I like that the one thing she knows nothing about is the one thing I do know. When I talk about surfing, she looks at me like I'm smart. Like I actually know things.

I'm not smart, I didn't go to uni. If a conversation doesn't involve the ocean or surfing, I have little to say. Britta will find that out soon enough, but I think I'd like to see as much of her as possible until she does.

So, I guess I'll ride this wave until it gets frothy and hope I don't get too hurt when her time in LA is over.

CHAPTER TEN

Britta

My lunch of organic roasted chicken and fresh vegetables may be the best meal of my life—sorry, Mom—and Archie pays before I even see the bill. I offer to pay him back, but he refuses, and I don't fight him about it. I saw the prices on the menu and chose one of the least expensive dishes, but I was still stressing about the cost throughout the entire meal.

Money will always be a little tight when you own a coffee shop that has three months to make enough money to cover costs for the rest of the year when business slows to a crawl without the vacationers. But things always work out somehow. As long as there are no major expenses. I agreed to this trip because the apartment was already paid for, and the

summer had been good, money-wise, thanks to my grief-avoidant
work ethic and excellent staff.

But Adam called this morning with some bad news that reignited a
bit of the panic I've only just been keeping in check these last couple
of days.

Britta's is attached to a bank of buildings that includes an old
community center that's being torn down to build an indoor hockey
rink. *Britta's* is the only business that's still occupied, but—like *Annie's*—it's an institution that locals go out of their way to frequent.

The building is old—at least a hundred years. Between our harsh
winters and hot summers, it takes a beating year after year. I thought
most of its issues were cosmetic, but one wall was apparently dam-
aged during the demo of the community center.

"It wasn't anything on our end," Adam told me. He knows since
he's the one who did the demolition of the other part of the building.
"There were problems with the foundation that weren't apparent
during the engineering inspections. We've got someone coming out
to figure out our options. I just wanted to give you the heads up."

He explained more details, but construction is his thing, not mine.
Mine is business, and the only thing I could hear while he talked was
how much it's going to cost me to fix *Britta's*. There's insurance, of
course, and we have time to figure things out, but the weight of it is
still heavy in my chest.

The entire conversation should have made me sad. Maybe angry.
But the only thing I feel is exhaustion.

The past five years of my life have been a losing battle to keep both
Mom and *Britta's* alive. Of course, logically, I knew that would be
impossible with Mom. But I fought hard to keep her healthy, happy,
and as much herself for as long as possible.

And she ended up suffering, anyway.

I may not have the energy to rebuild *Britta's* if the damage is extensive. Adam warned me that there's a chance the entire building will have to be torn down.

If that's the case, what's the point of rebuilding *Britta's*? It won't be the same place it was when it was Mom's. Even though I made changes when I took over, the building still held the history of Mom and her grandma—the first Britta—before her. Without the building, that history is just memories.

I don't have to be in Paradise to get lost in memories.

Case in point, right now. Stella snaps her fingers in front of my face, and I realize I've been lost right here. I'm not sure for how long, but Stella has her purse slung over her shoulder, and she and Archie are both standing, ready to go.

Dex, though, has a look of concern written in flashing lights on his face.

"You okay?" He asks for the second time today.

Or maybe he's asked more times than that, and I haven't noticed. "Yeah! I'm great! I think I just slipped into a food coma. That lunch was amazing." I tuck my phone into the pocket of Dex's hoodie I'm still wearing.

"Okay..." Dex says, like he doesn't believe me.

Which means I need to try harder to be happy. For the rest of the day, I've got to forget about everything that's happening in Paradise and focus on what's happening right here. Dex needs a stress-free day and support. I can talk to Adam later, when Dex isn't around, and find out what the engineers discovered. Then I'll figure out my next steps with *Britta's*.

"What's next, Liam?" I ask even more brightly, which wipes the concern from his face.

"You're really sticking to that?" The corner of his mouth pulls up, and for the first time, I notice a dimple in his cheek.

"Calling you by your first name?" *How have I never noticed that dimple?*

Dex nods.

"Yeeeeeep."

His entire face scrunches as he tries to suppress his grin. It doesn't work. His dimple grows deeper, and I think I can forget everything else if I focus on that adorable attribute of his face.

Stella sidles up next to me, swings her arm over my shoulders, and leans close to Dex. "We're still going to raid the samples at Rip Tide, right?"

"Stella!"

"Like Vikings on their way to an English village," Dex says over my reprimand.

"That's grim. We're not pillaging anything." I turn my scolding on him.

"Speak for yourself." Stella takes a last sip of water, fortifying herself for the journey ahead.

Then we file out of the restaurant where a waiting customer seems to recognize Dex and then wishes him luck. He seems relieved it's only one.

The rest of the afternoon is spent at Rip Tide headquarters where everyone we meet trips all over themselves to help us. But not in a fawning way, as though they want to impress Dex. More like, they respect him, so they want to help.

A woman—Emily—who has the perfect nose for her piercing leads us to the sample floor. And by floor, I mean an entire warehouse floor of an office building.

There are racks of clothes, and stacks of boxes that Emily tells us will have the sizes we need if we don't find them on the rack.

"That area there is the summer season that just ended." She points to a spot on our left where I already see a bright blue something I want to check out.

Emily indicates the areas for the other seasons, including the winter season that hasn't been released yet. And by "winter" season, she definitely means a California winter. Even from across the room, I can tell there won't be anything in that section that will cover enough of me to survive a Paradise winter. Too many straps and not enough sleeves and fleece.

"I'll leave you to it. Take what you want. Just be sure to get pictures with Dex tomorrow while you're wearing our clothes, then tag us," Emily explains, which sparks Stella to strike up a conversation about social media marketing.

Talking about the work she does for Georgia is the only thing that could keep Stella from stuffing bags full of clothes like she's on that grocery game show, where the people have to buy as much as possible in ten minutes, or something equally ridiculous.

I wander toward the summer section, smiling as I hear Emily compliment Stella on the Georgia Rose Instagram page and TikTok, both of which Stella manages. She doesn't get any recognition for it, because it's supposed to look as though it's all Georgia. But I guess anyone who is in social media marketing would understand that's not how things work.

So, I leave the two of them to talk and, to save time, start pulling things Stella might like. Dex stays close to me while Archie makes his way to the men's area. When I take a dress off the rack, Dex makes a "hmm" sound.

"What?" I hold up the bright pink dress to examine it more closely.

"That's not something I thought you'd pick out."

"It's Stella's style. She may want it." I try not to notice that Dex seems to know my taste pretty well.

He takes the clothes from my arms. "What's in this pile that's for you?"

I pretend not to hear the question.

"Brit-*ta*," he prods.

"Nothing yet. I haven't really found anything." The hangers scrape across the metal rod as I rifle through the clothes.

Dex's gaze drops to the growing pile of clothes in his arms. "Are you trying to find something for yourself? Or are you only looking for Stella?"

Stella, still talking to Emily, laughs and the sound echoes through the concrete and metal warehouse.

"I'll look for myself in a minute."

Dex does an about face and walks to Stella. They exchange some words I can't hear. Then she holds out her arms and he lays the clothes across them.

"Oh! Good choices, Brit!" Stella's excitement reverberates off the walls, giving her words a high, tinny sound. "Now look for yourself!"

Dex comes back, grabs me by the hand, and drags me to a rounder of t-shirts and shorts. He pulls things from them, and in a matter of minutes my arms are as full of stuff for me as they were with what I'd picked out for Stella.

"That's enough! I'm only in San Clemente for one day, not the entire month." The clothes are as high as my chin, and Dex still searches the racks. "It's going to take me hours to try this stuff on."

"There aren't dressing rooms." Dex is still pulling stuff for me. "If it doesn't fit, I'll bring it back or give it to someone else."

I'm about to argue more, but Dex stops me. "Most gir—*women* would be stoked at a free shopping spree."

As much as I'd like to debunk the stereotype, he's not wrong. Now that she's done talking to Emily, Stella's arms are so full, she looks like a walking laundry pile.

He stretches out his arms. "Your turn to look. Give me those."

After a second's hesitation, I dump the clothes into his arms. I put in a half-hearted effort to rifle through a stack of colorful T-shirts folded on a table.

"To be honest, I haven't shopped for clothes in a long time. Unless going to the same website once or twice a year to order the exact style of jeans and shirts I always wear, but in different colors, counts as shopping."

Dex shakes his head. "I reckon it doesn't."

I laugh, then add a shirt I might actually like to the stack in his arms. "Mom and I used to take shopping trips to Salt Lake City when we had the chance. I enjoyed shopping back then."

"Let's make it fun now. How about a little competition? You've got fifteen minutes to grow your pile higher than Stella's. The only rule is, you have to at least like what you pick." His eyes dance with a challenge I can't say no to.

So, I load Dex up with more clothes until Emily has to bring us a giant bag for them or he's going to tip over. I genuinely like what I pick, but I stop short when Dex points out the most gorgeous, long, flowy dress I've ever seen.

"That would be gorg on you," he says.

I think he might be right. Its straps criss-cross in the back and it's my favorite shade of bright green. I rub the silky fabric between my fingertips, which is even softer than I'd imagined. But then I see the price tag.

"It's way too expensive, and I'll never wear it," I tell him, but, ignoring me, he rearranges the clothes in his arms. Before I can stop him, he grabs the dress and shoves it into the bag. I reach inside the bag, but he clamps it close to his side, forcing me to pull my hand from between his rock-solid arm and side without the dress.

"*Liam*." I use my sternest voice. "You'll just end up bringing it back. I've, literally, got nowhere to wear it."

"Reckon you'll have to find somewhere to wear it then, because it's perfect for you." He raises his eyebrows just enough to convey he's ready and willing to go to battle over this.

"Fine." Then I realize exactly what event it will be perfect for. "I'll wear it when I take you to dinner to celebrate you being the World Champion of Surfing."

Archie comes up behind Dex as I emphasize the last words so they ring through the giant room like I've announced them over a microphone.

Archie breaks into a reluctant grin and follows my words with a rousing cry of "Liam Dexter!" And then Stella, who never misses any kind of celebration, big or small, breaks into a cheer of her own.

And underneath all the cheering, I swear I hear Dex mutter, "I'll win just to see you in that dress."

Chapter Eleven

Dex

The Rip Tide house is in San Clemente, near Lower Trestles, and right on the sand. It's not as big as the mansion Archie grew up in, but it's still a mansion. Stella and Britta both gasp when we walk in. From the street, it doesn't look big, but once inside, the whole place opens up with a view of the ocean that stretches north to Dana Point.

We eat in for dinner, watching the sunset from the back deck. Britta and Stella live next to a giant, cobalt blue lake surrounded by mountains which provides an impressive setting for sunsets that took my breath away when I was in Paradise.

Britta seems to have a similar experience as we watch the sky go through an entire spectrum of oranges, reds, and pinks. Her face glows

in the fading light, and I hope she's experiencing the same content-
ment I did in Paradise, watching the sun go down.

I get the sense life's knocked Britta down harder than she lets on.
I know the feeling. It's no different from being held under water by
a wave, running out of air, fighting to resurface. But the beauty of
a sunset can make you forget all of that, even if it's only for twenty
minutes. And I'm keen for Britta to leave her troubles behind.

I go to bed satisfied that she enjoyed herself today and felt some
peace—even if it's short-lived. But I hope it will be something that
stays with her. That hope lulls me to sleep and I rest better than I
can ever remember the night before a competition.

The next morning, I insist Britta and Stella ride down to the beach
with us. Archie doesn't love it, but we have VIP parking, and I don't
want them parking a mile away again. Surfing and beer go hand in
hand, and the fans will have eskies full of grog. I don't want any
drunks hassling the girls—*women*.

"Once we're down there, you've got to give Dex space. He needs
to focus," Archie lectures them as we climb into the sprinter.

"Yes, sir," Britta says, and I pull in a smile when she salutes.

She's wearing shorts I picked out for her that show off her very
long legs, but also the Rip Tide jumper I loaned her. And while I
stay focused—taking the front seat today instead of the one next to
her—I am picturing her in that green dress.

I'm keen to see her in it.

That's as far as I'll let my mind wander away from the wave. I've
got to surf both fearless and smart.

Before we park, I turn to Britta and Stella in the backseat. "Once
we're parked, I've got a routine to stick to, so Archie will help you
get settled. When I stop talking, it's not meant to be rude. It's what
I do to get focused and then stay focused."

Archie gives me an approving nod, and once we park, true to my word, I pop on my headphones and turn on the music that helps me tune out everything but the wave and how I'm going to surf it. I don't see where the girls and Archie go, but he'll take care of them while I head to the locker room. I barely acknowledge the other surfers. The smallest of nods is all we offer each other.

In the locker room, I stretch. I'll be in the first heat with Jack again, so now it's my job to prepare myself. Archie will do everything else—checking me in, double checking the conditions, getting a schedule for the day's heats and taking the girls somewhere to watch. Maybe the beach, maybe the stands, maybe the box that team and family members watch from. None of it is my concern.

I feel a tap on my shoulder and turn to see Britta. Archie is behind her scowling, which means she's probably disobeyed orders. I feel a little irritated at the interruption, even if it is her.

She taps her ear, and I pull off my headphones. "Remember, it's a dance, and you know all the steps."

With a soft smile, she turns and follows Archie. My irritation disappears.

Even though I shouldn't, I watch her go, smiling to myself. My pulse slows to a more normal rate as I return to my music and focus on my breathing while allowing Britta's words to mix in with my routine. With every breath, my chest fills with confidence.

For whatever reason, Britta's encouragement is as motivating as all the pointers Archie has given me. She's reminded me I can enjoy myself while I compete. I can win because I *love* surfing.

I know this wave, and I know how to ride it.

I know how to anticipate its direction and move with it.

I know how to win.

My pulse does the thing it always does when I want something, slowing to a hard, steady beat. Everything around me goes fuzzy except the one singular goal. I dial into that beat, focusing on its rhythm until I hear a low hum of *win the title*.

And that's what I go out to do when the two-minute horn blows. Because Jack has priority, I don't get a wave until he takes the first one. And he's known for waiting until he gets just the right wave, letting the clock tick down so his opponents get nervous and take any wave they can to beat him.

I'm already at a disadvantage with the high score he gets to keep from yesterday. But I'm not going down without a fight.

I scope the horizon for a good set. Jack sees it and surprises me by taking the first wave. I don't watch him drop. I'm already setting up to take my wave. I've got a lot of points to make up.

Before he finishes his last maneuver, I've caught my wave. But the second I pop up, I realize I've miscalculated. The wave isn't powerful enough to score anything higher than a five. I need sevens and eights or higher if I'm going to beat Jack. I do what I can with the wave—a few carves, a basic one-eighty—but nothing that's going to wow the judges.

When the scores are announced, Jack's is a seven-five. Mine is a five. That puts him far enough ahead of me that he can sit out as many waves as he wants. He can let me work to catch up while he saves his energy for the perfect wave.

My breath is short and choppy as I recover. Every wave I see, I'm tempted to take. The more I try to score, the more chances I'll have to get a high one.

But taking as many waves as possible is risky too. Surfing takes a lot of energy. If I waste mine going after a crap wave, I might not have enough power left for a good one.

I close my eyes and take deep breaths, repeating all my mantras and Archie's encouragement. When I open them again, a dolphin jumps out of the water, followed by another, then another. Dozens more are beneath the surface, all moving together in a coordinated dance.

Then I smile, remembering Britta telling me to enjoy the dance.

That's exactly what I need to do.

This is what I love about surfing—not just being one with the wave, but one with everything around me. Rocking up and down, waiting for the right moment, the right energy. No cell phones, no media, no pressing in from anything that runs our lives. Even with the pressure of competing, I'm free. There's no place I'd rather be.

And once I let go of the scoring and fear, I spot it: a perfect wave. I feel it even before I pop up and drop in.

The maneuvers I've been mapping in my mind for weeks come to me a half-second before I do them—like I'm being coached right there on the wave. I find the pocket, carve the face, then launch off the lip into an aerial, land it, and end with a bottom turn.

I'm able to ride the wave all the way in, giving a double thumbs up to the wave as a thank you. I get close enough to the shore that I can hear the crowd cheering, and I know I've rocked it.

But I still have at least one more wave to catch so that my first score will drop off, so I don't wait to hear my points before I paddle back out. Jack's already there, waiting patiently, cool as he always is, knowing he has priority. It's intimidating, which is exactly why he does it, but I don't let it get to me.

We sit and wait, bobbing up and down, our thirty-five minutes ticking slowly away. My score is announced. A solid eight point five. I pump my fist and don't miss when Jack sets his jaw.

With the score I just got, he'll wait as long as possible before taking a wave, to lessen my chances of getting another one, so I'll have to keep my low score. It's a smart move, but my last round was exactly the confidence boost I needed.

If only the ocean would cooperate. Time slips away, and the water stays glassy.

Just as I'm sure I'm done, and with under a minute left on the clock, Jack and I spot a wave coming in that looks good and both paddle for it. Once Jack takes off, I can too. The A-framer breaks perfectly right and left, and Jack takes right. I'm about to drop in left, but at the last second, something tells me to wait. I back out of the wave while he finishes.

I paddle for the next wave, hoping I've made the right call. Only seconds remain before my heat is over. I get in position. At the exact right second, at the same time the horn blows, I pop up.

The wave is a perfect-peeling left-hander, the highest one of the day, with an endless face. As soon as I drop in, I know this is my chance for a perfect ten. Adrenaline surges, and I pump my board to pick up speed. I carve and turn, then launch into an aerial, land it even better than the last one, and still have time to do some more maneuvers before the wave washes out.

I let the whitewash carry me in, diving into the water just before shore. I've done my best. I may have scored my highest ever, and I tremble with excitement.

After I pop out of the water, self-doubt creeps in. Even though I did a ripper job on that wave, I worry my score still won't be high enough to beat Jack. The crowd is already cheering, and I can't tell if it's for me or for Robbo.

I carry my board out of the water, running my free hand over my face, wiping away salty water that's come from more than the ocean. There's nothing I would have done differently on that last wave. If I lose to Jack, I'll have done my best, but I don't have any idea how I could have done better.

My feet hit the sand, and I hear my name, then my score. A ten.

I just pulled off the impossible and scored a perfect ten in the WSL finals.

The crowd roars again, and I wipe my hand over my face to hide my tears. But they can tell I'm crying. Before I know it, Archie has his arms wrapped around me and lifts me off the ground.

"You did it, mate! You did it!"

When he lets go, I make my way to the locker room, high-fiving fans standing on each side of the path to the surfers' area. I still have four heats left, but Britta and Stella are waiting at the bottom of the stairs when I get there.

"That was quite a dance, Liam," Britta says.

I pause long enough to return her grin before I drop my board and close the space between us. She doesn't have an apron on, so no strings to hook my fingers around. Instead, I wrap an arm around her waist and pull her close enough there's no way she can't feel how hard my heart is pounding under my orange jersey and wetsuit.

Her mouth curves into a smile, giving me the permission I've been waiting for.

I slide my other hand across her jaw, into her hair, but Britta is the one who rises to her tiptoes in the sand to press her lips to mine. She has on lip stuff that tastes sweet and fruity, and I feel bad for the salty, chapped lips she's getting in return.

Britta doesn't seem to mind. With her arms slung around my neck, she deepens our kiss, pulling a moan from my throat when she tugs at my bottom lip while lowering her heels back to the sand.

"If that's what I get for winning the first heat, what's in store if I win the title?" I tighten my grip around her waist, wanting to keep her close.

"I guess you'll have to win it to find out." She looks up at me through feathery lashes, and her tongue darts between her lips before they pull into a smile.

I've wiped out heaps of times, tossed so hard by waves, I've had a dozen concussions, at least. It's a crazy experience being washed around like that. Under churning water, it's impossible to tell what's up or down.

With the taste of Britta's lips still on mine, I feel the same disconcerting sensation of being pummeled by a wave. There's no up or down. Nothing else exists outside the pounding in my chest and my lungs grasping for air.

But wiping out has never felt this good.

CHAPTER TWELVE

Britta

If you'd told me a year ago, I'd fall stupid in love within a matter of minutes, I would have laughed hysterically. Falling in love is not on my to-do list. Or my bullet list. Definitely not on my shopping list. But here I am, picking up a value-size, heart-shaped pack of love.

There's no use denying it. I am utterly, hopelessly in love with...surfing.

Falling in love with a person is very much off the table. At least for now, and at least with Dex. Even if I weren't trying to find my bearings after losing Mom, Dex and I live very different lives. He has to be near the ocean, and I have to be near *Britta's*, which is nowhere near an ocean. So, despite the hottest, most toe-curling kiss of my life—second only to the last time Dex kissed me—an actual relationship with him is out of the question.

That doesn't mean I have no interest in being kissed like that again. Or even a few more times like that. Kissing only has to do with love when you want it to.

Surfing, though, has stolen my heart.

Sure, the attraction started with Dex's looks. His kisses flooded me with heat first, but the same fire surges through me as I watch him glide across a wave, moving back and forth over it like they're a perfectly matched pair of ballroom dancers. The ocean leads, but Dex is very much in charge.

It's both beautiful and terrifying to watch. At any second, the wave could do something unpredictable and trip up Dex's carefully planned choreography. Not just trip him. Toss him and turn him like a dryer full of rocks. I'm on the edge of my seat, waiting for what Dex and his beautifully dangerous partner will do next.

I'm brimming with a nervous energy, wave after wave, heat after heat. Dex barely has time to recover between his heats while the women surf theirs. Then he's back in the ocean again. Stella and I watch all Dex's heats from the box with Archie. The giant windows, and the box's position above the stands and the crowd, allow us a perfect view. But when we want a close-up shot, we turn to the live feed from the TV on the one windowless wall that doesn't face the ocean.

There are twelve heats total, thirty-five minutes each. First the men go, then the women, with the winners moving on to the next heats, until there are two men, and two women left. The best two out of three heats for each determines who the champions are.

My fingernails slowly disappear as I chew on them each time Dex's score falls below his opponents', but Archie stays calm through all of it. During the women's heats, he disappears, and I assume he's with Dex. Stella and I stay put. I want Dex to stay focused as much as Archie does. When Dex surfs, Archie watches with his arms crossed, barely commenting after each of Dex's waves, and only lightly when Dex's scores are announced.

I don't get the same level of pumping adrenaline watching the other surfers—probably because I don't know them personally—but I still get a rush of excitement and awe. Especially watching the women surf. Their grace and power make me wish I'd grown up riding waves.

Male or female, each surfer has their distinct style. But none of them has the same cooperative relationship Dex did with his perfect ten wave in his first, nerve-racking heat. As little as I understand about surfing, I'm positive that ride will be one for the history books.

After that heat-winning performance, Dex takes every wave with a confidence that easily leads to win after win. He has a few rounds that don't go as planned, but nearly every ride is riveting. None has the same magic that perfect ten wave did—not even the last wave he rides that wins him the championship title—but his strength, determination, and joy is inspiring.

When the horn blows at the end of the last heat, Archie erupts. The final scores haven't been announced, but everyone knows Dex has clinched the title.

"He did it! That little ripper did it!" Archie jumps, pumping his fist in the air, cursing up a storm in between happy cheers.

Then he runs to meet Dex, navigating the rocky beach more expertly than a mountain goat in the Tetons. He splashes into the ocean, crashes into Dex, and they both tumble into the water. When they regain their feet, they're still embracing and buried in each other's necks. I can't see their faces, but the live feed shows a close-up of their shaking shoulders. My eyes water, too.

From the loudspeaker, the announcer talks about what a huge win this is for Dex after two separate comebacks. Archie and Dex make their way out of the water, arms slung over each other's shoulders, and I get an even stronger sense of how close they are.

Witnessing their bond—how they belong together and have all this history—I realize they're not just friends. They're brothers. Archie's getting as much delight out of Dex's win as Dex is, and that's what family is really about; people who know you well enough to cry with and for you, whether from joy or grief.

Suddenly, I'm flooded with a homesickness I haven't felt since I've been here. Maybe it's the emotion of the moment, but I miss my Dad. I miss my brothers. I miss all the people in Paradise who feel like family. Most of all, I miss Mom.

Stella and I wait in the box, watching out the window, as Dex and Archie make their way up the beach. It's slow going as microphones are shoved in Dex's face and he stops to make comments. The volume on the TV behind me is too low to hear what he says over the talking and cheering of the others around us.

But during one quick interview, Dex's eyes drift to the box until he finds me. Then he sends me a big wave. The surrounding crowd follows his gaze, and suddenly the spotlight is shining on me. Not a literal one, obviously, but I feel as hot as if it was. I return Dex's wave with a much smaller one, then retreat further into the box, away from view.

And a second feeling hits me, almost as intensely as the homesickness that's left me unsteady.

This isn't my place. I barely know Dex. I'm not like the other people in this box who've been watching their family and close friends, not just today, but for years. I'm not Dex's support system. I'm just a girl who showed up today because he kissed her once—now twice—and she likes the way he looks without a shirt.

And when I look at this whole situation in that light, I sound a lot like a groupie—or whatever girls are called who chase surfers. In hockey, those girls are known as puck bunnies. Are they called surf bunnies in surfing? Am I a *surf* bunny?

"We should go congratulate him." Stella tugs on my hand, but I stay planted.

"I don't want to get in his way."

"Uh, judging by the way he greeted you after his first win, you won't be 'in his way.' I get the vibe he'd love for you to be more 'in his way.'" Stella makes liberal use of air quotes each time she repeats my words.

The fact Dex may want me to be "in his way" is exactly why I shouldn't be. I don't want to give him the wrong idea about what his kiss meant or why I'm here. I enjoy hanging out with Dex. I want to have fun while I'm in LA. But not *that* kind of fun.

Kissing is one thing. Anything beyond that belongs in relationship territory, at least for me. And relationship territory feels even more dangerous than surfing in shark territory.

I'm even less interested in being the second trophy Dex takes home tonight. Dex doesn't seem like that kind of guy anymore, but I've scrolled far enough back on his Insta to see pics with a lot of different girls. And there is no shortage of girls in bikinis surrounding him right now, and by the looks of it, he doesn't mind.

So, I stay in the box while Dex goes on the temporary stage to receive his huge silver chalice-looking trophy. He and Caitlin Simmers, the women's champion, get sprayed with so much champagne, they sip it from their giant champagne-glass-shaped trophies. When he holds the trophy over his head, his smile is so big that I want to be down there celebrating with him.

All day, I've watched the wave here peel down the middle, moving with equal power in opposite directions. That's what I feel like now. Part of me wants to be by Dex's side, celebrating this huge win like I've dreamed of it for as long as he has. Like, I really understand how important this is for him because I've loved surfing my whole life, not just for the past eight hours. The easiest thing to do would be to give into temptation and join the party below and let our attraction lead wherever it will.

The other part of me knows this is all temporary. The stage and stands will come down. The event tents and portable structures will be stored away. Anything we start while I'm here, stays here. Dex will keep traveling the world to surf. I'll go back to my regular life in Paradise, which, I worry, will be even less satisfying than before if I get pulled too far into Dex's more exciting life.

So, I use every ounce of willpower to keep from going to the beach where he can see me again. I watch as he does quick media interviews. There are a lot of congratulations in between and other people to talk to. I have a bird's-eye view of it all and am happy to watch Dex celebrate from afar. Stella is in the mix somewhere—Stella is *always* in the mix somewhere—but I've lost sight of her.

There's food in here, so I gorge myself on chips and guac while Dex gets all the praise he deserves. Eventually, people walk up the path away from the beach and the crowd thins, and I spot her talking to Dex and Archie. She points up at me, wiping away any question about what they're talking about.

I wave to Dex, who lifts his trophy again, then motions me to come down to the beach where they are. I hesitate, still feeling pulled in two directions, but I can't ignore him. Mostly because he's the number one surfer in the entire world, but also because he's my ride back to my car.

I head in their direction, but before I get far, my phone dings in my back pocket. When I see a message from Adam, I immediately worry it's about *Britta's*. Adam doesn't just call out of the blue to say hi, and after our conversation yesterday, I've been expecting to hear from him.

I push play on the message and listen to Adam's gravelly voice. "We're going to have to make some hard decisions about whether *Britta's* can be saved. Call me ASAP."

The air grows close, pressing in on me as I listen to the message a second time.

I should have known things wouldn't go as planned if I left. Trailing my fears about a casual relationship with Dex, Adam's message feels like a sign.

I don't miss Paradise, but I have a sudden longing to be with everyone there. I should take care of *Britta's*—no matter who it belongs to now—because it was Mom's. I should carry on her legacy. I should take care of my dad and help my brother Bear and Cassie plan their wedding, taking Mom's place as the core of our family.

I want to call Adam right now. I *need* to call him. But not here.

Whatever hard decisions need to be made can't be made at the beach, after Dex's win. Not with people filing past me, brimming with a happy energy that comes from being part of something incredible, even just as a spectator.

"Britta!"

I turn at Stella's voice. Archie and Dex are with her, all walking my way with huge smiles, pulsing with an excitement I can feel from ten feet away. An excitement I chose not to share a few minutes ago, but now I can't even fake.

"We're celebrating tonight!" Stella says, and I force a smile as the three of them approach. "Rip Tide is throwing a huge party, and we're invited."

I face Dex but keep an arm's-length distance between us. I dodge his hug when he puts his arms up. "That was amazing! Congratulations! I knew you could do it."

I want to say more about how incredible he was to watch. How I held my breath after an aerial when he was so far in the whitewash, seconds passed before we knew whether he'd landed it. When he came out of the wave, standing upright, my heart rose to my throat, and I wanted to throw my arms around him.

"You're going to come tonight, right?" Dex asks, his face bright and shiny. "You're welcome to stay another night at the house. That's where the party will be. The execs are ordering in all kinds of food and getting a DJ."

"There will be famous people there. *Stars*, Britta," Stella says with actual stars in her eyes.

Which makes what I have to say even harder. If I stay there another night, I risk Dex expecting more than I have in me to give right now. Or, worse, expecting only a one-night stand. And, yes, we're both grown-ups capable of being honest with one another, but I can't add an awkward conversation with Dex about expectations to my already full plate.

"I'm sorry, Dex. I don't think we can." I feel more than see Stella's disappointed expression, but I can't avoid it on Dex's face. It goes deeper than not having me in his bed tonight, and for a fleeting second, I wonder if I've lost more than a chance to party with celebrities.

"What? Why?" Stella asks.

With a deep breath, I turn to her, away from the confusion that's replaced the disappointment on Dex's face. "There are big problems with *Britta's* to figure out. My laptop is back at the apartment, and I need to look at finances. And I already told Annie I'd come in tomorrow. I don't want to cancel on her again." I throw out every reason I can find. They're all legitimate, but somehow that's less reassuring than it should be that I've made the right choice leaving.

"Maybe I'll see you when you get back?" I keep my voice neutral, no sign of expectations.

"I hope so," Dex says with a wishful optimism that nearly undoes my resolve to leave.

CHAPTER THIRTEEN

Dex

The ride back to the house is quieter than it should be after I've just been named the world's best surfer. We should all be celebrating. I should be overjoyed every time I see my distorted reflection in the silver trophy that takes up my entire lap. It's so big, I can barely see Britta in the captain's chair next to me.

This win is what I've wanted more than anything since I started surfing—at least, before surfing was added as an Olympic sport—and I shouldn't care that the trophy is digging into my legs, or that I won't get to see Britta in her green dress tonight.

As happy as I am, the disappointment that's she's not staying to celebrate with me weighs even more than this award.

"Thanks for coming," I say as we turn down the street to the house.

"Thanks for inviting us. The whole day was amazing." She smiles, but there's a tentativeness she didn't have before.

"I hope everything is okay with *Britta's*."

"I'm sure everything will be fine," she says in a voice too high and too certain, but then there's a bit of a loosening in her posture. "I hope it's nothing that will cut my trip short."

"What?" Stella turns in her seat to face Britta. "You're thinking about leaving?"

My lungs refuse to take in air while I wait for Britta to answer.

"I'm just saying it's a possibility. Things are falling apart there without me." She stiffens again, like she's preparing to dig in her heels if Stella tells her to change her mind. "But you don't have to leave if you don't want to. You should stay until Georgia needs you. Finish your vacation."

"*You* should stay and finish your vacation until your family actually needs you," Stella shoots back and faces the road again.

Silence falls over all of us with an awkward thud. No one says a word until we pull into the driveway of the Rip Tide house. There are other cars parked there, and the house is already full of people waiting to celebrate with me. I realize I may not have time to say goodbye to Britta the way I want to.

She's out of the van the second Archie comes to a complete stop. I jump out to follow her, but the prize I thought I wanted more than anything slows me down. Britta is through the front door before I've made it halfway up the walkway.

By the time I walk in the door, she's on her way up the stairs to the bedroom where she and Stella slept. Before I can follow her, voices shout, "Congratulations!" and I'm squeezed into a giant group hug.

"Mum? Dad? What are you doing here?" Shock freezes me in their arms and those of my thirteen-year-old brother, Jordy, who's wrapped around my back. "Is Chloe here, too?"

"She has school, but we couldn't stay away! We got in this morning," they say together as they release me. "We watched the live coverage on TV."

Four years ago, after I fired Dad as my coach and manager, things were dicey between us. I asked my whole family not to come to competitions anymore. I made up an excuse about them needing to focus on Jordy's surfing career and getting my sister, Chloe—who's twenty-four now—through uni. I don't think anyone believed me, but it was better than saying the truth out loud; Dad knew I couldn't stand the pressure he put on me, even if he saw nothing wrong with what I was doing. But I couldn't ban only him from my events. If Mum, Chloe, and Jordy came without him, he'd think they were siding with me.

This is the first time they've come to a competition since then. It's been hard for them not to be there. It probably near-killed them not to watch me win today in person, but they flew halfway across the world to be here anyway, whether I won or lost. They respected my boundaries, but found a way to support me.

There's no way I can go after Britta now.

"I can't believe you're here." I look into Mum's teary eyes; genuinely happy they went to so much effort.

"Bro, that was so gnarly!" Jordy holds his hand up for a high-five.

He was a big surprise to all of us when he was born the first year I was in the juniors. Most of Chloe's childhood was spent being dragged to my competitions across Australia, but Jordy's been lugged around the world. At least he was until four years ago.

Chloe surfed some, but she decided early on to blaze her own trail and went to uni after a gap year. She's just started med school.

Jordy, though, wants to follow in my footsteps. I hope Dad's learned from his mistakes with me, and that Jordy will do better under the pressure than I did at his age.

"Good on ya, Son." Dad slaps me on the back then sniffs back the deeper emotions trying to escape.

"Thanks, Dad." I hand him the trophy. "Feel the weight of this beauty."

Dad hefts the trophy, smiling reluctantly. It was hard enough for him to say he's proud of me.

We move into the sitting room where Jordy takes a turn lifting the trophy like he's won it, then taking a selfie with it. Archie comes in at some point and gives them all a hug—except for Dad. Dad's mostly a handshake guy.

Soon after, Britta and Stella come down the stairs with their Rip Tide bags, and I meet them at the bottom step.

"I feel bad taking these," Britta says, holding the bag up.

I shake my head and take the paper bag from her, plus the one Stella's carrying. "I'll take them to the car for you."

Once we're out the door, away from my family and the other guests, I lean in close to Britta. "You promised me dinner. I'm going to hold you to that, and the green dress."

That puts the smile I know on her face as she opens the back door of her car. "As long as my family doesn't need me to come home, we're on."

"Then I'm crossing all my fingers they don't." I set the bags in her back seat. When I turn, she's behind me, close enough I could kiss her again. But unlike the other times, I worry that would be the wrong move here.

I wave goodbye instead, then watch her and Stella drive away.

Within minutes, more people show up. My agent, Marta, the Rip Tide execs, other Aussie surfers who were at the finals to support me and Jack. Matthew McConaughey.

The house fills with people, music, food, and drinks. Everyone wants to talk about my win, my meteoric rise over the past year, and—the kicker—what I have planned next. I try to answer the questions as best

I can, but the only thing that's certain is that all I have planned for the future is more surfing. Hopefully, more wins go along with that.

The party is an absolute cracker, especially after the pressure I've been under. The tension that's been curled, snake-like in the pit of my stomach, disappears in the music and the one beer I allow myself. But my mind keeps drifting back to Britta. Over and over, I find myself wishing she were here.

I'm throwing the bull with Kelly Slater when Archie finds me. "Can we chat for a minute, mate?"

I'm surprised by how serious he is at a party. He should be four beers in by now. He leads me to a back room where my agent, Marta, sits on the white leather sofa.

I send Archie a questioning look as I take the chair next to him and across from Marta. He answers with a micro-lift of his eyebrows that I have no idea how to interpret.

There's an ice bucket full of drinks on the table between us. I eye a Corona, but reach for a water instead.

"What's so important it can't wait until after the party?" I ask while twisting the cap off.

"That was a huge win today." Marta leans back in her chair and crosses her legs.

"Thanks."

I wait for her to say what she's really thinking, because it's not about surfing. She couldn't care less about surfing. All she cares about is how I can make money from it. That's why she's my agent now instead of Dad. She sees the surf companies who represent me and other pro-surfers as the multi-billion-dollar businesses they are. Dad saw them how they wanted us to see them: as fellow surfers who are family.

It was a nice thought. Except the execs were all driving hundred-thou-sand-dollar cars to their vacation homes while I was camping in the back of trucks to save money while surfing at competitions sponsored by their companies or shooting promotions for their products.

"We're going to get you more out of the win than some prize money and a trophy." Marta doesn't smile, and while I don't want to talk business right now, I trust her to do exactly what she's promised me. When my surfing career is over, I'll have enough money to retire without worrying about anything but where I'm going next to surf for fun.

"Awesome. Do it. Let me know what you need from me." Marta and Archie handle all the business stuff I'm not smart enough to understand.

They've got the education for it. I didn't finish secondary school, so I usually excuse myself from any conversation with Marta and let Archie do the talking. Which is what I have every intention of doing as I push myself up.

Marta's look puts me back in my seat. "I'm talking Olympics, Dex. You need to be part of this conversation."

"Olympics?" I'll gladly stay in my seat to talk about my chances of going to the Olympics. I might have been one of the two Australians in Tahiti six weeks ago if I hadn't gotten injured in 2022.

Archie rests his elbows on his knees and leans toward me. "Your comeback this year has grabbed the attention of sponsors and USA Surfing."

"USA?"

Archie nods.

"Why?"

"Your Mum's dual citizenship, for starters, which gives you a connection to America. Besides that, you've lived in the States three years and have a visa, so you may already qualify as a permanent resident. And most importantly, you've just proven you can beat the Aussies, but they don't want you." Archie counts off his fingers as he lists each point, but it's the last one that gets me.

"What do you mean, my country doesn't want me? I'm Aussie."

Archie holds up his hands to stop me. "Not your country, mate. The Olympic committee. You've been in their sights the last two Olympics, and you've crumbled or been injured."

"They still got their medals with Wright and Robbo," I mumble, but it's not a valid defense.

I doubt I'd consider myself if I were on the committee. I crumbled before even getting close to the 2020 Olympics, and my back injury took me out of contention for the 2024 games. That alone would be enough for the committee to be skittish about considering me, but add my age plus years of bad behavior when I was younger to the equation, and Archie's right. I wouldn't want me either.

"The real problem is whether you've spent enough time in the States over the past three years that you can qualify as a permanent resident. If so, you'd only need another two years to gain citizenship." Marta inserts, as though I'm actually thinking about surfing under any other flag but Aus's.

"They'd hate me back home if I surfed for America, and I spend as much time traveling out of the States as I do living here." I wag my head left and right, as much to say no as to shake the Olympic idea from my brain.

But it's already taken seed there. Because Archie may be right. The only way to live out my dream of surfing in the Olympics very well could be under another country's flag, and America is the only one I'd even consider.

Mum's dad was American. He met my Australian Gran when she was a nurse in Vietnam and he was a doctor. They married, but her tour ended before his did. She went home to Aus, already pregnant, to wait out the last few months of his service. He was killed when the helicopter he was in was shot down by enemy fire.

Mum never knew him, but his parents made sure they were part of her life. When she was old enough, she spent a few summers in San Diego with them. And because her dad was an American, it was easy for her to get dual citizenship. But she's never spent enough time in the States for her own kids to qualify for citizenship. Her history is my connection to America.

"You don't have to decide today," Marta says, but I recognize that tone. She's going to be pushing this idea. "In the meantime, I've already got an immigration lawyer looking into what it will take for you to gain citizenship in time to be considered for the 2028 USA team."

I look between Archie and Marta. Things are moving really fast. "We're sure the Aus team won't want me?"

"Not gonna happen, Dex. Put it out of your head. You surf for America or you don't surf in the Olympics." Marta's bluntness shouldn't surprise me, but I look to Archie to shut her down anyway.

He sucks in his lips and tilts his head to the side, like *sorry, bro.* "Look at the Aussies coming up behind you."

When I drag my eyes back to Marta, she meets me with an *I told you* expression.

But Archie's words have already convinced me. Aside from the fact that if he's trying to talk me into surfing for America, he must really think I have no chance of making the Australian team, we've spent a lot of time assessing the rookies and younger guys on the tour who are making their marks. They're younger than me, they haven't had the injuries I have, and even though they come from all over the world, the best ones are all from Aus.

"The American bench is a lot shallower, and as the host nation, they'll likely have a bigger team." Marta shifts on the couch to drill me with her determined gaze. "That's another reason USA Surfing has you in their sites. With the games in Los Angeles, they want to make sure the gold goes to an American, even one who's technically Australian."

When she goes quiet, Archie jumps in. "If you made the team, you'd be surfing Malibu, Huntington, or Lowers—all waves you know well."

"So do the other Americans. They're even more familiar with those waves," I say.

"And you just beat them, yeah?" Archie sends me a smug smile and holds out his fist.

"Can't argue that." I bump my fist to his, feeling my resolve to only surf for Aus crumble faster than I did as a rookie on the Tour. "How long would the process—what's it called?"

"Naturalization," Marta answers.

"Yeah. That. How long would it take if I decide to do it?" Still a big *if*, but I'm not counting it out. "And would I have to give up Aussie citizenship?"

"Five years, and you'd have dual citizenship." Marta tries to smooth a wrinkle from her trousers as she talks. "You've had a visa for the last three. If you've spent enough time in the States, and paid taxes here during those years, you could get citizenship as soon as two years from now."

I turn to Archie, who says, "I'll look back at our travel schedule once we hear from the immigration lawyer about residency requirements to see if you've met them. Taxes is a question I'll pass along to your accountant."

Worry sits at the slightly turned-down corners of his mouth. It's barely noticeable, but enough for me to tamp down my rising hopes.

"And if I'm not considered a permanent resident? Then what? There's only four years to the next Olympics."

This situation feels a lot like the Marta trying to smooth that wrinkle out of her trousers with only her hands—impossible. I don't remember if I've paid taxes in the US or Aus, but I do know I spend most of the year chasing waves. Some of those are in the US. Most aren't.

Odds are, I'm not becoming an American in time for the 2028 games. Even if, by some miracle—or, more likely, bribery—I meet the citizenship requirements, there's still the intense training and basic luck I'd need to stay on the Championship Tour for the next three years. The US coaches won't look at me if I don't keep winning.

The whole thing sounds impossible.

But just as I'm about to give up hope, I remember that at the beginning of this season, winning the world title seemed impossible too. But intense training and a bit of luck earned me the Duke Kahanamoku trophy. And I'd love to see an Olympic medal next to it.

An Olympic medal, more than any other trophy, legitimizes the sacrifices an athlete makes to be the best in the world. Not finishing secondary school or skipping university doesn't matter with an Olympic medal hanging around your neck. A fella doesn't have to be book smart to get one. He only has to know his sport and his competition.

The Olympics are the ultimate for any athlete, and I want to be that athlete.

I can handle the training it will take to get on the team; it's the legal stuff that's the biggest *if*.

"Is there any way to speed up the immigration process if my years here don't already count?" I ask Archie, even though Marta is more likely to have an answer. I have a sliver of hope left that I'm not prepared to lose to a blunt *no* from her.

Archie lifts his palms in a shrug. "I reckon marrying an American would speed things up."

He's joking, but Marta sits taller, her interest piqued. I stand and slap Archie's shoulder with a laugh, then bolt for the door. "If that's my only option, let's pray my days here count, then."

I've got a party to get back to, and an actual win to celebrate. That's what I'm supposed to be doing, not entertaining impossible dreams.

I'm almost to the door when Marta says, "Is that girl you kissed today American?"

With my hand on the knob, I turn around. Marta's foot tick tocks side to side, a sure sign she's cooking up some plan. But it's the way Archie slowly sits up that has me more worried.

"Yeah, she is," he says with a hint of excitement.

"What's that got to do with anything?" My eyes dart between the two of them.

"How serious are you two?" Marta asks.

"We barely know each other."

Music and laughing come from the other side of the door, but I can't open it. My head buzzes, trying to put the puzzle pieces together that Archie and Marta are laying in front of me.

"You like her though," Archie says.

I shoot him a warning, but I don't deny what he's said. He'd call me a liar if I did, and he wouldn't be wrong.

Marta taps at her phone. I should walk out right now, but I'm stuck waiting to see why Marta, who never smiles, looks like she just cracked the recipe for chicken salt.

She looks up, still smiling, and shows me her phone screen. There's a blue header up top with an official-looking seal and a title that says something about naturalization. "Three years to citizenship if you're married to an American."

I burst out laughing. "Britta may be on her way back to Idaho by the time I get back to South Bay. She will be for sure if I ask her to marry me."

Marta doesn't join me laughing. "If she's gone, then, depending on what our immigration lawyer says, you might want to consider Bumble or Tinder or whatever app will put you on the fast track to finding an American to spend the rest of your life with. Or at least the next three years."

I shift my gaze to Archie for backup that what Marta is proposing—no pun intended—is insane. But all I get is a forced laugh.

I stare at him until I finally find my words. "Yesterday Britta was a distraction, and now you're seriously considering I marry her as a backup plan?"

"I just watched you win the Title after kissing her. She may be exactly the distraction you need." Archie smiles, having officially—along with Marta—gone completely mad.

CHAPTER FOURTEEN

Britta

Stella stays silent for a solid five minutes after we leave the Rip Tide house. This is a record, and I worry I've broken her. We shared the same dream of living in LA someday, but her driving reason was to rub elbows with celebrities. She's never wanted to be one herself, but she's fascinated by fame. The party tonight was a dream come true for her.

"I'm sorry, Stella," I say when I can't take the silence anymore.

"You should be." She sits up taller. "Now, what's going on with *Britta's*?"

"I don't know yet." I pull onto the freeway, relieved that Stella seems to have forgiven me. "I need to call Adam when I get back to the apartment. Things were too loud at the beach, and it would have been harder to call at a party."

"This humidity is killing my hair. I shouldn't have bothered straightening it." Stella tugs an elastic from her wrist and pulls her dark hair into a ponytail. "We've got an hour's drive ahead of us. Why not call Adam now?"

And there's the Stella I know and love, bouncing from one topic to another.

"It'll be boring." I reach for the stereo, but Stella swipes my hand away.

"Just because I don't have any ownership in *Britta's* doesn't mean I don't care about it. If you're worried enough to pull me away from a celebrity-filled party, then I get to be privy to the conversation." Her penetrating stare leaves no room for argument.

"Fine." I press the call button on my steering wheel. "Call Grumpy Adam."

A loud ringing fills the car, followed by my brother's too serious, "Hey, Britt."

"Hey." I smile, Adam's familiar voice settling my nerves. "Stella's here, too."

"Hi, Stella. I'm at Dad's. He wants to talk to you."

A quick shuffling follows as Adam hands off the phone. "Hi, honey!"

Dad's cheerful voice is so close, I can picture the smile lines around his eyes. I've missed those lines and that face. "How are things in the big city? Have you been relaxing like I told you to?"

"Yeah. I spent the day at the beach watching a huge surf competition. Stella and I had a great time." I echo Dad's cheerfulness, even as a sliver of regret needles me about not celebrating with Dex after he'd been so generous. "I'm just a little worried about *Britta's*."

I get right to the point to keep my mind drifting back to Dex.

With no more prompting, Adam launches into the long list of problems we face with *Britta's*. He has years of construction experience, so when he says the foundation is the biggest problem, I trust him. One option—an expensive one—is to jack up the building and try to repair the water-damaged parts of the foundation.

But the age of the building makes that a risky option, plus the fact the wooden frame of the building has termite and water damage itself. It may not survive being lifted, and with a heavy winter expected, the job would have to be done soon and quickly before the snow comes.

"Will insurance pay for any of it?" I ask. "*Britta's* is barely in the black now."

All the money I've saved has to get *Britta's* through the winter and most of the spring before the busy summer season.

"Maybe," Adam says. "But more expenses will pop up as we go. That's the way it always is with construction. With every estimate, tack on at least another ten percent."

I slow down as the cars in front of me brake, illuminating the night with hundreds of red taillights. "We have to do whatever it takes to save *Britta's*. I can come home tomorrow."

Stella shakes her head so vehemently; she may throw out a disc. Dad, on the other hand, was so worried about me leaving that I'm surprised when he doesn't tell me to pack my bags and get on the road immediately. Instead, he and Adam are both quiet.

"We're not making any decisions tonight," Dad says, finally, in a more decisive way than I've ever heard from him. "Let's take the next week to think about it while you enjoy your time in LA. Once we have a better idea of exact costs, if you still want to come home, then do it."

I want to argue, but then I remember I've promised Annie I would help her at the coffee shop. I don't want to go back on my word, and volunteering there will also give me something to take my mind off *Britta's*. Another week in LA might appease Stella, too.

"Are you sure?" I ask.

Stella lets out a sigh of relief.

"There's nothing you can do here until I put together an estimate," Adam says. "That will take a few more days, then we'll need to decide together what to do."

I stiffen at his *together*. The decision should be mine.

The anger I was determined to leave back home threatens to creep through the tiny opening I've given it. I feel it burrowing through my sternum. But a familiar sound in the background catches my attention, and I change the topic.

"Are you watching *the Sound of Music,* Dad?" My forced cheerfulness comes out sounding as unnatural as it feels.

Mom spent the last year of her life watching that musical on repeat. All of us have it memorized. Not just the songs. Every line.

Dad lets out a sad laugh. "I'm used to it being on in the background."

I don't have words. Dad is lonely, which only deepens my concern that I should come home. He needs me even more than *Britta's* does, and I'm about to tell him again that I can be home by tomorrow night, but he speaks first.

"Honey, we didn't get a chance to talk before you left. I got the feeling you were avoiding me," he says in his soft voice.

"Not you, Dad. Saying goodbye. I hate it." I glance at Stella, who looks out the window as though that will give me the privacy I suddenly want.

Dad takes a breath. "I understand why you're upset Mom didn't leave *Britta's* to you. You have every right. You put your life on hold to run it. But I think Mom wanted you to pick up your own life after she was gone."

As gentle as his words are, they leave me reeling.

"She should have known I would carry on what she and her grandmother created." The words come out on a staggered breath. I've thought them a thousand times, but never said them out loud. It hurts too much to think Mom didn't know me as well as I thought she did.

"She knew you'd do it out of duty, but not out of love, and she didn't want you to be saddled with that obligation if it wasn't your choice," Dad says.

His reasoning doesn't make things better, but I can't pinpoint why. Maybe because there's a truth in it I'm not ready to grapple with.

"But I don't have a choice now, and I *do* love *Britta's*," I say finally.

"You can love something and still let it go when it's time to say goodbye." His gentle tone holds me so close we could be in the same room.

"I don't want to do anymore goodbyes, Dad."

"Maybe it's time you did." Dad doesn't exactly scold, but there's the quiet urging of a loving parent in his tone. This is advice I can't easily dismiss.

We say I love you and hang up. I'll consider what he's said, but I'm not ready to use the g-word with him or *Britta's*. It's too soon since I had to say it to Mom.

I'm lost in my head when Stella says, "Real talk, Britta. Why did you want to leave instead of staying for Dex's party?"

Traffic picks up, and I press the gas. I change lanes and speed past the car, moving too slowly in front of me.

"Britta..." Stella prods.

There's no bypassing her question, so I take a deep breath. "I worried I'd given him the wrong idea about why I was there."

"What do you mean?"

"I don't know... I just... he kissed me, and I kissed him back. Then he said we could stay at the house again, and I was afraid if I said yes that he'd have expectations I wasn't going to deliver on." Hearing the words out loud doesn't make them more convincing.

"Why not just tell him you weren't going to sleep with him?" Her question is valid, but also annoying because I'm supposed to be the older, wiser cousin.

I throw up my hands. "I don't know. I panicked."

Stella studies me from the other side of the car, her eyes digging into me, searching for the secrets I've tucked away.

"You ran," she says. "That's not like you."

"I was worried about *Britta's*." That's my only excuse. It's not like I can tell her she's wrong. I've never had a problem setting boundaries with guys.

Stella lets out a frustrated sigh that forces me to look at her. "I know how important *Britta's* is to you." She reaches across the car and squeezes my hand gently before letting it go. "But my career is important too, and that party tonight would have been an amazing networking opportunity."

I wince at her words. "What do you mean? You work for Georgia."

"Yeah, and Zach and Georgia will move back to LA once her project in Paradise is done," she says this like I should believe it, just because Georgia has been saying she's going back to LA since she came to Paradise. "And I want to take on more clients before then so I can move here, too. I can do some work remotely, but I can't build the clientele I want in Paradise."

Traffic slows again, and I mull over what she's said. "So, if Dad and Adam had said I needed to come home right away, would you have stayed in LA without me?"

When she doesn't answer, I glance at her long enough to see her blink in disbelief before she speaks.

"I've got a little over a week until Georgia's show starts again. We're living next door to the World Champion of surfing and his friend who starred in a TV show and who also is the twin brother of Frankie Forsythe. And... AND, their best friend is Rhys James." Stella puts her palms up, like *duh*.

"Okay, fine. When you put it that way, you have a pretty excellent opportunity here." I weave around a car as two lanes merge into one.

"Yeah, so do you, Britt."

"What do you mean?" I'm taken back by her words and nearly miss the red taillights in front of me and have to slam on my brakes to avoid rear-ending the car in front of us.

"I mean, you used to want to go somewhere bigger than Paradise. You wanted your own business, your own life, and you gave that up when your mom got sick."

I keep my eyes pointed forward. She's not telling me anything I don't already know. Occasionally, I let myself imagine what my life would be like now if Mom hadn't gotten sick. But it's a pointless exercise. Those opportunities I gave up are gone, and I'd give them up again.

"What else was I supposed to do?" While traffic is stopped, I face her. "Dad couldn't take care of Mom by himself and run the grocery store at the same time. And my brothers have their own businesses. They did what they could, though. We all did."

"I know they did. You all pitched in." Stella scoots closer and pulls me into a side hug. "But you're the only one who doesn't see that you gave up the most. The internship in LA. The chance to live somewhere you weren't Pete and Heidi Thomsen's daughter or Adam, Zach, and Bear's sister. The chance to be who you really are instead of how other people define you."

I close my eyes, tempted to sink into Stella's hug, but we're in the middle of traffic. And I'm not ready.

In general, I try not to think about what I gave up to take care of Mom, because when I do, I get angry. Not just at her because *Britta's* isn't mine, but also at my dad for not selling the store so he could take care of Mom full time. At my brothers for not having the same expectations or pressure to care for our parents because society thinks it's a woman's job.

At Mom for getting sick.

That's the one I feel the guiltiest for. Logically, I understand it's not her fault. She didn't ask to get Alzheimer's in her fifties. She didn't want to leave Dad alone or miss seeing Bear get married. Adam and Evie are ready to have kids. Mom would have loved having grandkids.

None of it is fair. That's what makes me mad. And being mad over things I have no control over leaves me feeling like a spoiled little girl. That's not who I am. I'm the girl who holds things together. It scares me to think that person could disappear if I admit that I'm angry.

Because life isn't fair, right? No one gets it easy. Childhood dreams aren't reality for anyone. But I'm uncomfortable with the thoughts Stella's brought up for me and I'm not sure how to sort them.

"Thanks, Stella." I pull away from her as traffic starts again. "I really appreciate you looking out for me. I'll commit to staying at least until you leave."

"Good girl." She pats my head like our Grandma Sparks used to do to us. "And don't run from Dex anymore, okay?"

My mouth drops and I choke out a "What!" before coughing a laugh. "I'm not running from Dex."

I *feel* Stella roll her eyes. That's the magnitude of her disbelief. "Yes, you are. But what are you really afraid of? That you were going to have to tell him no tonight? Or that you might catch feelings for him?"

Now it's my turn to roll my eyes. "People don't just *catch* feelings."

"Not if they don't let themselves," she counters with a smug smile. "Is that what you're doing?"

I pull my lips in tight, refusing to answer her questions. I'm already uncomfortable enough thinking about them.

Stella gets the message, because she pulls out her phone and scrolls through Tik Tok. She chatters about what she's watching and shows videos to me when we're stopped in traffic.

I answer when I have to, but I'm back in my head, thinking about what both Dad and Stella have said tonight. There's a lot to consider, especially when I get honest with myself about what I want for the future.

Maybe it's not *Britta's*.

Maybe it *is* Dex.

Or maybe it's neither. I'm not sure. But I'm open to the possibility of finding out.

CHAPTER FIFTEEN

Britta

S tella and I get home late. We've had a long day in the sun, we're both dead on our feet, and I've told Annie I'd be at the shop when it opens at six a.m. But when I crawl into bed, I can't fall asleep. My mind keeps turning over everything that's happened today.

Introspection isn't my favorite, and I've had to do a lot of it t. Squished in between examining my anger towards Mom and grappling with regret for not taking Stella's career into account, is the realization that I *did* run from Dex. And I did it on a monumental day for him he'd invited me to be part of. He's been nothing but generous, and I chose not to have a mildly awkward conversation about "expectations" with him.

The truth is, I think I used that as an excuse because I *am* afraid of "catching" feelings for him. And I'd really rather not. I don't want the heartbreak of saying goodbye.

But I remember Mom saying something when she was first diagnosed with Alzheimer's: *I won't let fears about my future get in the way of enjoying my now,* and maybe she was right

Mom had squeezed the most out of life first. Some people would have traveled and checked as much as possible off their bucket list. Mom focused on loving everyone, giving as much of herself as she could before that self disappeared.

Except that part of Mom never disappeared, even when she couldn't give much more than a smile. Her friendly and open nature is why everyone remembers her. Not her coffee or ebelskiver, but the fact she made and served them with all the love she could.

Remembering Mom like that opens a place in my heart that's been sealed shut. Relief and acceptance slip in, loosening the stranglehold guilt has had on me. With that loosening, the tears I've held back for so long come freely. The distant sound of waves lapping the shore lulls me to sleep.

The next morning, my eyes are red and puffy, and I look like I got even less sleep than I did—which wasn't much. I'm so tired, but I feel lighter than I have in...I honestly don't remember how long. The waves that sounded far away and gentle last night are louder, crashing with the energy of high tide, reminding me of Dex, his kiss, his win, and the possibility of achieving the impossible.

The last two days with him and Stella, and even Archie, were exactly the break I didn't think I needed. My life since Mom got sick has been one of routine and schedules. When the unexpected happened, it usually came as an emergency. I've lived in fear of something happening that wasn't scheduled.

Staying an extra day in San Clemente wasn't on my calendar, but it was the best day I've had in years. I couldn't have anticipated how much I'd enjoy watching a competition for a sport I barely knew anything about, or that I would fall in love with it. Everything about yesterday was unpredictable, in the very best way. Maybe that's part of what made me run too. I'm used to pulse-racing anxiety—not happiness—that comes with not knowing what's next.

The time both with and watching Dex was a reset button. I feel invigorated. I'm excited to work with Annie, not just to stay busy, but also because there may be something I can learn from her I can use back at *Britta's*.

But I don't want to think about going back to Paradise today. I'm living in the now, so even though it's only a little after five a.m., I send Dex a message. He's an early riser, but I hope he's got his phone on silent if he's let his alarm have a day off.

> **Dear World's Greatest Surfer. Thanks for everything yesterday. I'm sorry I left so suddenly. I owe you dinner. When do you get back?**

Thirty minutes later, as I head out the door for *Annie's*, my phone dings. I dig it out of my purse. It has to be Dex, and my lips kick into a grin when I see his name on my screen.

> **Dear World's Greatest Barista. Thanks for being there. You DO owe me dinner. Be back next week.**

My laugh at his greeting morphs into a frown. If Dex is gone for a week, and I leave LA when Stella does in ten days, that will only give Dex and me a couple of days to hang out. The lightness that had me floating only a few minutes ago leaks away.

Ten days also doesn't give me time to do much for Annie. And Britta's will still be closed...

All things to consider.

I arrive at *Annie's* a couple minutes before Annie, who gives me a forced smile that holds little happiness. She looks even more fatigued than the first time we met.

She unlocks the door, and I follow her in. After locking the door behind us, Annie lets out a deep sigh, then locks on a smile that doesn't reach her eyes.

"How was the competition?" She takes a chair off a table and sets it upright.

"Amazing. Absolutely incredible to watch." I follow her lead and set more chairs back in place. "You heard Dex won, right?"

Annie nods, and a flash of joy tugs the edges of her lips higher. "Didn't I say he was magic on the water?"

My face warms as I nod. I meant the competition was amazing, but Annie wasn't off in assuming I meant Dex. He was the best part of it.

We talk more while setting up the dining room. I give her as many details as she asks for, but I sense an unnatural quietness in Annie. I don't know her well, but one day watching her interact with customers and employees has given me a pretty good sense of who she is.

A safe place. *Annie's* isn't just a refuge for people from their busy—often difficult—lives. Annie herself is too.

I imagine most of the time that brings her a lot of joy, but I wonder if it's a heavy burden to carry when your own life has been turned upside down.

As we prep the espresso machines and workstations, I muster up the courage to ask her a real question, hoping I won't overstep.

"Is everything okay, Annie?"

She takes a breath, like she's considering how to answer. "Diva is scheduled to come in at six, but the bus is never on time. Mitzi's baby is sick, and she doesn't have childcare for him, so she won't be in today. Hopefully Sergio can work both shifts."

"Whew." I wipe my hands on my apron, already breaking into sympathy sweat for Annie. I'd only planned on volunteering for a few hours, but that won't be enough. "I can stay. We'll make it work."

Annie's shoulders relax, and she leans in my direction. "If I thought I could do without you, I'd say no. I'll just say thank you instead."

"I'm happy to help." I chew my lip, not wanting to push, but still feel like she hasn't answered my question. "But... how are *you*?"

Annie pauses, then drops her head and shakes it. "Tired. I'm tired, Britta. You heard about my Keesha's accident?"

"Your daughter?"

She nods.

"A little."

"She's been in a rehab center, but my insurance is pushing for her to be released, and she's going to need full-time care when she comes home." Annie wipes the already-shining metal counters with an energy like a genie might appear to grant her three wishes.

I bet I could guess what her number one wish would be.

My heart tugs with my own memories of my family and me coordinating our schedules and lives around Mom's care.

"Have you got help?"

"I've got plenty of friends and my church who have offered." Annie stops scrubbing and leans against the counter with her hand on her hip. "But I'm stretched in two directions when I'm here instead of with Keesha."

I bob my head in sympathy. "I get that. My mom had Alzheimer's. My family and I spent five years juggling our businesses and her care. Most of her care fell on me." I take the rag from Annie and rub down the counter opposite the one she's worked on.

"When did she pass?" Annie asks gently.

Not *if...* When. "

She knows without being told. That's what makes Annie a safe place.

"End of April, but I'm still surprised some days when I wake and remember she's gone."

"I'm sorry, Britta. You're too young to lose a parent." Annie rests a warm hand on my shoulder, which, somehow, is more reassuring than a hug. As if she's saying *I'm here for you* instead of *I'm so sad for you*.

"Yeah, it is." I face Annie again. "I miss her every day, but I don't think I'd change anything, even if I could. It was an honor to care for her."

Annie nods slowly. "No one will take care of Keesha like I will. I know better than anyone what she needs."

"We felt the same about Mom, too. We didn't want to put her in a nursing home. That's not the best decision for every family, but for us it worked, but it wasn't easy. None of us could have done it alone and still run our own businesses." I point to the espresso machine. "Can I make you a coffee?"

Annie tilts her head in a yes. "I've had a big chain make an offer to buy *Annie's*."

It's my turn to be surprised. "Would you take it?"

"I don't want to, but if it comes down to choosing where I'm needed most, the answer will always be Keesha." Her mouth twists with the impossible choice she's already considering.

"I'm here for whatever you need, Annie. At least for another week and a half." Last night, when I agreed to stay as long as Stella does, ten days seemed like a long time. Now it seems too short.

"Like I've said, you are a godsend." Annie reties her multi-colored apron over her caftan—a rich purple today—then walks to the door and flips over the closed sign. "Time to open."

Over the next six days, I'm with Annie every time she flips that sign and says those same words. And I'm still there when she leaves for the day to take care of Keesha and the afternoon shift manager shows up. I help through the lunch rush, then head back to the apartment between two and three.

I'm always exhausted when I get there, but Stella and I find something different to do every day. Walk a new beach looking for shells and sea glass. Try a food we've never eaten before. Shop cute boutiques along PCH.

The only thing that doesn't change is how much I enjoy the sunshine and the soothing *shush* of the ocean.

The more time I spend at *Annie's,* the more responsibility Annie gives me; leaving me in charge while she runs to the rehab center to check on Keesha; trusting me to balance the books; and even asking me to write the schedule for the following week. It's all stuff I've done thousands of times at *Britta's,* and the familiarity of the tasks eases some of the longing I feel for my coffee shop. *Annie's* feels like a little piece of home.

Today, Annie left me completely in charge while she met with her daughter's doctor to talk about moving her to a rehab center. I was so happy to help. Like, happier than I've been in a really long time.

And I really enjoy working with Mitzi and Diva, but I also like the other baristas who work there. Manny, who's putting himself through college; Carla, who lost her home when she couldn't pay her hospital bills after getting hit by an uninsured driver; and Sergio who's learning all the ropes so he can open his own coffee shop in El Salvador once he has enough money to return home.

At the end of the shift, Annie comes back to the shop and sits at a table doing some paperwork, but I feel her observing me. When I hang up my apron to leave, she catches me.

"Can we talk in the office?" she asks, and I follow her to the tiny room at the back of the shop that barely has space for a desk and chair, let alone the stacks of papers on both.

Annie glances around like she's just realized there's nowhere for us to sit, then shrugs and leans against the desk.

"I'm just going to come out with it. I need to sell so I can take care of Keesha, and I could really use your help until then, if you can stay longer. Unless..." She catches my eye and doesn't let it go.

"What?"

"I'd rather you bought *Annie's* than some chain that will ruin everything I've built." Her eyes burrow into me, unearthing the dream I've had to start a business of my own. The dream I set aside to run *Britta's*.

"I'm not sure if you're in a position to buy," Annie continues. "Or if you've even thought of staying in LA for good, but if you're interested, I'd sell to you before anyone else."

"Buy *Annie's*?" Even after our conversation the other day, I'd never thought about buying *Annie's*.

Her chin plunges up and down. "More than just the business. I own this property too. I think you're the person who could do right by my baby, so I'll sell everything to you for less than what the chain is offering. Are you interested?"

I stare at Annie. I should say no.

I don't.

CHAPTER SIXTEEN

Dex

There are perks to being a world champion that go beyond the title and a cool trophy. Within a day of my win, major companies have reached out to Marta with opportunities for me to promote their watches, energy drinks, beer, SUVs, and even skin care products. She's brokering so many deals for me that I'm nearly ready to forgive her marriage proposal blunder.

Even better, Rip Tide is *very* happy with me, and they want me to be happy with *them*. They have heaps of reasons for wanting me to stay with them once my contract expires. And all those reasons have dollar signs in front of them, which is an enormous relief. I've got the right people who will make sure the money I earn right now turns into enough money to set me up for life, no matter what happens.

The day after the finals, the Rip Tide execs offer to let my family and me, plus Archie—who's family too—stay at their beach house for a week. There is only one answer to their offer, and we graciously accept. We spend a lot of time surfing, just for fun. It's been ages since my family has done that together, and I love seeing how much Jordy has progressed. When Dad was my coach and manager, surfing together meant training. It meant not letting him or me down.

This is better.

We find other things to do besides surfing. We drive down to San Diego where Mom spent time with her American grandparents. She doesn't have family there anymore, but she shows us the places she used to love. Then we go to the zoo, which is ripper.

My whole life has been about surfing. Every family vacation we took was to waves that were on the Junior Tour, then the Challenger Series. After my first year in the Challenger Series, Dad was the only one who came with me. Mom wasn't there to be a buffer, and I can see now that I started drinking in part to relieve the pressure he put on me.

Now at competitions, it's me and Archie, sometimes my nutritionist and trainer, and only an occasional beer. I like it that way.

While we're wandering around the San Diego Zoo—in front of the elephant enclosure, to be exact—Archie takes a call. Not two minutes later, he pulls me aside from my family.

"That was Marta on the phone." Archie laces his fingers together and puts them on top of his head. This is what he does when he's worried. "I passed along all your travel info to the lawyer, but unless he can find some loopholes, it's not looking good. Between traveling and your back injury in 2022, you spent most of your time outside the US. And you've paid taxes in Aus, not the US."

I haven't forgotten about being part of the USA Olympic Surfing team, but things have been so good with my family, I've tried not to think about it. Partly because I didn't want any bad news to get me down, but also because I worry Dad will full on lose it if I mention surfing for the US instead of Aus.

But mostly because I don't want Jordy to feel any pressure to live up to my reputation. He's already talking about when he wins the WSL Finals. I admire the confidence, but experience has taught me those expectations—whether from yourself or others—can be crushing.

"We knew it was a long shot, right?" I shrug, not wanting Archie to see how disappointed I am or my family to wonder what's got me down.

"There are still options," Archie's serious tone doesn't match his shrug, like he's *not* seriously considering me marrying an American as one of those options.

We both know he is. But he's the only one of the two of us. I haven't forgotten the idea, but only because it's crazy.

I shake my head and walk back to my family. The elephant, on the other side of the enclosure from them, lifts her trunk and makes a trumpeting sound. Jordy, a few feet away, makes a loud *pawoooo* sound in return that makes us all laugh.

I just want to enjoy this and not worry about how I'm going to get to the Olympics. Now that Archie and Marta have put it in my head, I'm not ready to give up so easily. I'll find another way to get there, but it can wait until my family goes home.

The week goes by too quickly, a thing I never thought would happen before, when Dad and I were working together. I actually enjoy my time with him. But, by the end of the week, I'm ready to get back to LA, not only because I feel off-kilter when I'm not training, but also because I want to see Britta.

I'm already picturing her in the green dress, but in the texts we've exchanged, I've held back, reminding her of that promise. She's spending her time at *Annie's*, so our texts and calls are sparse, but my thoughts about her aren't. And I let them linger as long as they want, because

I'd rather think of her than obsess about how I'm going to get to the Olympics. That's all up to the lawyers at this point.

But on the day Archie and I drive to LA to drop my family at the airport and go back to our apartment, the 2028 Olympics take up more real estate in my brain. I've tried to stay focused on my family while they're here, instead of that pipedream, but I can't anymore. There are too many signs that I should make that dream a reality.

Literally, signs. Even though the games are four years away, billboards along the 405 freeway already advertise where the venues will be for track and field, gymnastics, and swimming. There aren't any for surfing, but the officials will announce which wave it will be soon. Lowers, Huntington, or Malibu. All waves I've won on over the years.

We pass another Olympics billboard about diving, and my pulse slows, the surrounding noise grows quiet while everything in the periphery of my vision goes soft. Only one thing comes into sharp focus. An image of me surfing a perfect wave at Lowers, scoring another ten. Only this time the prize is a gold medal.

When I hug my parents and brother goodbye at the airport, Mom holds me longer than I expect, then presses her hands to my cheeks. "You've got something big in your sights. I don't know what it is, but I see it in your eyes. Whatever it is, Liam, you make it happen."

I break into a smile. Mum may live on the other side of the world from me, but she still knows me better than anyone.

"We've got to go, Kim," Dad says before giving me a side hug. "Keep on the tour, Dex. No messing about."

"Will do, Dad."

He means well, so I take his encouragement the way he intended, even if my chest tightens.

Archie and I climb back in the Sprinter van, wave goodbye, then grab the freeway back to South Bay. It's a fifteen-minute drive, but as soon as we exit the on-ramp, we come to a complete stop. Red brake lights stretch in front of us as far as we can see.

"I want this, Arch," I say, staring ahead. I don't have to tell him what *this* is.

"Yeah, mate. I know. We'll make it happen." Archie cracks open the window and leans his elbow out of it.

We move forward a foot or two, then stop again. Archie taps his fingers on the steering wheel while I bounce my legs. We're a couple of racehorses, pawing at the dirt, ready to go. Ready to *win*. All we need is someone to open the chute.

When the untapped energy in the van reaches a tipping point where we may both jump out of the van and run home, Archie breaks the tension. "Sure you don't want to give the marriage idea a whirl? The media's already shipped you and Britta. You get along. She's pretty. Doesn't seem like one of those needy girls."

I laugh. He's joking, but only half.

"Yeah, she's perfect. I'll plan to go back to Idaho with her when she leaves. Waves are pretty good in that lake she lives on. Shouldn't be a problem training there." I try to joke back, but I come off more sarcastic than anything.

"No need to get defensive, mate." Archie turns up the stereo, ending our conversation.

Smog hangs over the city, trapped by the unseasonably hot day, and the setting sun creates a gloomy haze. Exhaust pours from the cars around us, making the atmosphere more miserable. I've been so stoked since the Finals—even going into them—that I had to come down sometime. Thinking about my Olympic dreams being just out of reach and about Britta leaving soon brings my euphoria to a screeching halt.

I've reached the goal I've been chasing since going pro. I'm in an exclusive club of thirty-one men, if you count the winners of competitions held by predecessors to the World Surf League. Now I want entry into a more exclusive club. I want to be an Olympian.

I can't let a bunch of paperwork get in the way of my dream, but the marriage idea is straight-up crazy. The last thing I need is a wife. I'm gone for months at a time. What woman wants to follow her husband around the world to sit around waiting for him to surf? Sometimes in remote, bug-infested camps without Wi-Fi or even hot water.

Britta and I have a connection. There's no denying that. I felt it the first time I saw her. I think she's felt it too. That or she's expert at faking it in her kisses.

But it would take more than attraction to be married to someone like me. Even if it was a fake marriage.

Which, again, is straight up insane.

I turn down the stereo and mumble, "Sorry, Arch. Lots of head rubbish going on right now, but it will all get sorted. One day at a time, right?"

Then Archie and I find something else to talk about besides the Olympics. There's not another Championship Tour event until January when the first one will be at Pipeline on the North Shore. I'll spend the next four months training for that wave, mentally and physically. Between surfing and promotional things for Rip Tide and other companies, Archie and I have plenty to plan for.

Our fifteen-minute drive takes half an hour, but that's LA. It's dusk when we pull into our apartment complex. Archie parks, and I gather my bag and my trophy. Our arms are full as we lug our stuff to the walkway leading to our unit.

Ahead of me, Archie says, "Lights are on at Georgia's."

I crane my neck around my trophy to follow the direction of his finger. Sure enough, the lights are on, and a shadow figure crosses in front of the window. I wonder if it's Britta. I also wonder about Archie's sudden interest in electricity and who's using it.

"Cracker observation, mate."

Archie smirks over his shoulder. "Just pointing it out in case you want to drop by and say hello."

"Maybe propose?"

Archie lifts his shoulders. "If it comes up." Then he slows to fall in step with me. "Joking aside, we'll figure out a way to get you to the Olympics."

His confidence gives my own a jolt. If Archie says he'll figure out how to get me to my next goal, he'll do it. "You work on the legal stuff. I'll work on staying in top form."

"Right. Olympics, here we come."

I smile, then allow myself one last glance at Britta's apartment.

CHAPTER SEVENTEEN

Britta

I'm kicking back on the couch watching *90 Day Fiancé* with Stella while thinking about Annie's offer to sell me her coffee shop. I've given myself a million reasons I'd never be able to do it, but I can't shake the feeling of excitement at the idea of owning a coffee shop on the outskirts of LA, a couple blocks from the Pacific Ocean.

My phone buzzes, and I pull it from the pocket of Dex's Rip Tide hoodie that I forgot to give back to him and have made daily use of since "forgetting."

"It's Zach." I swing my feet off the ottoman and stand. "Pause it until I get back, please."

Stella's shoulders fold in disappointment. "Hurry! I need to know if Rob cheated on Sophie."

"No one *needs* to know that." I step over Stella's legs, which she doesn't move from the ottoman, before taking the call.

"Hey, Zach!" I walk into the kitchen and sit on a barstool while Stella flips impatiently through the TV channels.

"Hey, Sis. How's it going?" My brother's cheerful voice is more muted than usual.

"All good." We make small talk for a few minutes—it's cooling down in Paradise; people had on puffy jackets here today, even though it was sixty degrees most of the day—while I wait for him to tell me why he's called.

"Listen, I've got some news I wanted to share with you first," he says finally. "The city contacted me about buying the land *Britta's* is on. Since it's right next to the new community center, they've decided it would be a good idea to own it so they can add on to the center in the next few years."

"Sooo, what would happen to *Britta's*?" I have an idea, but I'm not sure how to feel yet, other than stunned.

"They'd tear it down."

Hearing the words out loud immediately brings me clarity. "You told them no, right?"

"I wanted to talk to you first."

"Why? Did you think I'd say anything but no?" I sit up straighter on the stool and brace myself for whatever arguments Zach may be prepared to throw my way.

He's a realtor, so it makes sense the city would approach him. But he's also the most likable of us Thomsen kids. Zach has sweet-talked himself out of a lot of tight spots. Whoever approached him probably thought he'd be able to sweet talk all of us into taking the deal.

Wrong.

I'm immune to my brother's charm.

"I knew you'd say no, but I thought you might change your mind after I told you what we could do, so *Britta's* is yours." Zach has slipped into his deep, smooth-as-butter salesman's tone, which also means he'll be doing all the talking. "The city is offering a good price. Enough that, if Cassie were on board, we could renovate the apartment portion of her bookstore into a new *Britta's*."

I don't hate the idea. Cassie's bookstore is in an old building that once belonged to Mom's family, too. Moving *Britta's* there would make sense historically, but Cassie owns the building now.

"How would moving *Britta's* to the bookstore that Cassie owns make it mine?" I want something that's my own. Something I can pass down to my kids, if I ever have them, and if they wanted it. "And what would happen to *Britta's* if the bookstore closes or Cassie has to sell the building?"

"Those are all details we can work out later, but before we sell the plot *Britta's* is on now, I'll convince everyone to deed you their portion. You'll own the business itself and have the capital to re-open in a new location," Zach says with a confidence I envy, despite knowing it was hard-earned.

"Why not convince them to give me *Britta's* now?"

"If we don't move from the current location, do you want to be entirely responsible for all the repairs *Britta's* needs?" He has a good point, which is annoying.

Even though I've primarily run *Britta's* for the past five years, everyone has pitched in, working a few shifts a week, at least. When Adam took over Mom's other restaurant, the *Garden of Eatin'*, he bought her out. *Britta's* is the only thing Mom had to give us when she passed. It wouldn't really be fair to ask everyone to share the cost of repairs beyond what insurance covers, then ask them to give me the refurbished coffee shop.

"I'll think about," I tell Zach. "But I'm not sure if having the name to myself is worth giving up the shop itself. That's where the memories of Mom are."

"Yeah, I get what you mean." Though he's sympathetic, I hear the *but* in his voice. "We'd be saying goodbye to a piece of her history, but the memories of her are with *us*."

"I spent a lot of time there with her, Zach." I try not to sound defensive, but it's different for him. He doesn't have the same emotional attachment to *Britta's*.

"I know, but think about it."

We end our conversation, and even though I've promised him I'll consider the offer, all I want to do is go back to watching *90 Day Fiancé* and not think about anything. Because all I'm thinking about now is that I have to decide about whether I'm leaving with Stella on Monday or staying in LA by myself. To be honest, I was leaning toward staying. Annie needs me here. I still can't shake the idea of buying *Annie's* from her, but now I'm wondering if *Britta's* needs me more. I'm being pulled between doing what I want to do and what I should do.

It's the same feeling I had when Mom got sick, and I had to decide between taking an internship in LA or going home to Paradise.

I slide off the kitchen stool, but I barely make it to the couch before there's a knock at the door.

Somehow, I know it's Dex. Probably because I don't know anyone else in LA, but also, the knock sounds like him, patient and persistent at the same time. I've both expected he'd stop by once he got back and also felt anxious about it.

I'd be lying if I said Dex wasn't one reason I was thinking of staying longer. Over the past week, I couldn't stop myself from texting—and occasionally talking to—Dex, even knowing if I choose to leave, it'll be easier if I don't have to stamp out any sparks I've stoked to life.

At the same time, our first goodbye was the best goodbye I've ever had. Great kissing; very little talking; no use of the actual word *goodbye*.

Now that he's actually here, though, I'm frozen. I want to see him, but I also want to leave LA with no emotional attachments, and I need a second to think about which I want more.

"Will you get that?" I ask Stella.

She looks at me with her enormous eyes and a smirk that tells me she knows who's knocking, and she's not interested in throwing me a life preserver. "I'm not wearing a bra."

I don't think she's worn a bra since we got here. She's never really needed one to begin with, but she runs to her room and shuts the door before I can point out either of those things.

So I go to the door, making one quick stop in front of the mirror hanging in the breakfast nook. I've been at *Annie's* most of the day, and I look—and smell—like it. There's not a lot I can do beyond tightening my ponytail and smoothing away some smudged mascara under my eyes.

I open the door to see exactly who I thought—and, okay, *hoped*—it would be.

"Hi," Dex says, his dimple playing at the corner of his mouth.

"Hi." My eyes get stuck on his lips and that dimple. "Welcome back, Champ."

His grin grows. "Thought I'd drop by to ask when I could collect on that dinner you promised."

I open the door wider. "I can make you the best bowl of cereal you've ever eaten right now."

Dex shifts like he's going to come in but stays in the doorway. "I seem to recall something about a green dress in your promise."

The way Dex's eyes light up when he mentions the green dress sends a rush of adrenaline straight from my heart to my brain. I want to put on the dress right now, just so I can watch his golden-brown eyes grow darker. Looking at him leaning against the doorframe—wanting to yank him inside so hard that we collide, lips and all—I know what the right decision is.

My attraction to Dex is as powerful as a retreating wave. As hard as I try to resist its tug, I can't stop being pulled deeper...

Unless I get out of his path.

It's time to go.

I tip my head. "Will you hate me if I back out of my promise?"

His head cocks back with surprise, and I have to tell him the truth.

"I like you Dex, a lot," I say, and his face lifts so quickly, I hate that what I have to say will wipe away his smile. "But I just got some bad news, and I need to go back to Paradise. I'm leaving Monday."

His mouth drops, but in seconds he's schooled his emotions behind a pleasant grin.

"Your family needs you back that soon?" He asks so casually that he's obviously more invested in my answer than he wants to let on.

I nod. "*Britta's* does, anyway."

Dex studies me carefully, questions flicking in his eyes while I clutch the inside door handle, waiting. "Is that what you want? To go back?"

I shrug. "What I want isn't really important. People need me."

"People? Or your business? A business is made up of people, but *it's* not people."

I don't answer. I can't find the words.

Dex stands straight and makes a disappointed tsk. "Raincheck, then?"

I nod. "Next time you're in Paradise."

"Next time I'm in Paradise." He backs away from the door.

"See you then." I lift my hand, then drop it and slowly close the door as he turns toward his apartment.

The door clicks shut, but I take a few seconds before I'm ready to walk away. I did the right thing, stepping out of the current pulling me toward Dex. The disappointment I feel will pass.

I let go of the doorknob, turn around and nearly run into Stella.

"You are an idiot." Her hands are on her hips, and the fiery Italian half of her DNA is on full display. "You've got Dex and Annie both begging you to stay, and you're running back to Paradise to handle problems that can be handled by the people there."

"I wouldn't call what Dex said begging." I step around her without meeting her glare. "He refused my offer of cereal."

"Fine, then only Annie begged with words. Dex kept it to body language." Stella follows me into the hallway.

"I'm not talking about this, Stella." I head toward my bedroom to escape whatever lecture she's got cooking.

I can't deny what she said about Annie, or that, if a pile of money fell into my lap, I would buy her coffee shop. My pulse ticks up a notch every time I think about the possibility. But it's not realistic, and neither is anything long term with Dex, so why set myself up for disappointment?

"You should take the city's offer to buy *Britta's* and use the money to live your own dreams." Stella's statement stops me in my tracks, and she runs into me.

I turn slowly and face her. "You were listening to my conversation?"

Her cheeks color slightly, but she pulls her shoulders back. "It's not my fault you all are loud talkers."

"It's not your business, Stella." I step into my room, but she presses her hand to the door to stop me from closing it.

I drop my hand from the knob and glare at her.

"You know you get rude when you get defensive?" Stella glares back at me. "We're all family, so it is our business. Maybe not financially for me, but... heritagely. Britta was my great-grandma too."

"Heritagely? Not a word." With Stella blocking the door, I give up, closing it and walk into my room. But my hands need something to do, so I grab an elastic from my dresser and look at myself in the mirror while twisting my hair into a topknot. "If you care so much about *Britta's*, then you should understand why I need to go back and why I don't want to sell to the city and why I have to keep it running."

Stella catches my eyes in the mirror. "I do understand. I understand all of it. But I also understand that you're using *Britta's* as an excuse to run from your feelings. You're doing the same thing with *Annie's*."

I finish winding an elastic around my hair, then face Stella. "What are you talking about?"

"You're staying as busy as possible so you don't have to deal with your grief." Stella's voice softens. "It won't work. You can't keep running. You have to deal with the trauma. It's why you're here, Britta. It's why everyone encouraged you to go."

Stella's words stun me. I can't move.

"What trauma?"

Stella lets out a long sigh, edged with frustration. "You watched your mom die. For five years."

"That's not trauma. That's life." My voice cracks, and I back away from Stella.

She smiles sadly and moves toward the open door. "Georgia offered you this apartment so you could slow down and give yourself time to recover. Your family knows you need this break. Let them give you that gift. How else can they repay you for taking care of your mom all those years?"

Apparently, it's a rhetorical question because Stella doesn't wait for me to answer before stepping out the door and closing it behind her to leave me alone.

All alone, except for my thoughts. If those count, then I'm in a very crowded room. A crowded room every inch of my body wants to escape.

But where would I go that Stella's words, my thoughts, and my memories of Mom wouldn't follow?

I stare at myself in the mirror. Even in my reflection, I can't escape seeing Mom. I look too much like her. But I also see my dad in the shape of my nose, my brothers in the curve of my lips. I share so many similarities with all of them that even people who are strangers to me, but not my parents or brothers, have asked me if I'm their daughter or sister.

And I wonder if I've ever seen myself just for who I am, rather than who I am because of the family I'm part of.

I study my reflection more closely, searching for something that's only me. I can't see it yet, but I think I might if I give myself more time. I stare harder, thinking not only about what Stella's said but also Dex's question about what I want.

It's an excellent question that I can't answer. This is an unfamiliar experience for me, sitting with my thoughts, letting them sink in and take hold in a way I never have before.

Because Stella's right. I have been running. And I'm tired. And sad. Maybe even a little lonely. Mom was my best friend. Then she got sick, and I lost the person I told everything and counted on to help me make sense of my life. That person eventually didn't even know me anymore.

But I didn't know *her* either. That was the hardest part; watching Mom become someone else.

I stare so hard in the mirror that my vision goes fuzzy, except for a bright green spot in my closet.

My focus goes to the dress hanging there. The green dress I promised to wear for Dex. Dex, who makes me smile. Who makes me laugh. Who makes me *feel*. Whose kisses make the world around me go as soft and fuzzy as it is right now, before bringing it into sharper focus, full of color and depth.

Watching him reach his dream was awesome, in the truest sense of the word. But knowing even a little about what it took for him to get there is inspiring. He didn't rely on luck. He set high goals, then worked his hardest to achieve them.

I remember when I used to do the same, whether it was making straight A's, getting into a good university, or joining clubs and networking in order to get a prestigious internship after graduating from college. In the years after Mom got sick, I stopped setting my own goals. My only focus was on keeping her alive and comfortable for as long as possible.

I'm not ready to fall in love—I'm not sure I'll ever be. But running from the possibility—especially when the chance is so slim—isn't the answer. Why not use the next few weeks to figure out who I am and what it is I want?

And why not let Dex be part of that?

As hard as it is to admit, other people can handle *Britta's* right now. It's hard to imagine my life without *Britta's,* so if I decide that's part of who I want to be, I'll be managing the restaurant for as long as I can. This may be my one real vacation for a very long time.

The most important thing I learned taking care of Mom is that life is short. Why not squeeze the most out of it?

I take a deep, staggered breath, then reach for my phone.

> **Fine. I'll stay.**

Seconds later Stella whoops and another few seconds after that, my phone pings.

Stella has sent me a gif of a baby doing a celebratory dance.

I laugh, then examine the green dress for wrinkles. I'm going to need it tomorrow.

CHAPTER EIGHTEEN

Dex

For the first time in years, I take a true day off where I have no actual plans—other than throwing some shrimp on the barbie—schedule, or diet restrictions. I sleep in, eat donuts for breakfast, and veg. The only thing I don't skip in my daily routine is some light yoga and meditation, because today is about relaxing and doing whatever I want.

And watching the AFL Grand Final is what I want to do more than anything else. Even though watching the match will be more full-on than relaxing. It's basically the Australian Super Bowl, except Aussies don't wear pads when we knock each other around. We man up and get hurt, even the girls.

Not me, obviously. The only sport worth getting injured for is surfing. But I love watching the AFL. Archie does too. The match is scheduled for two-thirty in Melbourne on Saturday, which makes it nine-thirty on Friday night in LA.

Archie and I have been planning a barbie for weeks. We've got it heated and ready to go as soon as Rhys shows up. The match falls on a week when he's got a break from touring.

That's who I'm expecting a couple hours before match time when someone knocks on our door. So when I open it and see Britta, blonde hair swept up with a few tendrils framing her face, wearing the green dress I picked out for her, I nearly drop my second donut of the day.

"Hi." The word stumbles out of my mouth, tripping over its one syllable.

"Hi." Britta smiles, and it's all I can do to keep my eyes on her mouth and not the thin straps on her shoulders or the deep V of fabric leading to her...

I force my eyes back to hers. "I thought you were leaving."

She shakes her head. "I had a promise to keep. Can I take you to dinner?"

Now my eyes drop to my bare chest—I catch Britta's gaze following mine. The only thing I'm wearing is board shorts. I haven't showered. I haven't combed my hair. I have plans with two of my best mates, including one I haven't seen in ages.

But when I look back at Britta in that dress, I can't say no. I motion her inside. "Give me ten minutes to put on something more...better. Clothes, I mean, so I don't look like a dag next to you."

"I don't know what that is, but don't go to a lot of trouble. We can go somewhere casual." Britta follows me into the sitting room, where Archie's eyes nearly pop out of his head when he sees her.

"Britta's taking me to dinner," I tell him.

He keeps staring at Britta, so I raise my voice. "Archie!" His head swings to me, but his eyes are glazed over. That's how good Britta looks.

More than good.

Absolutely gorge.

She's always been a stunner, but that dress on her looks better than I imagined.

"Can you get Britta a drink or something while I get cleaned up?" I ask him, and he finally comes out of his daze.

"You're not staying for the match? Rhys is coming over."

Britta is about to sit down but stops with Archie's idiotic question. I send him a fiery glare at the same time she says, "You've got plans? Of course you do. It's a Friday night. We can go another time."

She moves so quick for the door, and I get so distracted by the low, strappy back of her dress that I almost can't stop her in time. But I come to and dash in front of the door as she reaches for the knob.

"The match doesn't start for hours. We've got time to grab dinner. After that, why don't you stay and watch with us? Stella, too."

She's about to say no, I can see it in her eyes, so I lay down my ace. "Rhys will be here... Rhys James."

I'm such a dipstick. I never name drop like that.

But it works. The no in her eyes is gone. "Stella will kill me if I don't say yes and she finds out."

"Go tell her. I'll take a quick shower, then pop over."

With the smallest hint of a smile, Britta nods. Crisis averted.

After I close the door behind her, I face Archie, sure he's upset with me.

Instead, he surprises me with a goofy smile. Before he can say anything stupid about Britta being an American and tonight would be the perfect opportunity to propose, I run to the bathroom.

In record time, I'm dressed in trousers and my nicest button up. As I'm about to leave, there's another knock at the door. This time when I open it, Rhys is there in a jumper with the hood pulled up over his baseball cap. Dark sunglasses cover his eyes, and he's holding a six-pack of Balter. I barely have the door open before he rushes in.

"Shut the door," he orders, handing me the Balter, which he's gone to a lot of trouble to get, being an Australian beer, and my favorite. I'll allow myself one today.

I glimpse Stella in the hallway, staring with her mouth open, and wave as I close my door.

"Hello to you, too, mate," I say. "Bit warm for a jumper, isn't it?"

Rhys pulls down the hood and takes off his hat, but keeps the glasses on. "I'm sweating my bum off, and that girl still recognized me. She couldn't stop saying my name and kept getting louder. Paps will be here before the end of the night." He shakes his head with frustration before putting on a smile and swinging his arms around me for a quick hug. "What a ripper, Mr. World Champion! Good on ya!"

"Thanks. Couldn't have done it without Archie." I wag my head toward Archie, who's come in for his own hug.

"I watched it all. Cheering for you the whole time," Rhys goes on while hugging Archie. "We're celebrating tonight. I brought beer." He nods to the Balter I'm holding like we could have missed it.

"We'll have to wait for this one to get back from his date." Archie tips his chin in my direction. "And he invited her and her friend over."

Rhys's whole body sags when he looks at me. "Do they know I'm here? It won't be just the two of them if they do."

I shake my head. "They don't know anyone in LA."

"It'll be all over social media." Rhys looks ready to bolt until Archie claps him on the shoulder.

"No worries. They're cool." Archie gives me a steely look that immediately triggers a warning. "Plus, he's planning to propose to one of them."

Rhys's eyebrows shoot up.

I give Archie the finger, then shake my head. "None of that nonsense in front of the girls." I'll let him explain his bananas plan to Rhys.

I've got a date with a girl—a *woman*—in a green dress and for the next two hours, that's all that matters.

CHAPTER NINETEEN

Britta

By the time Dex knocks on the door, Stella has *almost* recovered from the shock of first, seeing Rhys James in the hallway, and second, being invited to a party where he'll be.

"I'm not going over there without you, Britt. So eat fast." She fans her hands up and down by her face.

"I make no promises, but Liam will probably want to be back by the time the game starts." I open the door to his smiling face.

He's wearing a white, short-sleeve button-up, light jeans, and flip-flops, and I think this is the most dressed up I've ever seen him. And while I think his best look is shirtless, this one totally works for him, too.

Before I can get more than a *hi again* out, Stella is by my side, clinging to my arm.

"Dex. I just made a fool of myself when I saw Rhys in the hallway. I think I said 'You're Rhys James' at least eighty-five times. Maybe more. I *petted* his sleeve to make sure I wasn't hallucinating." She presses her free hand to her forehead and shakes her head. "You need to explain to him I am *not* like that. I work for a famous person—not Rhys-level famous—but I can behave." Stella talks on autopilot, not stopping until I cover her mouth with my hand.

Dex laughs. "Why don't you go on over and tell him yourself?"

Stella swipes my hand away and nearly chokes on Dex's suggestion. "Absolutely not. I'm not going anywhere near Rhys James without both of you there to steer me away if I get stupid and fangirl all over him like some rabid..." she waves her hands, grasping for the right word. "Superfan."

"But you are a rabid superfan," I remind her.

"Exactly. Which is why I need you there." She grabs both my shoulders and gives me a gentle shake.

"All right, all right." I brush her hands away and face Dex. "Apparently, we have to eat fast, so what would you like? Burgers? Tacos?"

At this, Stella throws up her hands. "Absolutely not. You both look too gorgeous to eat fast food. Go somewhere good. But also fast. But really good, and not cheap. But not expensive. And close by."

Dex's mouth turns down in that way some people can frown and still look happy, and my pulse skips like a little girl on her way to the candy store with a pocket full of loose change she's swiped from her dad's collect-all box. (That little girl was me).

"Sushi?" Dex asks. "There's a good place right on the beach. It might be busy, but they'll usually give me a seat at the counter if the tables are full."

"Because you're Liam Dexter?" I'm teasing, but his slow shrug wipes the smile from my face. "Oh. For real?"

He nods, his cheeks growing a shade darker.

"I've never had sushi. Do you think I'll like it?" I don't want to flat-out say no, but, yeah, I've never eaten raw fish and hadn't ever planned on it. But I also never planned on dinner with the best surfer in the world. I'm keeping an open mind.

Dex blinks hard like he can't process what I've said, so I follow up with my own slow shrug. My shoulders are barely back down when he grabs my hand and pulls me through the door.

"You're about to find out how good it is."

I send Stella a panicked look, but she just smiles and joins the shrug party with one of her own.

Dex keeps a hold of my hand as we walk the half block to the board-walk, twining his fingers through mine when we reach the cement path paralleling the ocean. The sun hovers over the horizon, ready to paint the sky orange, pink, and red. I slow to take it in, and Dex tugs me to stand in the still-warm sand, out of the way of people walking, skating, and biking the path.

"We've got time to watch," he says, then a few seconds later. "It's a beauty, isn't it?"

I nod. "Reminds me of home. Except we don't get those shades of purple." I point to the lavender-laced clouds weaving through the rays of deep orange.

"Paradise has beautiful sunsets." He brushes his thumb across mine, sending goosebumps up my arms that prompt him to ask, "Are you cold?"

I shake my head, trying to regain my power of speech. When I do, I ask, "What do sunsets look like in Burleigh Heads?"

Dex swivels his head to look at me. "How'd you know where I'm from?"

I give him a long stare. "You may not be aware, but you have an internet presence. Google knows you really well and you have your own Wikipedia page."

He laughs and as the sun continues its descent, we step back on the cement path and continue our stroll. "I'm just surprised you looked me up."

"I got a little curious when I realized there was really such a thing as famous surfers and you happened to be one of them." I bump him playfully with my hip, and then we stay glued together from our fingertips to our shoulders.

"You could have asked me your questions instead. Google doesn't know everything."

A voice in the far corner of my mind sends warnings I shouldn't be letting Dex get this close—holding my hand, stroking my thumb, brushing my arm with his—but the combination of his deep voice and soft Australian accent drowns out everything else, including my worries about what happens when I go back to Paradise.

"Good to know. Tell me what sunsets look like on the other side of the world."

"I've seen a lot more sunrises than sunsets—the best waves are in the morning—and Burleigh Heads has the most beautiful sunrises in the world." Dex isn't looking at the sunset in front of us anymore. He's back home. I hear the longing in his voice.

"Do you miss it there?" The last rays of this sunset back light the angles of his profile. His strong brow, the round tip of his nose and his square jaw. They're outlined in orange and a hazy black. Breathtaking.

"I do." He looks at me, and in the fading light, his amber eyes take on a dark copper tone. "I go back a few times a year, usually when I have an event in Aus. But I haven't lived there permanently in over four years, but there are more promotional opportunities here."

We slow to a stop again and turn toward each other. His eyes drop to my lips and my heart picks up speed. Even though we've kissed before, this moment feels different. With those other kisses, there were people around. We were the center of attention. Lightning flashed between us, then disappeared as quickly as it had appeared.

But right now there's only us. A few people pass by, but they either don't recognize Dex or they don't care, which allows an intimacy Dex and I haven't had before. A slow, pulsing energy flows between us, drawing us closer together with a force neither of us can resist. Maybe we don't want to. Or maybe it's stronger than either of us. Whichever reason doesn't matter, because we're pressed too close together to care.

Dex leans in, and I rise to the balls of my feet, eyes closing in anticipation of tasting his salt-stained lips again.

Instead, I'm met with the shrill sound of a bike bell and someone crying, "On your left!"

With impressive reflexes, Dex grabs me by the waist and pulls me out of the way of the beach cruiser speeding towards us.

"Idiot," he mutters, then moves his hands to my hips and looks down at me. "You okay?"

"Yeah," I nod, breathless in a way that has nothing to do with nearly being run over. My chest rises and falls before either of us says anything.

"This is the place." Dex points behind me to a packed restaurant with outdoor seating lit with strings of big-bulbed lights. People laugh over the sounds of clinking glasses and a mixture of languages I don't recognize.

And while I'd rather be standing on the beach kissing Dex than eating raw fish, I let him lead me around the tables, through the back door to the host station at the front of the restaurant. People sit shoulder to shoulder on leather sofas in the small lobby and more line up out the door.

"Looks pretty busy," I say to Dex, maybe a little hopeful I won't have to try sushi tonight.

"No worries," he says with the confidence of a man who knows he's getting a plate full of octopus and eel, and whatever else sushi is made from.

The man at the station has his back to us and a stack of menus tucked under his arm. He turns to lead a group of people to a table and breaks into a wide smile as soon as he sees Dex.

"Dex! We've been waiting for you to come celebrate! What took so long?" He points to two empty seats at an otherwise full counter. "We thought when Archie called, he'd be with you, not a beautiful woman."

He gives me a slight bow, and I smile.

"Got tired of looking at his ugly mug. Thanks, Kenzo." Dex leads me to the counter where, as soon as the chef patting rice and fish together sees him, he lets out a loud yelp.

"World Surf Champion!" he cheers in a thick Japanese accent, and everyone at the counter—maybe in the whole restaurant—follows the chef's lead and lifts their glasses.

Dex's mouth pulls into a shy smile and, even in the dim light, I can see pink the color of the sunset rising in his cheeks. The chef hands him a small glass of something clear and Dex lifts it to the crowd. I expect him to down the whole thing in one swallow, but he only takes a sip, then sets it down.

"So, I guess they know you here?" I say as he pulls out the chair for me.

"Yeah, but if Kanoa Igarashi were here, these seats would be his."

"Who's that?"

"Another surfer. He's Japanese but grew up around here. Won silver for Japan at the Tokyo Olympics." Dex takes the seat beside me and opens his menu.

"Have you surfed against him?"

Dex nods.

"Did you win?"

He faces me with a smile. "Sometimes. But let's talk about you. What made you decide to stay longer?" He takes the menu I'm about to open from me. "You talk, I'll order. Chef always makes me something special."

"How will I know what fish I'm eating?" I reluctantly let go of my menu.

"You won't. That's the point. Then you're not afraid to try it because you're not picturing what it looks like alive." He lays the menu out of my reach, then waves the chef over. "Give us my usual and whatever you think we'll like tonight. Britta's never tried sushi."

The chef gives a small smile and a bow, then pulls fish off the ice in the glass case in front of us. He skins and cuts it with a quick efficiency I can't take my eyes off.

"You haven't answered my question. Why'd you decide to stay?" Dex leans close, his chin in his hand, and suddenly, I'm less interested in how my dinner is being made.

That doesn't mean I tell Dex that he was one reason I stayed. He's surprisingly humble about being the world champion surfer, but I get the sense if he knew I'd stayed to spend time with him, it would go straight to his head. So, I tell him about volunteering at *Annie's,* then without having planned to, I tell him all the problems with *Britta's* and my realization—thanks to Stella—that my being there won't solve the issues.

"You really love that place, don't you?" he asks.

I consider my words before answering. "My Great-Grandma Britta started it over sixty years ago, and my mom took it over and babied it all my life. I want to carry on the legacy."

Dex nods thoughtfully. "That's really noble, but you didn't answer my question."

"Yeah, I did. Mom's legacy. That's what I love."

Chef sets a long plate in front of us with what looks more like art than food. Each round seaweed-wrapped rice and fish concoction is identical, topped with a colorful mix of bright yellow mango and green avocado.

"Do you eat horseradish?" Dex asks.

"Weird question, but yeah. It's good on prime rib."

Dex laughs and scoops a bit of green stuff from a little plate, then mixes it with soy sauce in a tiny bowl. "Wasabi is basically green horseradish. Dip the roll in this first." He passes me the bowl. "Then put the whole thing in your mouth."

I pick up my chopsticks, one in each hand. His eyelids slowly drop closed, and he shakes his head.

"Did I mention I'm from a small town where my family owns most of the restaurants? I've eaten a lot of pretty authentic Danish food, but beyond that I've had limited options. I haven't used chopsticks very often." I try to explain, but before I finish, Dex is behind me.

He takes the chopstick from my left hand and moves it to the right. Then he gently positions my fingers around the sticks. Holding them is difficult, but Dex smells like cedar and pine in a rainstorm; it's very distracting but also very centering—like it's just the two of us right now.

When he sits back down, my skin still tingles from his touch. He watches me awkwardly dip my roll, then stuff the whole thing in my mouth. I can barely close my lips around it, but then there's an explosion of flavor.

I cover my mouth and point my chopsticks at the rolls. "Dat's reary good."

Dex laughs and expertly pops one in his mouth. I'm reaching for a second one when the chef puts another dish in front of us, equally artistic but totally different with a pink fish—salmon?—and cucumber in the middle.

Feeling brave, I take a roll from the second plate.

"When did you fall in love with surfing?" I'd rather keep the focus on him than on questions about why I'm staying in LA longer.

He cocks his head to the side and pinches his chopsticks together. "About four years ago."

"You've been surfing for a lot longer than four years." I try to imitate his pinching motion but drop one of my chopsticks.

"Yeah, but you asked when I fell in love with it." He helps me reposition my chopsticks in the right place. "That was about four years ago, after I decided I needed a new manager. My dad had always been the one making all the decisions, but I'm the one who hired Archie. That's what made my career mine, if that makes any sense." He glances at me for a reaction, and I nod. "That's when I fell head over heels in love with the sport I'd been doing for nearly twenty years by then."

I take in everything Dex has said, wondering how to ask my next question. "When you say your dad made all the decisions before, does that mean he was your manager?"

"What you won't find on google," he says, giving me a cheeky grin before focusing on the sushi again, possibly to hide the vulnerability I saw in that glance. "I started surfing because my dad loved it, and like any little boy, I wanted to be just like him. At some point, I also realized that it might be the only way to spend time with him. And, it turns out, I was pretty good at it, which Dad loved too. I started competing when I was around twelve years old. Dad became my manager, and we traveled to competitions all over the world. I can see now that my reason for doing it was because I wanted to please him and he wanted me to win."

Dex dips his roll, but his mind is somewhere else. "Don't get me wrong; Dad loves me. He's a great guy, but as the years went on, I felt a lot of pressure. If I didn't do well, he'd get upset. Not at me, necessarily, but it was hard to tell the difference. And in surfing, you can never win all the time. A bad wave, an injury, the wrong weather, or a better competitor can cancel out your skill in any competition. He pushed me hard, and it blurred the lines of why surfing had become my whole world."

"Oh wow. That's intense Dex." I didn't have the same relationship with my mom, but my parents were both so busy running businesses so they could pay bills and provide for us that spending time with them meant working by their sides. I'm not sure I've ever looked at it that way before and I feel some emotion building in my throat to see it this way. "What changed four years ago?"

"In 2015, I made it to the Finals as a rookie, which was a huge deal. But then I dropped in the ranks for the next four years. Dad was furious, and I started to see how twisted up surfing was in my head, yeah? I kept getting injured, and it seemed like he was less worried about that than he was about my sponsor dropping me."

He waves a hand. "That wasn't true, but like I said, things were twisted up with me. Archie helped me sort through things and offered to manage me since he wasn't surfing anymore. I put some distance between my dad and me, and things turned around."

I nod as though I get what he means. Then, I realize I do. I felt that when I left Paradise for college, and why I hadn't planned to go back after graduating. Not that I wanted to leave my family or the place I've always lived. More that, I needed some space to figure out who I was without them.

Then mom started behaving oddly and was struggling to manage the shop the way she had for over twenty years. She got her diagnosis, and I made the choice to go home.

Dex catches my eye and holds me with his gaze. "It took about a year of Archie's coaching, some therapy, and surfing for myself before I truly fell in love with it. So, I guess what I'm saying is, if you're going to devote your life to something—give everything to it—you've got to love it more than anything and you can only figure that out for yourself."

I consider what he's said, impressed with how smoothly he brought this back to me. "That's how you feel about surfing?"

"Yeah, I do. I love it more than anything now, but it took me twenty years to get there."

I have to think about that. His passion for surfing is something that fascinates me about him. I really admire it.

But I don't think I agree with him.

Sometimes you've got to devote your life to something because you love *someone*. I don't love *Britta's*, but I loved my mom—still do. I'm willing to devote my life to something because I loved her more than anything. I don't want her to be forgotten, and I'm willing to put aside my own dreams to make sure that doesn't happen.

I love what Dex has said, though, and I'll return to those thoughts, but I feel my truth solidifying too. I dip another piece of sushi and line up my words to make sure I get my point across.

CHAPTER TWENTY

Dex

"Loving surfing that much doesn't leave you a lot of time for anything else, does it?" Britta asks.

"Not much." I shrug and drop my eyes from hers.

It's a leading question. Is she asking if I have time for relationships? Time for her? I'm not sure. And does it matter if she's not planning to stay in LA more than a few more weeks?

The truth is, staying competitive *doesn't* leave a lot of time for anything else. That's why I just won the world title. I cut out everything else in my life except surfing.

But when I look at Britta, when I see her smile or hear her laugh, I feel the same rush of adrenaline I get when I ride a perfect wave.

Everything falls into place and my focus is entirely on her. I don't want to be anywhere but right here, right now.

Talking to her silences the surrounding noise in the same way the ocean does when I'm watching the horizon for a good set. There's anticipation and excitement, but also a calmness I only get when I'm rolling up and down with the sea. A peacefulness that comes from knowing a wave will always come. If not today, then tomorrow.

And I've basically just told her I don't have time for her.

I immediately want to take it back, re-explain, but I take another piece of sushi instead. Because...I don't know what I offer or what I'm willing to give up for a relationship with anyone, even her. She's not staying in LA. There's no life for me in Paradise, Idaho.

The realization sits heavy, and so I push through it. I don't want to ruin this night, which has been perfect so far. I want to keep it that way, so I'll hold on to the fantasy of Britta and me for another few hours. Reality can wait.

"Annie's pretty awesome, isn't she?" I say to change the subject.

"She's amazing." Britta sits up, and a happy energy returns to buzz around us. "She reminds me so much of my mom."

"Really?" I ask, picturing Annie's round dark face and grey-black braids while also remembering the very pale-faced Scandinavian look of Britta's entire family back in Idaho. I never met her mom, but it's hard to imagine a resemblance. And then I realize what she means and feel my cheeks light up. She didn't mean they looked similar.

"Annie does so much for people and everyone loves her for it. My mom was that way, too," Britta explains. "She drew people together and helped them find purpose. I love watching Annie do that here. In a city of millions, she makes everyone feel seen. You know what I mean?"

"Yeah." I nod. "When Archie, Frankie, Rhys, and I first came to LA to film *Surf City High,* she was a surrogate mom. She learned how to make our favorite Australian desserts; did she tell you that?"

"Yeah," Britta takes a roll from the new plate the chef puts in front of us. "By the way, sushi is delicious. I didn't expect that, but it is."

"Most people wouldn't dive right in the way you have your first time." I like that about Britta. She doesn't shrink from a challenge.

She looks down at the empty plates surrounding her. "I'll take that as a compliment."

"You should." I take a sip of water to wash down the lobster roll.

"Annie said she had a chain coffee store offer to buy her place." Britta lays down her chopsticks and sips her Japanese beer like she hasn't delivered a potentially devastating blow.

"She won't sell." I say it more to comfort myself than because I believe it.

"She may have to. Her daughter needs full-time care, and even with all the money people have donated to help her, she can't pay for the help Keesha needs." Britta's eyes wander to mine. "I've been there. It took my whole family rotating around our different businesses, helping wherever and whenever we could, to keep them running while we took care of Mom, too."

"Georgia's told me a bit. I know it was rough, especially on you." I glance at Britta, pleased to find her smiling softly at me. "Annie doesn't have much family around, but I can't see her ever selling to a Starbucks or another chain." The reason *Annie's* feels like a piece of home isn't just because of Annie. So many of our coffee joints in Aus hold near and dear to my heart because of the love they show their locals, and Annie shows that love to the people of LA.

Britta lays her chopsticks across her plate and stares at them. "She'd like me to buy it. She wants the new owner to keep working with the nonprofit to train unhoused people to be baristas. But there's no way I could come up with the kind of money I'd need to buy."

I nod along as Britta talks, wondering if she'd actually buy *Annie's* if she had the money. Would she want to move to LA permanently? I don't reckon she would, but there's a longing in her eyes I haven't seen when she talks about going back to Paradise and *Britta's*. And, hard as I try not to let it, Archie's marriage idea slips into my brain.

"If you had the money, and *Britta's* weren't in the picture, would you want to buy *Annie's*? Would you leave Paradise for LA?" The wheels in my head spin through possibilities. Archie's idea is crazy, but it might be an option if Britta wants to stay in LA. If it's something that would work for her, too.

Her mouth plays at a smile. She crosses her arms and leans forward on the counter. The thread-thin strap of her dress falls over her shoulder, and I tuck my hands in my pockets to keep from sliding it back into place.

"Dex..." she takes a breath, but I've lost mine in the sound of my nickname on her lips. "I think I might. I mean, if we're talking about dreams that will never come true, yeah, I'd love to try something new while still doing something I love. Because I do love having my coffee shop, I just feel stuck in Paradise sometimes." She tilts her head to the side. "Most of the time, actually."

Her voice is wispy, like dandelion fluff floating through the air, almost within reach before it's carried away on a breeze.

I've been pummeled by a rogue wave—*Britta would stay in LA if she had the money to buy* Annie's. As I recover from the surprise of that info, my crazy thought surfaces as a fully formed idea. Getting married could mean Britta gets her dream, too.

"What about you? Do you have an impossible dream now that you've reached the pinnacle of surfing?" she asks, as though she's read my mind, and cracks open a window of opportunity. "Or do you feel like nothing is out of reach now that you've won the giant champagne glass?" Her eyes sparkle in the light of flickering candle votive between us, like the night sky above is a campfire.

"The Olympics. That's my dream." I don't hesitate, even though I've only told my closest friends that's what I want more than anything.

"Ohh. That's a good one. There's no surfing in the Olympics, right? So it's even more impossible than my dream." Britta picks the crab off the top of a roll with no idea how wrong she is.

"Surfing was added in 2020." I fake being chill.

Inside, I'm on high alert, waiting for the right moment to drop in with my idea and ride the trickiest wave of my life to completion.

"Really?" She laughs. "I haven't watched the Summer Olympics since I was a kid. I'm always too busy to even pay attention during the summer. And there's no hockey."

"There's field hockey."

Britta raises a disappointed eyebrow. "Like I said, there's no hockey in the Summer Olympics."

I laugh, and she cracks a smile.

"So your dream isn't impossible at all. You could be on the Australian team, couldn't you? I mean, you're The World Champion Surfer." She emphasizes each word, like she did the first time she said them.

"Probably not the Australian team." *This* is my moment. "But possibly the American team."

"American team?" Britta's face scrunches into a confused expression. "Don't you have to be American to be on the American team?"

"My mum's got dual citizenship, so I have a connection to the US, but I don't have citizenship."

"And you'd need that to be on the team?"

I nod.

"What do you have to do to get it?" She picks another piece of crab off a roll, pops it in her mouth, then slides the tip of her tongue over her lips. "Whatever that is, it's fantastic."

"Crab. It's crab." I slide my sweating palms down my trousers. "Yeah, I'd have to officially immigrate and do heaps of paperwork. I've got a lawyer working on that. It's a long process, lots of hoops and waiting periods. We're hoping we can get it done in time for me to qualify for the next Olympics, but I'm not sure if that's possible."

"That sounds stressful." She props her chin on her fist, leaning close enough I could kiss her. "What about the Olympics after that? Could you be on the American team then?"

"Eight years from now?" I say, lifting my eyebrows and giving her a smile. "The Games are in Brisbane, so I'd want to surf for Australia, but I'm already getting old for this sport. I go up against guys ten years my junior. I think I can do the next Olympics in four years if I give it everything I've got, but to compete for the first time when I'm almost forty isn't even unreachable-dream level. It's impossible." I shrug, trying to hide how discouraging it is to say all this out loud and pick up another piece of sushi.

Britta grabs another piece of sushi. "So, then, the only other option is to marry an American, right?"

My head snaps up and I drop the sushi into the wasabi-soy sauce. I stare at her hand covering her mouth. Is she chewing? Or wishing she could take back what she's said? Her eyes sparkle, which may mean she's joking, or may just be the light bouncing off her blue irises. I can't be sure, but I don't want to miss my chance if she's serious.

"Funny story..." I suck in my breath, then I go for it.

I tell her Archie's plan, which suddenly doesn't seem quite so mad, knowing she has a dream of her own I could make happen if I add a twist of my own:

I give Britta enough money for a down payment on *Annie's*, and she marries me so I can become an American Olympian.

CHAPTER TWENTY-ONE

Britta

D ex gives me a nervous smile. If I hadn't already swallowed my
sushi roll, I'd be choking on it. I'll be lucky if I can keep it
down as it is.

"Did you just... ask me to marry you?" I feel a little queasy.

"Yes, but no. It'd be more of a business arrangement." Dex's words
come out even faster than usual, and in that nano-second, his entire
face turns as red as the tiny pepper on top of the sushi roll I just ate.

"A business marriage?" That sounds even less tempting than a
regular, old-fashioned marriage. "Do you mean a marriage-of-convenience? That's what they're called in the Hallmark movies my dad
likes. I didn't think they were a real thing."

"Forget I asked. I'm really sorry I made things so awkward. The whole idea is a bit gone. I shouldn't have even mentioned it—I blame it on Archie." Dex rubs the back of his neck and keeps his gaze down.

I crane my neck and catch his eye. "You didn't make things awkward. Thank you for sharing your dream with me."

He lets out a loud breath and sends me a nervous grin that's so adorably shy and sexy at the same time that I nearly change my mind about marrying him.

"Are you still hungry? Or have I made you lose your appetite too?" He points at the half-eaten plates of food.

I *hate* wasting food. But Dex looks so uncomfortable that there's no way my stomach can take anymore raw fish on top of a marriage/business proposal.

"You didn't make me lose anything, but raw fish is surprisingly filling." I sound too perky, which only adds to the awkwardness we're both pretending isn't pressing in on us. "Except we haven't got the check yet."

"It's already taken care of." Dex stands and tosses his napkin on the table.

"I was supposed to buy you dinner." I grab my purse and try to wave down Kenzo.

"Britta..." There's a desperation in Dex's voice that makes me drop my hand. "They don't let me pay here. Even if they did, after I ruined the night, I wouldn't let you buy me dinner. I owe you at least a thousand dinners for saying something so stupid."

Dex takes my elbow and leads me out the door. The air outside is cooler than it was when we went inside, and I shiver as the breeze from the ocean hits me.

If Dex notices I'm cold, I can't tell. He drops my elbow and puts at least a foot between us as we make our way to the boardwalk. There's no handholding or being protected from the wind. And I'm a little hurt that he's letting my 'no' to his marriage offer come between us, but also surprised by how much I miss the warmth of him.

I don't miss it enough to *marry* him. But I also don't want this business proposal—for lack of a better term—to come between us. Honestly, I'm flattered he thinks he could marry me, even if just for pretend.

So, I close the distance between us and slide my arm through his. "Liam..." no more calling him Dex—that's when things went sideways. "I'm really flattered you asked, and that you'd be willing to help me buy *Annie's.*"

He tenses, and for a second, I expect him to pull away from me. Instead, he lets out a loud sigh. "It's a stupid idea, but I'm just desperate enough to get to the Olympics that I lost my head. But it was Archie's idea, so blame him for putting it in my head in the first place."

"I just assumed an idea that bad had to be his."

Dex laughs and squeezes my arm close to his side. "Thanks for not bolting when I said it. Have I mentioned that it's been a crazy, intense week?"

I drop my head on his shoulder. "If I were ever to marry someone I barely knew, it would definitely be you."

"So, are you saying you'll think about it?" There's teasing in his voice as he slides his arm around my waist, resting his hand on my hip and sending a shiver of excitement up my spine.

Now it's my turn to laugh. "My family would disown me if I got married for any other reason than love. And I don't plan on falling in love any time soon. I need to figure out who I am and what I want first."

He taps his fingers on my hipbone. "Those are good reasons for not falling in love, but I've always thought falling was involuntary. Whether it's in love or because of the law of gravity. But if you've got the secret for how not to do both, let me in on it. I could win a lot more competitions if I could quit the habit of falling for girls and on waves."

I scoff at his naivete. "I can't tell you how not to fall in surfing, but in love, you avoid getting emotionally attached to anyone. Like you said, you don't let anyone get in the way of the thing you love to do."

"Is that what I said? I meant that if you love doing something, don't let anything get in the way of doing the thing you love. I didn't mean love a dream more than people, but I see your point." He drops his arm from my waist, but just as I miss his touch, he hooks my finger with his pinkie. "Sometimes dreams are so big, there's no room left for anything else, including relationships."

We're further apart, but maybe that's better. The way he's rephrased my words makes them sound harsher than I meant them. More selfish than plain old self-defense. Love makes goodbyes even harder, especially long ones. I don't want to go through that again.

But there is some truth to how Dex said it. "I was planning on a prestigious internship in LA, but then my mom got sick. I wouldn't change my decision to go back home and take care of her, but I want to take some time for myself now, before my life gets swept up in someone else's needs. Not that I don't want that someday, when I'm ready to be a wife and a mom. Just not yet."

The thought that chases my words is that Paradise might not be the best place for my personal growth or for finding the kind of man I could share my life with. My chest constricts, pressing on my lungs and slowing my pace.

Waves crash on the shore, but the dark hides everything but the sound. In the moonless night, I feel Dex's eyes on me as he moves closer, sliding his hand around mine.

"I feel the same," he says quietly. "I want all that someday, but not now when I have to prioritize my career." Dex pauses, then a breathy laugh escapes.

"What?"

"The fact we're both focused on what it takes to achieve our goals might actually make a business marriage work. We're not in love, so that won't hold us back from what we really want, but being married could keep us from falling in love with other people."

I've seen the fierce competitor Dex is on the waves, but this calculating side of him surprises me. There's a cynicism to it that doesn't vibe with his usual optimism, and I wonder if he believes what he's saying. On the surface, it makes sense. But if I already like Dex, how do I keep from falling in love with him if I marry him?

"You make it sound so easy..." I say, not hiding my sarcasm. "Being married without forming any kind of emotional connection. Wouldn't the INS—or whoever is in charge of naturalization—have to believe we were married for real? That's what always happens in my dad's Hallmark movies. Someone will get deported if they're caught marrying for citizenship."

"Hmm. Good point." Dex thinks for a few seconds. "We already have a connection—*I* felt it the minute we met, anyway—so there's no putting that genie back in the bottle. But that could work in our favor. Anyone who interviews us would see we're attracted to each other."

My heart dances. I'd felt that connection too, but I didn't know Dex had. I don't tell him that. And if he feels my pulse quicken, he doesn't react.

"We'd have to have rules to keep that attraction from growing," I say, surprising myself, since all this talk is purely theoretical. I'm not *marrying* Dex. "Lots of them, so we don't get emotionally attached."

We both go quiet until Dex mumbles, "Heaps of rules? Like what?"

I say the first thing that comes to mind. "Like no physical intimacy."

Dex goes quiet, and his steps slow. "None? Not even kissing?"

I shake my head, even though I already regret the words. "Absolutely not. It would confuse things. At least for me."

"But we'd have to kiss sometimes... for people to believe we were married." There's a desperate hopefulness in his voice that doesn't sound at all, like we're in a serious contract negotiation.

Which we're not, because I'm *not* marrying Liam Dexter.

We cross the two-way path toward our apartment building, but before we're off the path, a dog barks behind me, and someone yells, "Watch out! On your left."

For the second time tonight, Dex pulls me out of the way of oncoming traffic—this time a large dog running fast enough to pull his skateboarding owner behind him. Dex's arms tighten around my waist, our bodies pressed so close together I can feel his heartbeat under my hands on his chest.

Our eyes lock, and the air goes still, cocooning us in the sound of crashing waves and our own breath. I wait for him to kiss me, but as he leans close, loud voices come from the apartment building.

He lifts his gaze and loosens his hold on me. The windows are open in his unit and the next shout is definitely from Archie. Dex blinks, and with it, our ridiculous fantasy of being married disappears.

"Sounds like the match has started. We should head up." He lets go of my hand and picks up his pace, not quite leaving me behind, but not quite letting me catch up, either. As we get closer, I can make out Stella's voice, too.

"I guess Stella went over without me after all," I say as we climb the cement stairs.

"I texted Archie to go get her. Wasn't sure we'd make it back before the match started."

We reach the landing between our apartments, and in his glance, I catch a flicker of sadness. He blinks and it's gone as he reaches for his doorknob. "You coming in?"

I want to say yes, but I shake my head. Stella's already there. She doesn't need me. By now she's BFFs with Rhys. I don't have it in me to put on a happy face and pretend I didn't just turn down Dex's marriage proposal. The awkwardness between us would be too noticeable.

"Well, thank you for the dinner." His voice is more formal than I've ever heard it.

I send him an apologetic smile, then step close enough to kiss his cheek. "Thank you, Dex. And I'm sorry."

The next morning, Stella shuffles into the kitchen, looking tired and possibly hung over. I went to bed before she got home, so we didn't talk. Honestly, I didn't really feel like talking, anyway. All I could think about was Dex's proposal, and I'm not sure he'd want anyone to know he asked me—sort of—to marry him.

In case she's mad, I hand her the coffee I've made for myself as a peace offering. She takes a long, loud sip, then sinks into a barstool at the counter. "Mmm. That's good."

"I'm sorry I didn't come over last night." I set up the French press to make a second cup of coffee.

Stella waves away my comment while she sips from her mug. "Dex said the sushi upset your stomach."

"Oh, yeah. Something like that. I definitely felt off after dinner." That's not an outright lie. My world *did* get tipped on its axis. "Did you have fun? How was Rhys?"

Stella rolls her eyes. "Let's just say my decade-long crush on him is officially over."

"What! Why?" This news is almost as surprising as Dex's proposal.

"He's soooo boring in real life and full of himself. Every time I asked him a question, he'd give me a one or two-word answer. I tried to ask him about the AFL—"

"—What's that?"

"*Exactly*. That's the game they were watching last night. No one's heard of it besides Australians, so obviously I had questions." Stella gives her shorts an annoyed tug, then sits back down.

"Maybe he was just into the game." I take the stool next to her to wait for my cup of coffee to finish brewing.

"You can watch a game and have a conversation at the same time. The two are not mutually exclusive. It's not like you're going to distract the players from throwing their ball in the right direction." Sometimes Stella likes to be the center of attention, so I take what she says about Rhys with a grain of salt.

"Dex was weirdly quiet too," she says. "Not I'm-too-cool-for-you quiet, like Rhys, but not as funny as he usually is. Did something happen at dinner?" She holds my eyes. I look away.

I stare at the French press, willing it to finish and give me an escape, while also debating if I should tell her. Probably not, but I've got to tell someone, and Stella is right here. Plus, for as much as she talks, she knows how to keep a secret.

"He proposed to me last night," I blurt.

Stella sips her coffee, unfazed. "Proposed what?"

"Marriage."

Her eyes go wide, and she sets her mug down so hard, coffee flies out. Whatever the opposite of unfazed is—fazed?—she's that. She's extra fazed. Fazed and confused.

"He asked you to MARRY him? Like with a ring and someone recording the whole thing?"

"Not quite that. More like, 'let's have a business arrangement where we get married so I can be an American and you can buy *Annie's*.'"

"Shut. UP." She slides off her stool, splays both hands on the counter, and leans so close I can smell the vanilla lotion she likes. "He *Proposal*ed you? Like in that movie with Sandra Bullock and Ryan Reynolds and the eagle that snatches the dog?"

I reluctantly nod. I should have never let her watch that movie when we were younger. "Yeah, I guess so."

"Britta, please tell me you said yes. *Please* tell me you're the star of your own real-life romcom that co-stars the current World's Greatest Surfer, who also is *Australian.*" Stella grabs my shoulders and shakes me. "I need all the details. All. Of. Them."

My phone buzzes in my pocket, and I'm surprised to see Dad is calling. We've already got a call with the whole family scheduled tonight to talk about *Britta's,* which somehow slipped my mind until right this minute. Maybe because I'm still a little in shock about being proposed to. By a famous, world-champion surfer—as Stella just pointed out—which puts my "no" in a more questionable light.

I click on the answer button and Dad's face pops up before Stella can shake anything else out of me. "Hi Dad! Say hi to Stella!"

I turn the phone and Stella's face transforms from a searing glare at me to her biggest smile for my dad.

"Hi, Uncle Pete! Britta's got big news!"

I flip the phone around so fast I drop it. As I scramble after it, I mouth, *don't say anything,* to Stella. She cups her ear like she can't hear me, and I get close enough for her and only her—not the rest of my dad who's asking where I went—to hear me.

"I told him no." I cover her mouth before a *WHAT??* can explode from her mouth. "I will tell you everything after this call."

"Fine," she mumbles through my hand.

I carry the phone to my room and shut the door, then put on a smile for my family. "Hi! It's so good to see all of you."

They respond with muffled hi's. Something is off. They're too quiet and not making eye contact. Even Georgia isn't smiling, and she smiles all the time. She's kind of known for it. Literally, it's a thing she's famous for.

Dad puts his screen closer to his face. "Everyone is already here, so we called you now instead of waiting until tonight."

"Ohh-kay." The very-serious vibe is making me nervous.

"We should get right down to business," Dad says.

That's when I'm certain things aren't going to turn out the way I want them to. Dad's not a "down to business" guy. He's more of a, "let's wander down a few tangents, then forget what we're talking about," kind of guy.

"The city has offered a good price for *Britta's,* and I think we should take it," he says, going from point A to point B at bullet-train speed.

Meanwhile, I'm still at the station wondering when the steam engine is going to arrive. "Excuse me?"

I look at my brothers one by one until Adam finally speaks up. "I don't like it either, Britta, but the repairs *are* going to be really expensive."

"How expensive?" I ask.

"Basically, we have to tear down the whole building and start from scratch—the foundation isn't salvageable and it would be more expensive to lift what we have and fix the foundation than it would be to rebuild. Selling to the city is the more reasonable option, but it sucks." Adam's mouth pulls into a tight line that tells me he's no happier saying it than I am hearing it.

I look at the faces of my family, lined up on my screen in tiny squares, expecting one of them to jump in. When they don't, I say what they should. "Then let's tear the whole building down and start from scratch. That's what Mom would want." My throat is dry, and tears sting my eyes.

"I don't think she would, Britta," Dad says softly.

Zach and Bear both nod before Zach says, "The city has made us a good offer, Britta. We can split it five ways."

"Or," Bear butts in, "we can use the money to convert the living space attached to Cassie's bookstore into a new location for *Britta's* and transfer the ownership to Britta the way it should have been done in the beginning. It's ridiculous that we are making a decision that should be hers—she's the one who kept the shop running all these years, never mind the will."

"That's my vote," Zach says, and I wonder if he's already proposed the idea to my family.

"Mine too," Bear and Dad say at the same time.

"Financially, it makes the most sense," Adam mumbles. "But I don't like it. I want to keep *Britta's* as much what it is now as we can."

I don't say anything. My chest squeezes so tight I can barely breathe, let alone talk. When I finally take in enough air to speak, all I can whisper is, "What about Mom?"

Bear is the first to answer. "The city wants to expand the indoor ice rink into a bigger community center and the center is still going to be named after Mom. She loved hockey, and she loved Paradise. It's still a tribute to her, in my opinion. And we could still have *Britta's*. It's just a different location."

Naming the community center after Mom was one condition Bear and I asked for when we convinced the city council to fund the ice rink. But having Mom's name on a building isn't the same as having the coffee shop she spent her life building. It has my name, but *Britta's* was always mom's. The community sees it that way. I see it that way. Giving up the location feels so wrong.

"Or you can take your portion of the money from the sale and do whatever you want with it, honey," Dad says. "If you want to put it toward the new *Britta's,* the store will be all yours. But I think the way this needs to go is obvious."

"Are you kidding me right now?" I search their faces, but no one seems to be joking. "I've spent most of my life working at *Britta's*, and I don't get a say in what happens to it?"

"Of course, you do." Dad's sincere tone sets loose the tears I've been holding back. "We all want what's best for the shop, but even more, we want what's best for you. Mom worried you wouldn't ever leave if you came home to take care of her. She begged me to talk you out of giving up your internship." His breath hitches. "But... I wanted my whole family together for the little time we had left."

I sniff and wipe my cheeks.

"I think that's why she didn't leave *Britta's* to only you, Sweetie. She wanted you to have choices, not force a future on you that might not be the one you would otherwise choose. She was being kind, and she was being a good mom when she made that decision." He swallows hard, then looks at me so close through the screen, I feel like we're in the same room. "And I'm telling you, too. Paradise will always be your home, but it doesn't have to be your only home."

I appreciate what Dad's saying, but without *Britta's*, I'm not sure how Paradise can be home. In a matter of weeks, the tether that's held me to my hometown has unraveled strand by strand, and I can't tell whether I feel unmoored or...free.

"*Britta's* has been as much a home to me as Paradise," I say. That's as close as I can get to saying goodbye to *Britta's*.

"Honey, home isn't a place. It's the people you love," Dad says quietly. "And we'll always be here for you, no matter where you are. There's a lot that's happened in our family these last few years—all the extra faces on this call are proof of that—and there will be more changes. That's how we keep growing and moving forward. We all want you to have an opportunity to choose your own path—wherever it leads—knowing that we will always be with you on that journey. Just like Mom is."

One by one, they all nod. And I realize, my family is giving me permission to live my own dreams, even though I'm not sure what those are anymore.

Then last night's conversation with Dex comes back to me. *If Britta's wasn't in the equation, would you want to buy* Annie's?

I hadn't thought twice about my answer.

"How much money is there if we sell to the city?" My question comes out staggered and painful.

Following my dream means letting go of *Britta's* altogether.

"About forty thousand for each of us," Zach answers.

"I'm willing to give you my share, Britta," Bear says.

"No way, Bear." I don't even have the words out before my dad and brothers follow with the same offer. "I couldn't let any of you do that."

While I don't want to take the money, I can't help thinking about how two hundred thousand dollars would be a good-sized starter fund on *Annie's*. Not enough to buy it outright—not even close with the value of both the business itself and the beach-adjacent property it's on. But I could do it. I could have my coffee shop in LA, live by the beach, and make a new start on my own.

Then I realize something. "Will you be able to open the new *Britta's* if you give me your shares?"

One at a time, my brothers and dad shake their heads.

"Then no. I won't take it. I don't know what I'll do with my share yet, but I won't take anyone else's."

Dad opens his mouth to say something, and I stop him. "But thank you all. Your generosity..."

I can't finish the sentence. The sacrifice they were all willing to make is so much bigger than money, but it's too big. I can give up *Britta's* if I know it will survive. A newer version is better than no version at all.

We talk a little more—and cry. It's possible there's more crying than talking until we finally give up and end the call with sniffling *I love you*'s.

Stella waits zero seconds before she comes into my room. "I heard everything. You Thomsens are loud." She throws her arms around me, and I cry some more.

When I finally get my emotions back under control, I say, "I have no idea what I'm going to do."

"You're going to buy *Annie's*!" she says confidently.

"There's not enough money." I haven't given up on the idea of buying *Annie's*; but I'll need a lot of financing. "This is LA, beach adjacent, and not just the business, the property, too. I might be a small-town girl, but I'm not naïve enough to think I can buy Annie's with forty thousand dollars."

Stella takes my face in her hands and looks me straight in the eyes. "Then you have only one more question to answer..." she pauses long enough for maximum dramatic effect. "Are you going to say yes to the Dex?"

Chapter Twenty-Two

Dex

Approximately eighteen hours after the most humiliating moment of my life—and I don't have a shortage of humiliating moments—the woman who witnessed it is on the landing. She peers over the railing as I carry my board up the stairs to my apartment.

My team lost the AFL match yesterday, I had to admit to Archie that I'd proposed to Britta and she'd said no, Rhys was bent out of shape about me inviting the girls over—Stella asked him a million and one questions—and I had a crap morning on the waves. So, I'm not exactly excited to see Britta and relive the humiliation of her rejection.

I told Archie all along that it was a stupid idea, then I went ahead and did it anyway, and made myself out to be a desperate idiot. I don't blame Britta for saying no—even though I think I'd make a pretty decent fake husband. It was a lot to ask—tying herself to me long enough for me to get citizenship.

The thing I'm most upset about that I did, though, is mess up the good thing we had going. She's probably decided to leave Monday after all.

"Hi Liam," Britta says when I reach the landing. Her greeting isn't cold, but it's not warm either.

"Morning, Britta." I angle myself and my board around her to my door.

"It's afternoon."

I pause long enough to really look at her, wondering if it wasn't a coincidence running into her. Maybe she was waiting for me. "Good arvo, then."

Her face screws into a question, but I don't have the energy to explain arvo is just a quicker—better—way to say afternoon. That's the beauty of Australian English. We get our point across without a bunch of extra words and syllables.

"Can we talk for a minute?" Britta follows me inside.

I set my board against the wall and sigh. "Can it wait? I'm knackered."

She stiffens, and I notice she's clutching folded sheets of paper. "No, it can't. It's important. But if you can't spare two minutes, I'll go."

She turns to leave, and I feel bad for snapping. It's not her fault I'm embarrassed. I was the idiot who asked her to marry him on our first official date. I can't be mad at her for having brains enough to say no.

"Wait, Britta." I grab her arm and gently tug her back. "I'm sorry. I'm tired and feel like a tool after last night, but I don't want that to get in the way of our relationship. Can we just forget about it and go back to being friends?"

Her eyes dart to the papers in her hands, and she bites her lip. "That's actually what I came to talk about." She meets my eye, and her cheeks turn a lovely shade of pink. "I want to be more than friends. I want to be business partners too."

I take a second to process what she's saying, but then she hands me her papers. "Here are my conditions."

I unfold them and read the words, *Britta Thomsen and Liam Dexter Marriage Contract.* My eyes bounce from the paper to Britta's face, then back again.

"What changed your mind?" The words on the paper are a blur, I'm so shocked.

"Long story, but basically, I've decided figuring out who I am means staying in LA, and what I want is a coffee shop close to the beach." She finishes with a clipped, *I'm certain,* nod.

"Good on ya, Britt." I return her clipped nod, because I'm certain I want her to stay in LA and take over my favorite coffee shop, too.

Her mouth tugs at the corner before she points to the "contract" I'm holding.

"It's not legally binding, obviously." Her voice skitters with nervousness. "But I trust you to give your word until we can have a pre-nup drawn up."

"A pre-nup?"

She waves her hand, like she's brushing away a minor inconvenience. "I want the money you give me to be a loan, so whatever legal paperwork we need to do to make sure that happens."

"I'd rather give—"

Her hand goes up and I stop. "Not negotiating on that one, but I'm willing to work with you on my other conditions... some of them, anyway."

I scan the numbered list, and because my brain can't think of any words to say of my own, I read Britta's out loud.

"Number one: no kissing in private." I nod. Disappointing, but not surprising. "Number two. No kissing in public, with the exception of kissing-appropriate celebrations."

I look up. Specifically, at her lips. "Like under the mistletoe or on New Year's Eve?"

She waves her hand at the list. "We can discuss details later if you agree to these conditions."

I read the rest of the list to myself. It's two pages long and covers a lot of ground like, absolutely, positively, no sex. That one she points out specifically and adds, "In private or public. Just to be clear."

"Public was never on the table. Just to be clear." I pull in my smile. "I hadn't considered holidays together, but I appreciate that you're willing to go to Australia for Thanksgiving."

"As long as my family gets us at Christmas," she says firmly.

"You're aware we don't celebrate Thanksgiving in Australia?"

"Hmm. I guess we'll have to go to my family then."

"No Fourth of July celebrations in Aus either." I raise an eyebrow.

"Paradise has a really great one. I guess we can go there instead." She doesn't crack a smile, and I get a sense of who's going to have the upper hand in this 'partnership.'

I go back to the list, trying to keep my face as unreadable as hers. Most of her asks are reasonable. Separate bedrooms. Separate bathrooms, with an aside that reads *non-negotiable. I shared a bathroom with three brothers.* Handholding only when absolutely necessary.

That one stings. Her hand is soft and fits perfectly in mine.

"You want me to teach you to surf?" I raise my eyes to hers. "I'll happily do it, but it will mean breaking the 'no touching' rule."

Britta leans in and reads the list over my shoulder, then points to rule number eleven. "No *unnecessary* touching. Touching while teaching is fine."

A thousand thoughts of what I'd like to teach her run through my mind. None of them appropriate. I bite back a smile as her cheeks grow pink.

"Do *not* say what you're thinking right now." She grabs the list from me. "I'm serious, Liam. We have to keep this arrangement professional, otherwise it won't work and one of us will get hurt."

"How can you be so sure about that? We've got awesome connection. Maybe we should see where things go. We might like being married to each other." I'm wondering if the Olympics are worth giving up anything but a "professional" relationship with Britta.

When doubt skitters across her face, I think maybe she's reconsidering the professional part too, but then she pulls back her shoulders and sets her jaw in a firm line. "We barely know each other, and we're very, *very* different. If we act on our feelings, what happens if we find out in another month or two that we're not a good fit? We're stuck together until you get your citizenship, because that's the agreement, right?"

I rub my fingers across my forehead and nod. "But if you wanted out, I wouldn't hold you to it."

Britta presses her lips together and moves her head slowly, side to side. "This only works if we both come out with what we want going in, and the best way to make sure that happens is to keep things friendly, but professional."

I school every emotion and put on my most serious face. "I agree, Britta. Whatever you have on that list, I'll do. I want you to feel safe. I never want you to think I'm taking advantage of your generosity or our partnership. I want this to work, but not at the expense of your dignity or our friendship."

"Thank you..." Britta's shoulders relax, but not enough to release the tension still coiled at her neck. "But you should read the entire list before you agree. Especially the second to last line. That's the one I'm most worried about. It's a lot." She hands the list back to me, and I go to the second page, all the way to the bottom.

I breathe a sigh of relief when I read it. It's by far the easiest thing on the list. "Not a problem."

Britta's jaw drops. "It's three hundred thousand dollars. That's how much I need for a down payment on *Annie's.*"

I reach for her hand, then question whether this is an "absolutely necessary" moment, and let it drop back to my side. "The money part is easy. Except for this apartment, I don't have many expenses. Rip Tide gives me clothes. The Sprinter van belongs to Archie, and I've saved most of my winnings. I expected you to ask for more. You should have, and you still can. My agent has brokered heaps of promotions for me since I won. You don't need to worry about money."

Britta breathes a sigh of relief. "Thank you. That means a lot. And I do feel safe with you. We both want the same thing: to reach our goals before getting into any long-term attachments. That's why we'll be excellent partners."

Her words should wipe away any of my worries. Instead, my enthusiasm for this whole thing takes a hit. Then my eyes bounce to the last condition, and my excitement is down for the count.

"This won't work." I fold the list and hand it back to her.

"What? Why?" She unfolds the papers and scans them, so I point to the last line that says *annulment proceedings to begin one year from the date of marriage.*

"This won't be a one-year thing, Britta. We have to be married for three years for me to get citizenship. I should have told you that. I thought I had."

Her face drains of color, and I feel my own cheeks heat. I was so close. I should have known this was too good to be true. Three years is an enormous commitment for anything, but especially for a fake marriage.

Britta goes to the sofa, sinks into it, and drops her head in her hands. All I can do is watch. The fact she hasn't bolted back to her place is tempting me to hope I might still have a chance.

Finally, she lifts her head. "Three years is a long time."

"Yeah. I get it if that's a deal breaker. I don't expect you to give up three years of your life for me. You've already given up years, taking care of your mum the way you did." I stay planted where I am, not daring to move forward.

She sits up straight and rolls her shoulders back. "It's fine. I can do anything for three years, but we'll need to add another condition. No dating."

"Easy. Archie's already made me follow that rule this season, but either way, I wouldn't want people to think I was cheating on you."

A look of confusion crosses her face before her eyes go wide. "I mean each other, too."

"We can't date each other?" I can go without other girls, but I'm more disappointed about not dating her.

"Strictly professional, Liam." Britta leaves no room for argument there, and I have to be okay with that. I *should* be okay with that. "Besides," she adds in a softer voice. "We'll be too busy chasing our dreams for anything else. That's the other benefit of this partnership. We contractually can't get distracted by the opposite sex."

A slow smile spreads across my face. She's right, of course. We'll keep each other focused by eliminating the biggest potential obstacle. "I think I'm going to like being married to you."

"You have to." She smiles. "That's number seventeen on the list. Right under splitting housework down the middle. I'll do the cooking, but you get dishes."

I laugh. "Fine, but I have a condition of my own."

"Only one?"

I nod. "That's an even split, right? I get thirty-two rules to follow; you get one?"

"I think so, depending on the size of your ask." She folds her arms across her chest and sits back, like she's planning to stay for a while.

I cross the room to erase the distance between us, but not enough to actually touch. I look down at her, lounging on my sofa, and a shiver of excitement runs down my spine at the thought that soon this will be an everyday occurrence. The two of us hanging out, laughing, teasing each other.

"It's a big one." I raise an eyebrow in a challenge.

She tips up her chin and lifts her own eyebrow, waiting. Then I lay out my non-negotiable.

"No more Liam. Call me Dex."

CHAPTER TWENTY-THREE

Britta

Moments after Dex and I agree to get married, he yells the news to Archie, who's in his room. From that point on, Archie takes over, and I see why Dex hired him as his manager. The next twenty-four hours are a whirlwind.

I figured we'd have to drive to Las Vegas for a quickie wedding, but within minutes Archie has found a same-day wedding service right here in LA.

"You can get married on the beach in Santa Monica without a permit. It's first come, first serve, and with just a few of us there, it won't be a problem." He's on the couch between Dex and me, feet on the edge of the coffee table and his laptop on his bent knees.

All I can see of Dex is his bouncing legs, which doesn't make me any less nervous. I mean, I know it's not an actual marriage, but I'm still getting married, and it has to look real, especially because Dex is a famous surfer. He's in the media enough that there will be extra scrutiny.

"Rhys can perform the ceremony if you want. He's still in town for a couple of days," Archie says.

"Rhys James is an ordained minister?" I did *not* see that coming.

"He got ordained online so he could perform Frankie's ceremony last summer," Dex mutters off-hand.

"Frankie is married?" I don't read a lot of Hollywood gossip, but I can't believe that news wasn't splashed all over. This day is full of all kinds of surprises.

"Not anymore," Archie says tightly, and I ask no more questions about his twin.

Dex's legs stop bouncing, and he leans forward so I can see him. "Is all of this okay with you?"

"The sooner we can get the naturalization process started, the better." Archie is all business, which makes this feel even less like a real wedding.

"Are you asking if I'm okay having Archie Forsythe as my wedding planner and Rhys James as the officiant?" I blink long and slow. "As long as Rhys sings the whole thing."

Dex and Archie both laugh, and Archie says, "I'll see what I can do. He may charge extra for the service."

"I just don't want you to feel rushed into anything," Dex adds more seriously.

I shake my head. "I don't... I mean, I *do*, but I'd rather get things rolling than wait. I have to talk to my dad first, though. And Stella, obviously. She has to be there."

"Of course," Dex agrees, but Archie shakes his head.

"You've got to keep this a secret," he says. "At least the real reason you're getting married. Not even your family can know. If it gets out, you and Dex will both be in a lot of trouble and Dex could be deported. He wouldn't be able to come back for competitions."

"I can't lie to my family." That's a deal breaker right there.

"Then don't. But you can't tell them the whole truth either," Archie says firmly.

I stare at him and decide that I don't like being managed.

But I don't have much choice if I want to buy *Annie's*. Or if I want to help Dex get to the Olympics. *Annie's* is my primary motivation for marrying Dex, but I also love the idea of being a part of him achieving his dream. Maybe I should be worried about how invested I am in his getting to the Olympics, but I can't help it.

Dex came to Paradise at the perfect time, a month after Mom passed, a ray of sunshine at the darkest time of my life. I'm getting *Annie's* and a new life out of the deal, but if marrying Dex gets him to the Olympics, I'll be happy to have returned the happiness he brought me.

"Okay, then." I push myself from the couch. "I'm going to figure out how not to lie to my dad while also not telling him the truth while you two finish this." I sweep my hand in a circle to indicate Archie's laptop and the million tabs he has opened.

Dex stands too. "All right then, I guess we're getting married."

An awkward moment follows where we both do what can only be described as a dance around how to say goodbye as an officially engaged couple without touching each other.

Finally, I jut out my hand. "It's a deal."

Dex's gaze drops to my hand, then back to my face. His eyes meet mine. In the distance, I hear waves crashing. The smell of the ocean permeates everything, and I'm reminded of the taste of Dex's lips.

He slides his hand in mine, slowly. His fingertips brush my palm, then my wrist. He doesn't shake my hand. He holds it, like he did last night—the last time we touched. Tenderly. Protectively.

"Deal." The word comes out as a whisper, but he keeps hold of my hand. The feeling of security that accompanies his touch is both comforting and terrifying. Suddenly, his soft expression transforms into wide-eyed horror. "I don't have a ring."

The breath I'd been holding comes out as a laugh. "It's okay. We can figure that out later."

He exhales and releases my hand. "Right. Rings can wait."

"You'll need a place to live, too," Archie offers without taking his eyes from his laptop.

"Together?" Dex and I say at the same time.

Archie sends both of us a look that can only be interpreted as a silent *duh.* "Everything has to be airtight if we're going to convince officials that this marriage isn't just about Dex fast-tracking the immigration process."

I hadn't really thought through *where* I'd have my bedroom and bathroom when I wrote up our contract. My only thought was to include every contingency.

"I sorta thought we'd keep things the way they are until Britta has to move out of her unit. Then she could move in here." Dex rakes his hand through his hair, clutching a handful.

"Into our two-bedroom apartment?" Archie asks.

"We're hardly ever here." His hair stands up where he's pulled at it, and he reminds me of Bear when he was a toddler. Completely clueless.

"Don't worry. I'll handle it." Archie goes back to his laptop.

"I need my room and bathroom," I say carefully. "It's in the contract."

Archie stops typing long enough to send me an exasperated look. "You realize that contract isn't legally binding, right?" He waits for me to answer, but I don't appreciate his tone, so I don't say anything. "You'll have your own space," he finally relents.

With that, I leave so I'll have some privacy when I break the news to my dad that I'm getting married.

Stella is waiting at the door for me when I walk in. "Well?"

"I'm getting married tomorrow." I walk past her, ignoring her pleas for details. If I don't call Dad now, I'll chicken out. Then he'll find out from the news, my brothers, or some other source, and it will break his heart.

He answers on the first ring. Of course. The one time he doesn't have to search for his phone is the one time I could use a few more seconds to breathe.

"Britta! Is everything okay, honey? I wasn't expecting another call from you today." The worry in his voice doesn't give me any time to beat around the bush.

"Everything's fine, Dad. I have some news to tell you, but it's good news." I hope he thinks so, but I decide to play it up more because he's going to take a lot of convincing. "Really, really good news."

"We can use some good news around here, but hold on a minute..." His phone goes quiet.

"Dad? Are you still there?"

"I'm here, just walking to the kitchen." His voice is muffled, and there's a lot of background noise.

"Dad, I can barely hear you."

"Almost there." Silence again. Except for the blood pounding in my ears.

The number one thing I don't miss about Paradise is the terrible reception and dropped calls. Every time the line goes quiet, my pulse fills in the absence by thumping hard.

As soon as I hear Dad again, I say, "When I tell you this news, I need you to trust me. I really am happy, and it's the best thing for me right now."

My phone buzzes. Dad is trying to FaceTime me. I sigh and accept the call. Then his face pops up in front of me, which doesn't make it easier to deliver my news.

"Okay, go ahe—"

"—I'm getting married." I don't let him finish his sentence. If I do, I'll lose my courage.

The shock on Dad's face I expected, but then Adam's face pops into the screen next to Dad's. "You're what?"

"Did you say you're getting married?" Dad asks, and the background noise gets louder and clearer.

"Who's getting married?" Zach yells.

I suddenly realize I've made a crucial mistake by forgetting it's Evie's birthday. I close my eyes and mutter, "No, no, no."

"You're *not* getting married?" Dad asks. "Thank goodness. I thought that's what I heard you say."

I take a deep breath and open my eyes. "I am getting married, Dad."

My entire family is at Dad's celebrating. Not just my brothers and their partners. Stella's mom and brother, too. Along with his wife and stepdaughter. Literally, everyone is there. Which means my private conversation with Dad is now going to be a family meeting.

"You're getting married? To who?" Bear's face fills the screen. He's my baby brother, but he's always been the most protective of me.

He's also the biggest of my brothers, and suddenly I'm a little worried about Dex's safety. I've got a lot of explaining to do—without too much truth-telling—but at least I'll only have to do it one time. So maybe this rip-the-Band-Aid-off moment is a good thing. If I can get them to stop asking me questions all at the same time.

I put my fingers between my lips and whistle. "Listen up!"

The room goes silent and more faces squeeze into the screen. But I have everyone's attention, so I let out as much information as I can in one long breath.

"LiamandIaregettingmarriedtomorrow,andIneedyoutotrust-methatthisiswhatIwantandnotaskalotofquestions."

A beat passes before Bear growls, "Who is Liam?"

"Dex. I mean Dex." I have to get used to calling him that again—I guess—since it's his one and only condition.

"I called it!" Georgia yells, followed by Zach's confused voice. "The surfer?"

And I'm swept away in a sea of voices and questions. I toss out answers to as many as I can and ignore the ones I can't answer. Like the one from Dad about whether I'm in love with Dex.

But when everyone goes silent, and Dad asks in a sad voice, "Did you say tomorrow?" I can't ignore him.

"Yeah. We don't want it to be a big deal—what with the media and everything. It's just going to be us and a couple of friends on the beach."

Dad's expression grows sadder in equal proportion to the increasing perkiness in my voice until the hurt on his face is unbearable.

"Who's walking you down the aisle?" He asks, and I am unprepared for the longing that fills my chest.

Thirteen was my wedding-obsession era. I imagined a big wedding with Mom and Dad both giving me away. I had a Pinterest board of ideas and everything. Mom and I worked on it together.

Then she got sick... and, well, you know.

"There won't be an aisle on the beach," I say weakly, without looking at his face. I officially hate video calls almost as much as I hate the deep well of sadness in Dad's blue eyes.

"If you could put it off a day," he says, slowly. "We could drive to California and be there for it."

"Or go to Vegas, and we'll meet you there!" My cousin Seb calls from somewhere off-screen.

I start to shake my head, then catch Dad's eye.

"Vegas is closer for us," he says carefully. "We could leave early tomorrow morning and be there late afternoon. You wouldn't have to postpone, and we'd be part of your big day."

If I'd only heard the pleading in Dad's voice over the phone and not seen it written wide on my cell screen, I could have said no.

But I dare anyone to look at Dad when he has that face and tell him no. I am reminded in this moment of something I've been so aware of but haven't thought about yet. Dad has lost so much. He lost his wife, partner, and best friend to a slow and miserable disease. He spent his life working toward a future he will never have and watched the toll it took on all of us.

Three years from now, I'm going to get a divorce, and he'll never know the real reason. I've shocked him with this announcement, but he's not telling me not to do it. He just wants to be there for what he thinks is a beautiful decision I've made. I feel like the worst daughter ever, but I can't tell him that either. Instead, I tell him I'll see what I can do.

Which is how, the following day, instead of driving fifteen minutes to Santa Monica beach and although I've never been on an airplane, Dex, Archie, Stella, and I meet Rhys James at a private jet at the Burbank Airport to fly to Las Vegas—a place I've never been—for my fake wedding day.

CHAPTER TWENTY-FOUR

Dex

Vegas isn't the most low-key place for a spur-of-the-moment wedding, especially with Rhys James in tow, but if Britta wants her family at our wedding, I'm not gonna tell her no. Even if I may not make it out of Vegas alive if her brothers get a hold of me.

Aside from Archie, Britta, and me, Rhys and Stella are the only two who know this marriage is a business arrangement. You can't keep something like that from your best mates. Rhys rolled his eyes, but understood better than I'd expected. Stella twists in her chair, bobbing with the energy of Italo Ferreira nine Red Bulls into the World Finals. I'm not sure if she's excited about Britta and me or because she's on a private plane with Rhys James. Probably the second, but she still found time before we boarded to pull me aside for a *hurt her and you die* talk.

"I wasn't keen on this idea in the beginning, but Vegas might actually be better," Archie says from the leather captain's chair across from me. Britta is to my side, across the aisle. If I want to look at her, I have to turn my whole body, and it takes every ounce of willpower not to.

"How so?" Rhys asks.

"We can make a bigger deal of it." Archie's eyes dart from Britta to me. "Still small and quiet, but it will look more realistic to the press and Immigration if we have Britta's family there."

"How will the press know?" Rhys asks, looking ready to jump off the plane even though we're already in the air. He's been burned by the media too many times—we all have, really. That's the reason Frankie's not here right now.

"Marta will have to alert them after the fact. That is, if we keep all of us being in Vegas—especially Rhys—under wraps long enough that the news doesn't get leaked before the ceremony," Archie twists open the cap of his water bottle with a calmness I envy. My hands are shaking so hard I don't dare try. "We have to treat this wedding as though it's the real thing," he finishes, then takes a long sip.

"I don't even have a dress," Britta says with a nervousness that makes me feel less self-conscious about my own nerves.

"Did you bring the green one? You could wear that." I'd love to see her in that again.

"I brought it, but it's not white." Britta chews on her thumbnail, her brows drawn together in a tight V.

"You're too pale to wear white," Stella offers helpfully, with absolutely no anxiety. In fact, I hope some of her excitement will rub off on me. "The green will be gorgeous. Dex, if you'll give me access to your social media accounts, as soon as the ceremony is over, I'll post about it. We'll control the news from the very beginning by releasing pictures of the wedding with a caption about marrying the love of your life in an impromptu ceremony."

She leans forward to look at Rhys, who's on the other side of me, next to the window. "You'll need to be in the pictures. Then the focus will shift from Dex and Britta to you officiating. That will ease some questions people might ask over the next few days and also mitigate any suspicion that could arise later when Dex applies to become a national. *His mate officiated*; that's good cred."

This is a Stella I haven't seen before, and one who's not fangirling over Rhys anymore. Not that I know her well, but she's young and usually shows her age. Now she's all business, and I wonder how Rhys is going to take it.

He tenses, and I wonder if he's going to tell her no way. He's not used to being talked to the way Stella just spoke—as though he's not a certified rockstar who needs to be tiptoed around because of his fragile ego.

I love the guy, but I have suspected over the last few years that he's surrounded himself with a team of people who are more interested in keeping him happy than they are in giving him sound advice that he might not like. I've never said as much, of course, but watching how this has unfolded so far has only confirmed those suspicions.

"You okay with that, mate?" I ask him. Maybe I'm just as bad as his usual entourage. But I also respect that his schedule isn't his own. It's packed tight, and it wasn't simple making time to be by my side today. That took major rearranging and made some people unhappy. I don't want him to regret his decision to be here.

His mouth twists to the side as he looks past me to Stella. Seconds pass before he speaks. "Yeah. That'll work." He sits back and closes his eyes, then says, "Tell me if you want to post stuff on my accounts too."

Stella pulls back in surprise, but I can tell she's trying to hide it. "Yeah, that'd be great. Don't you think, Archie? Makes the wedding even more believable. Is there any way we can get Frankie to come? We could do a whole *Surf City High* reunion and wedding party post."

Archie, Rhys, and I shake our heads at the same time, and Archie answers firmly, "Frankie won't be there." He pauses, and his next words come out less tense. "But I agree on everything else. If we play up the details, we take control of the story from the beginning."

"I'll have my manager send over my login info," Rhys says, his eyes still closed.

"You don't know your own logins?" Stella blurts. "That explains a lot," she adds, mostly to herself.

"What's that supposed to mean?" Rhys's eyes fly open, and he leans across me to see Stella again.

"It means your accounts are boring. They don't feel personal at all. I suspected you weren't the one posting. Now I know." Stella meets Rhys's gaze, refusing to back down from the truth about the social media personas he counts as one measure of his success.

"Boring? You think you could do better?" He's offended, but I hear something else too. It sounds like... curiosity. Definitely not the usual boredom that edges his voice so often these days.

"Yeah, I do. I run Georgia Beck's personal and professional sites, and I've increased her engagement by two hundred percent in the past eighteen months. *And* you know what never got out? That she and Zach were in a fake relationship when her show started. When you take control of your own story, you're the one who gets to tell it, not the media." Stella taps Britta's leg and points to Rhys. "Trade Britta places so I can show you what I'm talking about."

Rhys's eyes narrow and Archie and I look at each other, both holding our breath. Then, to our surprise, Rhys unbuckles his seatbelt and follows Stella's order.

Britta scoots by Rhys in the aisle, clinging to the back of the seats as she moves. She's wearing loose jeans and a Taylor Swift concert tee, but not from the Eras tour. Something older. Probably from before Britta started taking care of her mom.

Her legs brush my knees as she slides by me on the way to Rhys's seat, and her shaking is visible. Suddenly, the plane hits bumpy air, and she ends up in my lap instead of her seat, her long legs dangling over the armrest and my arms wrapped around her waist. Her shirt is soft and worn, and her hair—pulled up like usual—smells earthy and citrusy.

"You okay?" I should help her stand, but I keep my arms around her. Who knows when I'll have the chance again once we say *I do,* and the no touching rules are in effect.

"Fine," she force-laughs, her cheeks pink. "Sorry about that."

Archie offers her a steadying hand until she sits in her seat, and a rush of jealousy hits me with the force of a surprise windstorm. Before I can stop myself, I'm shooting a glare Archie's way. He gets to touch her, help her, settle her in, but I can't for fear I'll break one of her rules.

In a matter of seconds, his expression shifts from confusion to surprise before landing on a smug smirk, like he knows something I don't.

"Are you as nervous as I am?" Britta leans close to ask. "I mean, it would be weird if we weren't, right? Even if this isn't for real."

Archie raises an eyebrow. We've known each other long enough that I can read the question on his face. He's wondering if I want this to be real.

I'm not going to answer that, but I will answer Britta's question.

"I'm a bit toey." I catch Archie holding back a laugh, and my face heats.

"I should have added another condition to our agreement: you have to explain what all your Australian words mean." Britta nudges me with her elbow while clutching the armrest, and I'm reminded how hard it's going to be to follow her no touching rule.

"Toey means nervous or anxious," I say.

"That's one definition," Archie mutters under his breath, and I send him a warning to keep his mouth shut.

Luckily, Britta either doesn't hear or ignores him, because she doesn't ask what the other meaning is. My face would be even warmer if I had to explain the innuendo. Totally inappropriate for what else I might be nervous about on our wedding day, considering we won't be having a typical honeymoon.

Unfortunately.

Britta is a stunner. I hadn't really thought through what the next three years will be like married to her without any of the benefits of marriage. And I won't be dating anyone else, not that I want to.

Suddenly, the reality of what we're doing hits me hard. A year of no-dating was difficult. But three years of celibacy? No kissing even, while I'm married to a woman I'm seriously attracted to? That might be harder than training for the Olympics. It might be an Olympic event itself. If I win, I should get more than a gold medal. I should get a Vibranium medal.

My heart pounds harder than it has since the seconds before my score was announced in the last heat of the Finals. I reach for an airbag. I might yak.

"Are you alright, Li—Dex?" Britta puts her hand on my back as I stick the bag over my mouth. "You look a little green."

She rubs my back, which doesn't help with my hyperventilating. She's already breaking her own rule, and we're not even married yet.

I take the bag away from my face and between heavy breaths blurt, "We're not supposed to touch, are we?" The bag goes right back over my mouth when I finish. Depending on her answer, I may actually puke.

"It seemed necessary."

My back goes cold when she pulls her hand back.

I take a few more breaths before I sit up. "It was. Thanks."

This is what both of us want—no distractions. If I'm going to make the Olympic team, this is the perfect arrangement, and not just so I can become an American. With Britta as my wife—even in name only—I won't be tempted by other girls. I won't get sucked into relationships that would shift my focus away from training and winning.

And knowing Britta isn't interested in anything but friendship, with me or anyone else, will keep me from falling for her. No kissing. No touching. No feelings. It's exactly what we both need right now.

The rest of the hour flight to Vegas is pretty quiet, except for Stella outlining for Rhys all the things he could do differently with his social media accounts to combat some of the negative press he's had. Unsurprisingly, the more Stella talks, the deeper Rhys's scowl grows, but he doesn't stop her, which is interesting.

We land at McCarren airport where we're met by a black Escalade with tinted windows whose driver takes the five of us to the MGM hotel, and through a secret entrance to one of the most-exclusive hotels in the world.

"What is this?" Britta asks, looking at the courtyard and Renaissance-inspired (according to the website—I never learned that stuff) hotel hidden in plain sight.

"The Mansion," Rhys says, smiling for the first time. "Super-exclusive and super-private. The rooms are all villas with butler and menu service. Anything you want, just ask."

"Well done, Rhys." Stella's voice is almost a whisper, and her gaze is glued to the building.

Archie says nothing, even though I'm sure he's the one who pulled strings to get us rooms here. He'll let everyone think it's Rhys's doing, when really, it's for Rhys's benefit. The more Rhys's star rises, the more he values his privacy. I'm not the only one who's aware of what Rhys is sacrificing by being here for my wedding instead of relaxing at home, alone, before his next show. We're still his best mates, no matter how famous he gets, and I'm reminded of how much he needs us as his star continues to rise.

"Does my family know how to find this place? They booked rooms at the MGM." Britta stares at the cool yellowish stone and the pink flowering plants that are a world away from the heat and bright lights of the Strip.

"They have rooms here, too. We'll make sure they're brought here when they check in," Archie says.

"They can't afford this!" Britta panics.

"They're not paying for it," Archie pulls his phone from his pocket and steps away before Britta can argue.

While Archie makes his phone call, we walk inside, where we're met by a man in an understated, but obviously expensive suit.

"Welcome to the Mansion, Mr. James. I'm Marshall. We're so pleased to have you and your guests with us." Marshall stands stiff as a board and speaks so formally that I wish I'd worn something besides board shorts and thongs. "We've booked a one bedroom, two two-bedroom villas, and a four bedroom for your party."

"Is that enough for all of us?" I try to do a quick calculation in my head, but I'm not sure who in Britta's family is coming.

"I apologize. We don't have anything else. We gave you the last and only rooms available." Marshall leads us through a foyer with posh furniture and lots of deep red. He stops in the middle of the room and holds up a key card. "This is for the bride and groom."

He scans our group, trying to pick out who fits the description since none of us are acting like we're in love. Britta and I aren't even standing by each other. Rhys coughs and elbows me forward.

"I guess that's me." I take the key and send Britta a nervous glance. "Ready... babe?"

Britta looks at me like I've lost my mind before remembering she's the bride. "Oh, yeah."

Marshall's mouth curves into something resembling a smile. "Congratulations on your nuptials. Your entrance is down the hall, directly to the right."

I hold out my hand to Britta, hoping this is an appropriate hand-holding moment. Her conditions weren't specific on that point. I let out my breath when she slides her fingers through mine.

We walk down the hall to our room—*our* room—my palm growing clammier by the second. I wonder if the clamminess is only me or if Britta is just as nervous. We agreed to this marriage-of-convenience less than twenty-four hours ago, and already we've run into problems that her list of conditions didn't anticipate. Like staying in the same room.

Our villa is probably big enough to have two beds. If not two separate beds, then at least a sofa.

But I can't help hoping it doesn't.

CHAPTER TWENTY-FIVE

Britta

Dex and I both stare at the giant bed piled high with thick bedding and enough decorative pillows to supply my entire hometown. The room is bigger than both our apartments put together, and yet, the bed seems to take up most of it.

"I can take the couch," Dex says, and we both turn toward the plush, velvet seating across the room.

The back is straight, and it has those cylinder pillows that look pretty but aren't cushy. If it were the only piece of furniture in the room, we'd probably think it looked comfortable.

But... there is... The Bed.

"We can flip a coin." My eyes drift back to the bed, which looks very comfortable and definitely roomy enough for a married couple with a strict, no-touching rule.

If the person in that pair who insisted on the rule wasn't already questioning how strictly it needs to be followed. I've got to put a stop to that right now.

Dex drops his bag, then takes mine from my shoulder and carries it to the fancy bench at the end of the bed. He sets it there, slips off his flip-flops and falls backwards. The white duvet catches him with an inviting *whoosh* that reminds me of when I was a little girl and imagined what it would be like to sleep on a fluffy cloud.

"We'll take turns." Dex stretches his arms and laces his fingers before tucking them behind his head. "I get first go."

"When is it my turn?" I take a few steps closer to the bed, even though it's clearly *not* my turn.

Dex sits up enough to see me. I can't actually see his abs through his T-shirt, and that doesn't stop me from picturing what they look like, all activated in the crunch position he's holding.

"Whenever you want, Britta." His tone is neutral, but his eyes dance the same way he did across the waves.

I'm so tempted to lie down next to him, engulfed in the down bedding, pillows, and his arms. I'm exhausted. I can't remember anymore when I wasn't. I bet I could rest pretty well with Dex holding me.

Which is why I back away from the bed. "I'll take my turn tonight."

Dex nods and lies back down, closing his eyes. I study his profile but stay where I am.

If this arrangement is going to work, I can't give into any physical or emotional attraction. Of course, I'm longing for both, but love is not part of my plan for the next few years. I'm not ready yet. I have too many things I want to do first.

Dex and I have to stay in this room together. There's no way around it. If it were just the staff I was worried would ask questions about why Dex and I didn't sleep together—in the strictest sense of the word—I wouldn't care. I imagine that people in hotels like this are trained to keep their mouths shut.

My family, on the other hand, is not.

They would have all kinds of questions about why I was sharing a room with Stella instead of the man I'm marrying in a few hours. I'd get a long lecture from my brothers, Dad, aunt, and cousin about how marriage isn't a short-term business arrangement, it's a lifetime commitment built on love.

I don't disagree. That's been their experience, and it's worked out great. But that doesn't mean my experience should be the same.

Noise from the hallway draws my attention away from Dex. I have an idea of what—or who—it is even before the knock at the door.

Dex turns his head and looks at me.

"My family," I say to answer the question on his face.

He scrambles off the bed and drags a hand through his hair while I answer the door. I barely have it open before they swarm in—all thirteen of them. I expected seven with my brothers, their partners, and Dad. But Stella's mom, her brother Sebastian, sister-in-law, and niece are also in tow. The last two in, though, are the most unexpected.

Grandma and Grandpa Sparks, my mom's parents.

Dex shakes my dad's hand, looking more intimidated than he did when he paddled out for the World Title.

I don't blame him; I guess. Dad is a big guy, but his perpetual smile makes him look more like a big teddy bear than a grizzly. He's not smiling now, though. And neither is my brother Bear, who looks even scarier than Dad.

Fortunately, Georgia's smile makes up for everyone else's death stares.

"Dex!" She throws her arms around him, then waves me over so she can pull me in, too. She's half a foot shorter than I am, so Dex and I are both forced to curl into her neck.

"I predicted you'd fall for each other the minute I saw you together this summer!" Georgia exclaims. "I never dreamed you'd get married so fast, but when you know, you know."

Dex and I give each other a look across her shoulders that I hope no one else catches. Apparently, Georgia knows more about us than we do.

"Better than living together," Grandpa says in his gruff voice.

That's as close to approval as we'll get from him, and I'll take it. Grandpa's old school. If Dex and I were really in love, Grandpa would be more upset if we moved in together than he is about us getting married, even if we barely know each other.

So, I'll just keep letting him think that's what's happening here. The guilt I feel will get easier after a while—probably.

"These are some digs, Britt." My brother Zach scans the entire room, letting his eyes linger on the rumpled bed.

"What's the plan for this... event?" Dad's question hovers uncomfortably in the air, and he won't make eye contact with Dex or me.

I look at Dex. He and Archie said they'd take care of everything, so I don't have an answer for Dad, even though now he's looking at me, expecting one.

"Archie has it all planned, but we wanted it to be a surprise for Britta." Dex takes a couple of tentative steps toward Dad, who does his best not to encourage him.

Dex bites his lip and shoots me a glance, then pulls his shoulders back and puts on a confident smile. He moves close enough to Dad to swing an arm over his shoulder. "Before we do anything, we should talk. This is all fast—you have to be worried—and I want to marry your daughter, but not without your permission, sir."

"What?" I blurt out, but at the relieved look on Dad's face, I bite back my comment about being a grown woman, not a piece of property Dex is looking to take off my dad's hands.

"That's unnecessary, son." Dad pats Dex's lower back. "It's Britta's choice. I trust her."

"Thanks, Dad." I push back the lump in my throat, but there's no stopping the swelling guilt in my gut.

There's another knock at the door, and Adam, who's standing closest, opens it to let in Archie and Rhys.

"Good. Everyone's here," Archie says. "We've got tickets for the venue in two hours, so be ready to go in ninety minutes." He taps his watch and sets a timer.

"Tickets?" I ask. Who needs tickets for a wedding venue?

"You're Rhys James," my sister-in-law, Evie, says in a breathless voice, which elicits a growl from Adam.

Rhys dips his chin in a reluctant nod.

Evie turns to me, still awestruck. "You didn't tell me Rhys James was going to be here."

"I had to keep that part a secret. Sorry." I don't meet her gaze in case she can see Rhys isn't the only secret I have to keep.

"He's performing the ceremony," Archie says matter-of-factly before checking his watch. "Which is in approximately one hundred and eighteen minutes, so we should let the bride get ready."

"Yep." Georgia pushes everyone toward the door, including the three women who can't stop staring at Rhys. "Let's go. We've only got eighty-seven minutes until it's time to leave. Everyone be in the lobby at six-thirty... make that six-twenty-five."

"I'm a good flower girl," Stella's four-year-old niece, Charlie, says to me.

I squat down to get eye-to-eye with her. "I know you are! I hope you'll be mine."

Charlie throws her pudgy arms around my neck. "Mama bringed my dress."

I hug her back, and a tiny part of me wishes this were real, like Adam and Zach's double wedding where Charlie was the flower girl for the first time.

Hope leads Charlie out the door, and in a matter of seconds, I'm alone again with Dex. My fake fiancé. My soon-to-be—in less than two hours—fake husband.

Our eyes meet, and he looks as nervous as I feel.

"If you want to call this off, you can." He's five feet away, close to the door, looking ready to run.

"Is that what you want to do?" I hold my breath, waiting for his answer, not sure if I want it to be yes or no.

"No. But I will. I feel awful they think this is... real."

"Me too," I say, then let a few seconds of silence settle between us. "But it's okay. I'm a big girl and I'm making my decision with eyes wide open. It would only hurt them to know the truth, and this marriage is making me happy—just differently than they think."

He nods, then runs his fingers over the patch of stubble on his jawline before shaking his head. "I should shave."

A grin escapes before I can stop it. "Me too."

We both laugh, but the awkwardness between us has leveled down to an excited nervousness.

"We can make this work... right?" I'm not sure how that turned into a question instead of a statement.

Dex lifts his shoulders. "We've got no reason not to. It's the best thing for both of us." Then he points to the bathroom. "You can have it first."

Eighty minutes later, Dex and I are in the foyer waiting for my family. I've got on my green dress, my hair pulled into a loose, but fancy, updo and gold earrings dangling from my ears. This is the most dressed up I've been since my brothers got married. I'm pretty sure the same is true for Dex.

He's got on a button-up shirt, khakis, and real shoes—not flip-flops. They're black Vans, but still, shoes. He tugs at his collar every few seconds, and I don't know if it's because he's nervous or if it's because he hates collared shirts.

"Is this a hand-holding situation?" he whispers as the elevator door opens and Dad steps out.

I nod and slide my fingers through his. "Yes, please."

Dad's by himself, and his eyes are rimmed with red as he approaches us, and I brace myself for waterworks. He pulls something from his pants pocket, then stops in front of me.

"I forgot to give you this earlier." He holds up a gold ring with a tiny diamond. "It's your mom's and you don't have to use it as your own. But if you want it, I think she'd like you to have it."

All I can do is nod because the waterworks are coming from me, not Dad. The Bellagio fountains spring from my eyes, accompanied by an instrumental version of a familiar song I can't place, playing softly from speakers somewhere in the foyer.

Home. That's the name of the song by the guy with the same name twice—Phillip Phillips. The lines about taking on an unfamiliar road together fill my head, which only makes me cry more.

"Thanks, Dad." I take the ring from him, feeling its weight in my fingers before handing it to Dex. "One ring problem solved, but I still don't have a ring for you."

"We'll figure it out. Your ring is more important. Thank you, Mr. Thomsen." His eyes are a little red too, which pulls more tears from me.

The rest of my family arrives, and Archie herds us all to the waiting Escalades outside.

Before I can ask Archie where we're going, I'm crowded into one vehicle with my dad and brothers. I'm just as surprised as everyone else when the SUV stops to let us out on a wide walkway between two hotels. The cement path is lined on both sides with restaurants and other businesses catering to tourists. At the end of the walkway, there's a giant Ferris wheel with enclosed carriages.

As we wind our way through crowds of people, I don't see anything that looks like a wedding venue, and there are fewer businesses the closer we get to the Ferris Wheel thing with the blinking neon *High Roller* sign.

"Archie?" I pick up my dress and quick step up to him. "Is that where we're getting married?" I point to the slow-spinning wheel of death, my heart pounding.

Archie nods, pleased with himself. "Yeah. At sunset. It will be beautiful."

Against my better judgement, I let my eyes travel to the top of the Ferris wheel. The carriages sway back and forth, and I feel the blood drain from my face.

"What's wrong?" Dex's fingers brush the bare skin of my back.

I lean over with my hands on my knees. "I think I'm going to throw up."

"You've changed your mind?" Dex's question is laced with disappointment, but all I can do is shake my head.

"Britta doesn't like heights," Stella answers for me. "She's never flown before or been on a regular-sized Ferris Wheel, let alone one that's five hundred and fifty feet tall, so it's kind of big day for her."

I groan. Wherever she found those numbers, the information is *not* helpful.

"I'm sorry, Britta. I didn't think to ask." Archie's apology is sincere. He sounds as wrecked as I feel. "We can go back to the Mansion and have the ceremony there."

I take a deep breath and stand taller. I don't like heights, and, yeah, I'm a little afraid of them. But if I'm not afraid to marry a world-famous surfer who I've only known a few weeks in order to buy a coffee shop in a city ten thousand times bigger than the one where I've spent most of my life, then I can push past being afraid to say my *I do's* at the top of a giant Ferris wheel with a view of the sunset in Las Vegas.

"You okay?" Dex asks.

"I think so."

He moves in front of me. With the heels I'm wearing, we're nearly eye-to-eye. "Remember what you told me before my first heat at the Finals?"

I shake my head. The only thing I can think about right now is getting myself on that Ferris wheel without passing out.

"You told me to make it a dance. That's what kept me from panicking while I was waiting for the right wave." Dex's words are slow, calm, and confident. "That's why I won that heat. Your words."

My breathing slows. The pounding in my ears quiets.

"If you don't want to get married here, we won't," he continues. "But if you're okay with it, I'll hold your hand the whole time. I won't let anything happen to you. If you'll trust me right now—the way I trusted you on that wave—I'll keep you safe."

Dex's words flow over me, a soft breeze in the blazing heat, and my body cools.

"Let's get married," I say and put my shaking hand in his.

CHAPTER TWENTY-SIX

Dex

The bones in my right hand may never recover from the vice grip Britta has them in. The closer our compartment gets to the top of the High Roller, the tighter Britta squeezes, and the more my eyes water. Britta's dad is crying too, but for less painful reasons. Maybe he's crying because he thinks I am. Or maybe he's crying about his little girl marrying a guy whose only skill is surfing.

Rhys says some nice things about marriage and finding true love, so the ceremony looks real. Honestly, it feels authentic enough that some of my tears might not be from pain. I hope, though, that Britta's face is white from fear of heights and not fear of what she's getting herself into.

We both benefit from this arrangement, but I'm getting the better end of the deal. Britta is beautiful, smart, and ambitious. She would have figured out how to buy *Annie's* without me. She could have taken out a loan. I need her heaps more than she needs me.

Rhys perfectly times his speech so that he says the "do you take" part just as we reach the highest point of the ride. The sun turns the bright, gaudy lights of Las Vegas and the brown desert it sprung from into soft hues of golds, yellows, and reds. Britta gasps and loosens her grip on my hand, but I keep hold of hers, like I promised.

We don't have vows to exchange, just rings. Or a ring. I slip her mother's ring on her finger. It fits perfectly, and Britta wipes at her cheek. For a second, I wish this were real, for her sake. Then I realize it *is* real. Not the madly in-love part, but the marriage part is. We're officially husband and wife. Rhys just announced it.

He follows up with, "You may kiss the bride!"

This is for sure a necessary moment, and since I don't know when I'll have another chance like this, I decide to make the most of it.

I let go of Britta's hand in mine, and circle my arms around her waist, drawing her closer. The green dress is cut low in the back, and I smooth my thumb over her soft skin until it meets the silky fabric at the small of her back.

Her hands travel across my shoulders and around my neck. She's so close, I feel her chest rising and falling in quick breaths. The tip of her tongue darts between her lips. That's all the invitation I need to press my lips to hers.

The trick to riding a barreling wave is to make it last. The force of the wave pushes you forward, but dragging a hand along the wall slows you down. You can ride the wave for longer, all the way to the end, if you can slow down the momentum.

That's what I want now. The air buzzes with an energy that threatens to make this kiss end too quickly. I may never get the chance to kiss Britta like this again, so I slow it down. I run my hand up her back to the space between her shoulders, letting it rest there before deepening our connection.

I know Britta's rules, and I'm determined to keep them. But right now, all I want to do is break them and I think I can get away with it.

To be honest, there aren't many rules I *don't* want to break. But what I feel now is more than rebellion. The force of the wave barreling around us makes me want to pull Britta closer and keep her safe. So, it's not until she digs her fingers into my back that I rein in my desire.

I want to kiss her so much harder and longer, but even more, I want Britta to trust me. This marriage is primarily a business arrangement, but I want her to understand she's not a commodity to me.

I like Britta.

I like her a lot.

And I don't want her getting hurt in all of this, which, I remember, is the reason for all the rules: to avoid heartbreak. I need to remember that.

Britta breaks away first, letting her hands fall to her side, but our eyes stay locked. She smiles softly, and I can't stop myself from brushing her lips with mine one more time. Then our compartment fills with applause and cheering.

She takes my hand, and we turn to face her family and my friends. Ten minutes later, the wheel stops. Before the doors open, cameras flash in the crowd of people waiting outside the line of ticket holders for the High Roller. In a matter of thirty minutes, people have heard Rhys James is here and gathered to wait for him.

Stella steps off the Ferris wheel first. "Mr. James is here for a wedding and won't be signing autographs. Please respect his privacy," she says at the top of her lungs with all the authority of a girlboss.

I clutch Britta's hand and push my way through the crowd, only looking back once to make sure Rhys is okay. As big a star as he is, he hates this part of being a celebrity. He does whatever he can to avoid being mauled by fans, and he came here knowing it would probably happen.

But Britta's brothers have circled around him like they're trained bodyguards and not guys who just met Rhys a few hours ago.

"Your brothers are good guys," I say to Britta once we've made our way out of the flood of people. Ironically, even though it's my wedding, Rhys takes all the attention and Britta and I end up with a few moments to ourselves.

"The best," she says before pointing behind me. "I think I found our wedding cake."

I look over my shoulder at a Sprinkles Cupcakes vending machine. "Never had them, but if that's what my bride wants, that's what she gets."

While the Thomsen brothers escort Rhys to the waiting Escalade, Britta and I empty the vending machine of all its little cakes, forgetting we only have four hands between us. Both of us are trying to balance a dozen cupcakes each in plastic containers in our arms when I hear someone behind me say, "Dude! You're Liam Dexter!"

I turn to face a kid with wild blonde hair wearing board shorts and thongs. He's definitely a surfer. I can see it in his eyes.

"Yeah, mate. What's your name?" I'd shake his hand, but I don't have a free one myself.

"Brody."

"He's a big fan of yours," says the man next to him. He looks like an older version of the kid and has to be his dad.

"Yeah? Glad to hear it. I'd give you an autograph, but my hands are full." At that moment, a cupcake flies from my arms, upsetting the balance of the rest so that half of them attempt their own escape.

Fortunately, the containers don't open, but they'll be a bit smashed for sure. Brody and his dad scramble to pick them up for me, while Britta shifts back and forth, struggling to keep hers from falling.

"You must really love cupcakes, Dex." Brody tries to hand me one, but his dad takes it from him.

"Where are you taking these? We can help you," he says before taking a few from Britta too.

"Thank you," she says with a breath before smiling at Brody. "They're our wedding cake. We just got married."

I look at her, shocked. Pleasantly. I was holding back making the announcement, afraid she might not like it. So, I'm a bit pleased she's the one who said it first.

"Married?" Brody's dad asks.

Britta and I both nod. I can't see if she's smiling, but I am. I hope she is.

Brody and his dad help us carry the cupcakes to a waiting Rolls Royce Archie arranged for Britta and me. The Escalades are packed and ready to go with our family and friends. I assume Rhys made it inside one of them—the tinted windows make it impossible to see—because there's a crowd of people taking pictures of the cars.

Britta and I get a picture with Brody and his dad, which I'm sure will be our second wedding photo posted online, right after the ones I'm sure Stella's already posted. Then we give them two cupcakes for their help and climb into the car.

The last time we were alone, we weren't married. Now we are. I can't tell what Britta's thinking, but I'm in a bit of shock. She has to be, too.

"I guess I'm Mrs. Dexter now?" Britta asks with a sprinkle of teasing that breaks the tension

"Nah. I'm Mr. Thomsen." I wish I could take her hand, but I don't think she'd like that. At least she laughs at my joke.

"That works for me." She tucks a loose strand of hair behind her ear. "It's been quite a day."

I blow out a breath. "I'll say."

We go quiet again before I work up the nerve to say what I've wanted to since the minute she walked out of the bathroom in that green dress.

"You look really beautiful. This probably wasn't what you dreamed your wedding day would be, but I've never seen a prettier bride."

Britta's lips stretch across her perfect white teeth. "Thanks, Dex. It wasn't the day I planned when I was a little girl, but for a wedding put together in less than forty-eight hours and that I didn't have to spend my dad's life savings on, I have no complaints. Archie did an amazing job planning, and I'm sure Rhys pulled a lot of strings to get us in that secret hotel and on the High Roller last minute. You have good friends."

I nod. I do have the best mates, but I'm stuck on something else she said. "You really had wedding plans when you were a girl?"

She drops her head, and her skin flushes, but she laughs. "I was the only girl in a house full of boys, and a total tomboy. My mom let me play as rough as I wanted, but I was a flower girl a few times. To get me excited, we scrolled through Pinterest looking at weddings." Britta lifts her shoulder, and her dangling gold earring brushes her bare skin. "It kind of stuck. We kept doing it and had all kinds of boards for my future wedding."

"That's sweet…" I rub my hands down my legs. Vegas is too hot, and I hate wearing trousers. "I'm sorry you didn't get that today."

Britta tips her head, thinking. "Without Mom, the wedding plans we made together will always just be Pinterest boards. I'm not sure I'll ever get married for real. If this is my one and only wedding, I couldn't have asked for better."

I put on a smile, but the words 'married for real' sting. Like getting sprayed coming out of a wave. It's part of surfing, but it still hurts every time.

We're quiet the rest of the way back to the Mansion. When we climb out of the car, everyone is waiting for us. Archie has set up a dinner for all of us in the Mansion's private dining room, so we won't be bothered by onlookers. Britta and I sit by each other, but judging by the looks her dad keeps sending us, he's not convinced Britta and I are marrying for love.

We talk a little, but we're awkward with each other. What's more, I'm awkward with her in a way I've never been. Now that I'm not supposed to touch her, that's all I want to do. Our wedding dinner is likely one of the "appropriate" or "necessary" times we can touch, but I'm like a schoolboy hoping for a first kiss. Britta will have to take the lead, because I can't find what to do with my hands anymore, other than use them to shovel food into my mouth.

I wasn't this nervous at the Finals.

When dinner ends, Georgia suggests we head to the private pools. I look at Britta, who shrugs and says, "Sure."

Georgia's gaze skitters between Britta and me. "What are you talking about? It's your wedding night." She leans between us and lowers her voice. "I'm getting everyone out of your way. Go enjoy yourselves."

I can't look at Britta. Not while Georgia is smiling wider than a ten-year-old who's cracked their first sex joke.

"Whatever you want to do... babe," I manage to say before grabbing Britta's hand, all without looking at her. So, yeah, my hand may have touched a few other body parts before I found her fingers.

"If you two get into a swimming pool instead of enjoying the 'villa'...'" Georgia makes air quotes here, which only makes things worse. "You have for one night, I'll—I don't actually know what I'll do—be very, very disappointed, I guess." She's not smiling anymore as she turns to Britta. "Do we need to have 'the talk'? Is that what's happening here? Because I'll do it. We both know your dad would rather do *anything* but that."

What I learned about Georgia when she lived next door is that she doesn't take no for an answer. Ever. Britta has to know this better than I do, so I wait for her to respond.

"I'm twenty-six, not six, Georgia," Britta says. "I don't need the talk, thank you very much." Britta tugs at my hand. "Should we go to our room... *honey?*"

I nod. My mouth has gone dry. We're going to our room. As a married couple. To celebrate our wedding night.

I have no clue what that will look like without touching. I don't remember seeing a TV in our villa, and I didn't bring any board games. I don't even know if Britta likes board games. I should probably know that about my wife, shouldn't I?

Now that I think about it, there's a long list of things I should learn about Britta. Like her birthday. Her favorite color. Her favorite food. Whether she has allergies. That one is important. What if I accidentally kill her with peanuts or cats or something?

These are all my thoughts as we walk in silence to our room, which is bigger than the house I grew up in, but only has one bed. *One.*

As soon as the door closes behind us, Britta opens her mouth to say something, but I'm already blurting, "Do you have any allergies I should know about?"

She closes her mouth and shakes her head. "Do you?"

"Latex. I can't wear--"

Britta's eyes go wide. My face catches fire as I realize what she's afraid I'm going to say.

"*Goggles.* I can't wear goggles. If we were to go swimming, or some-thing." Why does the *something* sound dirty in this context? Why did I even say it? When else would I wear goggles besides to swim?

"Good to know," she says slowly before waving her thumb toward the bathroom. "Do you mind if I use it first? I think I'll sit in that tub, and I may be there for a while."

Sit in the tub? I picture Britta hanging out in the tub, fully clothed, then realize she means she's going to take a bath.

And now I'm not picturing her fully clothed.

I swallow hard. "Sure. Take your time. It's past my bedtime, anyway. I'll make myself a bed on the couch. Can I brush my teeth before you... uh, bathe?"

"Of course."

We look at each other for a few seconds, then I grab my toiletry bag and make my way to the bathroom.

Ten minutes later, I'm on a couch that should be more comfortable than it is, based on how much this villa costs per night, listening to the water run as Britta fills her bath, reminding myself to not get distracted.

CHAPTER TWENTY-SEVEN

Britta

I step into the tub, then sink all the way in, letting the hot water swallow my entire body. I can almost stretch my legs straight; the tub is that big. I squeeze my eyes shut and stay under for as long as I can hold my breath, hoping when I reemerge it will be without the crushing guilt I've felt since stepping off the High Roller and touching blessed solid ground again.

A normal person would feel guilty for not telling her family the whole truth about why she's getting married, but that's only part of what's eating me up. The main thing I don't think I'll ever get over is the fact that I got married today and didn't think about my mom once during the entire ceremony.

Maybe it's because it happened so fast or because I was ten seconds away from a full-blown panic attack through the whole thing, but I didn't miss her. And I should have. This is a day we planned together. Sure, the wedding looked nothing like my old Pinterest boards, but that's not the issue.

I'm not sure I can forgive myself for forgetting her today.

And I wonder if the main reason I did is because I had Dex by my side, holding my hand. For the first time since Mom passed, I didn't feel like a part of me was missing. I felt whole again—my heart intact—even though I was doing something that feels wrong. But right. But wrong.

I let all that's happened and all my thoughts and regrets cycle through me for a long time—until the water is lukewarm and my fingertips are prunes. I almost turn the hot water on again, so I can stay in longer, but I don't want to be alone with these thoughts anymore. I haven't found a resolution, I've just grown more used to the questions, I guess. So, I climb out and put on my pjs.

Not sexy ones, and to be honest, that makes me a little sad too. The wedding ceremony wasn't anything like what I'd pictured, but it was still amazing. I faced my fear of heights and got married in the sky with *Rhys James* as the officiant. I mean, come on. How could I be disappointed about that?

But the wedding night?

That won't be anything like I imagined.

Aside from not sealing the deal—as they say—I'm going to be sleeping by myself. Dex won't be holding me or telling me he loves me. We won't be talking about how happy we are that we finally tied the knot or that we can't wait to spend our lives together.

Maybe I'll have that someday, but it won't be tonight.

The lights are out when I tiptoe to the bed. As I pull the covers up to my shoulders, I listen for any noise from Dex. I can barely make out his form on the couch, but I don't hear anything. Not even deep breaths that would show he's asleep.

"Dex?" I whisper.

"Yeah?" he answers a few seconds later, and my chest loosens.

"Thanks for holding my hand today... I mean, on the High Roller." I stare at the unfamiliar ceiling above me, the outline of the molding growing more visible as my eyes adjust to the dark. "I couldn't have done that without you."

"You wouldn't've had to if not for me," he scoffs.

"True," I laugh, then pause. "But you made me feel safe."

"Good. That's what I wanted. That's all I want for you with this whole thing—to feel safe." His voice always has a hint of laughter in it, but not now. That, more than anything, underlines how sincere he is.

The room fills again with a lonely silence that makes my heart pound almost as much as it did when I saw the High Roller.

"Dex?"

"Yeah?" The sound of his voice quiets my pulse.

"You were really nice to that kid today." I smile at the memory of the way Brody's face lit up when Dex talked to him like they were already friends.

"That surprised you?" He shifts on the couch, and I can see the outline of his torso sitting up against the arm of the couch.

"No. Not at all, but it was still nice to see."

"He caught me on a good day," he deadpans.

"It was a good day, wasn't it?"

Dex lets out a breath. "Yeah, it really was."

We go quiet again, but the loneliness is gone. I'm not ready to go to sleep. I want to keep talking, but this is nice too.

"I was worried you might be sad because your mum wasn't there," Dex says softly, and my breath hitches.

"I wasn't, Dex," the words rush out. I couldn't stop them if I wanted. "I didn't even think about her, and that scares me. It scares me even more than that stupid, giant Ferris wheel we got married on."

My breath comes fast and heavy. I will *not* cry. Not on my fake wedding night. It won't change anything. I can't go back and miss her while I was saying "I do" to a business arrangement.

Dex is quiet, and I wonder if he's thinking the Olympics might not be worth three years with a crazy person who breaks into tears if her mom is mentioned.

"Sorry. I didn't mean to put that on you." I control my voice until the end when *you* comes out in a stagger.

From across the room, Dex lets out a frustrated sigh that only makes me feel worse. Then he pads across the room, probably to the bathroom. Except he stops next to the bed, his shadow falling over me.

"Move over," he orders.

Without asking questions, I scoot to the center of the bed, and Dex climbs on, pinning the covers around me as he lies on top of them. He slides his arm under my head, pulls me close to his chest, and wraps his other arm around me.

"I call necessary hugging." His lips brush the top of my head in what may be an accident or a kiss.

I hope it's the second, because I'm already nestled into his chest, wishing the down comforter wasn't between us, while burying my head into it to muffle my sniffling.

I don't fool Dex. He rubs my back and whispers things like, "there, there," and "let it out. I've got you." Which only makes me cry harder, because it's been a long time since someone's had my back.

There are no platitudes. No, "it will be okay" or "things will get easier with time." Because it won't ever be okay that Mom wasn't here and I didn't miss her, and I also hate the thought of things getting easier the longer Mom is gone. I don't want her to be gone *now* or in the future when my memories of her start to fade.

"What do you think it means that I forgot her today?" I ask when my tears slow enough I can form the question without making that weird choking sound that comes with crying.

"Do you mean while we were getting married in one of the world's tallest Ferris wheels, even though you're scared of heights? And maybe marriage, too."

I let out a small laugh.

"I think it means you were too terrified to think of anything besides what was happening in the moment. Nothing else." Dex's hand is cupped around my shoulder, and he caresses my bare skin with his thumb.

I take a deep breath, wanting to let go of the weight I've carried for years, but that's become unbearable since Mom passed. "I don't want to forget Mom, but I'm afraid that's the penance I have to pay."

"Penance for what?" Dex's voice is calm, like what I've told him is totally normal.

"Being mad at her for getting sick. It makes no sense, but I am. It's not her fault, but I gave up everything I had planned because I wanted to take care of her." Not only have I never said these words out loud, but I also haven't articulated them to myself.

But saying them brings clarity to my feelings, and I shed a fragment of the shame I've been carrying. "She raised me to be whatever I wanted, to go wherever my heart took me. Then, because I'm her only daughter, her illness brought me home before I could do any of the things I wanted to do."

I feel Dex nod. "She asked you to come home?"

I've asked myself the same question, because I honestly don't remember. "Nobody tried to stop me."

"Hmm. You regret going home?" He drags one fingertip at a time slowly down my shoulder.

I don't answer right away, because regret isn't what I feel. Anger? Yeah. Resentment? Yes. But not necessarily regret.

"I wouldn't change going home instead of taking a job in LA. I'd care for Mom all over again. The only thing I'd change is her getting sick." I push out a frustrated laugh. "See why it makes no sense that I'm mad at her?"

Dex makes his "ah" sound that I'm learning is what he does before saying something he wants you to think isn't much but is actually pretty deep.

"Makes perfect sense to me. It's how I feel about my dad pushing me to surf."

I tilt my chin toward the outline of his jaw. "You love surfing."

"More than anything." He looks down at me, and I turn over to rest my chin and hands on his chest, which I realize as the duvet between us shifts, is bare.

His skin is warm, and I brush my thumb over his shoulder, the way he did to mine. There's only enough light in the room to see shapes, not his eyes. But I feel them on me, studying me, weighing whether to open up to me the way I have to him.

"Remember how I told you I was ten when I told my dad I wanted to go pro?" he says. "That's all it took for my pipedream to become his dream. Suddenly surfing was less about us connecting than it was about me earning money for it."

"That's a lot of pressure for a ten-year-old."

"It's a lot of pressure for any surfer. You put up heaps of money before you ever start earning." He tucks one arm under his head, but the other one stays draped across my lower back.

"That's true of any sport, isn't it?"

"Yeah, but other athletes don't travel internationally for months at a time before they're pros, hoping to win enough smaller events to qualify for the paying events." There's no bitterness in his voice, just acceptance.

"You did that?"

Dex nods. "A football stadium can be built anywhere, but the only place to surf is where the waves are, and a good wave depends on the seafloor, time of year, and wind. The type of seafloor—reef break, sandbar, beach break or the like—and the wind speed, duration, and how large the fetch determines how the wave breaks."

I hold back my joke about *Mean Girls* and fetch, and instead raise my hand, like I'm in a high school science class. "Professor Dexter, will you explain what fetch means?"

Dex laughs, and his chest expands. Then I lose track of time as he explains to me how waves are formed—math was my best subject, not science—what makes a perfect wave for surfing, and the differences between the waves he's surfed. He explains why surf competitions are held all over the world and how waves are scored differently—so no one has an unfair advantage. His stories of traveling to Indonesia, Tahiti, Brazil, and other far-flung places, sleeping in tents or in vans to save money, away from home for months at a time while he was still a kid, are fascinating. His descriptions of the biggest waves, though, are both interesting and terrifying.

"A barrel wave, like Pipeline in Hawaii, is created by the wind and the shallow reef it comes off." He uses his hands to imitate the shape of the wave and the reef. "It's the reef that makes it so perfect but also so dangerous. You get pummeled by that wave and hit the reef, you're in for a serious injury. I've seen it happen to more than one surfer, and anyone who surfs it regularly has stories of close encounters."

"I had no idea surfing could be so dangerous."

I picture myself at sixteen in my little high school, thinking I was tough playing hockey with the boys and studying hard so I could go to college because it was my only way out of Paradise. Dex, though, was traveling the world, sometimes by himself, working at a restaurant when he was home to earn enough money to get to the next event. The next wave.

"Chasing waves isn't just a saying. It's how pro-surfers live," he finishes with a small yawn.

"I never thought about that. How did you go to school?"

"I didn't," Dex huffs. "In theory, I was home-schooled, but the only proper teachers I had were experience and the ocean."

"Really? You didn't have to do schoolwork?" I push myself up to meet his eyes.

"Dad did it for me until it got too hard for him."

Talking about waves and what he'd learned from traveling, Dex sounded confident and proud. Now I can barely hear him. His words are drowned out by the shame in his voice that's easily recognizable. I've heard the same in my voice.

I lower my head back to the crook of his shoulder before sliding my hand across his chest. I hold him just enough that hopefully he feels safe.

"What do you mean, 'he did it for you?'" I ask slowly.

Dex runs his hand over my entire arm until it comes to rest on my shoulder. "How many rules are we breaking right now?"

I scoff. "We'll worry about rules tomorrow. Don't change the subject."

I hold my breath, hoping he keeps talking, but also hoping we both forget the rules tomorrow.

After a sigh, Dex says, "Dad did the work I was supposed to do and submitted it as if I'd done it. He thought it was more important for me to be on the waves than reading *Lord of the Flies*."

"Honestly, Dex. He wasn't wrong about that. I hated that book."

His laugh rumbles over me. "At least you understand what people are talking about when they say, 'it's *Lord of the Flies* in there.'"

"Unless you've seen pre-teen boys kill each other, they're exaggerating."

"I have *not* seen that."

"Because *Lord of the Flies* is a stupid, depressing book, and William Golding had a stupid, depressing view of humanity." No one should feel bad about not reading that book, especially someone like Dex who's a good guy.

"Good to know."

"Seriously, Dex, you've done really well for not going to school much." I may be too comfortable right now, because it feels totally natural when I curl in closer to him, my leg over his, wishing there wasn't a blanket between us.

He presses his palm into my skin and slides his hand down my arm, then back up. "I've done well at the one thing I know how to do, because it's the only thing I'll ever be able to do without an education. Surfing is all I've got going for me."

I disagree, but that's not what I say.

"So, do you regret giving up everything else to do it?"

He shakes his head. "Nope. It's like you taking care of your mum. The only thing I'd change is what it did to my relationship with my dad. But if I changed that, I wouldn't be where I am."

Dex rearranges the pillow behind his head, then pulls me closer. "Take your mum. If she hadn't gotten sick—which no one could have changed—you wouldn't be the Britta you are today either. You wouldn't be risking everything to start a totally new life. You wouldn't even know how much you wanted this new life, yeah?"

Something brushes the top of my head. Maybe his cheek. Maybe his lips. I hope it's his lips.

"Not to minimize what you've been through and all the sacrifice it took to get through it," Dex's voice grows softer, more serious. "But from where I stand, the results are pretty awesome and with so much happening, it's not the least bit surprising that you didn't think about your mum. I didn't think about mine either, and she's still around. I haven't even told them."

In the quiet that follows, Dex's heart beats steady under my cheek, and I try not to think of him as my husband. If I let my mind go there, my lips will follow. And if I kiss him, the rest of my body will want to follow, too. We're married, after all. It would be easier to get lost in each other's bodies than to sit with the hard things we're unloading on each other.

But I can't leave Dex carrying my baggage without helping shoulder his.

"What did going pro do to your relationship with your dad?" I ask quietly.

"He became my manager and my coach instead of my dad." The bitterness his voice lacked before is there now.

"Do you think you'd be the world champion if he hadn't coached you?"

Dex shakes his head again, but more slowly. "The reason I'm world champion is that I fired him four years ago. I quit surfing to win for him and went back to doing it because I love it. That's what helped me win, not him telling me I could do better." Dex's words come out faster than usual, like he's expelling them.

I suck in my breath. "Is that why things were weird between you when he came to San Clemente?"

Dex shifts and smiles. "You saw that? You ducked out so fast, I didn't think you noticed my family was there."

"I noticed, and I'm sorry. For leaving, and for the way things are with your dad." I circle my fingers over his chest and feel his skin prickle.

"His pride won't let him get over it, not just because I fired him, but because he knows he did a crap job as manager. He let people take advantage of me, because he thought a handshake meant more than a contract. He cares more about the money he cost me than I do." His fingers find the spot where my t-shirt has crept above my waist, and he runs them along my exposed spine. "I still love him, but he wants his job back, and I want my dad back, and it puts us at a bit of an impasse."

I search for words but come up empty except for the truth. "I'm at a loss for what to say. Sorry isn't enough."

Dex presses his palm to my back. "You listened. That's enough."

His hands are rough and chapped from spending so much time in the ocean. The broken skin and calluses are evidence of how hard he works at what he loves. When I saw him surf, I thought I understood why he loves it. If I hadn't, I wouldn't have agreed to help him achieve his dream of going to the Olympics.

But I didn't understand anything that first day watching him on the waves.

His gaze catches mine, and both our chests go still. If he kisses me now, I won't stop him. I won't be able to. Every part of me wants it.

But instead of pressing his lips to mine, he brushes them across the top of my head. "Look at us, talking like an old married couple."

My breath comes out in a loud laugh that hopefully covers my disappointment, which quickly passes anyway. Dex did the right thing. We're married in name only, and we have to keep it that way.

Now that I know what he's sacrificed to be the best surfer in the world, I better understand how much he loves surfing.

So much that I'm not only safe being fake married to him, I'm also safe here in his arms, saying things I've never said out loud. Because I realize now, he'll never love anything as much as he loves riding waves.

There's no danger of us falling in love.

Even though, at the moment, I could stay here forever.

CHAPTER TWENTY-EIGHT

Dex

When I wake up the next morning with Britta still in my arms, I dare to hope it won't be the last time. I wish I could wake up like this every morning except without the kink in my neck and my arm stiff. I'm used to waking up with some part of my body hurting; I'm *not* used to waking up at peace with the world and my place in it.

Talking to Britta did that for me. My friends don't even know how uneducated I feel around most people. When they surfed professionally, they had tutors. They all finished Year Twelve. Archie has a university degree—only because his dad made him get it, but I'd take that type of dad over a dad who convinces you that you're such a good surfer you don't need a high school certificate.

What sixteen-year-old doesn't want to believe that? It only took a decade, heaps of minor injuries, and one major one to make me realize I don't have other options if surfing doesn't work out.

Britta didn't try to convince me I'm more than a surfer, and she didn't judge me for my lack of education either. Which makes me trust her even more.

While we say goodbye to her family, we're totally at ease with each other—holding hands and being affectionate. Because the news of our wedding is out, there's a bit of media waiting for us outside the hotel, and we keep up the act. Our legs even touch inside the Escalade on our way to the airport.

It's not until we're safely in the air and Archie announces he's got a place for us to live that things get weird. Britta, sitting next to me, our shoulders brushing, suddenly leans away.

"Wait." Across from Britta, Stella looks up from her magazine, which, ironically, is plastered with the face of the rock star sitting across from her. "You're not staying at the apartment with me?"

Britta looks at Archie, who shakes his head.

"It's gotta look real from the start. We talked about this," he says to her. "It's better if you two move into the beach house right away."

"The beach house?" Britta and I say together at the same time Stella says, "What about me?"

"Yeah, my dad's beach house," Archie says, as though it's obvious. "No one's using it. You can stay there for now until you find a place of your own. You too, Stella. I don't care. It just has to look like Britta and Dex are living as a married couple."

"How nice is this beach house?" Stella asks with a slightly calculating expression. "Like run-down chic, beach-adjacent? Or somewhere Rhys would stay?"

"Somewhere Rhys *has* stayed. Very comfortably, I'll add," Rhys answers, not looking up from his phone.

"Cool. I'm in." Stella smiles, ignoring Britta's sharp look.

"Why don't you stay at your dad's beach house?" Britta asks. "That makes more sense. Dex and I can stay at the apartment. I'll take over your portion of the rent."

Archie shakes his head. "If I wanted to live there, I'd be there already. The house will give Dex a bigger image of success. The more successful he looks; the more companies will want him promoting their brands. And you'll have a place right on the beach."

I rest my fingertips on Britta's knee to nudge her to let it go.

But Britta doesn't get the message. She shifts in the large captain's chair, putting more space between us. "Do I get a say? Or am I the silent partner in this arrangement?"

"And so, the fun begins," Rhys lets out a low laugh, then his eyes drop to his face on Stella's magazine. "Don't believe any of that," he says to her. "I never dated Gigi Paris. It's not my fault she and Glen broke up. I barely know her."

Stella shrugs and opens the magazine again. "Like I told you yesterday, I can help you take control of your own story."

"You're not a silent partner," I say to Britta over Rhys and Stella. "You have a say in all of this."

"I'm just trying to help." Archie puts up his hands but sounds irritated.

I send Archie a look, warning him to keep his temper in check, then I turn to Britta. "The house is nice. You'd have your own bedroom and bathroom, and I'd still be within walking distance of good waves. But we can figure something else out if you're uncomfortable or want to pick something out yourself."

We hit a patch of light turbulence, and the small plane rattles. Not a lot, but enough for Britta to grab the hand I've got on my armrest. Her face is white, and her jaw clenched tight. I guess fearing heights also includes airplanes. Which also explains why she was so nervous on the flight here. It wasn't just about marrying me. I wish she'd have told me.

I flip my hand over and lace my fingers through hers, then put my other hand over both of ours. "I've got you," I whisper. "It'll pass."

Almost as soon as the words are out, the turbulence is over. Too soon for me. Even though Britta is gripping my hand as tight as she did on the High Roller, she lets go before I'm ready.

"How close is it to *Annie's*?" She clutches her hands on her lap, still nervous, but not needing me anymore.

"Ten minutes, unless there's traffic. During the summer, you'll want to bike the boardwalk to get there." I try not to stare at her long, slender fingers. "I meant what I said about you having a say. If you don't want to move to the beach house, we'll find somewhere else."

"We're only five minutes walking distance from *Annie's* now."

"Yeah, but Archie's house isn't surrounded by bars and restaurants. It's quieter."

She nods with her whole body, then asks Archie, "How much is the rent?"

"Nothing. No rent."

"Your dad is letting us live there for free?" Britta's eyes tighten at the corners.

Archie presses back into his seat without meeting Britta's gaze. "He won't know."

"He won't know?" Britta blinks. "Your dad just has so many beach houses lying around that he doesn't notice if someone moves into one without paying rent?"

Archie narrows his eyes and sucks on his cheek. "He thinks I live there."

The house doesn't hold good memories for Archie, but his dad gave it to him, anyway. Archie's letting us use it, not only as a gift for us but also as a gift for himself. He hates worrying about the upkeep on a house he doesn't want but can't sell.

"So, then, circling back..." Britta draws out her sentence, and I have an idea what's coming next. "Why don't *you* live there, and Dex and I can stay in your apartment?"

Archie shakes his head before she's even finished the question. "Because I don't *want* to live there."

She opens her mouth, but I touch her arm to stop her. "It's a really nice place. Very posh."

Archie's got his reasons for not wanting to stay there. If he wants Britta to know them, he'll tell her. She looks between me and Archie a few more times before seeming to understand there's some history that justifies Archie's reasons for living in a basic apartment instead of his own house.

"Don't be a dummy, Britta," Stella says without looking up from her magazine. "Live in the posh beach house."

Britta turns up her palms in surrender. "Okay."

The rest of the trip goes by quickly, with no turbulence, which is a bummer. I enjoy holding Britta's hand. I like Britta. A lot.

This is a problem. We haven't been married forty-eight hours, and already I can't stop thinking about waking up with her in my arms. It was hard enough just holding her on our wedding night. My willpower was stretched to the limit. I don't seem to have any left to help me redirect my thoughts away from her.

The curve of her full lips. The way her hair sweeps across her forehead, highlighting her blue eyes. The way my thumb fits perfectly in the groove between her waist and hipbone. The way...

"Dex?" Archie stares at me, and I come back to myself. "You coming, mate?"

Everyone else is filing out of the plane—including Britta—while I'm sitting here daydreaming about her.

How am I supposed to focus on surfing if all I can think about is how to break all her rules about no touching or kissing?

And now, here we are... about to move in together.

I push myself up and grab my bag from the overhead compartment, then follow Archie out the door. Britta is ahead of us, holding back her blonde hair to keep the wind from wreaking havoc with it as she walks the stairs to the tarmac. Her wide-legged jeans show off the length of her legs, and the t-shirt tucked into them emphasizes her slim waist.

When she glances over her shoulder and smiles at me, my breath catches. I smile back, but not before she turns back around, loops her arm through Stella's and bends close to tell her something.

"Dex?"

It's Archie. I've stopped moving again.

I lift my chin, then hurry down the last of the stairs while he waits. A black SUV waits for us—Rhys, more specifically—and the girls climb into the backseat.

"What are you thinking, mate?" Archie asks, like he doesn't already know the answer.

The driver closes the door to the SUV, and Britta disappears from my view.

"Being fake married is already heaps harder than your no-dating rule." I'm still staring at the spot where Britta stood a few seconds ago.

"Yeah. I thought it might be. Think you can keep it together until our Azores trip? You'll get a few weeks' reprieve there. Maybe we make time for Pipe, too." He looks at me and raises his eyebrows.

I nod.

Archie can tell I've got a problem.

Britta has become the distraction she wasn't supposed to be.

CHAPTER TWENTY-NINE

Britta

Two days after I become Mrs. Dexter (or Thomsen-Dexter...possibly Dexter-Thomsen—we're still workshopping it), I put a down payment on *Annie's*—in cash, thanks to Dex. That same day, Stella and I wheel our suitcases into the white marble foyer of Archie's dad's beach house—he and Dex close behind—then try not to trip over our jaws when they hit the floor.

I stop in the middle of the entrance, tip my head back, and gaze into an array of crystals hanging from a giant chandelier. Sunlight pours in from the window that frames the chandelier, hitting the crystals before being reflected into a thousand tiny rainbows to dance in its rays.

"Archie?" Stella's voice wobbles beside me, where she stares at the same thing I am.

"Yeah?" There's a hint of nervousness in Archie's tone, and I suspect we both have an idea what's on Stella's mind.

"How rich are you?" She rotates to face him, and I do the same. As impolite as the question is, I want to hear the answer.

"Like I said, this is my dad's place." He shifts my duffle bag he's carrying from one shoulder to the other and doesn't meet our eyes.

"Then how rich is he?" Stella asks.

This time I elbow her for being rude, even while I stare at Archie, waiting for his answer.

"None of your business." He walks between us toward a staircase tiled in the same white marble as the rest of the foyer. "Come on, I'll show you your rooms."

Dex follows, stopping long enough between Stella and me to mutter, "billions rich," before grabbing my suitcase handle and wheeling it to a doorway that I now realize is an elevator.

"This house has an elevator?" Stella's words bounce off the white walls and high ceiling, stopping Archie's ascent up the stairs long enough for him to let out a loud sigh.

"We'll meet you up there, mate!" Dex calls cheerfully.

Archie answers with a terse nod before continuing his climb while the three of us and our too-big suitcases squeeze into the shoebox-sized elevator. When the doors close, Dex and I are pressed so tightly together, our chests touch.

The hint of longing in the soft smile he sends me stops my breath. I turn in a slow, half-circle to escape his dark, widening pupils ringed with gold and to settle my staggering-drunk pulse. Every part of me touches him in my attempt to put space between us, until finally, we're not chest to chest, but butt to... not chest. Not even waist. Lower.

And this is not better.

His balmy, coconut scent fills the tight space and makes me want to dive into the ocean with him—a feeling I'm trying very hard to avoid by not getting too close to him, literally and figuratively. It's hard enough not to find some excuse to touch him whenever I'm within an arm's-length. And the little I learned about him on our wedding night made me want to get to know him better—to share that closeness with him again.

The tight quarters on the airplane yesterday were torture. Dex didn't make things any easier with the way he kept brushing his fingers on my leg or arm. And now I'm pressed up against him in the Slowest Elevator Ever about to catch fire every time he brushes against me.

"Did anyone press the button?" Stella asks after eternities pass and we still haven't reached the second floor. "I don't think we're moving."

She answers her own question by reaching past me to push the round *up* button. The elevator stutters to a start, and she tips into me, forcing me even closer to Dex.

"Oh, my gosh! I'm so sorry!" she exclaims, but I don't miss the grin she's trying to hide.

Fortunately, the ride is short. As soon as the door opens, I push my way past Stella, gasping for Dex-free air and space.

Archie's waiting in the hallway and leads us to a closed door. "This one's all yours, Britta. Unless you'd rather share with Stella."

"Up to you," I say to Stella, forcing my eyes wide so she knows the right answer.

I begged Stella to stay another week and somehow she talked Georgia into it. Good thing, too, because, despite her shenanigans on the elevator—or maybe because of my reaction to them—I need a buffer here between Dex and me.

Stella grins at me, then turns to Archie. "If you've got a room for me, I'll take it. Britta snores."

"You can have your own room." Archie laughs, then twists the knob, and the door swings open.

I send Stella a withering glare for both her snoring comment and her unbuffer-like demand for her own room, before stepping past Archie into a space half the size of the entire house I grew up in. There's a sitting area with a fireplace, a giant TV hanging on the wall, and an office nook. The colors are all soft blues and light beige, reflecting the view of the beach and ocean outside the sliding glass door that leads to a patio.

And the bed? That's big and fluffy enough to rival the one Dex and I had at the Mansion. I wonder if he's thinking the same thing, but I don't dare look, afraid he'll see how hard I'm fighting not to think about his arms around me, holding me, letting me cry.

"Are all the rooms this big?" I ask Archie.

He shakes his head. "Dex wanted you to have the primary bedr oom."Now I look at Dex, whose slow shrug is followed by an even slower smile. "Least I could do."

I look back at Archie. "You really don't want to live here? This room is bigger than your entire apartment."

Archie lets out an exasperated sigh. "Bigger doesn't mean better. I have reasons for staying where I am."

Before I can come up with any other arguments, Archie leads Stella out the door to her room. "There's a bathroom between your room and Dex's, but if you don't want to share with him, maybe you can use Britta's," he says as they walk down the hall.

Which prompts me to open the door on the opposite wall from the bed, which has to lead to the bathroom. I gasp before I have it all the way open.

"I thought you'd like it," Dex says behind me.

I turn slowly, taking in the white marble, dark wood, and tasteful touches of gold. "This is the biggest bathroom I've ever seen."

He laughs. "Check out the size of the tub. Figured you'd enjoy a soak in that."

"I can't wait." I run my fingertips along the curved edge of the free-standing porcelain bathtub, then look back at Dex.

Red creeps across his cheeks and, like a rock over still water, my heart skips.

"Where's your room?" With my thumb and pinky, I twist Mom's ring around my finger.

Dex's eyes don't leave mine as he wags his head toward the hall. "Right across the hall."

"So... close?"

He nods.

I swallow.

And Stella yells. "Britta, you've got to come see this!"

Dex and I huff a laugh at the same time, our eyes still locked, before I walk past him, closer than I need to in this giant bathroom, because, as I've already admitted, I'm like a bear to honey. I can't stop helping myself to Dex, no matter how sticky the situation might get.

"Coming!" I call, then follow her excited voice to a room only slightly smaller than mine, but with a life-sized picture of the whole squad from *Surf City High*.

She spends the next ten minutes asking Archie and Dex random questions about the show's winding character arcs that are so specific, neither one of them can answer. Dex just laughs, but Archie's energy depletes faster than a pin-pricked balloon leaking air.

In a moment of silence, when Stella spots a pod of dolphins and runs to her room's balcony to watch them, Dex says, "we'll leave you girls to unpack. Archie and I are going to catch a few waves while the surf's good."

"Oh... Okay." I'm not sure why this surprises me—that Dex will go on with his regular life, like nothing's changed. Technically, nothing really has, even if my life has taken a one-hundred-eighty degree turn in the past four days. "Maybe I'll see you later tonight, then?"

"Maybe." Dex bobs his head up and down, then turns to leave.

He's almost to the door, and my stomach is somewhere near the floor when he stops, pivots, and lets his mouth slide into a mischievous grin. "Unless you'd rather leave unpacking for later and take your first surf lesson instead."

My stomach may as well be bungee jumping, the way it shoots back up into my chest when Dex's brown eyes—two smooth, shimmering espressos—meet mine.

"I would absolutely rather surf with you," I say without even thinking about it.

Only when Archie closes his eyes and, in a tiny, almost imperceptible motion, shakes his head, do I wonder if I should have said no.

But the thought gets lost in Dex's dimpled smile.

CHAPTER THIRTY

Dex

Instead of walking out the back door and surfing a perfect, curling wave, we drive fifteen minutes south to a beach with a nice, fluffy wave, just right for a beginner. Archie's not happy about it, but he'll get over it. I'm also not the one who has to go with Stella to rent a longboard, since there was only one at the house, and she wants to learn too. That's Archie's job.

My job is to teach my wife how to surf; a job I plan to enjoy.

Britta and I head to the beach while Archie and Stella find a board. We drop our stuff, and Britta peels off her T-shirt and shorts to reveal a colorful bikini with enough blue to highlight her eyes and little enough fabric to show off her shape. She's tall and thin with the right amount of feminine curves, but not so many that she'll have trouble popping up on her board. Lotta fellas prefer more up top, but I like a girl with a more athletic build.

Far as I'm concerned, Britta's got the perfect body. But I might be biased because she's got a cracker personality, too.

Either way, I hate to cover up the view, but I hand her a wetsuit—one a girl I dated left behind. "You'll want this. It's cold out there, and it'll protect you from board rash. Wax makes the deck rough as sandpaper."

While Britta sticks her feet into the tight legs and shimmies the neoprene suit over her thighs, I try to keep my focus on her board, pointing out the curved nose, flat deck, the sides we call rails, and finally the fins. At last, she's done shaking her hips side-to-side in a motion that makes me too hot to even think about putting on my wetsuit. Climate change has nothing on me. Ocean temps are about to rise another degree or two once I get in the water.

I help Britta zip up, then carry her board into the water. When we're waist deep, I strap the leash onto her ankle before holding the board so she can get on. "First thing is to teach you how to balance on your board and how to paddle."

Foamy waves roll around us, bobbing Britta's board up and down and making her wobble.

"Scoot up a bit more," I tell her, steadying her board. When she doesn't move, I shift from the front of her board to the side where I can hold the board's rails, one arm stretched across her back to the opposite rail from me.

"You don't want to be too high up toward the nose," I continue, ignoring the way my arm brushes her neoprene-covered butt with each gentle roll of the wave. "You gotta find the sweet spot where you feel steady. Don't fight the wave. Roll with it."

After a couple minutes, her breathing levels out, and I feel her sink into the board a bit, trusting it, herself, and the ocean. "I think I've got it."

"Feels alright, yeah?" I loosen my grip on the other side and slide my hand to her lower back. "Next is lifting your chest. Ever done yoga?"

Britta nods.

"Hands on your board, next to your heart, then peel your chest up, like in an upward dog or cobra."

She nods, and in one fluid motion, moves her hands and lifts her chest, following her breath like she's on a yoga mat, not bobbing in the ocean, and it's so beautiful—*she's* so beautiful—that I want to applaud.

"Good on ya', Britt. Beaut move."

She glances over her shoulder at me, her wet hair falling across her opposite shoulder. "Really?"

I nod, feeling like I've had the wind knocked from me, but in the best way.

Suddenly a rogue wave, no more than a foot, rolls under us, and I lose my hold on her board. Britta panics and slips off into the water. She goes under before she can find her feet, and the retreating wave pulls her into deeper water.

The board strapped to her leg doesn't help because she can't get her legs under her. I dive under the board and swim around her kicking legs to pop up behind her.

"Hold still so I can undo the leash," I say quickly before going back under to unstrap her from the board.

Without the board, her toes scrape the sand, and I hold her hand, helping her forward until we're both in waist-level water again. White-wash carries the board to the beach, but I keep hold of Britta, until she's steady again. I move in front of her, so I can see incoming waves and she can see the beach isn't far away.

"You alright?" With one hand on her hip, I use my other to push back the hair from her face, fighting every urge to kiss her.

Her head moves up and down in quick jerks and she grips my biceps so tight her nails dig into my skin. "Just scared me."

Another wave threatens to pick her up, and she gasps.

"I've got you. Just hold on to me." I circle my hands around her waist and lace my fingers together. "Slide your hands around my neck."

Her eyes go wide with fear.

"Trust me. We're going to work on getting comfortable with the movement of the ocean—it's always moving, not like a lake."

Britta's breath slows, and one at a time, she slides her hands from my arms, over my shoulders, to the back of my neck. We lock eyes. I smile and take a deep breath. Her fingers go soft, and I pull her tighter to me.

"Close your eyes," I whisper, brushing my nose across her cheek.

She takes a slow, deep breath, then lowers her lids. I slide my hand higher on her back, between her shoulder blades, and drag my thumb along the side of the zipper that would be so easy to undo.

"Dance with me, Britta." My voice scrapes with the memory of her glowing in her green dress on our wedding day, my hand on her bare skin.

"I haven't learned these steps." Her words skip with a nervous excitement that sends my pulse racing.

"I'll teach you. Put your feet on mine."

She steps onto the tops of my feet, and with the next gentle wave, I push up from the bottom so we roll with it. On its return, I let it carry us backwards. Then I do the same thing again and again.

"Feel how the salt makes you more buoyant?"

Britta dips her head up and down. "The water feels heavier, somehow. Denser."

"Just flow with it, and you'll float."

With each wave, Britta relaxes a little more, letting the ocean carry her instead of fighting it. Trusting me to keep us steady as we move to deeper water. Not so far that I can't touch, but deep enough that we have to duck under a few stronger waves. The more comfortable she gets, the more she loosens her hold on me, slowly trusting her own ability to read the wave and flow with it.

Until, finally, she floats to my side, keeping her fingers twined through mine but otherwise standing on her own, and we move up and down, dancing together. Letting the waves carry us where they will without losing our hold on each other.

And I know, as well as I know the ocean, that I never want this moment to end. I want Britta by my side through every up and down. Through every rogue wave that may pummel us. Through the next three years and beyond.

I want Britta forever, but I promised her I wouldn't fall in love.

I'm in so much trouble.

CHAPTER THIRTY-ONE

Britta

Over the next week, while Dex surfs in the early morning, I head to *Annie's* to not only help but also to get to know the crew and the business that will be mine in ten days. Maybe I should be worried about how fast things are moving with the business, but it feels right.

Annie made continuing the Employment Training Program for Unhoused Residents of South Bay a condition of the sale, and I'm excited—if not a little intimidated by that. I would have wanted to continue it anyway, but making the sale conditional on keeping the program showed both my commitment to it and made things a million times easier to keep the funding Annie used for it.

I think Mom would be proud of me. Everyone in my family has been calling to see how things are going with *Annie's* and to encourage me.

The sale of *Britta's* hasn't gone through yet, but once it does, I'll use my portion to pay back some of the loan Dex gave me. Dad's portion too, because he won't take no for an answer. I still won't take my brothers' though. The only way I could let *Britta's* go is by knowing there will be a new one with the proceeds from the sale.

As it is, I'm glad I won't be there when my *Britta's* comes down. I'm also relieved that *Annie's* is keeping me too busy—and excited—to mourn the end of an era.

To my family's credit, any suspicions about whether my impromptu marriage to a famous surfer has anything to do with where I got a down payment for *Annie's*, they keep to themselves. Just like I keep to myself questions about just how *much* money Dex has made surfing.

I mean, obviously I do some googling, so I have a rough idea. Between earnings from winnings, sponsorships, and product placements, the answer is... a lot. The size of the estimated number actually makes me like Dex even more. Not because he has money, but because it doesn't matter to him that he does.

He doesn't drive a fancy car, have a lot of things, or wear expensive clothes. He doesn't even wear shirts most days—and I'm not complaining about that. Best of all, he doesn't have the attitude that he's better than anybody else, just because he has money. He treats everyone the same, from the baristas at *Annie's* to the celebrities who occasionally stop him to say hi. He's best friends with Rhys James and never even mentions it.

Running a business in a resort town, I've noticed how some wealthy people act like their money makes them better than people with outdated clothes and beat-up trucks. Not all of them, of course, but enough that I sort of expect it. So, the fact that he—and *billionaire*-adjacent Archie, for that matter—choose to live a middle-class lifestyle is admirable.

Basically, Dex is a pretty great guy.

Which—to quote him when something potentially catastrophic happens—is *a bit of a problem*.

The last thing I need right now is to fall in love with my husband. But the more time I spend with Dex, the more that risk increases.

It doesn't help that after our first surf lesson, every afternoon, once I'm done at *Annie's* and he's done surfing, Dex takes me back to the same beach to continue our lessons. Stella and Archie usually come too, so it's not like we're alone.

But it feels like we are.

Every time he touches me, I lose all sense of anything else. All I can feel is his skin on mine. All I smell is coconut oil and sunshine. I only see him. I only hear *him*.

And I really want to taste his kisses again.

"I honestly had no idea it would take this long to learn how to surf," I say to him at the end of our first week of lessons, after I've finally stayed upright long enough to ride a wave all the way to the beach.

We peel out of our wetsuits, then lie face-up on the beach, eyes closed, warm sand under our towels, the sun lingering on the horizon. I'm exhausted, but Dex is resting up before he catches some last waves. He'll have to paddle out a ways to get past the "fluffy" ones I've finally conquered. That's when I'll sit up and watch.

This is the routine we've established, and I can't tell what gives me a bigger adrenaline rush: surfing myself or watching him.

When I hear Stella's laugh and Archie's heavy footsteps, I open my eyes and sit up.

"Well done, Stella." Dex says to her. "You're almost not a grom anymore."

"What's a grom?" She reaches past me to grab a towel from her bag, dripping cold water on my bare stomach.

"Stella!" I wipe the water away and grab Dex's Rip Tide hoodie, which is technically mine now by virtue of possession being nine-tenths of the law.

"A rookie or a newbie," Dex answers.

"She had a good teacher," Archie says.

"Sure. But did you see Britta out there?" Dex—always the competitor—shoots back.

Archie scoffs. "If she comes out every day, she'll be ready for a bigger wave once we're back."

I pop my head out of the hoodie, not sure I've heard Archie right. "Back from where? Are you going somewhere?"

Archie glances at Dex, who drops his head, letting Archie take the question. "The Azores."

"Where's that?" I assume somewhere close—like Lower Trestles or Huntington—until Dex shoots Archie a glare before turning to me.

"Middle of the Atlantic—a thousand miles off the coast of Portugal," he says in a tone heavy with apology.

"Oh." I'm surprised he hasn't mentioned it, and maybe a little hurt. Which quickly changes to annoyance with me for feeling anything at all and with Dex for acting like he needs to apologize for not telling me. What we have is a business arrangement, not a relationship.

"When do you leave?" I ask in as neutral a tone as I can manage.

"Tomorrow night," Archie answers.

"That soon?" Dex asks, digging his toes into the sand.

"Look at your calendar, mate. Everything's right there." Archie isn't just reminding Dex of his schedule. It sounds like he's reminding Dex what he should be focused on... and that's not me.

"I'm leaving tomorrow, too. I told you both that." Stella says to Archie and Dex, the protectiveness in her voice making things even worse. She's probably thinking Dex shouldn't be leaving me alone.

But I'm a big girl. Just because this will be my first time alone in LA, doesn't mean I can't handle it.

"Sounds fun," I say too cheerfully. "Good waves there, I'm guessing."

Stella tosses her towel on her board, then peels her arms out of her wetsuit. "I'd stay if I could, Britt. But Georgia needs me back in Paradise. They start filming Monday."

She looks at me, but her voice is barbed with blame directed at Dex and Archie, and they know it.

"We don't have to go," Dex says to Archie.

"Whatever you want, mate," Archie holds up his hands. "But you gotta get in more than these little waves here before Pipe."

"Nobody has to stay for me." I don't tiptoe around what everyone knows we're talking about. I push myself up and brush the sand from my butt. "I've got plenty to do with *Annie's,* but it's stuff I can do alone."

That's a lie and they all know it. I've got remodeling plans to make, materials to find, supplies to order, account books to look over. I could use help just running errands. But I don't appreciate being handled like a crystal vase packaged in bubble wrap and labeled FRAGILE. I'll be fine by myself. In fact, it will be nice to finally have some time alone. I haven't had that in years.

"You could come with us," Dex says to me with a nervous anticipation.

My brain lights up with a rush of dopamine, tempting me to say yes, but Archie answers before I have a chance.

"No, she can't. You need to stay focused. Your training is already off this week." His voice rises. Not with anger. More with frustration. "You married Britta to get to the Olympics. Remember that."

"I haven't forgotten I have a wife," Dex says in a low, gravelly voice I've never heard. "That's why I want her to come with us. I don't want to leave her here alone."

Heat simmers between Archie and Dex, then prickles my skin as it travels to my chest and settles there, heavy and claustrophobic. It's the same feeling I had when my family told me what they'd decided about *Britta's*. Once again, I'm being left out of decisions that are about me. Dex and Stella don't think I can be alone, and Archie doesn't want me around.

So I do the one thing I can do: pretend I'm fine until I am.

With my back to all of them, I rummage through my bag and take out my wallet. "Are you surfing, Dex? I'm going to grab a snack to tide me over until we leave. I'm starved."

Without waiting for his answer, I walk toward the weathered snack stand, hoping it's actually open. I can't tell with my eyes watering, which fills me with a frustration that only makes them water more.

I shouldn't be upset. I can't even pinpoint why I am. Partly because Stella is leaving. That was always the plan—for her to leave before I did. But that was when this trip to LA was a long vacation, not a complete change in my life's trajectory.

And maybe I'm upset at Archie's reminder that my job as Dex's wife is to give Dex a legal path to the Olympics, then stay out of his way so he can focus on surfing. That was the deal I not only agreed to but also worked into my list of conditions.

Maybe I'm also a little afraid I've made a mistake buying *Annie's* and staying in LA instead of going back to Paradise and everything—and everyone—that I know. I am fine to be here alone, but I'm also nervous about it. I hate driving in this traffic and have been able to avoid it. I don't want to go to restaurants by myself or be alone in that big beach house. I'm used to being surrounded by people and now I won't be. I've traded all that comfort in for a fake marriage and a very expensive investment that could both go completely wrong.

The closer I get to the snack stand, the more my lungs burn and the shorter my breaths get. By the time I get to the sidewalk, I'm gasping for air. I bend over to stop the world from spinning, my hands on my knees, head below my heart.

"Britta?" Dex's voice is close, and his hand is on my back before I see him. "You alright?"

I nod, my breath already slowing at the sound of his voice and his touch, but I stay bent over and I'm humiliated that he's seeing me lose it like this.

"You sure about that?" He rubs his hand down my back, then up again.

I take a deep breath, stand upright, and give Dex a smile that's mostly real. "Yeah. I'm good."

He tips his head and studies me, letting seconds pass before he says, "I'm sorry about the trip. It's been scheduled for months. But why don't you come with me?"

I make a sound that's both a huff and a snort and could only be created with a lump in my throat. "I'll be okay here by myself. I'm just... tired. And I'll miss... uh, Stella."

Surprise crosses Dex's face. "Of course, you're okay here by yourself..." He lifts a shoulder. "I just like being with you. That's why I invited you. The Azores are gorgeous. You'd like it there and once you take over ownership of the shop, you won't be able to travel much, if at all."

The warmth in his honey brown eyes tempts me to say yes. California is the furthest I've ever been from Paradise, and I probably should take some time for myself while I still can. Traveling to another country sounds magical, especially with Dex. And I do love watching him surf, but...

"Would I have to fly?"

"Um, yes," Dex says. "It's in the middle of the ocean."

"Yeah, well, that's a deal breaker for me. I've sworn off air travel. And there's this little coffee shop idea I've been bouncing around." I shrug to emphasize how casual my little coffee shop is. "But I hope you have a great time."

Dex laughs. "Come on, Britt. If you can marry a fella you hardly know—one whose only skill is totally useless outside of the ocean—why are you so afraid to fly?"

"You have lots of skills beyond surfing, but you make a good point about the flying." I'm about to say maybe, but then something else comes out. "I can't."

He lowers his head and frowns, then looks back at me. "Even if I promise I'll follow all the rules?"

Now I let out a genuine laugh. "No, Dex. I'm not worried about that. I'd love to go, but I've never been out of the country. I don't have a passport."

A slow smile spreads across his face, and his relief is palpable. "We've gotta fix that, then. You've gotta be able to travel the world at a moment's notice if we're going to be married."

"I don't remember that being one of your conditions." My heart pounds. I'm wading into dangerous waters, but I follow the pull of the tide anyway. "But it's not too late to amend our contract."

"That's possible?" Dex moves closer, and his smile is replaced by a look I haven't seen before. Both serious and tentative. "Maybe we could make some changes to the kissing parts, too?"

Dex jokes a lot. He's not doing that now. He wasn't joking when he called me his wife or got in a tiff with his best friend over it. He wasn't joking when he said he wanted me to go to the Azores with him.

And I *want* to go. So. Much. Not just because I've always wanted to travel, but also because I'm really going to miss him.

I've loved almost every moment I've spent with Dex, even before we got married. The only moments I haven't loved are the ones where I've forced myself to keep my distance from him. The times when I could have touched him but didn't and every time I've said goodnight before going to bed alone, then waking in the morning wishing Dex were there.

"Maybe." I can barely speak.

Cautiously, Dex slips a hand around mine, then looks at me with a question. *Is this okay?* I don't pull away, which is all the answer he needs to step closer while brushing his thumb across the top of my wrist.

"Maybe more than kiss, Britta?" He leans his forehead against mine and my pulse takes off faster than if I were mainlining triple espresso shots. "You're so much more than a way to the Olympics for me. You stopped being that the second you became my wife."

"Your wife?" I haven't forgotten we're married, but hearing him say I'm his wife adds so much more weight to our agreement.

He's called me "my wife" twice today. Both times, the words have taken my breath away. I suspect they have the potential to always do that to me. Like when I crest the last mountain before dropping into Paradise Valley. Suddenly there's the lake shining turquoise blue in the center of it all, a sapphire set in gold. I've driven into that breathtaking view a million times, and I could do it a million more without ever tiring of its beauty.

Hearing Dex say *my wife* feels like going home.

And I'm terrified.

That's not what this relationship is supposed to be.

"What are you asking, Dex?" I whisper the question, both afraid and excited for the answer.

Dex puts a few inches between us, then lifts my chin to meet his eyes. "That we quit acting like what we feel—what we've both felt since the day we met—is a short-term business deal and see if it could be the real thing; a long-term deal."

There's an intensity in his gaze that I've only seen on the day of the Championship when he was determined to beat the odds and win. It's a look that dares me to rush in without thinking, without measuring the costs of getting in over my head and being pummeled by waves I'm not ready for.

When Dex lets go of my hand to tuck a wet strand of hair behind my ear, I catch his hand and clutch it by my side. In another day he'll be gone, and I don't want to let him go until then. "How long are you in Portugal?"

"A week. Maybe two. Depends on the waves."

I nod. Everything always depends on the waves.

And then, because waves are unpredictable, and I don't know when I'll have the chance again, I step into Dex's arms, slide my hands over his shoulders to the nape of his neck and kiss him hard enough to silence the ocean lapping the sand, the people squealing with delight in the water, and my own doubts.

CHAPTER THIRTY-TWO

Dex

I carry Britta's kiss with me halfway across the world, all the way to Portugal. I'm not sure if her kiss meant *yes* to making this a proper relationship, or *maybe*. I don't think it meant no. Not when I can still smell the sea in her hair, taste the salt on her lips, feel the warmth of her skin where I slid my hand under her jumper—*my* jumper—to her bare back. I remember every second. It's all I can think about.

Literally, I forget everything else, including Archie sitting next to me on our sixteen-hour flight. That's a little on purpose. I'm still irritated with him for implying all Britta means to me is a ticket to the Olympics. Britta didn't act offended, but Archie can't go around saying stuff like that, especially now that Britta and I have opened up about how we really feel.

When we finally land, our plan is to island-hop around Sao Miguel, Terceira, and Sao Jorge, following the wind and the swells. I haven't been to the Azores in years. They're remote and less crowded than Nazare and other sites in Portugal. Santa Catarina off Terceira rivals Hawaii's Pipe with a freakishly quick drop into an instant barrel that skims across shallow reef. It'll be good practice before the first Championship Tour event at Pipe in January and the perfect place to refocus on what should be my one and only priority: surfing.

At least, that was my intention. I should be stoked about the swell when we get to Santa Catarina. The wave coming off the reef is perfect, and I get a rush of adrenaline watching it. But after paddling out and dropping in, I wipe out.

I do the same thing again and again and again. Even when the swell dies down, I still get raked over.

Finally, the last time I get tumbled over the reef, Archie waves me in. I climb over the rocks to get back to shore, breathing hard and hurting everywhere, probably bleeding somewhere. I hand off my board to Archie before I'm close enough and he has to lean farther to yank it from me.

"Let's go, mate, before you get hurt. Your head's not where it's supposed to be." He tucks my board under his arm and leaves me to scramble over the last few rocks.

"Yeah? You got something to say about where it is?" I catch up to him, then shake my head hard enough the water from my hair sprays him.

Archie turns. "Somewhere south of your shoulders, shoved up pretty far."

We glare at each other for a few seconds before walking to our rental car and heading back to the resort where we're staying. I'm a whacker, fighting with my manager and best mate. But everything is off being so far from Britta, worrying she might be lonely or that she might need help with *Annie's*. I'm not even able to contact her because the Wi-Fi here sucks and the time difference makes it hard to connect for more than a few minutes.

Things don't get better over the next few days. We extend our time in Santa Catarina based on the wind and swell reports from the other waves we plan to surf. Sets are still ripper here, and I hate walking away from a wave before I've conquered it.

Problem is, I can't quit thinking about Britta. On or off the wave, she's front and center in my brain. Every morning before Archie and I head for the beach, I check my phone to see if I've got enough bars to call or text her. On our fourth morning there, as we're walking out of our room, I finally do.

I stop in the middle of the hallway; afraid I'll lose reception if I move.

"This wind changes, and you're going to miss your wave." Archie's voice is as tight as his clenched jaw as he watches me typing into my phone.

The wind is predicted to change this afternoon, so we're checking out and moving on today deeper into the bush. Who knows what the reception will be like there?

"Just checking in with Britt while I've got service." I'm not keen on taking orders from him at the moment, so I type slower than I usually would.

"She's seven hours behind. It's the middle of the night there."

A growl works its way up the back of my throat, and I pull my lips in to keep it from escaping. I hate it when Archie thinks about things I don't. It's why he makes a good manager, but right now he's a pain in my butt. "Then she'll get it when she wakes up and know that I'm thinking about her."

"You wanna get on with it and tell me what's wrong, or you wanna keep messing around?" Archie's got me by half a head, and he uses those inches to hover over me.

"You were a tool to my wife." I don't back away. I've taken him in a brawl before. I can do it again if that's what it comes to.

Archie pulls back, looking genuinely surprised. "When?"

His scoffing tone riles me even more. How can he know everything except when he's being a jerk?

"You told her she's only good for getting me to the Olympics." I throw out my hands, challenging him.

Archie blinks hard, like I've slapped him. "No. I reminded *you* that you married her to get to the Olympics."

I shake my head for lack of anything better to say. I hate it when he uses facts to win an argument. "Doesn't mean you weren't a jerk the way you said it."

Archie's eyes go wider, like he has no idea what he's done. "Mate, I wasn't saying it to her. She's got way more on the line here than you do. I'm trying to protect her from *you*."

"Protect her? That's my job. She's *my* wife." I move closer so our chests are inches apart, both of us puffed up and ready to go.

"Yeah?" His face turns a darker red than his hair. "Have you thought about what happens if you don't make it to the Olympics because you lose focus and fall off Tour or get injured again?"

I stare at him, beginning to think I may have it wrong about who's being a jerk. "I don't make the team," I say finally.

"Right." He pokes me in the chest. "In the meantime, Britta's gone quarter of-a-mill in debt to you, given up falling in love with any other blokes, and risked going to jail for you. I see what's happening between you guys and it's going to lead to disaster, mate. You're going to lose your head, same as you did the first time you fell off Tour, and she's going to end up with a broken heart. This is supposed to be a business arrangement, but that's not what's happening, right?"

Archie emphasizes his right with another poke to my chest. I brush his hand away, but not with any anger. That's been washed away with the realization that I, in fact, am the tool. "I hear what you're saying," I mumble.

"Then pull your head out of your backside and decide whether you can really be in a relationship and stay at the top of your game—based on what I've seen since we got here, you can't," Archie's face is bright red now, and he's absorbed all the anger I've shed. "If I'm right, then don't toy with Britta. You mess up this relationship, it hurts her more than you, but you'll have to live with that. Got it?"

I drop my head. "Got it."

Archie turns and stalks down the hall, leaving me behind. I glance at the bars on my phone—still there—before I tuck it away and jog to catch Archie.

He's fast and is on the elevator before I can get there, so I take the stairs. I'm standing in front of the elevator doors when they slide open. Archie's face is back to his normal color, but he still meets me with a glare.

"Thanks, mate," I say. "You're right. I appreciate you looking out for Britta."

He nods, and his mouth pulls into a half-smile.

There's something neither one of us has thought of, though, but his worry about me getting hurt again made me think of it and take what he's said even more to heart. It's a legitimate worry, getting hurt. Surfing is a dangerous sport. I haven't met any pro who hasn't had a concussion—or half-a-dozen. Most have had other serious injuries, too.

"I need you to do something else for me," I say as Archie and I walk toward the car.

"What?" Archie keeps walking, only half paying attention, so I grab his arm to stop him.

"If I get injured again—something like last time, or worse—" At this, Archie raises his eyebrows.

My back injury took nearly six months to heal. There aren't many worse injuries. At least not the kind you can recover from.

"I don't want Britta taking care of me," I tell him. "She may feel obligated, but she's not. She's not giving up anymore of her life. At least not for me... Will you make sure she's not left responsible for me?"

Archie nods with his whole body.

The rest of the day, I work hard to push thoughts of Britta out of my mind every time she breaks in—which is a lot. She responds to my text by midafternoon for her, but late for me. I don't respond.

We've been in the Azores for four days and I haven't caught a single decent wave. It's not Britta's fault, it's mine, but it's tied to thoughts of her—that's obvious now. By the next morning, I'm feeling clearer, and my focus is better. I want the Olympics, which means I need to win at Pipe in January.

Once I focus on what I should be, I catch my first good wave that afternoon and I don't wipe out again in the Azores.

CHAPTER THIRTY-THREE

Britta

I was okay the first few days after Dex and Stella both left. I had plenty to keep me busy, and Stella texted me about a million times to make sure I was okay. Dex called and texted too and sent some pictures of where they are, but the time difference made it difficult to really communicate.

Then Stella's texts slow to a trickle. Obviously, she hasn't forgotten me, she's just busy managing Georgia's socials now that *At Home with Georgia* is back on air. But I've spent the past five years talking to her every day, and it's weird not to. I've always been surrounded by family—even when I went to college, I was only an hour away and came home often.

For the first time in my life, I don't have that, and I didn't anticipate how lonely I would be without it. Especially in an enormous
city full of unfamiliar faces.

To make matters worse, as soon as Stella's texts stop, Dex is basically unreachable. I don't think he's ignoring me. He's just in
a really remote area. But, for whatever reason, his unintentional
silence makes me feel more forgotten than Stella straight-up ghosting
me. I miss talking to him, and I hate being alone in a great big house
that still doesn't feel like home.

Days stretch into a week filled with too much space and quiet for
my thoughts to replay our last words.

Our last kiss.

Did I make a mistake kissing him that day on the boardwalk? I
didn't answer his question about whether our marriage could be
more than a business arrangement, but my kiss left little room for
interpretation. In the moment, I meant that I'd like to see if our
marriage could be a "long-term deal."

But in the week and the distance that separates us, I grow less sure.
I hate missing Dex as much as I do. I hate worrying that this dull ache
will become more painful the longer we're together. Leaving is part
of his job. And it's part of why I agreed to this—he'd be gone too
often for me to get attached.

Now, here I am, only a few weeks into being Dex's wife, and I'm
already attached to him like weeds to Velcro.

The second week Dex is gone, I spend as much time at *Annie's* as
possible. Mostly because I'm days away from taking ownership, but
also because it's too noisy and busy for me to get lost in thoughts of
Dex. When I'm not there, I'm on the phone with Dad or my brothers, getting their advice about everything from business practices to
renovation ideas, and counting down the days until they arrive to
help with renovations.

When I'm home alone, it's too easy to give into my loneliness and pull-on Dex's Rip Tide hoodie, then check my phone at least a thousand times an hour to see if he's answered my texts or tried to call even though my phone stays silent.

I should be thrilled the day Annie turns over the keys to me and slips her apron over my head. I will officially have too much to do to think about Dex. This is the first day of owning my first business that's completely my own. It's the start of a (mostly) new store, a new direction, a new life.

But even though Annie is staying on a few hours a week for the first few months to help with the transition, I am terrified. Capital T, *Terr-i-fied*.

I don't tell Annie this, of course. Her step is a thousand times lighter after she turns the *Closed* sign for the last time and walks out the door. But I'm overwhelmed by a thousand different emotions. I sink into a seat and spend the next hour sitting alone at a table, staring at the espresso machines, small kitchen, white wood-paneled walls, and the *Surf City High* picture of Dex and his friends.

It's all mine, and there's no one here to celebrate with me. Bear and Adam are on their way from Idaho, but I told them they didn't have to be here until tomorrow, when we'll be able to work a full day. I wish I hadn't. I wish I could make the first cups of coffee in my shop and toast my success with my family.

And with Dex. I wish he were here, too.

I'll be able to toast with my brothers tomorrow, but I don't know when Dex will be back.

Annie's will be closed for a week while I renovate before re-opening—new name still to be determined. There's a lot to do before then. I have a plan drawn up of what needs to be done and where to start, but I'm too overwhelmed to look at it, even if I could find the motivation to turn on an overhead light. Instead, I rest my arms on the table and drop my head into them.

Dusk settles outside. The dining area grows dim with only the light outside the front door shining through the tinted plate-glass window. I'm not sure how much time passes. I fill the time by giving myself an internal pep talk. It's a good talk with lots of *you've got this* and *you're living your dream*. I don't believe everything I say, but I've almost convinced myself to at least look at my list when there's a knock on the locked front door.

I pick up my keys and clutch the pepper spray attached to them. I'm not expecting anyone, and the neighborhood can feel a little sketchy after dark. But I felt that way about *Britta's* when there were thousands of summer visitors I didn't know in town. The two large shadows outside the glass door, though, have me worried enough to pull out my phone in case I need to call the sheriff's department. But as I creep closer, the shape of the shadows grows surprisingly familiar, until I'm certain who they belong to.

I unlock the door and swing it open so my brothers, Adam and Bear, can walk in.

"What are you two doing here?" I throw my arms around them one at a time, feeling my strength return when they squeeze me tight.

"We knew you'd need us sooner than you thought you did," Bear says, with his arm still slung over my shoulder.

"You know me too well." I wrap my arms around my giant baby brother's waist and hug him again, tight enough to almost stop the tears threatening to fall. Adam pats my back, and I pull away from Bear and face them both. But then Adam screws up his face, and I sense an oldest-brother-lecture coming on.

"We brought ebelskiver pans in case you want to add those to your menu." Adam has two tones: gruff and tender. They're both combined now, and I'm as surprised by his words as I am by his early arrival.

"I hadn't planned to, but I think that's a great idea." A way to bring Mom and *Britta's* here.

Adam offers me a half-smile that disappears as quickly as it appears. "Where should we start with getting you ready to open?"

I resist the urge to hug him again. Bear could take it, but Adam holds his emotions close. The fact he's here is as emotive as he'll get to saying he's always going to look out for his little sister, no matter how far away she lives. I tuck back my smile and jog to the table where I've left my overwhelming to-do list. I hand it to Adam, and wait as he reads it, the lines between his eyebrows growing deeper by the second.

When he finishes, he sighs and presses two fingers along the middle of his forehead to his temple, then hands the paper to Bear.

"I'm glad we came early," Adam says, and I brace myself for the rest of the lecture that never comes.

"It's a long list, Britta." Bear's deep voice rumbles loudly, but gently over me.

"We'd better get started if we're going to get it all done," Adam says to Bear.

"Tonight?" I take the list back from Bear and check my watch. "It's six o'clock. Why don't we get dinner and start tomorrow morning?"

Adam lets out another long sigh, and I'm sure he's even more annoyed with me than he's letting on, but then Bear says, "We have to be on set Monday. We've only got four days to get everything done before we drive home."

I nod, relieved I'm not the only cause of Adam's irritation. He's the contractor on the cottages Georgia is renovating for her TV show, which means he ends up on camera more often than he likes. But since his wife, Evie, is Georgia's design partner and co-star, he has a hard time saying no when the camera points in his direction.

"You drove?"

"How else was I going to get all my tools here?" Adam is already headed for the door, which he walks out of on the tail of his rhetorical question.

"In one day?" I ask Bear, who nods before following Adam.

They must have left before the crack of dawn to make the fourteen-hour drive, which makes the gesture even more meaningful. I flip on all the lights, really smiling for the first time in days. Maybe for the first time in a week. Probably since Dex left.

When my brothers come back inside, Adam's got his tool belt strapped on and his arms full of ebelskiver pans while Bear is carrying his plumber's kit. Bear goes straight to the restrooms to check out the toilets that regularly leak and clog. Adam goes straight for the kitchen.

He does construction work for a living nine months out of the year, but during the summer months, he's got his own restaurant—the best one in Paradise. He's a trained chef, so he only needs one look at the kitchen before he's got ideas about how to rearrange things to flow more efficiently. They aren't big changes. We don't have to tear anything out or move appliances—thank goodness—but moving prep stations and service areas will still take time.

While they get started, I grab us some dinner from a great Mexican fusion place around the block. We take a twenty-minute break to eat it, then we work until midnight. We're up early the next morning and work for twelve hours straight and do the same the next day and the next.

Watching how quickly they get things done, I'm both grateful they're here, and embarrassed that I didn't ask them to come sooner. I should have known how much I'd need them.

For their part, Adam and Bear are both surprised how easy it is to get the supplies they need—including industrial-strength toilets—but I've already learned this is one advantage of living in a big city. You can always find what you need, and you don't have to wait for it to be shipped.

They only ask one question about Dex, and not until the last day they're here: *where is he?*

"Surfing." My face warms when they simultaneously raise their eyebrows.

"He can't take a break from *surfing* to help his wife open her coffee shop in the major city she's just moved to?" Bear doesn't hold back his judgy tone.

"In Portugal. He's surfing in Portugal," I answer, staying focused on the paint touch-ups I'm doing.

"That's not better, Britt. He should be here helping you with this place," Adam says firmly, leaving no room for argument. "You gave up your whole life to do this."

I try to defend Dex, anyway. "I'm sure he would have been if he'd known how much work it was going to be, but the trip was already planned before we got married, and he's getting ready for a big competition in January. Surfing is his job."

You'd think Bear was Adam's twin instead of Zach, the way he and Adam both scoff at the same time, in the same way, before saying in unison, "that's not a job."

"Well, it's Dex's job, and he makes good money doing it." I set down my paintbrush and wipe sweat from my forehead with the back of my hand.

I can't be mad at my brothers for thinking the same thing I used to. And the way our marriage came together doesn't look good. They barely knew Dex when they came to our over-the-top celebrity wedding ceremony on a Ferris wheel in Las Vegas. He hasn't tried overly hard to connect with them—he's not nearly as connected to his own family as I am to mine, but there also hasn't been time or opportunity.

I don't blame them for being concerned Dex isn't here, but I can stick up for him. I feel obligated to. Maybe because we said goodbye with a kiss and the possibility of more than a fake marriage. Or maybe because

I can't stop wishing he were here. Whatever the reason, even if I'm not ready for him to be my actual husband, Dex doesn't feel like just the "guy I married" anymore.

I want my brothers and dad to respect what he does and see for themselves how amazing he is. That a piece of me is missing when he's gone, and he's my refuge when he's here. He feels like laughter and tears, comfort and warmth.

Dex feels like... a partner. And I wonder if that's what having a husband is supposed to be like, which sends me back to being even more terrified than I was when Annie handed me the keys to her shop a few days ago.

"Is that where you got the money for this place, Britt?" Bear asks, innocently enough, but I hear subtext in the question. *The money from Britta's couldn't have been enough for a down payment.*

"He helped some," I mumble. I can't tell the whole truth, but I won't flat out lie.

A few feet away from me, Adam takes a nail from between his lips and hammers a loose bit of baseboard back into place, then asks, "Is that why you married him? For the money?"

I shake my head hard. "No, it's not."

It's not a lie. I wouldn't have married Dex just for money, and I'm going to pay him back.

"Are you in love with him, though?" Bear's voice rises an octave, and I hear the worry there.

My brothers are protective, but not *over*-protective. Mostly, they stay out of my way, unless they're sure I need help. I realize now that they're here not just because they knew I'd need help with the shop, but also because they think I need help with Dex. Like I've been conned into marrying him, or something. Their suspicion is obvious.

What's not so obvious is how to answer Bear's question about whether I'm in love with Dex. I'm not *not* in love with him. But am I in *love* with him? Do I want to be?

So, I answer the only way I can. "You'll like him once you get to know him. Dex is a great guy."

Adam says in his quiet, but authoritative voice, "you should be with someone because you love him, not because he's a good guy."

I hand him my paintbrush so he can touch up the spot on the baseboard he's nailed. "That may be how it's worked for you and Evie—you and Cassie, too, Bear—but I'm not really interested in loving someone like that at this point in my life." *Why does that feel like a lie?* "What Dex and I have works for us. We enjoy being together, but we're also okay being apart."

I think that's true. It feels true in my head. And it's the agreement Dex and I have. We keep each other focused on the most important things by not being a distraction or allowing each other to be distracted by the opposite sex.

"Then you're going to get bored with each other real fast," Adam says. He's always been the most cynical of all of us.

So, I'm surprised when Bear feels the same. "Yeah, Britt. You're missing out if you don't ache for someone when you're apart. You don't get the high that comes when you're back together. There's no better rush than that."

I'm quiet for a minute—that's exactly how I feel about Dex. Does that mean I'm... in love with him?

Oh gosh.

I pivot slowly toward Bear. "That's how you feel about Cassie?"

Bear nods and sighs at the same time. "My chest is on fire I want to be with her so bad."

I look at Adam, who rocks his whole body in agreement.

I miss hanging out with Dex, but no part of my body is burning with the need to see him again. I mean, there's a dull ache, but not anything so big that I'll have the best rush of my life when he gets home. I hope he gets home soon because it's more fun when he's there, and the house is too big for just one person. But I don't think either of those is a sign I'm in love with Dex.

My brothers and I work in silence for the next hour with only Adam's guitar-heavy playlist playing in the background. It's after ten when we're finally ready to pack up for the night. Most of my list is done. The rest I can finish with help from my barista crew before I reopen as...

Not *Annie's*. I want to build on what Annie has done, but I want the store to be mine. But I still haven't landed on a name. Everything has happened so fast that a new name has been low on the priority list, below getting married to get the money to buy *Annie's*, then make all the fixes it needs.

With both things checked off my to-do list, I can finally focus on what to call this place. That's what I'm thinking about as I rinse paintbrushes and roll up the tarp covering the floor. I'm so focused, I barely register the soft tap at the door. Adam hears it before I do and walks cautiously to the door, putting out his arm for me to stay behind when I follow.

But I push his arm away when I see who's there. I run to the door, adrenaline rushing so quickly through my veins, I can barely turn the key in the lock. When I throw open the door, happiness and relief wash over me.

Dex is home.

CHAPTER THIRTY-FOUR

Dex

Britta's got white paint on her cheek, more of it on her clothes and in her hair, and she looks exhausted. Oh, and she's got two giants standing behind her, their arms crossed, shooting daggers at me from the same blue eyes Britta has, but angrier. So much angrier.

Her *brothers*.

I realize I should've brought Archie for backup. He would have run at the first sight of them, but I'm faster than him, which means they would've got him first. But now I'm in the direct line of fire with no escape.

Except Britt throws her arms around me and says, "You're home," with so much relief in her voice—and in the kiss that follows—I forget for a second that I was fearing for my life. Then I glimpse her brothers and reality hits me again.

I reckon she is happy to see me, but she's also got to put on a show for... whichever brothers these two are. Then I worry where the missing brother is—lying in wait for a surprise attack? I wouldn't blame him. Because the other thing that's clear, as I take in the changes to the shop, is that I left Britta alone when she needed help. Not that I'm all that handy with a hammer, but I should have been here, and I didn't even consider it.

I pull away from her and drop my arms to my side. "When you weren't home, I figured you might be here. I was worried you'd be alone."

My eyes dart to the long-haired brother—Adam, he's the one with the man-bun—but quickly retreat at the searing glare he's got trained on me.

"She wasn't alone. We came down from Idaho to help," the other brother with the bushy beard—Bear, that's his name; because he's as big as one—says in a deep voice, and I can't tell if he means to scare me with the tone of his voice or if he's just stating a fact.

"So, the place is yours, then?" I ask Britta, which is a stupid question. Of course it is. "I'm sorry I wasn't here to help. I shouldn't have gone."

"All mine." Britta smiles and turns in a slow circle with her arms out. "If I'd known how much work I was in for, I would have told you to stay. Luckily, Adam and Bear showed up to save the day."

"Yeah... that's incredible." If she meant to make me feel better, it doesn't work. Not with her brothers staring at me like I'm the biggest doofus this side of Joe Rogan.

They're not wrong. That's the worst part. I've got no defense for leaving, other than *I was trying not to fall in love with your sister, who happens to be my wife.* I get the feeling they're already suspicious about mine and Britta's relationship, so anything I say is likely to muck things up even worse.

But I try anyway. "What can I help with?"

Britta shakes her head. "We're done with the big stuff, and I'm too tired to do anything else tonight. Adam and Bear leave early tomorrow, so I say we head home and get some rest."

She slips her arm around mine, and it feels so natural, I take her hand like her brothers aren't even there. I wish it was real.

"You sure there's nothing I can do?" I ask as she reaches for the light switch.

"Bear, grab the lights in the back, will you?" she says before turning to me, the dim light only making her glow more. "You can help me clean all this up tomorrow."

I scan the room, taking in paint cans, rollers and brushes. Canvas tarps cover the floor and dust covers everything else. So, I haven't missed my opportunity to help. There's still heaps of work.

"And help me think of a name." Britta squeezes my hand and bounces on her toes. "It can't stay *Annie's* without her here."

"End of an era." Even though it's still a construction zone in here, I see the changes Britta's already made. Fresh paint, new tables and chairs, different counter set up. Still *Annie's,* but with an update.

"Why not *Britta's*?" I ask as we walk hand-in-hand to the door.

"I thought about it, but it doesn't feel quite right. *Breakfast at Britta's* was always my great-grandma Britta's, even after Mom and then I took over. I think I want something that's all me." Britta lets go of my hand to lock the door, then takes it again. "I'll ride with you, if that's okay."

She waves to her brothers before I can answer. Doesn't matter. I'm keen to have some time alone with her without her bodyguards.

But our ten minutes alone as we drive back to the house isn't what I hoped. Not because of Britta. She's got heaps of questions about my trip that I try to answer, but my mind's on her brothers who looked ready to murder me and what Archie said back at the resort about my needing to be more aware of what Britta's sacrificed for me and how I shouldn't forget that. His words ring even truer now that I've seen all the work Britta did in her coffee shop without me there.

What if her brothers hadn't shown up? What if the waves in the Azores had been really stellar? I would have stayed longer, leaving Britta totally alone with a mountain of work to do in a place where she hardly knows anyone.

I knew she'd be getting the keys to *Annie's* while I was gone. I should have canceled the trip. But I didn't think twice about what my being gone would mean for Britta. My only concern was surfing. My only concern *is* surfing. Always has been. I've lived my whole life around it, and everyone close to me has lived their life in a way that makes it possible for me to surf.

That's not right. Especially in a marriage.

But I also can't change it if I'm going to stay competitive and make the Olympic team. Surfing has to stay my focus, as much for Britta as for me, otherwise she's sacrificed for nothing. I've got nothing else to contribute to this relationship other than the one thing I know how to do.

That's all I think about as we drive home in silence. By the time I pull into the garage, all I want to do is climb into bed. I'm knackered from traveling. I feel like a complete whacker, and I really don't want to socialize with Britta's brothers.

Adam and Bear haven't arrived yet, so I tell Britta goodnight and head up the stairs to my room. I only get halfway when Britta calls from the bottom.

"Dex! You'll have to stay in my room tonight."

I turn and blink.

"My brothers are staying here." Her cheeks turn pink, and that's all the explanation I need.

I nod. "Got it. I'll see you in a bit then."

After a quick shower, I go into Britta's room. I don't know when she did it, but she's already moved some of my things there. Probably before her brothers got here to make it look like this is a proper marriage.

But, maybe because of what I said before I left, about wanting to be more than a fake couple. Maybe her kiss that day was a yes, not a maybe.

Now, how do I tell her never mind?

I could sleep on the couch in the sitting area, except it's small and covered with Britta's folded clothes. Her brothers must have brought more than themselves and their tools when they showed up because boxes labeled *Britta* are stacked around the couch. They must have brought some things from home for her, which are now serving as a subtle reminder to me she hadn't planned on staying more than six weeks before I proposed the marriage that I promised would be strictly business.

The easiest thing to do tonight would be to fall asleep before she gets into bed and avoid any temptation to act on our feelings for each other. But as tired as I am, that's not what happens. I'm still wide awake, lying on top of the bed, wearing more clothes than I've slept in since my mum quit putting me in pyjamas, when Britta tiptoes in.

She goes straight for the bathroom, and for the next twenty minutes I listen to the buzzing of her electric toothbrush, then running water. Light peeks from under the door, and when the toothbrush, then the water stops, I hear her bare feet pad over the tile floor. Hard as I try, I can't stop myself picturing Britta changing for bed and wondering what she'll put on.

I hope it's something easy for me to say no to. Thick, flannel pyjamas under a floor-length robe. A retainer or other orthodontia. One of those green face mask things women put on in the movies might do the trick.

The door opens and muffled footsteps follow as Britta makes her way across the plush carpet to the bed. Steam from the bathroom follows her, making the room more humid than the air outside.

"You still awake, Dex?" Britta whispers as she climbs under the duvet.

I should fake sleep.

I don't.

"Yeah."

"Can we talk for a minute?" Her voice ripples through the surrounding air, and I couldn't say no even if I'd really wanted to.

"Reckon we can talk as long as I can keep my eyes open." I turn to face her, propping my head in my hand. "What's on your mind?"

"I'm wondering what's on yours. We didn't really finish talking before you left, and we didn't talk at all while you were gone." Britta flips on her side, peering at me through the dark.

I can't see what she's got on below her waist but she's wearing a jumper on top, and I should be relieved, not disappointed, about that. "I'm sorry. I didn't realize reception would be so shoddy."

She nods slowly, like she wants to believe me, but doesn't quite. "I guess I'm wondering if you still want to make this... our relationship... more than a business deal." Britta's words are careful. "I'm asking..." she continues. "Because—and maybe you're just tired and I'm jumping to conclusions—it seems like something's changed. But I need to know where I stand and what to expect, because when you came home today... I was really happy. Happier than I've been in a long time."

I'm surprised by her directness. Britta is good at saying what's on her mind, but not with feelings. Those she keeps tucked away like a Christmas present bought in July.

If she'd been less direct, maybe I could think of something to say besides the truth, but I can't. She deserves my honesty.

I roll to my back, then scoot close enough to slip my arm around her and pull her to my chest. "My feelings for you haven't changed Britta. The first few days in the Azores, all I wanted was to be back here with you. I couldn't think about anything but you."

Britta snuggles closer, resting her duvet-covered leg on mine. "I missed you, too." Her arm comes from under the covers to cross my chest, and I can hardly breathe I want her so much.

But I can't risk ruining our arrangement. I'm even more sure of that now than I was after Archie pointed out all the sacrifices Britta has made for me, and all that she could lose because of me. As if the fact I didn't see it for myself would be enough evidence that I'm not ready to be a real husband to Britta, but then I come home to find her brothers here to help her with what I'd left her alone to do.

"But..." Britta says.

"But what?"

"You're not saying everything. You couldn't think about anything other than me, *but...*" Britta tips her head to peer at me, and her hair brushes my jaw. It's damp and silky, and she smells fresh and clean. There's a scent of lemon and vanilla, and I'm not sure if it's from her lotion or shampoo.

I hug her closer and kiss the top of her head. "Britta, there's nothing I want more than to be with you, which is exactly why I can't be."

Britta pulls away and sits up to stare at me. In the dim light, I feel more than see her eyes drill into me, and I try not to squirm. There's more to say, but the way she's studying me makes me keep my mouth shut.

"Because I'm a distraction?" she says finally.

I shake my head. "You're not the problem. I am. If I can't stay focused, I won't make the Olympic team, and then you will have married me for nothing."

Her lip tugs. "I got my coffee shop out of the deal, and I can help you stay focused. You said I'm the reason you won the Finals."

She drops back to my chest with her chin resting on her hands.

I can't stop my hand from resting on her lower back or my thumb from dragging along the top of her pyjama pants. "No. You got a loan from me to buy it. A loan you insist on paying back."

"That's only fair, Dex. Two hundred thousand dollars is a lot of money."

"Being married for three years to a guy who only knows how to do one thing—surf—is a long time."

Britta lifts her shoulders in a slow shrug. "Unless we decide three years isn't long enough."

Britta tips her chin, and my breath catches. I could kiss her right now. We could take a chance that we could last longer than three years. Maybe even forever.

But that would be selfish on my part.

"Britt, I was focused at the Finals because you were there. But being halfway across the world from you messed everything up. I wanted to be with you instead of on the wave."

"Did you ache for me?" she whispers.

"Ache?" That's a good way to put it. "I ached from wiping out a dozen times in a row because I couldn't stop thinking about you."

Britta slides her hands from under her chin and wraps her arms around my chest. Her cheek is warm against my sternum. "You're not doing a great job convincing me we shouldn't try being a real married couple."

I scoff. "I left you when you needed me here. My self-interest over-powered any worries I had that you'd be alone. Worse, I didn't even consider the fact you might need help with *Annie's*. All I cared about was my dream, not yours."

"You offered to cancel the trip. I told you not to."

"I could have canceled it weeks before, but I knew I was falling for you, and I wanted to run from those feelings."

"You didn't run fast enough," she says, and I let out a small laugh, because she's deadset right. "I can hear your heartbeat."

"You mean pound?"

"Yeah. Why is it pounding?"

"Because I'm trying to tell you I don't have it in me to be the husband you deserve." I wrap both arms around her back. "And it's killing me."

"I don't think that's true, Dex." Her breath skitters across my chest.

"Trust me, Britt, I've never done anything this hard."

She shakes her head, rubbing her cheek and chin against my too-thick jumper. I wish I could feel her skin against my bare chest. "That's not what I meant. I think if it's killing you to tell me we can't be together, then you're probably exactly the kind of husband I need... you're just not ready to be right now."

I don't know if she hears my heart stop, but it definitely does. I wanted her to understand, but I didn't think it'd be so painful.

"That's what you're trying to tell me, right?" She pushes herself up until she's sitting cross-legged next to me. "Our focus can't be on each other. It has to be on the reasons we got married in the first place—so you can get to the Olympics, and I can start over here with my store."

I hate that we're not touching anymore, but the distance makes it easier to say what I have to. "I'm going to be gone for weeks at a time on the Championship Tour—maybe months, if things go right. You can't go with me. You've got *An*—" I catch myself. "Your soon-to-be-named coffeeshop and all the employees counting on it to succeed."

Britta nods, then raises her eyes to meet mine. Even in the dark, the intensity of her blue irises bores straight through me. "Falling in love would distract us from what's really important."

I wince at the way she's said it, even though she's mostly right. "Not from what's *really,* really important, but from what has to be really important for the next few years."

"So we have to stop ourselves from growing anymore attached." Britta uncrosses her legs and pulls her knees to her chest, wrapping her arms around them. "How do you think we should do that?"

"We follow the rules you already made," I say firmly, now that we're on the same page at the same time.

"Hmm."

"What?" I peer at Britta. There's too much hesitation in her hum.

"I kind of hate myself for making so many rules. I mean, we're already breaking the not sleeping in the same bed one, and we'll have to break it every time someone visits who thinks we're really married."

She's got a good point. Plus, her bed is more comfortable than mine, and not just because she's in it.

Fine. It's mostly that.

I sit up against the headboard, careful not to touch her. "We're adults. We can set our own boundaries together. We're both aware we have to prioritize our careers right now, so anything that could jeopardize our focus is off limits."

"So we definitely keep the no sex rule. Too much emotional attachment for me if we don't follow that one."

"Agreed." *Reluctantly.*

"Ditto with kissing."

"Okay." I officially hate Britta's rules now, too. "No touching?" I say hesitantly.

I'm relieved when Britta shakes her head. "Way too hard." Then she bites her lip, and I worry about what may come next. "Do you think we could handle hugging? Maybe even cuddling? I mean, just as friends, obviously, but I come from an affectionate family. We're always hugging—except for Adam—and I miss it. I *need* it, Dex, especially when I'm so far from everyone I know."

I open my arms, because I've found one sacrifice I can make for Britta, no matter that I'll be taking the very real risk of falling even harder for her. "Hugging and cuddling definitely is a must."

CHAPTER THIRTY-FIVE

Britta

Twice now, Dex and I have proven we can share a bed like an old married couple who've been together for fifty years and don't have sex. After our talk, we keep the cuddling to a minimum, and we definitely don't kiss. Even though we're in the same bed, newly married, and we're really good at kissing. But we've set boundaries, and we're going to stick to them.

After my brothers leave early the next morning, I assume Dex will move his stuff back to his room, but he decides to wait until after he's surfed and helped me at the coffee shop. Thank goodness, because while we're cleaning up the renovation aftermath, Dex gets a call from an INS agent.

I can tell that's who it is when his face loses color, and he says, "yes that's correct. I'm married to an American."

We both knew we'd get a call at some point, but we're both surprised it's happened so soon.

The call doesn't last over two minutes, but Dex's face is still ashen. "She says she'll set up interviews with both of us after she does a home visit."

"A home visit?" I feel the color drain from my face. "When? Why?"

Dex shakes his head. "She didn't say. She'll just show up one day to make sure we're living in the same place as a married couple."

We both know what will happen if she doesn't believe us. Dex will be deported, and I could be arrested.

"Move into my room. At least until we don't have to worry about any surprise inspections. And we've got to tell each other everything about ourselves." Panic claws its way from my stomach to my chest. "I can't remember your parents' names. Do you even remember mine? I do *not* look good in orange, Dex." I don't even know if orange is standard prison color, but I'm not taking any chances.

"You're right," Dex nods. "But we'll be fine, yeah? We've slept in the same bed with no problems."

"Exactly. I'm not worried." I go back to scrubbing down the espresso machines to prove just how unworried I am.

"Me neither." Dex picks up two half-full cans of paint, stopping just before he steps outside. "Pete and Heidi, right? That's your parents' names?"

I nod and he smiles before lugging the cans to the small storage unit out back. We spend the rest of the day not being worried about the fact we'll be sharing a bed tonight and for the foreseeable future.

It's not until after we're home and Dex has moved all of his stuff to my room that we face the reality of our situation. We'd be safer from each other if we slept in separate beds, but we have no idea how closely the INS will look at our living arrangements. Will it be enough to *look* like we share a room without actually sleeping in the same bed? Or will they show up one day when Dex doesn't make his bed and starts asking questions we can't answer about how often we sleep together?

So we go with an abundance of caution approach and climb into bed together.

I've just erected a dividing line of pillows between us when Dex scrambles off the bed and goes to the thermostat on the wall.

"What are you doing?" I ask.

"Turning the A/C down really low. If I have to wear pyjamas, it's got to be too cold for me to take them off."

"Good plan. Take it down to sixty—Fahrenheit, not Celsius." I have no idea what cold is in Celsius, but I do know two things. This room can*not* get any hotter if Dex is going to be sleeping in my bed.

When he climbs back under the covers, he rolls over on his back and crosses his hands over his chest.

"Let's talk baby names," he says.

"Baby names?" There's obviously been a miscommunication. Maybe Celsius has a second sexual meaning in Australia.

"For your shop. That baby." His voice is so dry, there's no way to miss the teasing in it.

"Ha." I flip onto my back, accidentally brushing his elbow with mine. Just that smallest touch makes me want to be closer to him.

"We can still cuddle, right?" I ask him. "Especially with it being an icebox in here?

He answers by pulling me into his arms, and I rest my head against the boniest part of his shoulder so I can't get too comfortable. Just to be safe.

"How about Britta's Brew? Or Britta's Beans?" Dex asks.

"I don't want my name on it. I want people to understand it's a coffeeshop just from the name, but I don't want it to be about me. The shop is really about people like Diva and Mitzi." I keep my eyes on the ceiling, because I'm focusing. I will *not* get distracted by Dex.

"So, you want something that will draw attention to the work you're doing with the homeless?" He asks, also speaking to the ceiling.

"No. That feels performative, like I'm doing it so we can all feel like we're doing something complicated to solve an easy problem, when really it's the other way around." I reach up to still Dex's fingers tapping my shoulder, and somehow our hands end up linked. "That, and I don't want anyone who works for me to be defined by their circumstances."

Dex huffs a laugh.

"What?"

"You're really good at putting other people first. I reckon that's what I like most about you." He squeezes my hand. "But also, the reason we have to keep this between us at a business level."

"I've never shared a bed with a business partner. Probably because my brothers have been my only business partners."

"Yeah?" His chin scrapes the top of my head when he looks down at me. "Archie and I have shared lots of beds—'specially in the early days. This is standard business operations for me."

I laugh.

"Never kissed him, though." Dex goes on. "Or anyone else I've been in business with. You hold that rare honor."

"Maybe we should change the subject."

Dex doesn't miss a beat. "How about Deja Brew?"

I roll the words over my tongue. "I like it, but I think I want something a little more sophisticated than whimsical."

We go back and forth with a few more ideas until Dex suggests West Coast Brew.

"It's good, but not quite there." Then it hits me. "West Coast Roast! What do you think?"

"Perfect," he says with a yawn. Within minutes, he's asleep in my bed.

The next morning when Dex comes downstairs, I assume he's getting ready to surf. Then I notice that he's not only wearing a shirt but also real shoes, not flip-flops. The only other time I've seen him in both shoes and shirt was on our wedding day.

"What's the occasion?" I hand him the flat white I've just made with the gourmet espresso machine in the fancy kitchen.

"We've still got work to do at West Coast Roast, right?" He sips from his mug, then raises his eyebrows in approval.

"Don't you have your own work to do? You've been out of the country for two weeks."

"Out of the country *working*. I told you I'd help, and I'm going to help… but we should probably leave before Archie shows up. I've done my yoga and meditation, but surf will have to come later."

One thing I've learned about Dex since we've been married is that he's very dedicated to his training routine. His mornings always start with yoga or strength training—either with a video or his personal instructor—then surfing. His meals are more balanced than Simone Biles on a beam and he has a strict bedtime. At least, he does when he sleeps in his own bed.

Dex's discipline is impressive. But also, a little disappointing, because I doubt he'll deviate from our decision to keep our relationship strictly business. Or at least, mostly business with a healthy slice of friendship. Business platonic?

I'm not as certain about my ability to stick to our decision, but at least I can trust Dex not to swerve from our plan.

And I wonder what would have happened between us if Dex didn't need citizenship and we'd let our relationship grow organically. Would we be where we are now? I think our chemistry would be the same—amazing—but maybe we'd also be considering marriage for all the best reasons. Like love and connection.

Or maybe nothing would have happened without the motivating factors of citizenship and money. We wouldn't have gotten married, and our relationship would have fizzled. I'd be back in Paradise opening a new *Britta's* in Cassie's bookstore and Dex would be here focused only on surfing.

It's hard to say. But I sort of like the idea that our marriage-of-convenience is the leavening agent that's set everything in motion. With a little kneading and baking, Dex and I might just create something delicious.

CHAPTER THIRTY-SIX

Dex

When we get to *West Coast Roast*—it's going to take a minute to get used to calling it that—Britta seems anxious but settles down when Diva, Mitzi, and a few other baristas show up to help us put the store back together. Most of what we have to do is cleaning, arranging tables, and putting up pictures and other decorations.

Most of us are in the dining room scrubbing build-up from tables and chairs while Diva and Sergio are at the prep stations getting all the ingredients stocked and in place.

"I finally settled on a name," Britta says to her crew over Teddy Simms singing *Funeral* over the speaker. "West Coast Roast. What do you think?"

The silence that follows is worse than when you ask a girl "what's wrong?" and she says "nothing."

"It's nice," Mitzi answers, finally.

"Nice?" Britta stops in the middle of wiping down a table and peers at Mitzi who's on her knees cleaning the chair on the other side.

"Yeah. Nice," Mitzi says nervously. "A little formal, but I like it." She scrubs double time, like she's making up for Britta slacking.

"Formal?" Britta's eyes stay glued to Mitzi.

"She means it sucks," Diva yells from across the counter.

Britta's mouth drops open, and I'm searching for some way to change the conversation when I spy the old, framed *Surf City High* photo Annie had hanging up leaning against the wall. I've always loved that picture.

I run—not walk—to pick it up. "Hey Britt, you're not putting this back up, are you? Can I have it?"

My ploy works, and Britta turns from Diva to me. "Why wouldn't I put that back up? It belongs here."

"It's old and embarrassing." I shift the large frame to rest on my hips and scrutinize it. I hated being on the show, but I loved the time I spent with my friends.

"Aren't you two married? It'd be weird not to put it back up." Diva has no problem expressing her opinion, which I respect, but I don't want to look at my face every time I come in here. I didn't have a say when this shop was *Annie's,* but I ought to now that my wife owns it.

But Diva's not done. "You gotta play that up, girl. Fill this whole place with pictures of your famous man. That'll bring in the surfers and the tourists. Wife of Liam Dexter making their coffee."

Britta looks from me to Diva, then back again, like she's actually considering what Diva's said.

"Don't make it about me, Britt," I say, but her lip is already curling into a smile.

"I won't make it about you, but I could make it about surfing," she says.

Mitzi stands, shifting side to side until Britta looks at her. "You could call it Frothed."

"Frothed?" Britta's brow wrinkles, and I realize she doesn't get why it's actually the perfect name.

"Frothing is a surf term," I tell her. "It means excited or stoked, but froth is also the foam left after a wave breaks."

"I like the idea of a word that's used for coffee and surfing." Britta's eyes scan the room, bouncing over everyone here but not seeing us. "We could fill the walls with surfing pictures, make it a whole theme." Then she really gets stoked. "Dex, do you have an old board you could sign, and I could hang up?"

Spoiler Alert. I don't say no. I couldn't say no to Britta if I tried.

Over the next five days, after getting a logo made and ordering signage and product, I help Britta hang one million pictures, not just of me, but of every local surfer I can get a signed picture from. Both of us know it's a bad idea to make this place about me when we're not planning on staying married.

But she still puts up that old *Surf City High* picture and my signed surfboard. And who knows? Maybe this partnership will turn into something more if the timing is ever right.

By the end of October, *Frothed* is ready to open. The only person not frothing about Britta's shop is Archie. Not because he doesn't like Britta or coffee, but because I've missed a lot of training. I'm off my schedule, which is the opposite of what was supposed to happen when I married Britta.

"We've got ten weeks until Pipe," he says as we sip flat whites the morning of the official November First grand opening of *Frothed*. "Good swell is supposed to be coming in there the next few weeks, and you need the practice. I think we should make a trip."

I start to tell him I can't leave Britta alone when *Frothed* has just opened, but his look stops me.

"You stay on the Tour and make it to the Olympics; business could be even better for Britta. Her star rises with yours." Archie grips my shoulder. "You're so close. Don't lose focus now. Britta's got what she wanted out of your deal. Now let's go get what you want."

"And what if INS shows up while I'm gone?" I glance at Britta. I don't want her to deal with them by herself.

"Then it looks like you're out-of-town working, and Britta gets to answer questions without worrying whether yours will match hers. She can brief you before you get back." Archie flips up his palms and pulls his shoulders to his ears, waiting for a rebuttal.

I haven't got one.

Archie's right. I've got to get back on my game. He's said it before. If I don't make the Olympic team, Britta's made an enormous sacrifice for nothing. She took a leap of faith, leaving Paradise and opening this place. I'm also responsible for some of its success. As long as I stay on the Tour, I'm a draw to this place.

The popularity of surfing is growing heaps. By the 2028 Olympics, people are going to be watching. If I'm there, it can only be good for Britta's business.

All morning I've watched her smile at customers, taking orders, while also making time to compliment and encourage her crew. I'm chock-full of pride watching her. I *want* this place to work. Not just for her, but because this community needs her the same way they needed Annie.

"You're right, mate. Make the travel plans, and let's go catch some waves," I say to Archie, then wave goodbye to Britta.

By the time she gets home that night, Archie's got us booked to Oahu, and I have to break the news to her. This is the first time I've ever wanted to stay home instead of surfing a wave like Pipe.

We eat a dinner of fish, quinoa, and veggies on the patio where we can watch the sunset, but the sky is dark before I tell her.

"When do you leave?" Is her first question.

"The fifteenth."

"How long will you be gone?" Follows quickly after.

"Two weeks, at least. Depends on the swell." I try to get a read on her reaction. She attempts a smile, but I can't tell if it's forced because she's tired after her long day or if she's sad I'm leaving.

"You'll be gone over Thanksgiving? I thought I'd invite my family, if Archie's okay with them staying here. I won't be able to get away from *Frothed*." There's no mistaking the disappointment in her voice.

"Yeah. I forgot about Thanksgiving." Now I feel like a real dimwit, even though it's not a holiday I've ever celebrated—not even since living in America. I'm usually traveling in November.

"I believe it's in our contract," she teases, and I breathe out a laugh.

"I'm sorry, Britt. I promise not to miss Anzac Day."

Now it's her turn to laugh. "What's that? And are there gifts involved?"

"Only flowers for veterans, similar to your Memorial Day."

"I'll add it to my calendar." Her smile morphs into a yawn. "We probably need to make a schedule of when we'll be together if we want INS to think we're really married, but I'm too tired to do it tonight." She squeezes my hand. "I'm going to shower and climb into bed. Are you coming up soon?"

The first few nights sleeping in the same bed were awkward, but now it feels completely normal. Nothing's happened beyond talking until we both fall asleep. Staying in her warm bed, though, makes it harder to get out in the ocean with the mornings being as cold as they are. And knowing I'll be leaving for a few weeks has already got me thinking about the kiss she gave me the last time I left.

"In a minute." I tell her. It's probably best if she's asleep before I get there. I don't think cuddling will be enough to tide me over while I'm gone.

"Okay." She turns toward the stairs, and I watch her climb them, but halfway up, she stops and leans over the railing. "Dex?"

"Yeah?"

"Thanks for all your help with *Frothed*. Not just with the money part, but everything. Your support and confidence have kept me going." She sends me a soft smile.

"It's nothing, really. I haven't done much. Your brothers did most of the heavy lifting." I try to lower my gaze, but her eyes won't let me go.

"I can always count on my family to support me, because we're family. They believe in me because I'm part of them." She narrows her eyes, examining me. "But it's different with you. You just believe in me because I'm *me*. That means everything, Dex."

My chest swells. "I'm glad I could help."

She pushes herself from the railing and takes a step, but stops again and looks at me. "That's a talent, Dex, believing in people. Remember that when you think the only thing you're good at is surfing. That's what you *do*, and you do it better than just about anybody. But it's not who you are. You're so much more than just a surfer."

Britta continues her climb up the stairs, leaving me speechless.

Over the next week, while I get back on my training schedule, Britta is consumed with everything there is to do with running her own business. We hardly have a time to talk, let alone sync our schedules. She's often asleep before I get in bed, and she gets up even earlier than I do.

We've got exactly what we wanted. No distractions. Complete focus on our careers.

Except, my surfing doesn't get better. It doesn't suck, but I'm not in the kind of form I'll need to be come January.

Even when I come off a wave pleased with my ride, I don't get the same confidence boost I've always gotten before. I still love surfing, but it doesn't consume my every thought like it has for my entire life.

Now there's a Britta-sized hole that only she can fill.

The afternoon before I leave, I come home from my surf sesh to find a giant dry-erase calendar taking up half the wall in the laundry room. I always come in from the outside door here so I can drop my towel and boardies in the wash without tracking sand through the house. Britta's hung this calendar in the one place I won't miss.

I peer at the squares for the last two weeks of November. Britta's already filled them in with her own commitments. It's the same thing every day: *Frothed 5:00 am—2*. She schedules herself for the morning shift, then usually ends up staying until closing at six.

I'm relieved to see *Family Here* written across the week of Thanksgiving, but seeing the same daily schedule written day after day reminds me I'm leaving Britta here alone when she needs me. I might not be actual help when it comes to handy stuff like her brothers, but I'm good—make that excellent—at moral support. Especially when it's for Britta.

Frothed is a huge undertaking. Aside from running her own business, Britta is also training people to make a sustainable living—some of them for the first time. There are criteria she has to meet in order to keep her funding and standards that her employees have to reach in order to qualify for the program that's designed to lead them to housing and future education opportunities. Britta's not just making coffee or running a business. She's keeping single moms and kids off the streets and in secure employment.

I uncap the whiteboard marker hanging from twine next to the calendar and write in everything on my schedule that I can remember. It's Archie's job to keep track of my events and everything else, but it's not his job to communicate with my wife, so I fill in as much as I can.

I draw a question mark after writing *back from Oahu* on November 29th since we don't have return tickets yet. But I'll make sure we're home as close to that date as possible. Then I circle the Saturday that follows it a half dozen times. In that square, I write DATE NIGHT.

That will give me something to look forward to while I'm away. Because, the thing I've figured out this week is that pretending I'm not in love with Britta is as much a distraction as being in love with her, but not even half the fun.

In fact, it sucks.

CHAPTER THIRTY-SEVEN

Britta

M y watch buzzes with a text but *Frothed* is slammed with a line out the door, my new trainee, Josh, needs a lot of guidance—*heaps*, as Dex would say—and someone laid a plastic spoon on one of my ebelskiver pans while it was hot, so I'm short one pan until I can clean that mess up. I don't have time to look at my watch, let alone respond to a text if I did.

It's hours later before I do. I smile when I read Dex's name, then reach for my phone when I see he's attached a picture. I pull up the message and laugh.

> **Hey darl, I've done my husbandly duty and filled in the calendar.**

Only takes me a second to suss out darl is short for darling. Aussies are pros at clipping words.

I tap the picture and pull it big enough to see it's a closeup of November thirtieth—the day my family is scheduled to leave—and the words DATE NIGHT.

My first thought is Dex has made the most romantic gesture I can think of. My mom and dad did the same thing for each other. If they didn't schedule time together, it wouldn't happen. Mom swore it's what kept their marriage strong through really difficult times. Dad kept their date nights going even after Mom didn't understand what he was doing.

My second thought—the one that opens a hole in my chest—is that Dex is teasing. He wouldn't realize that the words *date night* sent a triple surge of excitement, hope, and nostalgia through me. With the memory of my parents and the longing to someday have what they had, heat surges through my veins.

Because maybe I already have what they had at the beginning of their marriage, but I'm too focused on ending up hurt if I act on my feelings. Maybe, despite what Mom always taught me, I'm letting fear about my future get in the way of enjoying my now.

I go back to work and spend a few minutes considering how to answer in a neutral way so that if he's not teasing, he'll understand I'm looking forward to an official date with him. But if he is teasing, I don't want him to know how much I wanted him to not be.

I can't think of anything. It's already been a few hours since he texted, and I don't want him to think I'm avoiding answering, so I just go with what I know how to do best. I'm direct.

> **I hope you're being serious.**

I hold my breath as I push send.

My face is only slightly blue when his text comes in soon after.

> **Deadset.**

There's no holding back my grin now. Or my relief.

Except Dex is leaving tomorrow, and I haven't spent much time with him since *Frothed* opened. As busy and crazy as my life has been, I miss him. I thought, when we decided not to have a real relationship, that staying busy would be enough to fill every empty place in my heart. I'm a little afraid of what it means that being busy isn't enough.

But also, a little excited.

Does that mean I'm ready for love? Maybe. But I'm still not sure I'm ready for the pain and heartache that so often goes hand-in-hand with loving someone. A hand in mine through life's difficulties, though, would be nice. A shared calendar with regular date nights; waking up next to someone, or—better yet—in his arms; having a person to laugh and cry with; necessary hugs. I think I might be ready for all that, even if with Dex's schedule, it would mean a lot of days and nights alone, too.

> Will I see you before you leave?

> I've got an event tonight but will try to cut out early.

I debate whether to give his reply a heart or a thumbs up, but what I mostly feel is disappointment we won't have more time together, even if he leaves his event early. A thumbs down feels too dramatic, so I go with the thumbs up. It's really my only option.

Then I go back to work, less stressed and a lot lighter than I've felt in days. The question that keeps rolling through my head, when I'm not making coffee or doing one of the thousand other things I have to do, is why I thought it would be easier to keep distance between Dex and me instead of staying close enough we can buoy each other up.

I don't have an answer until I get home after seven pm, exhausted, hungry, and ready for human interaction that doesn't involve any kind of work. But the house is dark, and Dex isn't home. I'm alone again.

I make myself some spaghetti, including extra for Dex, in case he gets home soon. Around eight o'clock, I put it in a Tupperware and stick it in the fridge. When the clock hits nine, I can barely keep my eyes open.

I take a quick shower, then climb into bed. I'm asleep before my head hits the pillow. So dead asleep that when someone says my name, I gasp awake, not sure where I am or who's standing over me.

"It's just me, Britt," Dex whispers.

"What time is it?" I'm still disconcerted.

"Around eleven. Sorry I'm so late."

I roll onto my back to see him better. "That's okay. I crashed early. What time's your flight tomorrow?"

He put it on the calendar, but my head's still fuzzy.

"Seven am. We're leaving at five."

So, we won't get time together before he goes. I don't say that aloud, but he must sense it because he brushes a lock of hair from my forehead, a gesture that sends pinpricks of fire down my spine every time he does it.

"Mind if we cuddle tonight?" he asks.

I don't have to think about it. I've already made space for him before I answer. "I'd like that."

Dex climbs in, and I find the space that's become so familiar to me in the pocket between his shoulder and chest.

"I like the calendar," he says, pulling me close.

"I like to know where you are. You don't feel so far away when I know you'll be home again." If I were more awake, I could be less vulnerable. I could just say *I like schedules.* It would be the truth, just not the whole of it.

But the work of keeping my heart locked is exhausting. I've always been able to bury myself in work. Work kept me from breaking down in tears every day Mom got a little worse. I can't do it now. Not when I have a chance at more happiness than pain.

"I like being able to schedule time with you," Dex says in a tone that is both teasing and serious. "I've missed you. I'm going to miss you even more these next two weeks."

I scoot in closer, breathing in his scent, locking it into my memory for the next two weeks or more. The fact I'm holding Dex as close as I can is the only way I can communicate how much I'm going to miss him. I don't have any words left. I let his warmth and the sound of his breathing lull me back to sleep.

The next morning, we oversleep fifteen minutes and have to both rush out the door with only a quick *see you soon*. Maybe if we'd had time, there would have been a kiss. Last night feels like a bit of a turning point. We didn't say it explicitly, but I think we both want to go back on our decision to keep things professional. I think we agree that a business marriage sucks.

At least I hope we do, because by the time I get to *Frothed*, my chest is cinched so tight I can hardly breathe, and I think I understand what Bear meant when he said being in love means aching when you're not with your person.

I've just unlocked the door when my phone pings. Once I'm inside, and I've flipped on the lights, I pull up my messages.

> **Wanted to kiss you goodbye. I'm a sook. Can I kiss you hello when I'm back?**

> **Always.**

It turns out that Hawaii has much better reception than the Azores, and there's only a three-hour time difference instead of seven. That means some late nights for me, but we call every day. Our conversations are usually short, because three hours is still a big difference, but we text throughout the day as well.

Being able to talk to Dex makes the first week go faster than it should have. I still miss him, but I'm not as lonely as I was during his Azores trip.

And the second week he's gone, my family and Stella's family arrive on Monday to prep for the Thanksgiving holiday. The chaos and commotion that arrive with them don't leave any space for loneliness and barely any to miss Dex.

I don't hear from him on Monday, but the date circled on our calendar gets one day closer as I make an X through the Monday square at the end of the night. Dad nods when he sees it, but his approval quickly disappears after asking when Dex will be home for the holiday, and I have to tell him he won't.

"Australians don't celebrate Thanksgiving. He didn't realize he was training over the holiday." I shrug off Dad's question and the eyes of everyone else waiting for my answer. "He's in Hawaii prepping for his big competition in January."

When more questions come, I use some of Dex's explanations he's given me. "Surfing isn't the same as football where you have a field or a stadium in every town—he has to go where the waves are."

Georgia and Evie both try to dig into the relationship part, but I give quick, shallow answers. Then Stella comes to my rescue and redirects the conversation like a boss. I suspect Georgia picks up on what we're doing, but by Tuesday she stops pushing, and I stop feeling so anxious about my family discovering the real reason I married Dex.

That worry is replaced with a different one when Dex hasn't returned any of my texts or calls for the second day in a row. I try to push my concern aside by telling myself he's just busy surfing, but something feels wrong.

The day before Thanksgiving, I close *Frothed* a few hours early so I can cook with my family. This is how we celebrate: cooking and eating together. This is the first big holiday we'll be celebrating without Mom, but we've felt her loss for years. She used to be at the center of all the holiday cooking, but the last few years we couldn't even let her in the kitchen for fear she'd hurt herself.

In a way, it helps that we're not at home celebrating. Her absence is less noticeable in this house where we've never had a family celebration before. But that only lasts until we start baking and cooking. When the smells of her recipes for cider-brined turkey, stuffing with apples and sausage, and candied sweet potatoes waft through the air, we feel Mom there with us. But there's something different about it. Sorrow, of course, but maybe we've all worked through enough that the joyful memories—that I think were harder to focus on when she was here, but not herself—rise to the surface.

Pretty soon we're swapping stories about the mom she'd been, along with bites of whatever dish we're working on. We talk over each other, laughing at our different versions of events from our childhood. An occasional leak springs from our eyes as we talk about Mom, but it hurts less. As much as we all miss her, we're eventually able to talk about what she went through with Alzheimer's and how grateful we are she's not suffering anymore.

We're able to remember her how she'd want to be remembered instead of watching her slip away right before our eyes. In a way, it feels like we have her back, and I'm grateful to have my family around me for Thanksgiving. It wasn't easy for them to arrange this trip, but they did it and I can feel so much healing from this time together.

It's amid all the chaos in the kitchen that I feel my phone buzz in my apron pocket. I pull it out, relieved to see Dex's name.

"Hey," I answer, then walk outside to the back patio for some privacy.

"Britta?" Instead of Dex, Archie's on the line, the worry in his voice loud and clear from the other side of the ocean I'm looking at.

"Archie?" My heart is already in my throat. "What's wrong?"

"Dex is hurt."

Chapter Thirty-Eight

Britta

I clutch the phone closer to my ear, hoping I've misheard while sure that I haven't. "How hurt?"

Archie's pause wipes away any thread of hope I might have held onto. "Bad. He's in hospital."

"What do you mean, hospital? What hospital? Here?" On some level, I realize that's not possible, but I throw out a desperate wish that Dex is closer than the middle of the Pacific Ocean.

"He's in the ICU at Queen's Medical Center in Honolulu."

So still in Hawaii. Worse, the Intensive Care Unit.

"What happened?" I whisper and sink into a patio chair.

The sun dips orange and pink rays into the horizon, painting the surface of the ocean with reds, violets, and hints of blue. I want Dex here to see it, his arms wrapped around my back and shoulders so we can watch it together.

"He was paddling out. An enormous wave crashed in front of him. He couldn't dive under fast enough and got pummeled hard. I thought for a minute he wasn't coming back up. That's how long it took for him to surface." Archie holds nothing back. There's more than worry in his voice. He needs to process what's happened to his best friend. "But then he got hit by half a dozen more colossal waves."

"Did he hit his head?" I ask, dropping my head in my hand.

I know surfers risk getting knocked out under water every time they wipe out—especially on a wave like Pipeline that breaks over shallow reef; more things I've learned from Dex, but this is the first thing he's told me I wish he hadn't.

"The doctor says his brain scan looks similar to a soldier's who's been caught in an explosion." I feel Archie's fear across the line.

"Are you saying he has a brain injury?" I glance up when I hear the back door slide open. A staggered breath escapes when Stella sits down next to me.

"This isn't Dex's first concussion, Britta," Archie says slowly, which is worse than a simple yes or no. There's no easy answer to whatever is happening with Dex.

"What does that mean, Archie? How many has he had?"

Stella mouths *what happened*, but I just shake my head. That's all I can tell her.

"A lot," Archie continues. "By my count, he's had at least a dozen concussions. Probably more."

"A dozen? Are you serious? Why is he even still surfing?" I already know the answer to the last question, but I don't understand how Dex could love something so much that he'd risk his life to do it.

"It's what every pro-surfer does." Archie pauses, as though he's giving me time to process everything he's said and make the connections on my own. I don't want to do that. I want Archie to tell me that Dex isn't as bad as I'm imagining.

I've seen brain scans. Mom had plenty of them, and I was there every time the doctor explained what they meant. I had a front-row seat to the deterioration of Mom's hippocampus, her entorhinal cortex, her temporal, frontal, and parietal lobes as the neurons in her brain stopped functioning. I know what a shrinking brain looks like in pictures, and I know what it looks like in real life.

"Archie, just tell me how bad it is. Can he walk? Talk?"

"That's what I'm trying to explain, Britta." The uncharacteristic gentleness of his tone makes my pulse tick faster. "This wipeout was bad. One of his worst... but not *the* worst. It's the previous concussions that've made the damage so bad this time."

"Archie, *please* just tell me." I can't stop the bouncing up and down of my legs until Stella puts her hand on my knee. I grab her hand and cling to it. I'll drown if I don't.

"The hospital has to run a lot more tests, so there's nothing conclu—"

"—Archie! Is he paralyzed? Can I talk to him?"

Another pause from Archie fills in the last pieces with the worst I'd imagined.

Stella stands and slips her hand from mine. "I'm getting your dad."

As she runs inside, Archie answers my question. "Right now, he can't walk. He's got bleeding in his brain, so the doctors have cut a hole in his skull to release some of the pressure from swelling. He can say a little, and he understands us, but—"

"—Who's us?"

"The doctors. Me and...his parents."

Now it's my turn to go quiet as the picture grows darker. Archie knows too much about this accident for it to have happened in the last few hours. For Dex's parents to have traveled from Australia to Hawaii, the accident couldn't have even happened today.

A shadow passes over me, and Dad takes Stella's place by my side.

"How long has Dex been in the hospital?" I ask.

I grab Dad's hand and hold tight. I count back the days to the last time Dex and I talked or texted, then answer my question.

"Monday? Why did you wait until today to call me?" My voice raises, and I try to stand, but Dad gently tugs me back down.

Archie takes a breath. "I wasn't sure Dex would want me to call you. He doesn't know that I am now."

"What? Why?" There's no keeping me in my seat now. I shake off Dad's hand and walk to the edge of the cement patio where a low wall separates the property from the sandy beach and the ocean fifty feet away.

"I can only guess, because he's not able to say much." Archie talks slowly, and I sense him searching for the right words. "But when I told him I'd call you. He shook his head and said, 'it's off.'"

"It's off? What does that mean?"

"When we were in the Azores, Dex made me promise that if anything happened to him, you wouldn't be left caring for him." Archie's tone is firm now—protective—but I'm not sure if he's trying to protect me or Dex. "Surfing is risky business. He didn't want you to feel obligated to care for him the way you had to for your mum if it came to that."

I'm knocked silent with Archie's words.

"But I'm his wife. Why wouldn't I want to care for him?" I'm feeling both defensive and guilty, replaying all the conversations I've had with Dex about Mom. How I don't regret giving up my own dreams to take care of her, even while I resent the fact that I felt like it was my duty as her daughter.

"You're his wife in name only. He understands that. If he can't keep his part of your arrangement, he doesn't want you to feel you have to, either."

In name only.

The words are true, but painful to hear. I'd started to think of myself as Dex's wife.

"I should be there, Archie." My voice is a whisper.

In the distance, a wave crashes on shore before being sucked back to sea to be reformed into another wave. From here, the sound is gentle and soothing. Up close, they'd be so loud, I wouldn't have heard Archie's next words.

"He won't want you here, Britta. Not yet. Not until we know exactly how bad it is. I'm sorry. But I still thought you should know. The story will be picked up by the sport reporters soon, and I didn't want you to hear it from them. "

I appreciate Archie sounds like the words are as hard to say as they are to hear, but that doesn't mean they don't knock the wind out of me like a punch to the gut.

"Okay." It's the only word I can get out between trying to catch my breath.

"I'll keep you updated."

That's the last thing I hear Archie say. I end the call before a goodbye can follow.

Chapter Thirty-Nine

Britta

M y eyes bounce from my phone to the ocean. I'm not sure which one I hate more right now. The thing that's hurt Dex or the thing that made it possible to deliver the news to me.

"Britta?" Dad says behind me before putting a hand on my shoulder. "What's happened?"

I push back tears and turn around, knowing the truth has to come out now for a lot of reasons, but mostly because I don't have the strength to dance around it with my family.

"Dex is hurt." That's as much as I can get out before my throat threatens to close.

"How bad?" Dad's eyes are soft with concern, and I know he's as worried about Dex as he is about me.

"Really bad. He's in the hospital. He can't walk. He can barely talk. A severe concussion. He's been in the ICU since Monday."

Dad nods, and I wonder if we're both thinking of Mom's last days when she couldn't walk or talk either. "He needs you there."

I drop my gaze to the grains of sand blowing across the patio. "He doesn't want me there."

The only sound that follows is the wind clanging the metal clamps against the cement poles the volleyball nets are attached to. There's a dark rhythm to the clinking, like the ticking of a clock running out of time.

"Hmm," Dad huffs thoughtfully. "Want and need are two different things."

I'm so surprised by his answer that I can't help but look at him. "What do you mean?"

Dad wraps his arm around my shoulder and guides me back to the chair I'd been sitting in before, then takes the one across from it.

"Why did you marry Dex?"

I search for some way to tell him, but no words that he'll understand come to me.

"The truth, Britta." He leans over his knees on his elbows with his hands clasped together. "It was obvious in Vegas that while you two are good friends, and there's... something there, there was also something missing—on both your parts. You get to walk your own path, Sweetie, but you don't need to hide it from me. Especially now."

I sigh, knowing that in this moment, I can't keep up the ruse, especially if Dad suspected it from the start. "He needs to gain citizenship to surf for Team USA in the 2028 Olympics, and I needed money to buy *Frothed.*"

I brace myself for Dad's disappointment. Hearing the words makes my arrangement with Dex sound more shallow than it is. Or, at least, than I thought it was.

"I'm going to pay him back," I add. "Dex didn't pay me to marry him. It's not like that." The more I try to justify what I've done, the more Dad's face grows weary, like he's aging right in front of my eyes. "We wanted to help each other reach our dreams."

Dad drops his head. Bear peeks out the glass door and raises his eyebrows. He wants to come out, but I shake my head. I'm not ready for this conversation to be between anyone but Dad and me. Bear drops his hand from the handle and turns back to the kitchen and the chaos there.

Dad lifts his head, and there's a steeliness in his eyes I've only ever seen when we had to decide whether to take extraordinary measures to keep Mom alive. His answer was no, and he wouldn't back down from it, even though it took me another day to see the wisdom of not prolonging her death any longer than we already had.

"I can respect that you two thought you were helping each other by getting married, but ultimately, you used a sacred institution for selfish reasons."

I'm shocked speechless. Dad's not a religious guy, so his use of *sacred* hits hard. I love my Dad, but I respect him too. I want him to respect me, so I scramble to find some kind of defense for what I've done. "I didn't think I was being selfish. I want him to go to the Olympics."

"And you planned to stay married to him forever after that? 'Til death do you part?'" Dad's words are gentle but prodding, and I can only shake my head.

"If your primary motivation for marrying Dex wasn't love, then you didn't do it for the right reasons. I thought your mom and I had taught you that." With each word Dad speaks, I sink further into the chair cushion, the implication of what I've done growing heavier and heavier.

Shame brings hot tears to my eyes. "I'm sorry, Dad."

His eyes soften. "You've got nothing to be sorry about in relation to me, but do you have any feelings at all for Dex? Because what I saw on his face on your wedding day can't be entirely faked. He wasn't saying yes to a business arrangement, whether or not he knew it at the time."

Maybe it's just his opinion, but Dad's words give me the courage to say what I haven't even admitted to myself. "I might love him, Dad."

Dad smiles. "Then you might need to find a flight to Hawaii."

I shake my head. "He didn't even want Archie to tell me he was hurt. He made Archie promise if anything happened to him, I wouldn't end up his... caretaker."

I tread carefully over the last word.

"Because of Mom?" he asks.

I answer with a nod.

Dad presses my hand between each of his. "None of us were prepared for what Mom would need from us. It all happened so fast. I have wondered since her... passing, if I put more on you than I even realized. Was it too much, honey? Did I expect more than I should have?"

I'm feeling raw and exposed, which might be why I decide in that moment not to protect him from the truth anymore. I've been wrestling with that truth a lot and I'm tired of keeping secrets.

"That expectation was heavy, Dad, and I'd be lying if I said I didn't resent it sometimes. You had to keep up at the store, I understand that, and the boys had a lot going on, I understand that too, but I gave up everything to fill in the gaps and..." I pause to make sure I'm okay revealing this much. I decide I am. "And no one seemed to even notice. Everyone seemed to ignore what I'd sacrificed to make Mom a priority. Like it was my job."

I turn my hand to better see his. His knuckles are swollen with arthritis and his veins corded from years of hard work, which almost makes me regret saying what I've said, but it also feels good to have finally said it out loud. "But I wouldn't do anything differently, either." I look up and meet his tear-filled eyes, which bring on tears of my own. "Does that make sense? I hate I had to watch Mom die the way she did, and I've been working through my resentment about that, but I'm so grateful I had the time with her, and I wouldn't take that back."

He sniffs and squeezes my hand tighter. "Oh sweetheart, I'm so sorry... and I am so grateful that you were there. It made all the difference, to us, but also to her. She was a different person by the time she died, but I know that inside, she was the same mother who loved you with her whole soul."

We embrace and I cry for my mother and how much I miss her. Dad cries too, and it's a beautiful moment for us to share. When we finally pull back, Dad puts both of his hands on my shoulders. "Do you care enough about Dex to be his caretaker if he doesn't recover from his injury? You don't have to, Dex is telling you to walk away, and we will support whatever you decide, but you have to live with the decision either way."

I picture Dex in a wheelchair like Mom's, needing to be fed and bathed, spending his days watching TV as he loses more and more of his motor functions. The idea of it presses on my lungs, making it hard to breathe.

But then I remember holding Mom's hand, wiping her mouth, helping her with the simplest tasks and how she'd smile her gratitude. I hated watching her die, but it was an honor to take care of her.

And Dex isn't Mom. He may not surf again, but people can learn to walk and talk again after a brain injury. As much as I hate he told Archie not to call me, it's a sign that his brain is still functioning.

I let out a breath and look at Dad. "I think I could take care of Dex, but I'm scared. What if it's too much for me? What if I change my mind?"

Dad's mouth forms a bittersweet line—not quite a smile, but not quite a frown. "I guarantee there will be days when it's too much and that you will change your mind every time you have an especially difficult day. That's what it is to be married. You recommit every day, through every big problem and minor inconvenience that comes your way."

I burst into a laugh that makes Dad blink with surprise. "So, what you're saying is, if I want my marriage-of-convenience to be more than that, I have to be prepared for a lot of inconveniences?"

Dad blinks again, his brow creased with confusion. "I suppose so."

I stand and kiss the top of his bald head. "Thanks, Dad. I need to get a flight booked for Hawaii."

Dad pushes himself off the chair and wraps me in a giant hug. "That's my girl."

I squeeze him back until a realization hits me so hard that my shoulders fall. "Airplane is the quickest way to Hawaii, isn't it?"

Inconvenience number one.

CHAPTER FORTY

Dex

My head doesn't hurt the way it did the first few days I was in hospital, but the doctors still keep the room dark and quiet. When they do reflex tests, my hands and feet respond, but the neurons in my brain are misfiring and I can't make them move. Mum's confident I'll relearn, but she's not the one who can't move.

If I could talk, I'd ask for Britta to be here with me. I'd take back my no when Archie asked if he should call her. So, I guess it's good I can't remember how to form words. She shouldn't be here for this. Taking care of her mum is one thing, but I don't expect her to do the same for her fake husband.

Doctors are saying I won't surf again. If they're right—and I've got every unmovable limb to back them up—Britta's got no reason to stay with me. I don't need to be a US citizen if I can't surf. Mum's already talking about taking me back to Australia for rehab.

I don't care if Britta doesn't pay me back. I never wanted her to. As far as I'm concerned, we're square. She's got no obligation to a broken surfer who can't do the only thing he was any good at to begin with. Even if thinking about life without her is worse than thinking about life without surfing.

I was just settling into the idea that we might have a real future together. Then I made the stupid decision to duck dive under a ten-foot wave. The water was too shallow, and the wave had too much power.

Now I've got a lot of time to sit with the worst mistake of my life. When I'm not sleeping, the thoughts that fill my mushy brain are about how one mistake has probably cost me everything. My career. My Olympic dreams. My *wife*.

Archie, Mum, and Dad take turns staying with me, and I'm grateful to them. But things are pretty lonely in my head, which is where I live with the words that I can't make my mouth form. I have no idea how many days have passed since my accident. Night bleeds into day, and nurses and doctors blend together. I'm not sure if they've been here a hundred times already or if this check is the first they've made.

I only know my sleep is often interrupted with questions about how I'm feeling, brain and reflex checks, and meals made up of foods I should recognize but are mushier than my brain.

So, when I hear someone who sounds like Britta whisper my name, I keep my eyes closed. This is just one more misfire in my brain. If I open my eyes, Britta will be gone, and a nurse whose name I can't remember will stand over me instead, asking me to answer her questions by blinking.

Then I feel a hand slide into mine, and I'm almost sure it's Britta's. I recognize her touch. She uses her other hand to curl my fingers around her palm and press them there.

"I'm here, Dex. Like it or not," she says in a whisper, the way the doctors and nurses do.

I've been in and out of consciousness for so many days that I may be dreaming, but the temptation to see if Britta is really there is too great. I open my eyes, expecting her to disappear.

But she doesn't. And even in the dim light poking through the vinyl blinds, I know it's her. Blonde hair pulled back as usual, looking tired, but her eyes still shine bright, blue hope.

I force her name from my brain to my lips. It comes out jumbled, like I've got a mouthful of rocks, but she smiles.

"Hi." She combs her fingers through my hair, and I lean into her palm. "I'm glad you're still smiling, even if you're a bit of a mess otherwise. Tough day at the office?"

I couldn't tell I was smiling. I suspect I'm crying, though. My cheeks are wet and my eyes blurry.

Britta lets go of my hand long enough to pull a chair next to the bed, then folds my hand into hers again. "If you don't want me here, I'll go."

I muster all my strength to move my head from one side to the other. It's barely a micro shake, but I hope she sees how much I don't want her to go.

"I'm going to take that as a *yes, Britta, stay*, but blink once to confirm."

The laugh in my chest comes out as a loud breath as I close my eyes and open them again.

"Good, because I got on an airplane and flew across an entire ocean to get here, Dex. An *ocean*. Full of water. I could have died in a fiery plane crash and drowned at the same time." Britta keeps her voice barely above a whisper, but it still bounces up and down with humor.

It hurts my head to laugh, and my eyelids are heavy, but I force them open in order to see Britta's smile.

But instead of a smile, I'm met with tears. "Did you really think I wouldn't want to be here?"

Britta kisses my knuckle, then presses her cheek to it. "I'm not letting you break our contract that easily. If this is your way of getting out of training to be an Olympian, think again. I've already got a spot picked out at *Frothed* for your gold medal. It'll be good for business."

Only Britta could look at me in this bed, connected to a million wires and tubes and tell me I still have a chance at the Olympics. She's so confident, I almost want to believe her.

"You laugh all you want," she goes on, after kissing my hand again. "But I'm serious. I'm counting on you to fight for your dream."

Britta stands and leans close, then takes my face in both of her hands. "And I'm going to be right here next to you."

There's a fire in her eyes that sparks a determination in me to get out of this bed. To do whatever it takes to hold her in my arms and tell her I love her. That's what I want more than anything. Even more than surfing.

I concentrate so hard it hurts, but I'm able to move my fingers and pat the bed next to me.

Britta's eyes dart from my hand, then back to me. "That's a good start."

With a smile, she lowers the bed rails and moves my arm further from my side. She adjusts a few of the monitors to keep from unplugging anything as she climbs into the bed next to me. I let out a noise that I hope she understands is relief, the same way she understood what my tapping fingers meant.

There's not much room in the bed, but Britta curls up next to me, her head in the pocket between my shoulder and chest. Then she reaches behind her to position my hand around her waist. I can't hold her on my own yet, but knowing she'll help me get there gives me the first bit of hope I've had since I woke up in this hospital bed.

"You should know I don't do goodbyes," she says as she slides her arm across my chest. "You're stuck with me, whether or not you like it."

That's all the motivation I need to get back to who I am so I can show Britta just how much I like being stuck with her.

The End

Epilogue

SEPTEMBER 2025

D ex holds me tight as we bounce in the boat we've chartered to take
us from Malolo Island, where we're honeymooning, to Tavarua
Island and Cloudbreak, Fiji's most famous wave, where the WSL Finals
are being held this year.

Dex isn't holding me tight for my sake, but for his own. In the past
ten months, he's made more progress than his doctors expected. He's
learned to talk again, although his speech grows slower and more slurred
when he's tired. Walking came easier, but he's still a little unsteady on his
feet, and, sometimes, even off them.

But he's still not back to where he was before the accident. In fact, he
hasn't been back on a surfboard—or even in the ocean—since then. Dex
hasn't said he wants to surf again, but I catch him staring at the waves

out our bedroom window at least once a day. He wants to get back out there, not just to surf, but to compete. I see it daily in his eyes, and I've felt it in his body since the minute we stepped on this boat to go to the Finals.

Dex won't be surfing in them this year, but the organizers still wanted him here. The entire surfing community has rallied around him, cheering for his recovery. And if I know Dex, he'll get there. I predict he's back to compete in the Finals this time next year.

In the meantime, I keep him balanced, whether he's walking across uneven ground or riding in a boat. He keeps me balanced by reminding me to let other people help him and by coming into *Frothed* to make me take breaks. And we keep each other focused on what's most important: our relationship. We're committed to not letting anything get in the way of loving each other.

Our boat hits a wave hard, and I wrap my arms tighter around Dex's waist to keep him from getting knocked over. Even a few months ago, he might have fallen off his seat, his balance was still so off from the concussion. But with daily physical and occupational therapy, Dex is getting stronger every day. He tips slightly, but catches himself and can sit upright again on his own.

I smile, tuck my chin into my windbreaker, then pull my hood tighter to block the spray coming off the dark water as the boat slices through the waves. Dex pulls me close, wrapping his arms around my shoulders so I can bury my head in his chest. His embrace isn't as tight as it used to be, but I'm grateful for the strength he's regained just in the last few weeks. The fact he can still hold me at all is a miracle.

Don't get me wrong, there have been fights when he hasn't wanted to do the work, and I've made him anyway or when I've come home tired from *Frothed* and not wanted to walk the boardwalk with him or help him with exercises. Communication was tough before he recovered his language skills. Sometimes it still is when he can't say something as fast as either of us wants him to or when he can't find a word he's lost.

Dex's recovery is hard for both of us. Marriage is hard—we've had to get to know each other while Dex has been relearning the most basic skills. *Life* has been hard.

But so, so good. And made even better by the family support we've had.

My dad, brothers, and sisters-in-law have taken turns coming to help. During the summer, when they couldn't be here, I couldn't keep Stella away. Dex's mom has stayed for weeks at a time, and his dad has even visited.

Besides family-by-blood, we've had Annie too. Everything she's learned taking care of Keesha she's been able to use with Dex, too. When I'm not there, she'll often come over to use our home gym to help both Keesha and Dex with their physical therapy. And when I need someone at the shop, she's usually available to step in, now that Keesha doesn't need round-the-clock care.

Then, there's Archie, who wouldn't let us move out of the beach house and insisted on making one room a gym with all the equipment we'd need for Dex to do most of his therapy at home. Between that and the elevator in the house that meant Dex wouldn't have to take stairs until he was ready, we couldn't say no. Archie even moved in to make sure Dex had twenty-four seven care.

He moved out last week. I didn't realize he'd planned to, but his stuff was gone one day when I came home from work. According to Dex, Archie had decided we needed our own space after witnessing too many "displays of affection."

That's probably true. I think he also finally decided I was more than just a distraction for Dex.

"Look at this, Britta." Dex loosens his hold on me and nudges me upright. The rising sun breaks through the clouds, weaving strands of orange and yellow through an aqua sky dotted with white. At the same time as the sun, the moon sinks into the ocean, but for a few beautiful moments, they hover in the sky together, holding space for each other.

There's a metaphor for marriage in there somewhere, but the only words I can think to say are, "that's a beaut, darl."

Dex laughs. "Your Australian still needs work."

"Yeah?" I dig my elbow into his side, right where he's ticklish. "Your American needs some work, too."

"Lucky for me, that's one of the easier requirements for citizenship." Dex clasps his hands together around my shoulders and squeezes tight, pressing me close to his chest.

That's the first Dex has said anything about getting American citizenship since his accident. It's been a low priority compared to the question of whether he'll ever surf again. But I suspect he hasn't given up on his Olympic dream.

I hope not. I'm not going anywhere, so citizenship shouldn't be a problem.

When we arrive at our destination, I'm surprised that the Finals this year are a completely different setup than they were at Lower Trestles last year. Dex told me Cloudbreak is a reef break, so maybe I should have expected that the wave wouldn't be close to shore. Instead of structures set up on the beach, they're on stilts in the water to be closer to the wave. Spectators are lined up in boats around the reef instead of on beach towels under umbrellas on shore.

And Cloudbreak itself is so much bigger and more powerful than the wave at Lower Trestles that, for the first time, I'm relieved Dex can't surf it. I'd be worried he'd get hurt again on a barrel wave similar to the one that took him out of competition this entire season—maybe even forever.

The boat pulls up to the WSL structure and Archie, who's already there, waves from the large opening on the second level, then comes down the stairs to meet us at the makeshift dock.

"G'day, mates!" Archie calls before hopping to the dock to help Dex out of the boat.

He grabs Dex's hand to pull him up and out, while I steady him by keeping my hands on his back. The boat rocks, and Dex sways with it, but I see his determination to look stronger than he is, in front of the surfers he's competed against for years. As he steps onto the dock, he grabs Archie's arm and holds tight for a few seconds until he's balanced. Once he's steady, Archie stretches his hand out to me.

But Dex beats him to it. I hesitate taking it until Dex raises his eyebrows and gives me a next-to-invisible nod. Then I let him pull me from the boat onto the dock. I do some of the work, but he does most of it, which sends a flutter of excitement to my belly.

Dex and I have spent a lot of time in each other's arms over the past ten months and only slightly less time with our lips pressed together, but that's it. We're still not a "married" couple beyond an official marriage certificate and our wedding pictures that are still posted on Dex's Instagram account.

At first, Dex's injury made any kind of physical intimacy out of the question. But as he got stronger, we decided it could wait until when, and *if*, we went on a honeymoon. And that depended on whether we wanted to stay married to each other.

Our primary focus since Dex has been able to communicate again has been on getting to know each other. Dex has prioritized that even above his own recovery, insisting that we tell each other one new thing every day. He plans weekly dates and helps me problem-solve work issues on a daily basis, and he won't let me hold back telling him when I'm upset or mad or frustrated. He's always worried that his care will require too much sacrifice on my part, and he's made sure that doesn't happen.

When Dex got hurt and I went to Hawaii, I thought I *might* love him. I've learned since then that what I felt was attraction. What I know now is that I absolutely love Dex and can't imagine my life without him. If he never walks completely on his own again, if he always has trouble remembering words, if his surfing days are over, I will always love Dex.

Once both Dex and I are on the dock, applause erupts from the other surfers, officials, and judges in the WSL stands with us, but also the spectators crowded into the dozens of boats anchored around the reef.

Dex looks around, confused, until Archie nudges him. "That's for you, mate. Give 'em a wave."

Dex glances at me. I grab his wrist and raise both of our arms over our heads. He won't be able to keep it up long by himself, so he clutches my hand and waves with his other hand. As the applause grows, tears form in his eyes.

They fall down his cheeks when a commentator—Luiza Florence—holds a mic near Dex's face and a cameraman moves in close with his equipment. I let go of Dex's hand to step out of the way, but he pulls me back.

I try not to fidget while Luiza asks Dex questions. Being on camera has never been my dream, especially after a windy boat ride and my hair still tucked into my hood. I'm so nervous about how I look and what I should do with my hands that I barely hear when Luiza asks, "What do you attribute your amazing recovery to?"

Dex clears his throat and wipes the back of his hand under his nose before answering, "Britta." His voice cracks. "My wife. That's it. I wouldn't be here without her."

The interview ends with both of us in tears. Then we spend the rest of the morning and part of the afternoon watching five men compete for the World Title of surfing. Dex won't be the champion anymore. His win will go down in history, but that event may have been his last. We both know it. We've talked about it, but the day is still more emotional than we expected.

We stay long enough to see Jack Robinson take the title and boost the trophy over his head, same as Dex did last year, then we climb on our boat to head back to our resort. We could have stayed in a closer hotel, but when I insisted we come to the Finals—despite the very long flight over the ocean—Dex agreed only if we could make the trip our honeymoon.

I said yes.

That's when we both knew this wasn't a marriage-of-convenience anymore. Ours was a marriage-for-forever, inconveniences and all.

So, when we get back to our private hut on the sand, we barely get the door closed before Dex is walking me backwards toward the bed while I peel his shirt over his head. When the back of my knees hit the mattress, we stop long enough for him to ask if I'm sure.

"More than sure." I rise on my tiptoes and find his mouth with my own.

With my arms around his neck and my lips still on his, Dex lifts me onto the bed. I lay back, taking in all of him before he kisses me again.

"Happy anniversary," he whispers between the kisses that find their way from my mouth to the tip of my earlobe.

"Our anniversary isn't for another two weeks." My breath catches as Dex's lips trace a path down my neck to my collarbone.

"Do you want to wait until then to celebrate?" His kisses don't stop.

"No." I shake my head. "I want to celebrate every day until then, then every day after."

Dex stops long enough to flash a dimpled grin. "Ripper plan, Mrs. Thomsen-Dexter."

Then, for the first time—but definitely not the last—Dex and I really share a bed.

Thanks so much for reading *Britta & the Beach Boy!*
I hope you had as much fun reading Dex and Britta's story as I did writing it!
Want to find out if Dex makes it to the Olympics? How things are at *Frothed?* **Whose story is coming next?**
Get Britta's Bonus Epilogue at brittanylarsenbooks.com!
Did you know Britta's brothers and her cousin Seb have their own books?
Find the entire Love in Paradise Valley series on Amazon or in my Etsy shop Brittany Larsen Books
Stay tuned to my social media accounts and my newsletter for more info about my *Love in LA* **series.**
Subscribe to my newsletterthrough my website
Follow me on Instagram @brittanylarsen.books
Join my Brittany Larsen Books Readers and Fans group on Face-book

Acknowledgements

Dear Friends, Readers, and Rellys,

Gather round while I tell you how I, a woman who doesn't drink coffee, surf, or speak Australian came to write a book about a barista and an Australian surfer...

Actually, the story isn't that long. Basically, I liked the idea of a small town girl opening her own coffee shop in LA, I love watching people surf, I really love the way Chris Hemsworth talks, and I had NO idea how much work the actual writing part would take. Apparently, whoever first said *write what you know* knew what she was talking about.

Writing this story required learning a few languages I don't speak, and I couldn't have done it without help. Lots and lots of help.

To learn to speak coffee, I relied on my darling daughter, Emma who taught me things like, "a ristretto is still espresso, just pulled slightly shorter," and I'm still not sure what that means, but I think I got the coffee stuff right with her help, but also by not going into very much detail. If there's still a mention of Drake anywhere in this book, it's not her fault. She told me he's corny, but I was too tired to double-check I took the reference out.

Surfing has it's own language, too, and it's much more complex than "dude" or "hang ten." You guys, to write this book I had to learn how waves work, figure out what surfing words mean, then try to describe surfing maneuvers in a way that would make sense to 99.9% of my readers. The lovely Ellie Hall gave me invaluable input and encouragement, and you should absolutely read ALL of her books. I also used the Apple series, *Make or Break* as a resource, but unless you want to fall in love with surfing and some of the current surfers competing in the World Surf League, you probably shouldn't watch it. My whole family got sucked in and enjoyed every minute (warning: in real life, surfers curse. A lot).

Every surfer mentioned in *Britta & the Beach Boy*, except for Dex and Archie, is a real person, and I'm a fangirl of each one of them. Their athletic ability and dedication to the sport is equal parts beautiful, fascinating, and inspiring, Owen Wright's story, in particular. Dex's injury is based on Wright's. His recovery was long and hard, and included persistent fears he'd never surf again. Five years later, he medaled in the 2020 Tokyo Olympics. You can read his inspiring story in his book, *Against the Water*.

Of course, you know Australians don't speak American English. But did you know they have a lot of slang that goes way beyond *G'day mate* and *fair dinkum?* In fact, no one really says *fair dinkum* anymore, a sad fact pointed out to me by my Australian beta readers, Andrea Grigg and Chelsea Browning who not only read through my manuscript once, but many times over as I made changes to make sure I was getting things right. Dex and Archie wouldn't be Australian without them, and what fun would they be then?

There's American surf slang and Australian surf slang. Many words are the same, some are not. I probably went back and forth between the two, and I probably got a lot wrong. Seriously, surfers speak their own language, and I'm basically still in Surfer 101, so I apologize to all the surfers out there whose words I've probably mutilated.

I asked my readers in my Facebook group for help with names, and they really stepped up. Frothed is courtesy of Melody Williamson, Deja Brew is Marcia's creation, and West Coast Roast was the brainchild of my favorite sister, Amber Macias. Sam @sam.read.that came up with Rip Tide which my newsletter readers chose by a wide margin. (This will be my defense if Rip Curl decides to sue me). Thank you all!

Cathy Jeppsen continues to try to keep me organized. Bless you, Cathy. Lindsey Karol is taking a crack at it, too. Bless you, Lindsey. The only job harder than writing is trying to manage a writer.

Bookstagrammers are an indie author's biggest ally. Thank you to those who have joined my Street and Launch teams in order to help me get the word out about *Britta & the Beach Boy*. Your support both motivates me and makes it possible financially to keep writing. Your promotion and support are invaluable.

As always, I thought this book wouldn't be over 80k words (writers speak in wordcount, not page count, fyi), until my editor and storyteller extraordinaire, Josi Kilpack-Limb, got hold of it. She helped me fill a lot of holes with a lot more words I wouldn't have found on my own. Thank you, thank you, thank you!!!

My proofreader this round was Natalie Jacobs @natsproofsandedits who went above and beyond in working with my ever-changing manuscript and deadlines. 10/10 Would recommend. Thank you, Natalie!

Shout out to my two critique groups and the amazing women, authors, and friends who comprise them. My California girls: Melanie Jacobson, Teri Christofferson, Aubrey Hartman, Tiffany Odekirk, and Jen White. My SBBs: Josi Kilpack-Limb, Becca Wilhite, Nancy Allen, and Jennifer Moore. I count each one of you as a blessing in my life.

I have no greater blessings than my husband and three daughters. They are the best. End of story.

Finally, Reader, thank YOU!

About the Author

Brittany Larsen is the author of ten sweet romantic comedies and a couple of historical romance novellas set in the Old West. Her stories may range across time and place, but they're always about one thing: connection. They're guaranteed to make you laugh, and maybe even tear up a little.

Born and raised in Idaho, Brittany has spent the past twenty years (maybe even more) living the California dream... If that dream includes wearing sweatpants all day and gorging herself on red Australian licorice–the second-best export of the continent/country (Chris Hemsworth being the obvious first). When not writing, she teaches hot yoga, walks her dog, and takes naps. Her sweater-sporting, mini Aussi-doodle, Bo, is her favorite writing companion. But her favorite people are her husband and three daughters.

Made in the USA
Monee, IL
19 October 2024

68289259R00208